A SMALL-TOWN WESTERN AGE-GAP ROMANCE

Greta Rose West

COPYRIGHT

PUNK
ROSE

PRESS

ALSO BY GRETA ROSE WEST

WILD HEART: WELCOME TO WISPER

A Short Story

Join the newsletter for this short introduction into the Wisper world and for extra goodies and scenes. Sign up on my website.

gretarosewest.com

THE CADE RANCH SERIES IN ORDER (Series #1)

BURNED

BROKEN

BUSTED

BRAVED

BLINDED

THE WISPER DREAMS SERIES (Series #2)

RIVERS BETWEEN US

STORMS INSIDE US

MOUNTAINS DIVIDE US

LIGHT BETRAYS US

ACKNOWLEDGEMENTS

This book!

Jack Cade will clobber me for saying so, but I think I'm in love with Frank Sims. He stole my heart, crunched it up, and tucked it in his pocket. And don't anybody tell Finn. Fisticuffs will break out, and then it'll just big a big ol' mess.

My husband and I moved during the end editing process of this book, and I do not recommend it. Through packing at the old place to the thousands of trips to the trunk of my car, all I kept thinking was, "Frank needs me! Damn this moving thing. I need to finish this book!" But finally, here we are. It took a while, but man, was it worth it! And I'm still not unpacked. Thank you to everyone who listened to me whine about it and cheered me on, trying to convince me that the office I'd just finished in the old place would be even better in the new one.

Dear Sean, I love you. I wish you were my sweater. While you're not a big, hunky sheriff's deputy out West, you're my Desert/Midwest hunk. You're always there for me, my biggest fan and supporter. I fear for the safety of anyone who ever dares to trash my books. Thanks for always building my office furniture and hanging up the very specific set of blinds I need. :p

Thank you again, Peter Senftleben, my editor. I decree that you shall never quit your job. Fisticuffs would break out then too. ;) And Joanne, my steadfast copy editor, I wish you ALLLL the boba and books. <3 Thanks to you both for understanding the mess in my head.

Smooches to my beta readers for salivating over Frank and for making me go further and dig deeper. After eight books, it's still amazing to me the things I overlook or disregard, and I'm so thankful that you see them! Ie: Geri and the peach-stained porcelain. Blech. And M, you had me in stitches when you praised Frank's diet and when you squealed in the margin comments when he sat to put on his socks. If that's hot to you, then I know the way to your heart always.

To my ready team of ARC readers. Thanks for being patient this time. I was throwing new books out left and right with the Cade Ranch series, but they were all mostly done before I published Jack's book. This go around, I'm doing it all on the fly, so I appreciate your patience as I figure out what my process is and how fast (or slowly) I can put out a new book. Thanks for always being ready to devour a new story. You are my people.

A huge shout-out to my newsletter peeps. You have no idea how much I appreciate your patience and understanding. Thanks for sticking with me, even when my emails are few and far between and when they aren't loaded with free stuff. You know you've got a true virtual friend when they stick around for boring author updates.

I would like to thank Shane Smith and the Saints. *bats eyelashes* Like Gregory Alan Isakov did with the Cade books, SS&tS are fueling me with this series. I've been jamming out for months. And if Stevie Nicks ever reads this (snort, yeah, right), thank you, my Queen. I've had your voice in my head through writing this whole book. I heart you. Which leads me to thank my parents for subjecting my ungrateful ten-year-old ears to Fleetwood Mac. Their music lives inside me now.

Lastly, I would like to acknowledge all the hot dads in my social feeds. You are truly an inspiration! :p I think there's even someone called hotcowboydaddy. Oh, how I thank you!

For all the Moms…
*Step-Moms, Mom-Moms, adopted Moms, my mom, kinda
Moms, Dad-Moms, neighborhood Moms, and any other kind
of Mom.*
*Thanks for being there, and to Mama Rea, thanks for always
keeping peanut butter Cap'n Crunch stocked in your pantry
for me.*

There are themes of miscarriage/pregnancy loss and infertility in this book. If this is something that has affected you in your life, or you are sensitive to it, please read with caution. Of course my characters get their HEA in the end, but if you've read my other books, you know it's a struggle to get there. There are also brief descriptions of parental loss and abandonment, a result of illicit drug use.

CHAPTER ONE

FRANK

A WHILE BACK…

"THIS CABIN SHOULD BE in a damn magazine," Max said. "What're you gonna do now?"

We'd just finished the last task on our renovation list—installing new gray and white granite countertops with rock edges.

I shrugged. "Dunno."

"Any other projects you wanna work on? We could start plannin' the barn you were talkin' about? Get you a horse? You got enough room on the property for it." He patted me hard on the back. "Turn you into a real cowboy? You're from Texas; you should already be one. You got the hat."

I laughed. "Naw, man. Thanks, but I think I need to sit with this place for a while. Get used to it. We pretty much overhauled the whole thing." I'd only lived in the house for a month before Max and I'd started ripping shit up.

I wasn't one to make friends easily, but through his generosity and his willingness to work for beer, Max Gordon had wormed his way in. I knew now, if I ever needed help with anything, all it would take was a phone call. It went both ways. Friendship like that wasn't something a man took for granted.

I could count on one hand the people I held in a similar regard. My boss, Carey Michaels, the sheriff of Teton County was another. My partner, Abey Lee, made the list too, but I would never, ever tell her that.

"Yeah, we sure did," he said, looking around, appraising all the work we'd done on our evenings off and weekends for the last nine or ten months. Max had his hands full out at Milson Ranch every day as the ranch foreman, and he'd given up plenty of side gigs on the weekends as a carpenter to help me. I was grateful.

The stone fireplace and the foundation of the fixer-upper I'd bought a year ago were the only parts of the house that didn't feel different. New drywall, new reclaimed wood floors, new kitchen and bathroom. Almost everything was new.

But that old fireplace was a thing of dreams.

As a younger man, I'd pictured long nights cozied up on a couch in front of a fire, snuggled up with a woman, drinking a beer, maybe watching a movie, our kids making a mess on the floor with Lincoln Logs or a highly contested game of Monopoly. Christmas stockings hung over the edge of the mantel, with twinkling lights from the tree in the window, casting the whole room in a warm glow.

Unfortunately, in order to have that family, I'd need to find a woman to share it with. And that *definitely* wasn't part of my plan.

It'd taken me a long time to get here—to reno the house, but more importantly, to get to a place in my life where I didn't look at every woman I met with distrust. Didn't automatically assume they would take what they could from me and then hightail it out of Dodge.

It was too late for me now anyway. Surveying the cabin, appreciating the sturdy beams, new windows, the built-in bookshelves, and all new appliances—it was my biggest fear that I'd die alone in this house. It was also what I'd already accepted would happen.

Two more years, and I'd officially be an "old man."

Max lifted his hat from my side table next to the couch. "Alright, well, take it easy. Stop by the bunkhouse out at Milson's for a beer here sometime soon, before the weather gets bad. Buckey keeps bitchin' about the money you owe him for that poker game. He plans to rob you blind next time, although you could probably just arrest him."

I laughed, offering a hand. "Thanks, Max. This house is… It's a thing of fuckin' beauty. I can't tell you how much I appreciate your help."

At least I could die in peace in a house that was well built and clean. It suited me. And I'd chosen my new home carefully—far enough outside town so I wouldn't be bothered by people knocking on my door all hours of the night.

"It was nothin'. You did most of the heavy liftin'. All I did was hammer a nail or two." He shook my hand. "Enjoy it. That's all the thanks I need." Looking over my shoulder, he added, "You better get some books for them built-ins. Place looks empty without somethin' to break up all that dark wood."

My phone rang on my kitchen table, and when I closed the door behind Max and grabbed it, I saw it was my adoptive mom calling.

"Hi, Mama K."

"Hi, Frankie. How are you, honey?"

I tried not to scoff at the nickname. I wasn't thirteen

anymore. In fact, when I was thirteen, I'd hated when she called me "Frankie." It was too personal, too intimate, something my mama would've called me, and Mama K wasn't my real mama. At least, that was how I'd seen it back then.

"I'm fine. How are you and Eugene doin'?"

"Oh, can't complain too much. Listen, I wanted to ask you about the invitation I sent to Krista's party. Do you think you'll make it this time? We'd love to see you."

I had been hoping to avoid this phone call. I was sure she knew I'd sent her to voicemail the three times she'd called about it before. "Don't think I can get the time off work."

"Hm. I guess that Carey fella works you to the bone, huh?"

"We're a small outpost station. If we need time off, we have to bring in guys from Jackson to cover our shifts. It's just not a good time."

"Oh, well now, I understand that. I'm sure you've mentioned it before. But maybe you could ask? Just in case? I know Dad and your brother and sister would love to see you."

I hated breaking her heart, and from the crack in her voice, I knew I was, but it was easier for me to stay away from my adoptive family. The only thing going back to Texas had ever done for me was break *my* heart. I couldn't step foot in the state without thoughts of the parents I'd lost rambling around in my head. And I never let myself think about them or of how I'd had to figure out how to fight this world on my own.

Mama K chattered on about my little brother, Aaron. He was set to marry his high school sweetheart in the spring, and my sister, Krista, had earned herself a big promotion at her job, and Mama K and Eugene wanted to celebrate. My adopted siblings were both years younger than me, and we'd never been close. Going down to visit now would only be uncomfortable for them. Besides, I was better off alone. Always had been, and it wasn't about to change now at almost half a century old.

I didn't mean to, but I zoned out on Mama K, looking at the built-in bookshelves Max had suggested I fill. The longer I looked at the empty space, the more I knew I needed something to put in it. Suddenly, my life felt empty without books to fill it.

Maybe a trip to the library before my shift could fix that, and it gave me something to do so I didn't have to lie to Mama K about needing to get off the phone.

What kind of books does a nearly fifty-year-old man read? What was a subject I wanted or needed to know more about?

The library in Wisper, Wyoming was small and set up in an old house in the middle of town. I doubted it had the resources most libraries did, and I was betting a lot of the books were old and out of date, but they'd be good enough for me. What was so wrong with old shit anyway?

I had no clue what I'd want to read, but before I spent a fortune on a bunch of books I wasn't sure I'd like, I figured it'd be better to check some out, take them home, and see if I could get into reading as a way to pass time. A way to relax. Alone time was something I figured I had a lot of in my future.

If I found something I liked, I could ask the librarian to order more.

I walked the aisles, thumbing through the books on the shelves. The covers gave an indication if they might be my kind of thing or not. Avoiding anything cartoony or too… pink, I picked one out: *A Mountain Man's Guide to Home*

Décor. The title was ridiculous, but the picture on the front showed a living room in a log cabin that had been decorated in a style I didn't hate. I checked the year of publishing. Eh, well, it was fifteen years old, so maybe not the most up-to-date, but I just needed an idea about the direction to go in since I'd never really furnished a living room on my own before. Maybe seeing what others had done would spark some ideas.

Or maybe I could ask the librarian if there was a newer version or a better book.

Where was the librarian? I hadn't met the new guy yet. After Adalaide Fraser, the woman who'd been here since I was probably in diapers back in Texas, suffered a mild heart attack and decided to retire, the county had hired a new librarian—Sam somebody, probably some young kid fresh out of school. Maybe his work ethic leaned to the lazy side, and that was why he hadn't come out to greet me. The front door needed to be planed. It stuck in the frame, so you had to give it a good push to open it. There was no way he hadn't heard me come in.

A black-and-white picture of a Panzer tank caught my eye on the front of a book facing out from the bookshelf. *Hm*. A book about World War II strategies: *The Blitzkrieg Attack: Yay or Nay?* I pulled it from the shelf to read the description on the back. *Could be interesting.*

As I flipped the old, dust-covered book in my hand, noticing the rip in the shiny paper jacket, I heard a humming. Not a humming sound, but a person humming a song. It was a female voice for sure. Kind of a pretty sound, but I heard a bass thumping quietly. It sounded like a rap song was coming from the ceiling.

"Hello?"

No reply.

"Hello? Who's there? Sheriff's Department." I'd learned my lesson about not announcing myself as law enforcement when I'd nearly sent Mr. Brooks to the hospital with a stroke when I walked up behind him to offer to help him jump his truck. It was something to do with the gun on my hip.

Walking to the end of the aisle I was standing in, books in hand, I scanned the next aisle, but I found no one. Slowly, I made my way along the end of the aisles, and the humming became louder.

Finally, in the very last aisle against the back wall, a young woman balanced on a spindly wooden ladder, trying to fit a book on the highest shelf. She was listening to her music through earbuds, so she must not have heard me. The ladder's legs were uneven, and it teetered, but she used her thighs, adjusting her stance to counteract gravity. The feet of the ladder evened out, settling on the floor beneath her, and the satisfied tilt to her lips had me looking harder at the side of her face.

Her long skirt was blue, and so was her hair. It had been pulled into a bun on the top of her head and secured with a— was that a pencil stuck in there?

I cleared my throat.

Nothing.

"'Scuse me."

Still nothing.

Did this woman not have peripheral vision? Or was she ignoring me? Or was she just that lost in her song and the books? *Kids these days.*

I raised my voice. "'Scuse me, ma'am. You know it ain't safe for you—"

Her head whipped in my direction. "Shit!"

The ladder wobbled again, tilting to one side, and she lost her balance and tipped to the other while it hovered in the air for a second. She reached through the slats, trying to find some control. Her hand connected with the bookshelf, but the ladder had other plans as it leaned the opposite way she had intended, and books rained down around her. Dropping the ones in my hand to the floor, I took three steps forward and caught her like a sack of potatoes when she fell.

Her breath came out in an "oof," and then she was glaring at me from the cradle of my arms. "You scared the crap out of me," she griped loudly over the sound of the music in her ears, gasping and clutching at her chest. Her glasses were too big for her face, and they'd been knocked crooked. She looked at me with one eye over the top of the pink frames, yanking on the cord connecting her earbuds to her phone in her skirt's pocket. The earbuds fell out and dangled over my arm. "Thank you, but did you have to yell at me like that? You could've spoken in a normal voice."

"Pretty sure I tried that."

I stood there, holding this woman in my arms and looking in her eyes, having just saved her from breaking her arm or a leg, and she had the nerve to complain about my efforts to prevent exactly what had just happened? "Lucky I was here," I said, "or you'd probably be on your way to the ER right now with a broken tail bone."

She wiggled, hinting she wanted to be put down and pushing on my shoulder with her small hand, until it slid over my polyester work shirt to my neck. "If you weren't here, I'd still be upright."

Her skin was soft, and I caught a whiff of her perfume, or maybe it was just the way she smelled. It was a clean, fresh scent with a hint of… cookies? No, cake. I knew the smell since I hadn't allowed myself to eat that crap for a long time, but occasionally I dreamed about eating it. Usually, for a good day after the dreams, I smelled cake everywhere I went.

"Can you put me down, please?"

I could've. I didn't though. The warm feel of her body pressed against my chest was… nice. My hand flexed involuntarily around her waist, and with her eyes locked on mine, she licked her lips.

"Who are you?" I meant it to sound like a question, but it came out of my mouth as more of a demand. And how old was she? Suddenly, the question was burning my tongue. I didn't voice it.

She was definitely shaped like a woman, behind her eyes she was all woman, but the blue hair and the lack of age lines on her face told me she was a hell of a lot younger than me. Her skin was perfectly smooth.

"Sam Russo. Samantha but Sam," she said. "The new librarian."

Oh, Samantha… but Sam. Definitely not a guy. "I was expectin' a man."

An annoyed laugh escaped her lips. "Of course you were." She pushed again, and I let go, and she landed on her feet in front of me, her heavy black boots thunking on the floor.

She swiped at her skirt, adjusting it, and righted her glasses. "Who're you?"

Lifting my hand, I pointed a finger at the rank patch on my uniform, but we'd just gotten new shirts, so my name patch hadn't been sewn on yet. "Frank Sims."

She squinted through her glasses, then looked up. "You're a deputy?"

I nodded. I wasn't sure what to say, so I went with, "When you get yourself together, I wanna check out these books." Bending forward, I picked up my books, and when I tried to straighten, blue skirt and birthday cake invaded my face. I inhaled. It had been a long time since all my senses had been flooded with femininity.

What man of my age got turned on just looking at some young thing? Well, they probably all did, but I shouldn't have.

She turned, walking out of the aisle as she wrapped her earbuds around her phone and dropped them into her pocket. Her skirt swished behind her, and I followed.

"Do you have a library card?"

"Sure don't."

When we got to the checkout counter, she stepped behind it, grabbing a square card and a pen as she leaned over an antique secretary desk against the wall, balancing on one leg. She twirled around to face me. "Alright, well, I'm over-hauling the system. New memberships should be done online, but I just got here, so fill this out." She pushed the card across the counter. "I'll have to send it to the main county library in Jackson, and they'll mail you your card. *Then* you can check those books out."

"When?" I asked, amused at her annoyance, realizing it had been a long time since I'd felt the urge to laugh at anything.

"I don't know. Probably, like, a week. Maybe ten days."

"You want me to wait a week?" What a crock. By then, I could've bought and had both books delivered. Probably could've read them already.

"That's how this goes, buddy. Don't blame me. This library is as old as dirt. Everything is ass backwards. It'll take me some time to get it all organized and running smoothly."

Grabbing the pen in front of her on the counter, I completed her form, shielding it from her with my hand.

"Oh, please. I'm going to have to look at it anyway."

"You said you were sendin' this to another library, so

technically, it's my mail. If you read it without my permission, I could arrest you." No, I wouldn't, but she didn't seem to know that, and her indignation was kind of adorable.

"You— What?"

I signed the ridiculous information card and shoved it at her. Crossing my arms over my chest, I cocked my head to the side, daring her.

"Funny," she said, crossing her arms too.

Oh yeah. That was me. A regular ol' comedian. If I told a joke at the station, my co-workers would probably drop dead from shock.

"Samantha but Sam" looked like she came from a different era, a made-up one with her long skirt and pink cat-eye glasses. Her top was old-fashioned, too, like something from some frontier TV show. It was a white, short-sleeved getup, with frills around her upper arms and pearl buttons ascending the soft curve of her neck. Her eye makeup was accented with a black flip at the edges of her eyes. Except for her blue hair and combat boots, she looked completely different than any other woman her age, whatever that was.

I was still wondering.

Whatever number, it was too young for me. And I was too old for her. That was clear. My vision was going. I'd barely been able to read the damn library card application she'd made me fill out. Shit was getting all fuzzy when I tried to see things up close.

If that wasn't a definitive sign of old age, I had no clue what was.

As I contemplated the age gap between us, trying to remind myself that I wasn't interested in getting involved with anyone, never mind if she was beautiful or not, a group of little kids poured through the library door, their parents following behind, chatting and laughing with each other, and Samantha smiled.

Whoa.

She pulled the pencil from her bun, and the hair uncoiled and slipped down her back, like water, and I watched her gaze at the kids as they ran around like rabid monkeys, chasing each other and giggling. Her smile lit the whole place up. It changed the shape of her face and made her seem like a wholly different person than the one I'd just been holding in my arms.

She had me rethinking this whole library thing. What was the harm in coming back again? Once I'd gotten my card, I'd need to come back to get my books anyway. And when I'd read those, I'd need more, right? Not a lot of people used the library in Wisper, so maybe if I did, it would start a trend.

Yeah, right. Frank Sims, a trendsetter? But still. I'd be back. I knew that for sure as she blinked and one lone dimple deepened on her right cheek.

"See you Tuesday," I said.

Her eyes darted up to mine, and she threw that smile my way finally. "Okay. Thanks for... you know, saving me, even though it was your fault I fell." She was joking. The little smirk in her eyes told me so.

Nodding once, I knocked on the counter and left the library, thinking, *But how old is too old, really? There's no law about it.* Well, okay, there were a lot of laws about it, but if she was running a library, she had at least graduated college. If I wasn't wrong, she was in her late twenties, maybe even early thirties. Technically, I was still in my forties.

That wasn't so far apart.

CHAPTER TWO

SAMANTHA

ONE YEAR AND, LIKE, FOUR MONTHS LATER…

"DOES there have to be so much"—Mrs. DuBois lowered her voice as she flipped through the paperback copy of a steamy contemporary romance I'd handed to her—"*sex* in every book we read?" She stopped in the middle, focusing on whatever scene she'd landed on, and her eyes went wide, her mouth forming into an O.

An odd group of women occupied various mismatched chairs in the reading room at the Wisper, Wyoming public library, my new favorite place since I'd taken the job here over a year ago. I was a little nervous. I'd never been a part of a large group of friends like this. Technically, we weren't friends yet, just acquaintances, but I was hopeful we'd get there.

The last few years hadn't been a picnic.

Who was I kidding? They were hell.

Getting pregnant in grad school had been unexpected, and then losing the baby in a whirlwind of bleeding, ambulances, and surgeries wasn't exactly a day at the boardwalk.

There were several months when I could barely get out of bed. I couldn't find a reason to, and I cried most of the time. At one point, I wondered if I'd even finish my graduate degree in library sciences, the thing I'd been chasing for more than eight years.

Finally, I'd pulled myself up by my bootstraps, made myself shower and eat on a semi-normal schedule, and graduated. I took the job in Wisper and moved on a whim, but what I'd left behind in Florida was still like this big neon sign in my mind, flashing: *You're hurt! Don't forget! You can't have that thing you really wanted, the thing you thought would make you happy for the rest of your life.*

I could've used a big group of friends to help peel me off my sofa. But after a lot of soul searching, I was trying to move on. And if I could find some girlfriends who liked to read and then talk about the books? What more could a librarian want? But I'd been in Wisper for a while now, and the friends I'd made were still few and far between: Brady, who I'd known since childhood, Theo, Juneau, and Vern. Vern was really technically more like the library's occasional handyman, but he was nice to me, so I counted him. He'd fixed the front door for me once when it got so stuck in the doorjamb I'd had to crawl in through a window.

My gramps was my friend, too, probably my best friend, and looking back, I wondered why I hadn't come to Wisper sooner. Being around him was like sunshine on a cloudy day, which was fitting since he'd nicknamed me Sunny the day I was born. Short for Sunshine. Unfortunately, Gramps was recharging his own sunny disposition at my parents' house in Clearwater while they were working on a project in Norway. At least, that's where I thought they'd emailed they were going this time. They rarely called. Why bother when email is so efficient?

But it wasn't just Gramps I missed. Giving up the dreams you'd once thought you couldn't live without was… lonely.

There was no one to blame for what had been taken from me, though, so I couldn't really call it "giving up" because I'd had no say in the matter. And if I could've continued to blame my ex-boyfriend, Tyler, I would have. He deserved some of my anger, especially because of his *"This is really messing up my plans for the future, Sam"* comment before I'd even been released from the hospital, but none of what had happened was actually his fault.

Sure, he could've handled it loads better. I mean, come on. He was five years older than me, with perfect credit and a pristine health insurance policy and, by the time we'd started dating, had already begun to thrive in his career as a project manager at a new tech startup. Now, while I was struggling to find myself, to force myself to adopt new dreams, he was off living the life he'd promised me before things had all gone to shit, with a wife and two kids, a swing set in the backyard, and yearly summer trips to the Adirondacks. But still, I couldn't blame him.

Sometimes, that made it harder. Harder for me not to blame myself.

But books? Books were the things I knew I could count on to take me away, to get me out of my head so I'd stop focusing on the blinking sign.

So I could breathe.

"This is a *romance* book club." Carly Eaton, another member of our fledgling club, was perusing a second copy of the same book Mrs. DuBois was still looking at like it offended her, but Carly seemed to be reacting much differently. An excited smile was spreading across her small features. She couldn't have been more than four foot, ten inches tall, but she was gorgeous, with her mahogany bob and bangs and deep brown eyes.

"No, Mrs. DuBois." I needed to interject before the older, more discerning member of our new group ran away with her knickers in twist. "Just because it's a romance club, that doesn't mean every book we read will have open-door sex scenes. There are lots of romances without any sex at all."

"Yeah, boring ones," Aislinn Burroughs said. She and her best friend Billie Cade had shown up for the meeting, but I hadn't known they were coming. "We should read a shifter romance. Those are the best."

Mrs. DuBois made a face like someone rubbed sulfur under her nose. "What's a shifter?"

"Oh," Billie drawled, "you're in for a proper education. Ace here reads all kinds of kinky stuff. A shifter is a dude who changes from a man into an animal, like a bear, dragon, or a wolf. Wolves are Ace's favorites." She wiggled her eyebrows suggestively.

Mrs. DuBois clutched at the neck of her red cashmere sweater, throwing a doubtful look at Billie. "Oh my."

"Yeah, apparently it's uber hot."

Now Aislinn was the target of Mrs. DuBois's silent judgment, but she was oblivious to it because she was visually impaired. If she wasn't allowing Billie to lead her, she used a walking cane. It was funny to me that Aislinn liked to read such explicit stories because of her prim and proper demeanor, with her perfect posture and long skinny legs, always crossed at the ankles. Sitting next to Billie, who was lounging in her armchair like this was her house and not the county-owned public library, Aislinn was the picture of poise. It seemed funny that they were best friends because they were complete opposites.

"But how is that"—Mrs. DuBois dropped the book into

her lap and scrunched her fingers in the air, whispering—
"*sexy*?"

"It's like super alpha-masculine or something," Billie answered, draping a thigh over her chair's arm, purple high-top dangling over the side. "How many people have signed up for book club, Sam?" she asked.

Ticking the names off on my fingers, I counted out loud. "Well, let's see. You, Aislinn, Mrs. DuBois, Carly, Juneau. Oh, Mrs. DuBois, is your sister joining us?"

She winced. "I think this is way too much feminism for Myrna."

"Okay," I said, kind of offended. I mean, did she think I couldn't come up with some good romance classics? I would've handed out *Pride and Prejudice* for our first book if I thought any of them would finish it. "Well, I think that's it then. Oh, wait. I can't forget Phil."

"There's a man in our romance book club? I don't think that's a good idea," Mrs. DuBois complained. "What self-respecting member of the male species would read one of these anyway?" She held the book up in the air, shaking it from side to side.

"Philomena Beasley," Billie said. "A *woman*. And why couldn't a man read a book like this? Men like sex and romance too."

She gasped. "Well, I never."

"Oh, I bet you have," Billie joked. "C'mon, tell us all how you wooed your husband. It's one of my favorite stories ever. It involves what Mrs. DuBois refers to as an 'aubergine.'"

Mrs. DuBois scoffed. "You really are insufferable, you know that? And of course I know Philomena. Who doesn't know that old bat?"

"Old bat? Look who's talking," Billie said, and she smooched a kiss in Mrs. DuBois's direction. They argued like mad cats, but they were weird friends somehow. Mrs. DuBois was teaching Billie to sew, and Billie was teaching her how to make TikTok videos. Mrs. DuBois even had a little bit of a following. People seemed to like her "uppity granny" schtick, though I wasn't sure how much of a schtick it was.

"All right," I said. "That's six. I was kind of hoping we'd get more people to join, but six is a solid start."

"Seven," Carly said, "including you."

"Oh, right."

The bell rang on the desk in the library's main room, and I excused myself to see who it was. The library was never really "busy," so we were having our preliminary book club meeting during regular hours. I wanted to gauge the ladies' interests and get to know them a bit better so I could find books that might challenge them or at least interest them. But they were all so different. I was suddenly doubting myself, wondering if I'd be able to find a book they'd all like.

My cell phone buzzed beneath my bra strap under my T-shirt because my skirt didn't have a pocket, and I ducked into the bathroom to pull it out. Hadn't I just said the library was never busy? Jeez. Now it was like a Costco all of a sudden.

"Hi, Gramps. Can I call you back? I'm hosting the first book club meeting right now."

"Sure, Sunny. But did you make an appointment with that doctor I told you about? My friend's daughter says she's the best reproductive doctor in Jackson."

I whispered, "Gramps!"

"What?"

"I don't want to talk about reproduction with you."

"I know, but Samantha, you haven't been to the doctor since the last surgery. I think you need a checkup, and I know you still have questions. So why don't you just go ahead and make the appointment? I'll come home and go with you, if you want."

God, he was the best grandpa. "Thank you, but you don't have to do that. I'm a big girl. I can go to the doctor by myself. I'll make an appointment, I promise, but right now, I gotta go."

"I'm gonna hold you to it, Sunny."

"Okay. I love you. Bye."

I regretted being tense with him as soon as I hung up. At least he cared to know what was going on with me, not like my parents, who I still hadn't even seen since *before* everything happened in Florida. The same parents who'd reacted to my miscarriage over the phone like it was a black mark on their shared calendar. Who has time to comfort their daughter when there were movies to be filmed?

Carrying my phone in my hand this time, I snuck out of the bathroom and headed toward the main room when the bell rang again. I turned the corner and saw Wisper's only female sheriff's deputy standing on the far side of the check-in desk.

"Hi," I said. "Is everything okay?" *Oh gosh, what is her name? Ally? Abby? Ugh.* I couldn't remember.

"Yeah. Uh, Ms. Moonlight told me to come. Juneau Moonlight?"

"To come to the library… why?"

"For the book club."

"Oh! You're not here in an official capacity?"

"No. Why'd you think that?"

"Um, 'cause your—" I motioned to her stiff brown uniform under a matching canvas coat. She was wearing a brown cowboy hat, and her white-blond hair had been pulled back into a quick bun at the back of her neck, but strands of it had fallen loose, and they framed her face. "Never mind. Come on. The ladies are in the back room."

"Is Juneau here yet?"

"Not yet. I'm hoping she's on her way. Come on back."

She followed after me, but I stopped and turned before we got to the reading room, noticing that she was armed with handcuffs and her gun. Yeesh. "I'm sorry. I didn't introduce myself. I've seen you around town, but I don't think we've ever properly met. I'm Sam."

She shook my hand, smirking. "Nope. We haven't, but I know who you are. I'm Deputy Abey Lee. I work with Frank."

"Oh, um, right. That's nice," I said, my cheeks heating and blushing. She was referring to her partner. Wait, did deputies have partners?

Whoever he was to her, he was also the man who came to my library every Tuesday. The same man who sat in an armchair and read a book he barely seemed interested in. And when he wasn't reading a book, he was reading *me*. Silently. He rarely spoke.

In fact—I checked my phone for the time—he would be headed here in less than an hour.

I looked down at my clothes. *Ugh*. My usual skirt and T-shirt would have to do, but maybe I'd have time to freshen my eyeliner before he got here. I mean, not that I was interested.

Although, he was extremely handsome, I may have noticed on occasion. But he had to be way older than me. His hair was graying, like, a lot, and he had kind of an old-guy air about him. Not like "grandpa old guy," but like, a distinguished older guy.

Fine. He was hot. Super macho, protective, law-enforcement hot. Tall and built like a mountain, if he could shift into a bear, he'd fit right into one of Aislinn's stories.

With a wave of my hand, I motioned for Abey to follow

me again, trying to fan my face discreetly with the other, but she chuckled under her breath, and I blushed harder. Did everyone know about the crush I had on my most regular patron?

We entered the back room, and I introduced her. "Everybody, this is Abey Lee. She heard about the book club, so she's joining us."

Abey removed her hat and pushed it out in front of her. "Yeah, but Juneau promised we'd read some LGBTQ books. I don't mind readin' about dudes and chicks, but I would also like to put my vote in now that we read some chick-on-chick love stories. Or dude-on-dude. I'm an equal-opportunity lesbian."

Mrs. DuBois squeaked, and Billie said, "I'm down. Right on, copper."

Abey sat next to Billie, and Billie spun in her chair, swinging her legs over the other arm. "How've you been? We haven't seen you since that whole Carey/Frannie drama. It's a good thing they tied the knot and started popping out babies. The angst was killing me."

Ouch. I tried not to show the wince on my face, but it was hard. No matter that it was a perfectly common thing for people to talk about. Pregnancy and babies always hit home like a punch to the stomach. Or more to the point, it was a punch to my barely functioning uterus and ovaries.

Abey laughed. "Can't complain."

Mrs. DuBois tsked, eyeing Abey's gun but trying to hide it. "Do you always wear your uniform, Deputy Lee?"

"Uh," Abey hesitated. "Yeah? Most the time, I guess, unless I'm sleepin', and then I'm naked."

Mrs. DuBois's face turned red, and the unintentional comedy helped the rush of sadness in my chest ebb a little. I stifled a giggle.

I'd assumed they would all know each other since Wisper was such a small town, but it was occurring to me that maybe they didn't. "Does everybody know everybody, or should we do introductions?"

"Wait," Carly said. "Where's Juneau Moonlight? I thought we were gettin' to meet a real romance author today."

"Oh, well"—I checked the clock on the wall—"she should be here any minute. She must be running late."

Billie raised her arm in the air, then let it flop back down to her chair. "I'm no romance author, but I'm Billie. I married Jay Cade, and I know you all know the Cade brothers. And this is Ace." She nudged Aislinn's leg with her shoe, and Aislinn swatted at it. "She's gonna be my sis-in-law soon. She's marrying Finn Cade."

An appreciative moaning sound came from Mrs. DuBois. Everyone looked at her.

She balked. "What, because I'm old, I can't think a man is handsome?"

"Not my fiancé, you can't," Aislinn said, and Mrs. DuBois arched a challenging eyebrow.

Carly giggled, then spoke up. "I'm Carly Eaton, and I have my own cowboy too. Buckey." She practically had hearts and flowers in her eyes when she said his name. "He works out at Milson's. We have three kids: Dora, Derek, and Drew. Seven, five, and two." She patted her chubby but still mostly flat stomach. "Here's number four. If it's a girl, we're namin' her Delilah. Deli for short."

Abey mouthed, "Deli?"

Billie snickered.

I panicked for a minute. I wanted to get to know these women, but I hadn't anticipated one of them being pregnant. I should have. It made me feel like a jerk. A person should be happy for a friend if they were having a child. And I wasn't *unhappy* about it, but—

"Good Lord," Mrs. DuBois said. "You and your husband certainly have been busy."

"Oh." Carly laughed, flapping a hand. "We're not married. He knocked me up in our junior year of high school, and we kinda just kept goin' from there. We keep sayin' we're gonna bite the bullet, but you know." She shrugged. "Life."

"What about you, Mrs. DuBois?" I asked, trying to steer the conversation away from the baby subject.

She threw a pointed look at me. "I'm *Callie* DuBois, but my friends call me Cal."

Smiling back, I let her know I'd taken her hint and would use her nickname from now on, instead of her married surname.

"I'm from Calgary, in Alberta, Canada, originally, but I married a cattle rancher and lived up near Billings, Montana for years. My husband Herbert died a few years ago so I moved here to be closer to my sister, Myrna. She also married an American. We spent a *lot* of time at the rodeos in Alberta when we were teenagers." She looked around the room, tapping the book in her hand with her long red acrylic fingernail. "And just so you know, I have *never* read a book like this."

Billie snorted. "Mmhm. Sure you haven't. Oh, before I forget, my mom-in-law is joining book club, too—Daisy— but she has to work today at the diner. She'll be at the next meeting."

Everybody nodded. Everyone knew Daisy because she worked at the only diner in town with her husband, José. And everybody knew José because he'd owned the diner for years and was an exceptional cook. My mouth watered just thinking about his signature fried chicken.

The front door slammed open in the other room, and then we heard, "Girls? Girls! Where you at?"

"That will be Phil," Aislinn said, shaking her head.

Phil appeared in the doorway, breathless and disheveled. "Oh, there ya are."

I understood Aislinn's reaction. Phil was very kind, but she was a whirlwind of a woman. She drove her rusted pickup around town, blasting Fleetwood Mac and Simon & Garfunkel, and she was loud, as in decibels, but also, she was a loud dresser. Today, she was sporting worn-out jeans with a bright yellow Jimmy Hendrix T-shirt under her black, shaggy faux-fur coat. Her gray hair was braided down her back, and she had purple reading glasses perched on top of her head. And I couldn't remember ever seeing her wear any other footwear besides her black and white checkered muck boots.

"Am I late?"

She was also the first resident of Wisper to welcome me back to the town I'd come to when I was a little girl to visit my grandparents. Phil had remembered me, and she'd made me yellow cupcakes with chocolate whipped-cream frosting on my first day as the new librarian, which, coincidentally, was also the first day I'd met sexy Deputy Frank—not that that mattered in the slightest. But Phil was an avid reader, and she was also a farmer, so she'd call me every couple of weeks to ask me to round up books for her to dive into at night, when she had a few minutes of downtime.

I kind of loved her, and I'd slowly been steering her closer and closer to the romance genre. She'd never read a romance book before she met me.

"Well, if it isn't *Cal DuBois*," she said in a tight voice, which was really unusual for Phil. "I didn't expect to find *you* here."

Cal responded through teeth clenched so tight, I thought they might crack, "Philomena."

Yikes. There was definitely some history between those two.

I intervened quickly. "Moving on. As you all probably know, I'm Sam Russo. I've been here at the library for a little over a year. Before that, I lived in Florida, but I came to Wisper a lot as a child. My gramps is Jessup Anderson. He used to run the *Wisper Gazette*, and my grandma, Josie, used to bring me to this library three times a week when I spent summers here. I'm really happy to be back, and I'm even more excited to find women I can talk to about books. The romance genre is my favorite, so I'm hoping I can find a lot of books that you'll love too."

Picking up another copy of the first book on my list from a small table set against the wall, I held it up in front of my chest. "If you haven't yet, grab a copy from the table. There's enough for everyone." When everyone had a copy in their hands, I said, "This one is really popular right now. It's on *The New York Times* Best Sellers list. It's a contemporary story, and it's all over Bookstagram, so I think it will appeal to a broad audience. I thought it would be a good choice for our first read. Then, we can get into more niche parts of the romance genre, like Aislinn suggested, and I hope you'll enjoy reading some of the classics too." Hugging the book to my chest like a dork, I said in a dreamy voice, "I love them all."

"What's Bookstagram?" Phil asked.

"I'll show you later, Phil," Billie said as an aside. "It's just Instagram, but the part that talks about books."

"There ain't one bit of that sentence that made sense to me except for the word 'book.'"

Billie snorted.

I tried not to laugh. I was really excited to have two older women in the group. If they could get along, they could add a whole different perspective to the stories we'd read. I was grateful they were putting themselves out there, jumping into the book club even though every other member was years younger than they were and some of the subject matter might feel questionable to them.

"Aislinn, I emailed you a link to download the audiobook. There's a coupon in the email, too, so it should be free for you. If anyone else wants the audiobook, let me know. And ladies, if there's a book you'd like the group to read, I've started a list out at the front desk. Just jot it down for me. We have to make sure it's available in more than just print to allow for our members to listen to on audiobook or read on their e-readers, if they prefer, but other than that, the only rule is that it has to be a romance. Oh, and no politics. Make love, not war."

Cal frowned, and no one else said a word.

Oh jeez.

I kept talking, hoping they'd just forget my joke. "Okay," I said. "Let's meet back here in a week or so, then we can better gauge how much time we'll need before we meet again. Really, this is informal. I want to set tentative dates so we can plan around our meetings, but we can be loose about them. The first thing you should know about me is that making a schedule gives me hives."

Really? Was no one going to laugh?

"That's fine for me," Carly said. "I'll be done in two days. Seriously, books are how I get through dealing with three kids every night, and then, when the big kids are at school and the baby's sleepin', it's my reward."

"Me too," Aislinn said. "My fiancé and I don't have children yet, but I'll probably finish in four or five days. It takes me a little longer because I listen to audiobooks, and if I set the pace too fast, I miss details."

Women after my own heart. It would probably only take me a day to finish the three-hundred-page book in my hands. Granted, I'd already read it, but I didn't mention that books were my escape too.

Carly lifted her purse from the floor. "We done for today? I gotta get back home. My mama's watchin' baby Drew, but he's in his fascinated-with-poop-and-boogers phase, and she can only last about an hour."

Cal made a disgusted sound in the back of her throat, and Phil laughed.

"Yep, we're done," I said, "and on that note, see you in a week."

The women all stood, chatting to each other and gathering their things, and I waited off to the side, hoping for the whole friendship thing to happen magically.

Of course it didn't.

CHAPTER THREE

FRANK

"FRANK, YOU HAVE TO TOUCH HIM."

Dr. Masterson was staring at me, waiting for me to respond while my overgrown puppy rubbed circles around her legs, drooling on her. Six months old and he was already tall enough to set his paws on the vet's shoulders if he stood on his hind legs.

"You know? Like, pet him." She scratched his fluffy yellow head. "Listen, I don't see anything wrong with your puppy, so if you want my help, I'm gonna need a little more information. The dog can't actually give that to me, you know, so you're gonna have to."

Running my fingers through my hair, I felt naked without my hat, but I didn't want to be rude and wear it indoors. "It won't eat. I don't think it likes me." I didn't like the sound of my own voice in the quiet examination room. The low timbre reminded me that I hadn't been alone with a woman in a long time. Dr. Masterson was married to a local rancher and had kids. I wasn't attracted to her, but my awareness of her *because* she was an attractive woman, combined with her younger age, had my mind wandering to the library.

The look on the doc's face got a little more severe. "*He* won't eat, and you don't think *he* likes you." Reaching behind her, she grabbed a bone-shaped dog treat from a blue ceramic jar on the counter. She held it out for him, and it disappeared. Just like that. "Well, he ate for me. Why don't you think he likes you? Puppies usually like everyone."

"He just sits there, lookin' at me. If he sees a squirrel or somethin', he likes that, and he runs around like a normal dog, but then when it's just me and him, he stares at me. And when I put his food down, he takes a few pieces and puts 'em in a pile he's been makin' by the door, then he just sits down again."

Now the doc looked like she might be losing her patience. "Frank, do you take him for walks? Do you play with him?"

I shrugged. I mean, I let the damn dog out to do his business, and he'd run circles around my yard. Wasn't that exercise? And I took him to work with me occasionally. My partner liked to take him for walks sometimes.

"Oh c'mon, Frank. You have to play with him. Throw a ball for him or take him for a hike. Puppies love to expend energy. He has a lot of it. You need to help him get it out." She looked me up and down. "You exercise every day, right? Take him with you."

I'd never had a puppy before. Dogs, sure, had a few, but never a pup. Older dogs were lazy. And I couldn't "take him with" me. I worked out at home, in my spare bedroom on a rowing machine and with a boxing bag. If I let him in the room, he'd probably break the rower and eat the bag. "Think he'd like to go to the library?"

"The library? Um, are animals allowed inside the library?"

Okay, so maybe that hadn't been my brightest idea, but I didn't want to have to take the damn dog all the way home and then drive back into town. Yesterday, he made me late for work 'cause I had to clean up remnants of the pillow he'd decided to steal off my couch and then rip to shreds in the night. He'd figured out how to escape his crate in my extra bedroom and had destroyed my living room. And he ate a loaf of bread off the kitchen counter. I hadn't found any wet spots, but I wasn't convinced he hadn't pissed on my rug too.

"If you have Doc Whitley fill out a form, you can claim him as an emotional support animal, and then you could take him to the library, although he might knock over the bookshelves. Maybe wait till he grows into his body a little and calms down a lot." To prove her point, the dog jumped at her. It looked like he was trying to dunk a basketball, he jumped so high.

Dr. Masterson laughed.

"I don't need a therapy dog."

"Okay, well, it was just a suggestion," she said. "Look, he's perfectly healthy. He's had all his shots, so you need to stop bringin' him here unless he gets worms or needs stitches, okay? Play with the damn dog, Frank. And for pete's sake, give him a name!"

When we were in my truck, waiting for it to warm up and watching snow falling lightly outside, I looked down at the dog, sitting shotgun on the floor and staring up at me. "What's your problem?"

He tilted his head.

I held half of my organic chicken wrap in the air above him, and he lunged, trying to get to it, but he couldn't reach without climbing on the seat next to me, which he wouldn't do 'cause he wasn't sure about me yet. The feeling was mutual.

"You want this? Here." I stuck it directly in front of his nose, and he scarfed it down. Took him about two seconds. "How am I s'posed to like you if you make me look like a liar to the vet?"

I'd had a dog who'd loved me, a rat terrier my ex-wife had named Boopers, but I lost him in the divorce. When my ex took him, there was no discussion. She just left, and the dog went with. I hadn't missed her once in eleven years, but I missed that dog every damn day, despite his name.

So I decided to get me a new one. I'd been called out to serve a woman with foreclosure papers south of Barton, and as luck would have it, she had a litter of goldendoodles. Well, maybe luck was the wrong word. Those poor dogs. The old woman hoarded dogs, and she hadn't paid her mortgage in two years. She knew she was up shit creek, so she gave the litter to me.

They were cute, and my quick internet search told me they weren't quite hypoallergenic, but they were good for people with allergies and didn't shed a whole lot, so I could take one to the station. The biggest one licked my hand and followed me around, so I took him home and dropped the rest at the no-kill shelter in Jackson. Thankfully, they were still young enough, and they'd all been adopted out quickly. The shelter's receptionist had texted me with the news, along with a not-so-subtle hint that if I asked her out, she'd say yes. I didn't respond. I wasn't interested in a quick romp in the hay with a random woman who liked the look of my ass. Been there, done that. Married that.

Besides, I had my sights set somewhere else.

That was four weeks ago, and this creature was still a mystery to me. He was a goofy, curly-haired pain in my ass, and I wasn't sure if his tongue could stay inside his mouth for longer than ten seconds, but he was nice enough, at least when he wasn't ruining my property. But we hadn't bonded yet.

"Never mind what the doc said," I told him. "Wanna go to the library?"

He yipped and tried to jump again, tangling himself in his leash, and I figured that was probably a "yes."

"Good," I said, shoving my cruiser into gear. "There's a woman there, and I go on my lunch break to see her on Tuesdays. I bet she'll like you. She likes anything cute and cuddly. She reads these old romance books, and she's always got a dreamy look in her eye." When I peeked down at him, he was gazing up at me with his head cocked again. I thought he might be smiling. Could dogs smile? I wasn't sure, but it looked like he was, and I took that as a good sign.

"She's a little younger than me," I said, wincing to myself as I admitted out loud, if only to a dog, the thing I was worried would stop Samantha Russo from agreeing to go on a date with me. But first I had to ask her. That was the preliminary hurdle. Today was the day.

Shelley's voice came through on my shoulder radio. "Come in, Frank."

"Yeah, I'm here. Relay."

"Aubrey called to report a break-in over at the bookstore. Carey and Abey are both out, so you better get your butt on over there."

"First," I told him, "you're gonna have to wait in the truck. I gotta take this call." Pressing the speaker button, I waited for the static to clear. "10-4. En route." Flashing my annoyance to the dog, I said, "Maybe you can use the alone time to think up a name for yourself."

I left him in the back seat of my running truck with the heat going and a window cracked for fresh air. He looked happy enough, licking his balls clean and listening to pop country on the radio.

"Thanks for comin', Frank." Aubrey George, the owner of Your Local Bookie, greeted me when I walked into her Main Street shop, the jingle bell on the door tinkling behind me. She looked flustered but in one piece. The front door or window hadn't been smashed in at least.

"You alright?" I passed her after I looked her over and went to check out the damaged back door in the stock room. It looked like the lock she had on it wasn't a strong one, like someone could force it open with a good shove. The door had a three-inch by maybe twelve-inch window set into the left side, and the glass was cracked, a few pieces littering the floor around the door, and the metal around the lock had crumpled in a bit, like maybe it had been kicked or hit with something heavy.

"Yeah. I'm fine. I was late openin' up this mornin', and when I got here, I found this mess. There's muddy shoe prints." She pointed by her feet to a smudged imprint on the tile floor of what looked to possibly be an athletic shoe. Likely a man's or a teenaged boy's shoe judging by the large size.

She followed me back out to the main room. "Now," she said, "before you suggest that it was my boys who caused this mess, I promise you, if they wanted to steal from me, they'd just take money from my purse. It wouldn't be the first time, but I don't think they'd damage the store, 'cause they know it's what pays for their video game obsession. Plus, it'd totally ruin their street cred if any of their friends found out they were in a bookstore without bein' forced." She rolled her eyes. "And I would beat 'em within an inch of their lives." She looked up at me sheepishly. "Just kiddin'. I don't beat my kids."

Walking around her, I looked behind the counter, but nothing seemed out of place. "Never said it was your boys."

She bumped into my back when I stopped to get a good look. "Well, it was *my* first thought, so I wouldn't blame you." She took a few steps backward, putting a proper amount of distance between us. "It ain't like those two haven't been in their fair share of trouble. You yourself hauled 'em to a cell at the station for stealin' from the Liquor Depot."

"They were lucky nothin' was damaged, and they only took one bottle of vodka on a dare." The owner of the Liquor Depot hadn't pressed charges, and Aubrey's boys hadn't had a chance to drink any of the vodka, at least not *that* time, so they got off scot-free, which, in my unoffered opinion, was part of her problem.

"Yeah, well, I love my boys, but I never said they had common sense."

"What was stolen?" I asked, planting my hands on my hips as I surveyed the rest of the small bookshop. Besides the back door and the mess on the floor, everything looked fine to me. There was no damage to the main part of the store that I could see.

"You get straight to the point, don'tcha? Um," she said, her eyes focused on my hands on my holster. Finally, she sighed and looked around too. "Twenty bucks in cash was taken from the till. I think maybe whoever it was knows how to work a cash register. There was a little over fifty bucks in there last night, but they only took twenty. Most people pay with cards or their phones nowadays, so I don't keep too much cash around. I close the register every night before I leave, but I found it open when I got here this mornin'. Whatcha think that's about?"

"Hm." It told me she wasn't being careful enough with her money, and that either the thief was really bad at their job, or it was someone who needed money but felt bad about taking it. So maybe not someone who needed it for drugs. Usually, the desire for a fix overrode the guilt. I knew that from experience. But who the hell committed burglary for twenty bucks?

"Are you always this talkative?" Mrs. George asked and laughed, her eyes finally landing on mine instead of every other inch of my body.

But it wasn't my job to make baseless assumptions. I needed more information. Besides, what was the point of saying words just to say them? What good did that do anybody? Seemed to me it was a waste of perfectly good mountain air. I didn't answer her. "What else was taken?"

"Nothin', not as far as I can tell."

"No other damage besides the back door?"

"Nope. Nada." She walked the length of the store, checking shelves, looking up and down, aisle by aisle, but she stopped in the middle next to a tall, round table. "Wait. There was a display right here. I know exactly what books are missin' 'cause I just made it last night before I closed."

"Are the missin' books significant somehow?" I asked, noticing under the store's bright lights how the shoeprints led from the table to the cash register and out the back door.

"No. I mean, altogether, they probably only cost thirty bucks retail. They were trade paperbacks, not first-edition hardcovers, but they were all classics. *The Catcher in the Rye, Journey to the Center of the Earth, Of Mice and Men, Oliver Twist*, and this one here, *The Great Gatsby*." She held up a blue book with weird-looking eyes on the front. "Guess the thief isn't a fan of F. Scott Fitzgerald."

The small paperback copy of *The Great Gatsby* dangling from her fingers was one I recognized. I couldn't disagree with whoever had stolen the other books. If I remembered it right from high school, the book was depressing as shit, and who wants to read about a bunch of rich people wasting their money?

I logged the stolen books in my pocket notebook. "You got cameras?" Not many store owners did in Wisper. We didn't usually have any upticks in petty crimes around these parts. Not anything too serious anyway, especially not down-town since the sheriff's station sat smack-dab in the middle of it.

Aubrey grimaced. "Um, I do have cameras, actually, but I need help settin' 'em up, and we've already discussed how my boys aren't the most helpful." Her husband dying on duty overseas several years ago left her alone with twin boys who hadn't become better behaved after their dad died. *Huh*. It was occurring to me that maybe it was why I was so hard on her boys whenever they found themselves in trouble with the law—which was often. They'd gone in the misbehaving dead-soldier-father direction, and I'd gone in the other.

"Might be difficult to find your thief without 'em, but I'll do my best."

"Frank, really, there's not much missin'. I only called you in case this is related to any other crimes or the person could be dangerous, though I'm thinkin' it was just somebody who needed money for food or somethin'. I probably won't even file a claim with my insurance. The deductible will probably cost more than the damage itself." She shrugged. "Why bother?"

"That's up to you," I said. "You got somebody you can call to fix your back door and install them cameras?"

"Yeah. You know my cousin, Max, right? He'll help me."

I made a note to text him myself to make sure it was done. "Okay. Anything else while I'm here?"

"No. That's it, I guess." Was I wrong, or did she look disappointed there weren't any other crimes for her to report?

"Alright then." I tipped my hat and headed toward the front door, but on the way, I noticed two local women in front of the shop, looking in the big front window at a Valentine's Day display of what I guessed were probably romance books. They were red and pink enough. "Mrs. George, you notice anybody out front last night or maybe the last few days? Any suspicious customers you remember? Anybody hangin' around out back when you parked?"

"Frank, c'mon. We've known each other a few years now. When are you gonna call me Aubrey?" She batted her eyelashes and flashed me a coy smile. "And no. I mean, other than the usual Wisper weirdos who come in, but you know all of them. And not one of 'em would steal from me."

Even if I hadn't been on the job, I would've ignored her question. "They might've noticed somethin'. Make a list of anybody you can remember comin' in here in the last week, please. And how 'bout you round up your credit card receipts. Then I'll talk to the folks that were here, see if they remember anything."

She shrugged again, her flirtatious smile dissolving when I didn't take the bait. "Sure. I'll do it after I clean up. I'll give you a call when I'm done."

I nodded and left Your Local Bookie, again taking stock of the state of the place as I went. I didn't see anything else out of the ordinary, besides the back door and the shoeprints, which were definitely odd. Whoever the culprit was, they went straight for the books first—not the cash register.

Now, what kind of thief would do that?

When the dog and I were standing outside the library, I checked my jacket. Since he didn't shed all that much, I wasn't covered in hair, but I swiped my hand over it anyway, just in case, and I took off my hat. I wasn't on duty, technically, so I didn't have to wear it, but I supposed it was habit. My hair felt flat, so I ruffled it a little and headed up the steps, hat in hand and dog chasing my heels.

My partner, Abey, came out the door in front of me, chattering with a group of ladies all buttoned up in winter coats. They smiled at me as I stepped off the sidewalk into the snow to let them pass, and one of the women, Billie Cade, roared at me like a lion, then winked, and she and Abey laughed.

"Have fun, ol' boy," Abey called out, and I flipped her off behind my back as I walked through the door.

"Oh my gosh!" Samantha gushed when she saw us, sitting cross-legged in her usual spot on top of the check-in desk.

I'd never seen a librarian like her before. Hell, I'd never seen anyone like her, period. She was a vision, and a colorful one at that, with her long, flowy skirt dotted everywhere with flowers. She'd changed her hair from blue to pink. I'd never admit it to anyone, but I loved the pink on her. It did something to her eyes, changed them somehow. They were… brighter.

Normally, she wore her glasses, but today her face was bare, and it allowed me to see them better.

"Who's this?" Hopping down, she kneeled in front of me,

scruffing up the dog's face, talking baby talk to him. "You're such a cute puppy. Oh my gosh, I wuv you. Gimme kisses."

The dog licked her face, and I frowned. *Gross.*

"What's her name?" she asked as she hopped up to grab her cell phone from the desk. When she kneeled in front of the dog again, she snapped his picture.

"He's a him," I said, and I realized it might've been the first time I'd spoken a whole sentence to her in months, even though I'd been coming to the library once a week on my lunch break for the better part of a year and a half. I was sorry it was such a short sentence and not the most interesting.

Her hair was down today, the straight pastel locks flowing over her shoulders and down her back. The smile on her matching lips was the purest I'd ever seen, like she was happy. You never knew what a person had inside them, but Samantha appeared to be content with life.

Her eyes lifted to mine, and I froze. I'd never seen anyone so beautiful, and down on her knees like that? *Shit.* Fuck all, she was sexy. I forgot the dog was even there for a second.

"Deputy?" she asked when I didn't answer 'cause my mind was still in the gutter. It'd take a backhoe to get it out. She looked at him, inspecting his camo collar. "I don't see a nametag."

I found my wits finally. "Haven't given him a name yet."

"He doesn't have a name?" Peeking up at me, she blushed. "Maybe you should call him Grumbly."

"Okay then," I said. "This is Grumbly." I'd do anything to get to see that pretty peach color blush across her cheeks again, and the dog did need a name.

"Oh, no. I was kidding because you—never mind."

She stood, and Grumbly jumped, raking his claws down her skirt.

"Dammit." I gave him a name, and now he was embarrassing me?

"Oh, it's okay." Samantha smiled at him, and the dog wrapped his big paws around her waist, looking up at her, tongue lolling. Resting her hands on his shoulders, she hugged him back, and it looked like they were dancing. It was safe to say I'd never had an urge to dance before, but I did now. "Aw, he's hugging me. You are just the cutest." She tickled her finger under his chin, and I suddenly found myself jealous of a mongrel.

"It's okay for him to be here?"

She looked around the library's main room. "Yeah. I mean, maybe there's some kind of rule about it, but I don't care. There's nobody else here. Just don't let him pee on the floor."

"He won't," I said, hoping that wasn't a miscalculation, bristling a bit at her pointing out that I was breaking a rule. I never did. Grumbly pushed off Samantha to begin his inspection of the library. He seemed to like the old, musty smell as he perused the first shelf, sniffing at each book he passed.

"Okay." She took a deep breath, then pressed her lips together. "So, um, are you on your lunch break?"

"Kinda."

Her eyebrows dipped down when I didn't say anything else. I wanted to, but I was so struck by her that sometimes I forgot to speak. The urge to swipe my thumb across her cheek was intense. I'd bet it was soft as silk.

I forced conversation out of my mouth. If there was anyone I wanted to talk to, it was Samantha. "Got the day off 'cause I had to take Grumbly to the vet, but then I took a call since Sheriff Michaels was busy. Always work to be done." It seemed Abey wasn't as busy as Shelley had thought, hanging out with her friends at the damn library.

"Is Grumbly sick? And are you really going to call him Grumbly?"

"No."

Her eyebrows rose this time, higher and higher, while she waited for me to say more. It wasn't my nature to be a chatterbox. I'd been alone a long time.

"Deputy, it's cool that you come to the library every week. In a way, it gives me hope. Nobody else does. But do you think you could talk to me? I mean, I get kind of lonely here, and you're here every Tuesday. We might as well talk."

"That'd be nice," I said, but talking wasn't what I wanted to do with her. "And call me Frank."

I'd been dreaming about kissing her for way too long. But I was out of practice talking to women, at least women I wanted to take to my bed, and that was the crux of the matter.

I'd thought for the longest time that Samantha's friend Brady was a suitor, so my plans to visit the library every week so I could get to know her had kind of died. But then I found out that, no, in fact, Brady was gay. Abey had filled me in when he and Theo Burroughs had gotten together, so I kept at it. Kept showing up. Maybe my divorce had put a damper on my confidence a bit, but it seemed to be making a comeback the longer I looked in her eyes.

"So, Frank," she said and smiled, "what else are you doing on your day off?"

I cleared my throat, trying to ignore how much I loved hearing her say my name. "I was gonna take Grumbly for a hike. Would you like to come with us?" Valentine's Day was only a couple days away, and I was betting she was a fan of the ridiculous holiday, but now that the words were tumbling out of my mouth, I didn't want to wait that long to take her out.

Her eyes grew huge, and she blinked. "Go with you?"

I winced. That had probably seemed pretty abrupt to her after more than a year of my Tuesday library visits. It wasn't like we never spoke. We did, of course, but just not a lot. Not after that first day. I never felt like she'd want to hear about my life. What could we possibly have in common, an old man and a beautiful young woman like her? When I was there, she was always on her laptop or busy setting up displays that she took pictures of for the library's Instagram page. I'd downloaded the stupid app just so I could see what she posted. The pictures rarely featured her, but I liked knowing what book she was talking about or what new thing she was into. Lately, it was growing herbs. She'd posted about starting up a seed exchange program for the library patrons.

She was still looking at me expectantly, waiting for me to finish asking her on a date. *Damn, man. You really are outta practice.* "The vet told me he needs to go on a hike. Thought I'd take a walk out toward the river. There's a nice path from here to there." Now I was groaning inside, realizing I sounded like I was ninety years old. Why didn't I just ask her to go shuffleboarding with me? Like I needed one more thing to make me seem older to her. Truth was, she had to be at least ten years younger than me, maybe more. I still didn't know her age. She probably had no clue what shuffleboarding was. I wasn't thrilled that I did.

"Thank you for the invite," she said, "but I can't leave work. There's an after-school tutoring group that comes later on Tuesday afternoons. Plus, there's a lot of snow left on the ground, maybe even ice." She turned to set her phone down, and when she turned back around, she blushed again. "But maybe we could go for a walk downtown after I get off? They salted the sidewalks down Main Street. I went for a walk last night."

I was nodding before she'd even finished speaking. I'd

known that. I was the one who'd called the county street department when they took their time getting to us. Wisper was a blip on their schedule, so sometimes they'd make us wait days for salt and plows.

"Yeah?" she asked in a tentative voice.

I wanted to say yes with conviction, but the only response I could seem to find was another nod. The little sparkle in her eye made the rest easy though. "Sounds good. Dinner?"

"Pick me up here at six-thirty?" She smiled at me, and my dick got hard. Oh, how I wanted Samantha Russo.

I wanted her bad. What in the hell had taken me so long to ask her out? And who knew it would be a damn dog to give me the courage?

A date wasn't a big deal. A nice meal with a nice woman. It didn't mean we'd get married. What was the harm?

It was occurring to me that my distrust of women, the thing that had convinced me for eleven years not to put myself out there, wasn't distrust at all. As I looked at the smile on her lips, I knew it was a fear of being disappointed, a fear of rejection, and a deep-seated fear I'd had since I was a kid that, once someone really got to know me, they'd leave.

But when I looked into her eyes, I wondered if Samantha Russo could be worth it all, and it seemed I was finally ready to take the risk.

CHAPTER FOUR

SAMANTHA

WHEN HE AND Grumbly left the library, Frank put his hat on and tipped it, then nodded at me. He did that a lot. He smiled, though, and my responding grin must've looked ridiculous.

Like it mattered. I'd been trying to rouse enthusiasm, but the library still wasn't very popular with the residents of Wisper, so as usual, Frank and I had been the only people there.

He was so cute when I'd mentioned breaking a rule. His nose crinkled up, his eyebrows crunching down, like it went against his very nature. *Hm.* It was the first time I'd ever considered him cute. He was always hot, no doubt about it, but today was the first time I'd pictured him as a little boy.

I'd always seen him as this hard, stern, giant of a guy. But he *was* cute. Adorable, really, the way he hung on my every word, the way his smile started in his eyes and then moved down to his mouth, and the way he pet Grumbly so lovingly without even noticing he was doing it when the puppy had sat next to him and leaned against Frank's leg.

But today, he'd really talked to me. He'd finally asked me out.

I had mixed feelings about it, though, because I still didn't know how freaking old he was.

Seriously though. Was he really going to name his dog Grumbly just because I'd suggested it?

Sometimes this little country town made me feel like I'd stepped back in time to a much simpler place where people were actually kind. You couldn't walk down Main Street without at least ten people saying, "Good day" or "Nice to see you." There were plenty of cowboys adjusting their hats at me all the time, saying, "Howdy, ma'am," or sometimes, "Hey, sweet thang, you wanna ride somethin'? I got me a big ol' bronco at home," and then they'd laugh and punch their buddies' arms.

I could've done without the latter, but still, it was like a bygone era where men were respectful even if they had no respect for you at all and where ladies wore skirt suits and slept in curlers so their hair was ready to be teased big the next day, like Cal DuBois.

There were lots of kids and teenagers, too, and they kept things modern with cell phones stuck to their fingers twenty-four hours a day, overpriced brand-name shoes, and bad attitudes. The mix of the two generations could sometimes be jarring.

I was closer to the kids' age at twenty-nine years old, almost thirty, but I felt like the older crowd. It was the main reason I was so excited about the book club. I had always been kind of a loner. I'd spent so much time alone as a kid, and the last few years hadn't improved that. My gramps said it was because I had an old soul, but it was more that I felt out of place. I dressed out of place, and I was just… different than most people my age.

I'd never been one to do what everyone else was doing to fit in.

Thrifting was my favorite thing in the world, besides reading, and I went resale shopping every time I had the chance, which wasn't often, usually because I didn't have a ride. I'd never learned to drive. There were a couple of small shops within walking distance, but unfortunately, I found more horse tack and used cowboy boots than I did vintage fashions or furniture, but finding a rare used item like an old dressing table or a hutch with bottle-glass doors was exciting to me, although living with Gramps definitely put a damper on the things I could bring home. His house was already filled to the brim with stuff. The man never threw anything away, so I had nowhere to put anything.

Hopefully someday soon, I'd get my own place, and then I could fill it with old traveling trunks and early American empire-style chairs.

My days might sound boring to some, but I'd had enough excitement in my life already, so this slow, small town seemed like the perfect place for me. Remembering the sounds of the grating traffic outside the hospital in Tampa, I thought, *If I never have to go back to a big, polluted, traffic-filled city again, I'll be—*

"Sam?"

"Huh?" I turned mid-thought to see my favorite author struggling to hold a heavy box in her hands. I hadn't even heard her come in.

My newest and best girlfriend in Wisper was a romance author, and she was a sight to behold, with her auburn shoulder-length curls framing her heart-shaped face perfectly. Like they'd been crafted by a sculptor, Juneau Moonlight's waves were big and wide, and they were always so shiny. "I'm so sorry I missed the meeting," she said as she plopped her box on the counter. "I had a phone meeting with my editor, and it ran late."

"It's okay. It was just a quick roll call basically. We made a plan to meet again in week or so." I tapped the box with my finger. "Are these the signed copies of the new Billionaire Brats book for the reading next month?"

"Yep," she said as I opened it, then grabbed my phone to snap a pic of her new book. The cover was hot, with a seriously physically fit man half dressed in suit pants, standing over a woman down on her knees, his tie wrapped around her throat. They weren't even touching in the picture, but the innuendo was there nonetheless. "There's one in there for you personally, a few for the library's collection, and I've got more in my car for the event next month."

"Perfect," I said. "Thanks. Oh, hey, we never discussed this, but were you thinking of keeping the reading small, like, with just local readers? Or I can totally promote this and get a bunch of people here."

"Oh, no. Let's keep it small."

"Are you sure? Don't you want to get the word out?"

"I guess, but I was thinking maybe we could just invite the ladies from the club and maybe a few others, and everyone could read a passage from their favorite romance book. And then maybe I could read a few paragraphs from the new release. We'll have food and drinks. Keep it light, and then we can post about it."

"It's Aiden and Aster's book, right?"

She nodded, glancing behind her at the front door. "*Aster's Billionaire Bad Boy.*"

"Sure," I said. "We can keep it local this time, but you've really got to try to get over this shyness, Juni. Your books are good. People need to know that."

"Yeah, yeah, thanks," she said, not even trying to hide the

change of subject. "Who was that big ol' hunk-o-man I just bumped into on my way in, and since when are dogs allowed in the library? I've seen him around town before. Isn't he the hot cop you told me about who comes in every week? I meant to tell you, I think Max knows him."

"Yeah, that's Frank. He's a deputy for the Sheriff's Department. He hasn't mentioned he knows Max—he doesn't really talk that much—but Wisper's so small, I'm sure your boyfriend and the hot cop are acquainted." I was still flushed from standing so close to him. My heart hadn't stopped pattering away inside my chest, but I was trying to act cool in front of Juni.

I'd only ever been that close to Frank one other time, when I'd lost my balance on my very first day at the library and he caught me at the last second before I fell on my ass. He held me in his arms, gazing into my eyes for at least thirty seconds longer than he'd needed to, and the whole time I'd been worried that I still had some of Phil's chocolate frosting on my face.

It felt good to be in his arms—not that I would ever let him in on that—but I'd been hoping since then that he might ask me out. I had been sure he would. I mean, the way he'd looked at me while he held me? All heat and intense gray-blue eyes. His lips had parted like he wanted to say something, but he didn't, and just before he lowered me to my feet, he squeezed his hand around my waist.

I had to excuse myself to the bathroom after he left so the Kid's Corner preschool group that had come in—or their parents—didn't notice the sweaty and overexcited mess I was.

Then he'd made it a regular thing. Other than one span of two weeks back in October, Frank showed up every Tuesday at eleven-thirty. He'd eat his lunch in his cruiser, and then he'd park his deliciously muscled ass in one of the library's under-stuffed, old armchairs and read a book, usually one about World War II or Vietnam.

But for the most part, the extent of the conversation I'd gotten out of him was a grunt or a mumble here or there. I'd thought maybe it was just me, but my friend Brady confirmed that Frank wasn't much of a talker with anyone.

I wondered why that was. And why had it taken him so long to ask me out? Was it the age thing? Obviously, there were a few years between us, but since I'd met him, I'd been dying to know what was going on in his head. And I guess there was the fact that, however old he was, he was most likely past the wanting-kids stage of life. That made him feel safe to me.

"Well, what's the story with him? There has to be one because you're blushing hardcore right now." Juneau cleared her throat, trying to pull my attention back to her, and she wiggled her eyebrows. It felt like I turned puce from head to toe.

"I think he finally asked me on a date. Or we kind of asked each other…? I'm not sure, but I was waiting for him to leave so I could freak out."

"Really?" She squealed. "He's hot. Good choice."

"Yeah, but he has to be years older than me, and he really doesn't talk very much. He's kind of grumpy."

"Oh, this is classic grumpy sunshine territory. You should know this. It's a trope I use all the time in my books, and Sam? It's hot. Give that grump a chance." She laughed. "You're lucky; you got grumpy sunshine and age gap all in one guy. You're a walking romance novel."

"Huh. I hadn't thought about it like that."

Juneau was smiling and nodding like the Cheshire cat.

"Anyway," I said with a flick of my wrist, trying to steer

the conversation back to the land of rational, "back to you and the reading."

She scoffed. "Never mind that. When's your date?"

"Um, tonight. Like"—I checked the clock on the wall above the cookbook alcove—"in six hours."

"What're you gonna wear? Something sexy, right? That man has naughty, forbidden sex written all over him. You could get some if you wanted."

I blushed again, a hot flash of need rushing over me because it had been way too long for me. Well over two years. Probably closer to three. But was she right? Was that what tonight was about? I mean, if it was only sex Frank wanted, would he have put in so much time with me? Granted, he barely spoke, but he appeared every week on time. If I was honest, I wasn't against a quick shag for the sake of shagging. But it didn't feel like Juneau was right.

Now, I just needed to decide if I wanted her to be.

Juneau looked me up and down. "What size are you? I think I've got just the thing for you to wear, if you need something. It's a wrap dress, so it'll fit any kind of curves you're willing to spill, and it's easy access if you want it to be. I'm gonna run home, grab the dress for you, and then we can talk about the reading."

CHAPTER FIVE

FRANK

SHUFFLING through the usually organized papers and files on my desk, I looked for the notebook I used to log the calls I went on. The one I kept in my jacket pocket was just for quick notes; the bigger one was where I wrote everything down. Shelley had set us up with the computer program the county provided to keep track of it all, but writing these things out on paper with a pen helped me to think things through. "Abey, have you seen my case log?"

Abey Lee, my co-deputy—and some days the bane of my existence—mumbled through a mouthful of chili. Her desk was a messy pile of casework and cracker crumbs. "Yeah. It's right here." Pushing a scattered pile of printed papers around, she lifted my notebook from underneath, and I snatched it from her fingers. "I needed a scrap of paper 'cause Max over at Milson Ranch called. His boss is pissed about somebody stealin' stuff outta the bunkhouse pantry. He wants Carey to look into it, but I didn't have anything to write Max's cell number on. I thought I had it but—"

"You can't just take shit from my desk and rip it up,

Abey. How many times I gotta tell you? And why didn't you just ask me? You know I have Max's number."

"Take a pill, Frank. You weren't here, and besides, those logs are just for your own personal organizational fits. It all goes into the computer system anyway."

She couldn't have texted me? "So? I like things how I like 'em. And why were you at the library earlier? You can hang out with your friends on your own time."

"Sorry," she said and then, under her breath, added, "stick-up-your-ass ol' fuddy-duddy."

"I heard that."

"I said it loud enough so you could." I grunted and Abey chuckled. "And for your information, I was on my lunch break."

I flashed a pointed look at her disgusting bucket of chili.

She shrugged, still chewing. "Shelley said you took a call at the bookstore. How'd it go?" Sprinkling grated cheese over the chili, she took another bite and spoke through the slop, "Oh my God, this chili is so good. We oughta sign José up for one of those cookin' competition shows. He'd win for sure."

"It went fine," I said, frowning at her general sloppiness. The woman couldn't keep her desk clean to save her life. I always had this irrational fear the mess on her desk would infect mine since they sat next to each other. "There was a theft there too. What's this damn town comin' to? People just helpin' themselves to whatever they want."

Pushing with her boots on the floor, she turned in her chair as I changed out of the emergency uniform shirt I kept in my truck for when I got called to a case on my day off. I pulled my old Army hoodie over my undershirt, and it messed up my hair. Leaning to the side, I checked my reflection in the front Main Street–facing window. Not that it'd matter too much if my hair was messy. It was short and gray. Couldn't do a lot with that.

"You look fine," Abey said. "Gettin' all gussied up for your date?"

I whirled around, trying not to show my shock. How the fuck did she know about that already? And of course I wasn't wearing a goddamn sweatshirt to a dinner date.

She smirked. "Small town." Tapping her temple with her finger, she said, "You hear the gossip every day. Did you really think you'd be the one to escape it?"

I grumbled, "Damn no-good busybodies."

She snorted. "You are a literal curmudgeon."

Narrowing my eyes, I glared at her, and she laughed and turned back toward her desk. "Well," she said, "so who asked who out?" When I didn't answer, she added, "Obviously Sam asked you. As if you'd even open your mouth long enough for that many words to come out."

"I asked her," I said, and I tried to leave it at that, but I should've known better.

"Really?" She spun back around. "Nuh uh. I don't believe it."

Carey slammed the door on the way out of his office. "Don't believe what?" he asked as he flipped through mail on Shelley's desk. Our receptionist wasn't any more organized than Abey. If Carey could find what he was looking for, I'd buy a lottery ticket.

"Frank asked the librarian out."

Carey paused, looking at me. "You did?"

"Yeah," I said. "What's the big deal?"

"Nothin'. Um"—he made a face and turned his head in Abey's direction so she could help him wiggle out of the conversation—"it's just that…"

She took a deep breath before she made it worse. "It's just

that you don't usually… um. You know, you're not the friendliest guy. No, that's not what I meant." She winced. "What I mean is—"

Carey changed the subject to shut her up. "Where's Shelley?"

Abey answered, focusing back on her food. "She ran down to the Discount Mart to get somethin' for little Liam's school project. Q-tips or cotton puffs or somethin'."

"She couldn't do that *after* work?"

"Don't look at me," Abey said. "You know that woman does whatever she wants. I ain't gonna try to stop her. Are you?"

Carey's face changed from annoyed to uncertain, and then he scrunched it up. "Tell her I said to go shoppin' on her own time."

"Yes, sir, Sheriff Michaels. Sure," Abey joked. "I'll do that right after I tell your wife she needs to feed you better so you ain't so grumpy in the middle of the day. Both of those comments would go over about as well as a fart in church."

"Nice," I said. "You got a mouth on you filthier than a trucker."

"And damn proud of it," she said, slurping another bite from her plastic spoon. "So fuck a duck."

Carey rolled his eyes and pushed out the front door as he fixed his hat on his head. "Be back in a bit. I'm headed out to take that call at Milson's ranch, and I will *not* tell Frannie what you said, unless you wanna get punched out by a sleep-deprived mother of a tween and a one-year-old."

"You two are a couple of grumpy buttheads," Abey said as the door closed. "Carey's usually much more chipper. What gives?"

"Got me," I said. "You'll have to ask him. *I* don't go around gossipin' about shit that ain't my business."

Abey smiled, turning toward her desk again, picking up a copy of *Country 4-Wheeling* magazine. She flipped the pages slowly, then dropped it on top of a book with a half-naked man on the cover who looked like he spent every workout on abs and shoulders. I was steering clear of that subject. "Oh, Frank, you dear, *dear* man. The whole town's gonna be talkin' about you after your date tonight. I'm takin' bets on how long till you yell at one of those busybodies or threaten to arrest 'em."

She snickered, and I grabbed my gun and holster, slung my badge over my neck, and got the fuck out of there.

"C'mon, Grumbly." He jumped up from the bed Abey had made for him out of old blankets in the corner and followed me to the door.

"You named your dog Grumbly? Oh my God!"

Her fit of laughter was the last thing I heard before I let the door slam shut behind me.

When I picked Samantha up, I was in awe as I gazed up at her standing at the top of the steps outside the library. She'd changed her dress. It was definitely shorter, and her legs were bare beneath it. The only protection she had against the brisk February air was a bright pink sweater she wore over her dress, and it kept dragging my eyes down to those bare calves. Wasn't she cold? I did like the look of her legs though. The longer skirts she usually wore kept them hidden. I couldn't remember ever seeing her wear jeans.

"You changed," I said.

She glanced down, fidgeting with the hem of the black dress two inches above her knees, the oversized sweater's excess fabric bunching up around her wrist. Her fingernails had been painted the same color pink as her hair. "I did. You don't like it?" She looked up, her eyes uncertain.

"Said nothin' of the sort."

Twisting her lips to one side, she frowned. "You didn't really say anything."

Shit. I was already blowing this date. "You're beautiful no matter what you wear." It was the truth.

That made her smile, and she stood a little taller.

"You ready?" I asked. "It's cold. I'll drive."

"Let's walk. It's not that cold."

"It's February."

"So?" she said, looking behind me. "The sunset is nice, and I've been sitting most of the day."

"Okay then." It was below freezing, and driving would be much more comfortable, but I wasn't about to argue with her on our first date. It got me to thinking though. "You walk a lot."

She nodded, slinging her big, flowery bag over her shoulder, clomping down the steps in her black combat boots. I tried not to let my smile show.

I'd been a keen observer of all things Samantha Russo for over a year, and the one thing I knew for certain about her was that she was kind and gentle, so the boots she wore, the colorfully dyed hair, and the flashes of silver from all the rings on her fingers and the tiny silver ball in her nose was all just a part of an armor she tried to project around herself. She wasn't tough. She wouldn't even hurt a spider. I'd seen her rescue them and carefully remove them from the library in a cup. She placed them in the grass outside and then watched as they crept away.

No, Wisper's librarian and the most beautiful woman in my world was nothing if not sweet.

"Don't think I've ever seen you drive."

She tsked. "Well, that may be because I don't know how. Oh, and I don't have a car."

Um... huh? "How's that?"

She shrugged. "I never learned. My parents traveled a lot for their jobs, and I usually went with, so it was never a priority. And when I went to college, and then grad school, I didn't need a car."

I fell in step beside her when she hopped off the bottom step, and we walked slowly and silently down Franklin to the corner. Before we crossed, she pushed her arm through mine, holding onto my forearm.

She looked up at me, and I nearly tripped and fell on my face. Her eyes this close up were the prettiest hazel color. I'd always thought they were just plain brown, but since she'd changed her hair, I'd started noticing the flecks of amber and green in them, and now, they sparkled at me.

"Where are we going?" she asked.

"Paulo's."

"What's that?"

"New restaurant downtown."

"Okay. That sounds nice."

She let go of me to adjust her dress, tugging at the hem again like maybe she wasn't used to the length or maybe her legs were cold. The slide of her arm against my side was warm, but she was shivering a little. It was barely noticeable, but I took my jacket off and draped it over her shoulders, then reached for her hand, guiding it under my arm again as we continued walking.

"Thank you."

"Don't you have a coat?"

"Yeah. It didn't go with my outfit."

I didn't respond to that, but the thought flitted through my head that maybe she was a little nuts. She'd lived through one

Wisper winter. She should've known better than to not have proper protection from the cold in the middle of February.

She looked up at the side of my face and, in a quiet voice, said, "It's weird that you're so forward."

"Weird?" I wasn't forward. I just didn't want her to stop touching me.

"Yeah, because you don't really talk. I thought you were shy, but—"

"I ain't shy."

"I'm getting that."

She squeezed my arm and faced forward as we walked past Henly's Gift Shop on the north end of Main Street. Henly's was a longtime Wisper staple, but we'd had a few new businesses like Paulo's pop up around town since Theo Burroughs had opened up the community center, Ace's House, in the middle of downtown, next to the station. He was rumored to be a billionaire, and apparently, he had a lot of rich friends. The Italian restaurant really was too fancy for our small town, but I'd heard the food was good.

"So," she said, "did you grow up here?"

"No."

"Oh." It took a minute, but she continued, "I guess I assumed because of your accent."

"Grew up in Texas."

"Where in Texas?"

"Little town called Risk. East Texas."

"I've never been there."

Not many people had. I'd lived other places in Texas before my mama died, but I worked hard not to think about them. Or her.

We crossed Washington Street, and Samantha's grip on my arm got a little tighter. Not that there was any traffic for me to protect her from, but I liked that she knew I would.

Stopping in the middle of the road, she pulled ever so gently. "Frank?"

I turned, and we were face to face. Seeing her in my leather jacket was some kind of turn-on. The jacket dwarfed her, but she'd settled into it like it was her own. I didn't think she noticed me watching out of the corner of my eye when she'd sniffed the collar. I was glad I'd made the decision to grab another shower when I'd taken Grumbly home. I'd even used the aftershave that had been sitting on my bathroom counter for more than a couple years, untouched.

"If you've changed your mind, it's okay. We don't have to go to dinner."

Pulling the sides of the jacket together to keep the warmth in when she shivered again, I stepped closer, a little confused. "Haven't changed my mind."

"Okay, it's just…" Her eyes were big and bright as she looked at me. Was she nervous? "You're barely talking to me. You give one-word answers, but even that feels like pulling teeth."

Barely talking? I'd just said more to her than I had to anyone in the last year, or at least, that was how it felt. Dammit. I needed to salvage this, or she'd change *her* mind.

Checking behind me for traffic that still wasn't there, I turned back to her and lifted my hands to her face. I held it, feeling my warm hands heat her cold cheeks. "I haven't changed my mind, Samantha. I'm quiet. I reckon it's just my nature, but I promise you, there's nowhere on earth I'd rather be."

CHAPTER SIX

SAMANTHA

WHOA.

Frank Sims was intense. It felt like he wanted to be on a date with me, but seriously, I was doing all the work, trying to coax basic information out of him. But when he looked in my eyes and promised there was nowhere else he'd rather be, I felt it in deep-down places. My core heated and zinged, and my mouth went slack.

Having his attention focused on me now that we were actually engaging in conversation—sparse though it was—felt really good.

His eyes zeroed in on my lips, and I wanted him to kiss me. I'd been dreaming about him kissing me for forever. Since that first day, when I'd fallen into his arms. It seemed like he wanted it, too, as he leaned even closer, but then he cleared his throat, turned us, and he dragged me to the sidewalk. "C'mon. You're freezin'."

"Okay." It was true. I was so cold, I thought my legs would freeze like popsicles. Whose bright idea had it been to walk to the restaurant?

The bossy way Frank had about him was alluring. Maybe

it wasn't bossy, per se, more like quietly confident, and I was drawn to it, to him, to his body like flicker to a flame.

It was the reason I did what he said without argument, but I was dying to ask him how old he was. The closer I got to him, the more lines I could see around his eyes, and the skin on the back of his neck above his shirt collar was tanned and tough, like he'd spent years in the sun. Maybe more years than I had been alive.

His stubbled beard was a mix of dark and light—mostly light—and even his eyebrows were going gray.

He was sexy. Sexier than any man I'd ever dated before.

The dress Juneau had lent me fit well, though she was a little more blessed in the chest department than I was, so the top part was loose. And it was definitely shorter than the skirts I usually wore, but it looked good with my boots, and the deep black hue had made my hair pop in the library's bathroom mirror, despite the fluorescent lighting.

Out of the corner of my eye, I watched Frank beside me, with my arm through his and my short, bubble gum–pink painted fingernails resting on his muscled forearm. I was comparing us. It was obvious he was older than me. Unless he'd gone almost completely gray at thirty, I would've bet he was quite a lot older than me. He was a lot taller than me, too, maybe six foot three or four.

He was more fit than anyone I'd ever met. The way his dark-washed jeans molded to his thighs and ass made my mouth water, and his shoulders were like two flesh-covered boulders that made the buttons of his long-sleeved Henley stretch and strain for safety back in their little buttonholes. I couldn't help noticing how defined his pectoral muscles were underneath. Seriously, what straight woman on planet Earth wouldn't? He'd given me his leather jacket, then pushed his shirt sleeves halfway up his forearms, and I'd wanted to rub my face on them to feel how warm they were. If he was cold, he didn't show it.

Hair covered those arms from his wrists all the way up and under his shirt. It peeked out from the neckline, and I imagined it everywhere on his body. I wondered if it helped to keep him warm, like a bear. *Ha.* Exactly like a bear in one of the shifter romances Aislinn had talked about. Would it keep me warm if we were naked and snuggled—

He grumbled, and I looked up at the side of his face again, freaking out for just a second, worrying he'd somehow heard my thoughts. *Ridiculous.* Thankfully, he wasn't a mind reader and was only side-eyeing a bunch of nosy people crowded around the door at the coffee shop, peeking at us as we walked by. Juneau was in there, and when I spotted her, she waved, wiggled her eyebrows, and gave me a thumbs-up. Next to her, Max Gordon, her severely handsome boyfriend, with his wavy blond hair under a black cowboy hat, shook his head, laughing, and kissed her cheek.

"Do you know Juneau?" I asked Frank.

"I know *of* her," he said. "I know every person in this town. Hazard of the job."

"Mm, yeah, I suppose you get to meet all kinds of people working for the Sheriff's Department. I met Juneau a little while after I moved here. She's really cool. She's doing a reading at the library next month."

"A what?"

"She's an author, so she does book readings and signings. She'll read a little from her new book for a group of romance fans. She writes steamy billionaire romance."

"Steamy billionaire…?" He looked perplexed as he worked the words over in his mind. A guy like Frank probably couldn't understand why anyone would want to read about sexy billionaires, especially since his reading genre of choice was nonfiction. I didn't explain any further. It was kind of fun to watch him squirm a little.

"Do you know her boyfriend?"

"Max? Mm, he's a buddy of mine. Helped me with some renovations on my property."

"That's cool," I said. "What kind of renovations?"

Placing his hand over mine still on his arm, he stopped walking, and I looked up at the building behind him. A big neon sign written in cursive lower-case lettering was pulsing "paulo's" in the fading daylight. Winter's shortened days had stolen the sunshine, but the blush of the pastel evening sunset was the perfect backdrop, and it set the purple sign off, making it glow in the darkening sky.

"We're here," he said, watching me like he was studying a puzzle he needed to solve. "Hope you're hungry."

What did I have smeared across my face this time? Hooking a stray strand of hair behind my ear nervously, I said, "Starving."

<hr>

"Whoa."

Settling into my chair while Frank held it for me, I was a little uncomfortable as I peeked around the restaurant at walls full of art and statues. There was even a waterfall feature in the middle of the room. We seemed out of place surrounded by such opulence, me like an immature girl, and Frank looked like he could be my—

I snorted at the thought.

Laying his cloth napkin over his muscular thighs as he sat, he eyed me dubiously and arranged his silverware on the table just so.

"Nothing," I said as an answer to the question he didn't

even ask. "It's just, this place is kind of over the top for Wisper, you know?"

"Heard the food is good."

A waiter appeared, setting two crystal glasses of water in front of us and handing over two menus wrapped in black leather he'd had tucked under his arm. Real leather, not that fake, stiff kind. The waiter seemed familiar, but I couldn't place him. Maybe he'd come into the library. Usually, I was good at recognizing my patrons' faces, but if I'd only spoken to them once, it was hard to commit them to memory. I was even worse with names.

"I'll give you a few minutes," the server said, and he smiled and walked away.

I opened my menu and almost sprayed Frank with a sip of water. "Fifty dollars for a steak? This isn't even a steakhouse."

"If it's good, it's worth it. If it ain't, we won't come back."

Come back? Was he already planning on a second date? I had a few questions for him first before I could commit to anything like that. And was he always so serious?

I wasn't used to spending money on food like this. Seriously, I didn't spend money on anything like this. I didn't *have* money. Not a lot anyway. The majority of my clothes were purposefully secondhand, and the most I'd spent on a meal in the last year was ten bucks at José's Diner. Talk about good food. Of course, my parents offered to send me money. They knew how much the county paid me to run the library, which was a paltry amount. And they had plenty to spare, but no. I didn't want their money. What I wanted from them was their consideration.

"Are you sure this is okay? I mean, obviously, I'll pay half, but we could go somewhere else."

His eyebrows fell slowly as I talked, and he fiddled with his silverware again, tipping the butter knife with his index finger until it was perfectly straight in relation to his fork. The rounded shape of the metal handle made it spin away from where he seemed to want it to stay. I thought he might yell at it or stab it into the tabletop. "You will not pay half. I asked you to dinner. It's on me."

"Thank you, but you don't have to do that. This isn't 1950. I can pay my way. And are you sure? José's has seriously good chili, and it's, like, five bucks with homemade dinner rolls and the best steak fries on the planet."

He scrunched his nose when I mentioned chili, and then his face morphed into a kind of stone-like wall, impassible like Caradhras Pass in *Lord of the Rings*. Snowy and impossible.

"You don't like chili?"

"Love it," he said, "but the smell of it lately turns my stomach sour. Abey eats it for lunch on the regular."

"Abey?"

"Deputy Lee. Blonde, annoyin'."

"Oh, right. I knew that. She just joined my book club. I don't know why I can't remember her name. It's unique enough." See? Case in point. I felt bad that I'd already forgotten her name, but when she'd come to the library earlier, she talked about Frank, so that was all I had been able to focus on. I knew who she was, though, obviously.

He grunted his agreement.

God, he made me nervous. It felt like there was an invisible energy between us, like lightning ready to crack. It felt like a good energy, but I didn't know what to do with it as it pulsed and grew.

A few minutes passed without a word from either of us while we waited for the server to make his next appearance. I looked around at the other couples and families in the restaurant while Frank watched a little boy two tables over as he played with green plastic soldier men on the arm of his chair. There was a smile trying to emerge on Frank's lips, but he was schooling it hard.

Then his gaze landed on me. I felt it, and I couldn't take the silence anymore. I needed to know what he was thinking. The not knowing was working me up into a ball of anxiety.

It just didn't make sense that a man like him would be into me.

Apparently, Frank couldn't handle the silence either, and when I turned back to him, we spoke at the same time.

He said, "You ain't payin' for dinner," while I asked, "Why's she annoying?"

"Wait," I argued. "You can't stop me from paying my half."

He smirked, cocking his head to the side. "Sure I can."

"No, you can't. Besides, that would be rude."

"Darlin', I wrangle criminals for a livin'. If you think I can't lock your wrists in one hand in under a second, you're sorely mistaken. And if you can't reach for your money, you can't pay." He seemed satisfied with that answer, and a tiny little part of me was hoping it was a promise.

"You're stubborn," I said, folding my arms across my chest and relaxing back into my seat.

"Wouldn't be the first time someone accused me of that."

"This isn't a promising start to our date. We're arguing already." It was true, but I'd surprised myself when I said it so boldly. His quietness intimidated me.

He sighed and sat forward, resting his elbows on the tabletop. "Samantha, I'm not tryin' to be difficult. Where I come from, when a man asks a woman to dinner, he pays. Or the woman does. If you'd asked me out, I'd let you pay. In fact, you can pay next time. Deal?"

Narrowing my eyes at him, I was trying to decipher if he was being honest, or if once he got me on a second date, he'd take it back and never let me pay. And technically, I asked him!

And then I reminded myself that I was a poor librarian, so why was I complaining?

With his elbows still on the table and his hands clasped together, he rubbed his chin slowly against his thumbs while he awaited my answer, eyes narrowed a bit, like he was calculating the chances that I'd give in.

Something about him made me want to please him. "Fine. Deal." I relented and smiled. "Thank you."

He straightened and smiled, too, a satisfied easing of a stress in his mouth, and in that small movement was the answer to my question. That was why I'd wanted to please him—to see his smile.

He'd only shown it to me a few times over the last year, once earlier today, when we'd agreed to dinner.

The sexy tilt of his lips was accompanied by more lines around his eyes and on his forehead, beneath the silver of his salt-and-pepper hair. It was cut into a military kind of style, but a lot longer on the top than an enlisted soldier, and it made me want to run my fingers through it. Was it coarse or soft? The hair on the sides and back of his neck had been shaved short, though, and it suited him, like he preferred things to be tidy and easy to control so they'd fit exactly in place.

Those lines around his eyes as his smile softened reminded me of the ever-present question in my mind. I blurted, "How old are you?"

The waiter interrupted before Frank could answer, and

when I looked up at him, I remembered his name. "Jason, right? I remember now."

"Yeah," he said.

"You came to the library looking for books for your psychology dissertation."

"Yep." After setting two empty wine glasses in front of us, he placed a wooden platter in the middle of the table that was topped with a large piece of artisan bread on a bed of fresh rosemary along with two small ramekins filled with butter. He wore black skinny jeans under his plum-colored server's apron, and his highlighted brown hair was curly and carefree. He was obviously closer to my age than Frank was, and it made me wonder what Frank thought about our age difference.

"Well, how'd it turn out?" I asked. "Your paper?"

"Good. I graduated before Christmas." He smiled at me and tilted his head a little. "You had just moved here. Am I remembering that right?"

"That's right," I said. "A little over a year ago now. Almost a year and a half."

He turned toward Frank. "And this is your f—?"

"You remember me, don'tcha, little Jason Dobbs?" Frank interrupted in his serious deputy voice. I thought Jason was about to be read his rights. "Do believe I arrested you a few years ago for disorderly conduct at the Fourth of July festival. Didn't you get drunk and urinate on a tree in the middle of town?"

It looked like poor Jason was choking on his own tongue. "Um, yeah. I mean, yes, sir. I'm sorry about that." He stepped back, lifting a tablet almost in front of his red face. "Are you ready to order, sir?"

CHAPTER SEVEN

FRANK

HER FATHER?

Definitely not the role I was aiming for.

The flirting idiot took our order—shrimp scampi for Samantha and steak for me. She ordered a glass of merlot, and I kept my water, and when he slithered away, she picked up right where she'd left off.

"So," she said again, "how old are you?"

My age wasn't anything to be embarrassed about, but the difference between us was beginning to glare. Our moron of a server looked like he was a better fit for Samantha's date than I was, by a mile.

No sense hiding it from her. "I'll be forty-nine in a week."

She gasped. "Forty-n—" If the red flush spreading across her cheeks was any indication, I was right that the gap between our ages was wide open. Maybe I should've looked up her background at the station before our date tonight so I could've been prepared, but it would've been a violation of her privacy.

"Frank," she whispered, looking around, making sure no one could hear her. "I'm thirty. Or I will be, also next week."

Okay, so nineteen years was a bit of a difference. I'd probably be six feet under by the time she reached my age.

Shit. She was only five years older than half my age. "When's your birthday?"

The warmth in her eyes when she smiled at me, though, was making it easier by the minute to ignore that fact. To try to forget our differences. But then I smiled, too, 'cause I just knew she was about to say—

"February seventeenth."

Raising my eyebrows, I crossed my arms over my chest, smug satisfaction written all over my face. "We have the same birthday."

"Your birthday is the seventeenth too?"

Maybe I could make her forget too. "It is. See? We ain't so far apart."

"There's almost twenty years between us, Frank. How can you say that?"

Then again, she *could* be my— *Jesus, Frank. What are you doing with this woman?*

"Frank? Where'd you go?"

Shaking my head, I tried to shake it off when she caught me in the realization that I was old enough to be her fucking parent. I didn't know what the hell to do with that knowledge. "Nowhere." I changed the subject, and with style, if I did say so myself. "So how did you get into the library sciences?"

"You know what that is?"

"I have a good guess, I think."

"Oh, well, there's a lot more to it than just the checkout person at the front desk. In a small town like Wisper, there are a lot of community building opportunities. Like, I've been thinking about starting a seed library and maybe a yoga class for senior citizens." She snorted at herself softly. "After I learn how to *do* yoga. But I've loved books my whole life. They were always there for me."

When she didn't add anything further, I nodded, waiting for her to go on, and it seemed there wasn't a better subject I could've asked her about. It didn't take but a minute, and she was talking around me in circles, sounding so in love with life and so intelligent. I was mesmerized by her.

"I love the research part of it too. It feels good to help people when they need information or want a certain kind of book, but really, I just love books. It's that simple. My parents traveled for their jobs. I spent summers here with my grandparents, but the rest of the year, I spent a lot of time in a hotel room, on a plane or train, or on a set. Books allowed me to escape the fact that I was a tagalong and a burden to my own parents. They barely cared if I did the homework my teachers would assign when they whisked me off on another trip. It was like they decided to have a kid and then went, 'Oh, maybe that wasn't such a good idea. Whatever, we'll just drag her along.'"

"A set?"

"Movie sets. I spent a lot of time on movie sets growing up."

"Your parents are actors?"

"Independent film directors. Husband-and-wife team. They were never really attentive parents, but they're creative and generous. Just not generous with me, not with their time. And not with each other. I'm actually kind of surprised they stayed married all these years. Better for tax purposes, I guess."

"I'm sorry to hear that." So maybe that was why she always had her nose stuck in a romance book.

Shrugging one shoulder, she said, "It's not a big deal. I got to see the world. It was an adventure, I suppose, and sometimes it was even fun. And it wasn't like they were neglectful, just not… warm or very nurturing. So I read about people who were or about fantastic worlds I could get lost in. I could ignore my parents' indifference to each other and to me, and they never complained when I needed a new book because it meant they could do what they wanted, and I'd comply. There's probably thousands of books out there with my childhood signature scratched on the last page. I signed every book I read and left it in the train or the hotel, hoping someone else would pick it up and read it."

"That's real sweet," I said, imagining her wide-eyed view of the world back then. But then I caught myself trying *not* to imagine what I had looked like when she was ten years old. I was twenty-nine then. "You're a dreamer."

I liked that. It fit the hopeless romantic I saw her as. But as I smiled at the thought, I realized what it meant—that she most likely had a lot of expectations and big ideas about love —and it sent red flags straight to my brain. I ignored them, too, or I tried to, but I lived in the real world.

Maybe she was right that this date wasn't a good idea. The last time I found myself caught up with a wishy-washy romantic, I lost my dog, my house, and all I got was a lousy divorce.

Her cheeks flushed at my dreamer comment, turning a pale pink color that matched her hair. But then her eyes shot to the door behind me. "Holy crap," she said. "Is that Vern?"

I turned to see for myself, and sure enough, there was Vernon Wexler, dumbest outlaw on the planet and definitely not the best dressed. Except tonight, he was mixing it up in pressed Wranglers, a gray suit vest and white button-down, and a spiffy, new black felt hat. He had a pretty woman on his arm who seemed just as confused as I was that Vern looked so good. She kept stealing quick glances at him.

Samantha called over to them and waved. "Vern, is that you? You look amazing. Hi, Millie."

Millie looked relieved to see Samantha. She released Vern's arm and rushed to our table. I stood, trying to figure out how to greet the guy I'd arrested more than a few times. But I wasn't a dick. If Vern was turning over a new leaf, I could accept that. It didn't mean I wouldn't still keep my eye on him though.

Peeking at me, Millie leaned down to hug Samantha. "I'm so glad to see you."

"Are you on a date with Vern?"

"I didn't think it was a date," Millie whispered before Vern caught up with her. "I think *he* thinks it's a date though." She caught a glance over her shoulder and straightened when he approached.

Sam stood, too, placing her cloth napkin on the tabletop after folding it into thirds. She smiled. "You look really good, Vern. I don't think I've ever seen you so dressed up."

"Thank you, ma'am." He tipped his hat but then remembered his manners enough to remove it inside a restaurant. When he pulled it off, I was surprised to see his head had been shaved, his hair only half an inch long. No more mullet for Vern.

Good on him. He did kind of look like a new man. And his date was beautiful, with her long, yellow-blond hair and sparkling sky-blue eyes. Vern's eyes were only for Millie; he was puffed up with pride, but I wasn't sure that was doing it for her. She looked unsure. He hadn't even noticed me yet.

"You guys look so good," Samantha said. "Can I take your picture for the library's Instagram page?"

"Why?" Vern asked at the same time the question popped into my head.

"I snap photos of all kinds of things, just so people can

see what a cool town Wisper is. I'm hoping to get our following up so maybe more people will come to the library." She looked at me. "Remind me to take a picture of the restaurant sign outside before we leave."

I nodded as Vern looked at me finally. Why did she have to take pictures of everything? Was that a generational thing? She'd already taken pictures of our drink glasses. Why on earth would anybody want to see that?

Millie smiled, turning to give Samantha a side view. She sucked in her trim stomach and fluffed her hair. "You can take our picture."

Vern seized the opportunity to touch Millie, wrapping his arm around her waist as Samantha pulled her phone from her bag under our table. "Thanks," she said, grinning at the odd couple, and she took a quick photo. "Well, enjoy your dinner. Oh, I'm so sorry. Millie, Vern, this is Frank." She motioned to me, smiling at me, too, and my heart skipped a beat. It stuttered into an uneven rhythm as she blinked, probably wondering what to call me.

Was this a date? Technically, it was, but we didn't really know each other. She wouldn't call me her boyfriend. If she did, it would've felt ridiculous. I was too old to be anybody's "boyfriend." "Frank's a deputy. He works for the Sheriff's Department."

Vern shrank back a step, releasing his hold on Millie. "Uh, yep. Pretty sure I knew that." He faced me. "Howdy, sir. I apologize for the trouble I mighta caused you in the past."

That stopped me in my tracks. This was definitely a different Vern. Before, he would've flipped me off and spat in my direction. What the hell had happened to the guy? Maybe he'd been doing some soul searching since his idiot best buddy had been carted off to federal prison. Carey arrested the guy, and Abey'd had the pleasure of hauling his worthless ass to the feds in Jackson after he beat his wife, neglected his kid, and broke all kinds of laws six ways to Sunday.

Now, Vern had a job at the community center. I'd even seen him around town helping people just 'cause they needed it. He didn't get paid to hang Christmas lights for Avery Fletcher at the flower shop after she'd dropped a bucket full of flowers, slipped on the spilled water, and broken her leg. No one asked him to deliver groceries to Veda Alderson after Carey had taken her license away 'cause she'd run her old Buick into the tree in her front yard for a third time, but he did it anyway. If the people of Wisper were talking about it, I was definitely hearing about it, and I'd heard plenty recently about Vern.

I stuck my hand out to him. "The past is the past. Good to see you doin' well, Vern."

The nod and small smile on his face as we shook was my good deed for the day; I wasn't known for being overly friendly.

Millie threw Vern some kind of look. Maybe she hadn't known about his many arrests, but I'd figured everyone in Wisper knew. Finally, she looked at me. "I've seen you outside the station. It's nice to meet you. My best friend is Devo. She works at Ace's House next door."

"I think I remember seein' you there. Nice to meet you too."

Vern held his hand out toward Millie, urging her on to their table when the hostess mentioned it was ready. I hoped he had enough cash to cover the fancy dinner they were about to order, but then I figured Theo Burroughs probably paid him pretty well. "Ma'am," he said to Samantha.

Millie responded with something that resembled half a smile and the other half a wince.

"Have fun," Samantha said as they walked away, and I

hurried around the table to hold her chair for her before she sat, but she didn't wait for me. Scooting in, she placed her napkin over her thighs again and looked up at me.

I thought there might've been a glint of defiance in her eyes, like she knew I was old-fashioned, but she didn't want to admit she was interested in those kinds of gestures from me.

Maybe that was generational too. The thing was, though, it had nothing to do with her being a "pretty little lady" and more to do with her being my beautiful date. I held the chair for everyone I ate with, man or woman. It had nothing to do with who they were but everything to do with who I was.

She interrupted my thought when she spoke. "Vern helps me sometimes at the library when I need something fixed. He does it for free. Isn't that nice?"

I nodded again, wondering if my neck would be sore later for all the damn nodding I was doing, and why she hadn't told me she needed help. I would've fixed anything for her, and I was there often enough.

"So where were we?" she asked as I sat. "Oh yeah. What about you?"

"What about me?"

"What was your childhood like? What do you want from life?"

I tried not to groan out loud. I hated lying to people, but in this instance, maybe a white lie was a better way to go. Part truth, part fib. "It was fine. I was adopted." I contemplated what to say next. Would she run? But I wanted to tell her. I took the chance. "And family. Always imagined I'd have a family by now."

She chewed the inside of her lip for a minute, staring into my eyes, then looked down, taking a sip of her wine and brushing over the family thing when she asked, "You were adopted? What was that like?" Some kind of look flashed across her face, but I had no idea what it was about.

"Mm," I said and shrugged.

"Your adoptive parents were good to you?"

I nodded.

"Are they still alive?"

"Yep."

"And do you have any brothers or sisters?"

"They adopted other kids after me, but I was grown by then, so we're not close."

"And what about your… birth parents?"

And here was the hard part. The less detail I gave her, the better off this date would go. Who wants to hear about a kid living alone on the street at thirteen years old, sleeping in train stations and under railroad tracks, eating food out of dumpsters, even stealing from restaurants and grocery stores? And that was *after* living in drug dens and sleeping on other addicts' filthy couches while the person who was supposed to be looking out for me was getting high in some back room, probably having sex to pay for her drugs.

"My father died overseas when I was ten, and then my mama got… sick." Sick of being a mother. Did that count?

"I'm so sorry."

"Don't remember it much. I was adopted in my teens, graduated high school, and then I joined the Army." Hopefully she was picking up on the finality of that last word. No use going back and crying over spilled milk. "The Army's where I learned to be a man. It's where I grew up. Taught me a lot."

"You liked the Army?"

"I did."

"What was your job?"

"MP."

Her eyebrows were doing that rising thing again. "I don't know what that is, Frank."

"Military police."

"Oh, so that's where you learned how to be a deputy?"

"Basically."

"What made you want to join the Army?"

I shrugged. "My dad."

She twisted her lips a little, taking her time before she said, "You're kind of clamming up on me again. Do you not like talking about your time in the service?"

It was a hell of a lot easier than talking about my childhood.

"Frank, why did you ask me on this date if you don't actually want to talk to me?"

I grumbled at her but then realized it was a fair question. "It's just that you went right for the heart of the matter. I haven't talked about this stuff in a long time. And…"

"And what?"

"Don't talk about myself very often."

"I'm sorry," she said, sitting forward. She propped her elbows on the table, cupping one hand over the other. "But isn't that the whole point of a date? To get to know each other? But I didn't mean to get too personal. We can talk about anything. What would you like to talk about?"

"You." It was the truth. I wanted to know what made Samantha Russo tick.

Did I see red flags everywhere? Yes. Did I care? Not so much.

Why was that?

Seemed I was taking all kinds of risks tonight. "I want you to tell me about the things you love."

"Why?" she asked shyly. I kind of liked her like this. I'd never really seen her as shy before, but then, I'd never really had a conversation with her. Not a personal one. Her bashfulness when I asked her about her dreams was more proof that she wasn't so tough.

"Why what?"

She blushed, and I swore I could feel the warmth rush over her skin across the small table. "Why do you want to know about me?"

Leaning toward her, I took her hand in mine before she could go for her wine glass again. "Many reasons, but when you laugh, it makes me feel hopeful. I haven't felt like that in a long time."

Hm. When it came out of my mouth, I knew it was the truth.

Her eyes softened, and she sighed. "Whoa."

Guess it was the right answer.

She didn't bring up age again, and we ate. She even mowed down some kind of cake with Chantilly cream on top, and I sat back, watching her with something akin to satisfaction in my chest and low in my stomach, warming the food I'd barely eaten 'cause I couldn't pay attention to hunger with the sound of her voice all around me in our little corner of the restaurant. Besides, the mushrooms that had come with my steak were drowning in butter, and I didn't even want to think about that shit coating the insides of my arteries.

Talking with her hands, she made big sweeping movements while she described traveling through Italy and France, pulling bread apart and stuffing it into her mouth before she finished a sentence. It was charming, and her zest for life was sexy. She talked about fancier dinners than ours in castles in Scotland and at the top of the Eiffel Tower, and I listened, but a small, far-off part of my mind remembered all the diner and fast-food dinners I'd had in comparison. Cans of beans and sweet corn. I was glad I'd brought her to Paulo's, but something told me she really would've been just as happy at José's Diner.

Our age difference was bothering her though. I could tell every time a terse little frown appeared on her face when she made mention of something I knew nothing about, like bands she liked or concert festivals she wanted to go to, movies I hadn't seen, or books I hadn't read.

Truthfully, I couldn't stop guessing what she had looked like or what she'd been doing at different points in my life. She was one year old when I'd joined the Army. A baby. As sappy as it sounded in my head, I felt pride when I realized I had been protecting the freedom she would grow up in. But still, I felt flat-out old sitting across from her.

The background music in the restaurant played quietly over speakers in the ceiling. I didn't recognize the songs, but Samantha did, and she hummed along during the pauses in our conversation. There weren't that many, but mostly she talked and I listened.

I was enraptured by her, getting swept up in the tender sound of her voice, when suddenly an old song popped into my head—"You Give Love a Bad Name" by Bon Jovi. There was a line in that song that my mama had played over and over. Something about the first kiss was your first kiss good-bye. It was the soundtrack to the downfall of my childhood. She'd listened to it obsessively, had a tape of it she'd recorded off the radio, and it lived in our old, beat-up car's tape deck.

And then another song pushed its way through—"Free Fallin'" by Tom Petty. I remembered hearing it on my way to enlist the day of my eighteenth birthday. I hadn't wanted to free fall into anything back then. Hearing that song on that day pushed me even harder to sign my name on the dotted line. It pushed me to join the Army, to ignore all my fears and dreams and just move on. Just live, even though I wasn't sure what I had been living *for*.

I'd had an okay life. My childhood was a sad one, that was for sure, but now, I had a lot to offer to the world. I had no problem paying for this stuffy, overpriced dinner. I was good at saving my money, planning for the future I'd probably never have. I still didn't want to "fall" into anything. It just wasn't me, but maybe I could ease my way into something.

If I found the right something. The right… *someone*.

Samantha kept talking. She let me pay for dinner without argument, and once or twice, her hand twitched toward mine while we walked back to my truck parked in front of the library.

When we were there, I held the door for her while she threw her bag up onto the seat and climbed in after it, and her little black dress rode up her thighs. It fit her well and had my imagination running circles around propriety, but it wasn't her usual garb. I liked her hippie skirts better. They suited her.

Still, it was hard not to stare, but I didn't want to give her the wrong impression. I kept my attention above her waistline, but out of the corner of my eye, I watched her cross her legs. I was hoping Grumbly's shed fur wouldn't be covering her ass when she got out. I should've cleaned my truck before I picked her up. In fact, it was unlike me not to think of it, and it irritated me that I hadn't. That damn dog really was a pain in my ass.

Remembering my emergency winter preparedness duffel in the back seat, I pulled a wool blanket out and covered her legs. A silent smile was thanks enough, but then she opened her millennial mouth. "Thank you, Frank, but you really don't have to drive me home. I could've walked."

"You ain't walkin' home in the dark alone in that dress. Not on my watch."

"That's kind of sexist, you know."

"It ain't sexist. It's common sense. It's cold, and I'm a cop, remember? I know exactly what could happen to someone like you on a dark road at night." Not to mention she'd probably freeze to death.

I was smacking myself mentally for not using my auto starter, but I shut her door and climbed in the other side, and when I finally did start the truck, she asked, "Someone like me? What's that supposed to mean?"

"Someone beautiful and... delicate." And young. Sure, she was an adult, and it wasn't like she was barely eighteen, but she was still a fuck of a lot younger than me.

She smiled but then caught herself and scrunched her face up. I wasn't trying to sound like a jerk, but damn, the floral scent of her shampoo, her warmth, and the smell of her skin wrapping around me in the truck was like a drug, an aphrodisiac, and I couldn't concentrate on what I was saying.

I couldn't remember the last time I'd experienced anything like it. Maybe I never had. I'd definitely never wanted to kiss someone so much in my near forty-nine years. I had to force myself to focus on my hands on the steering wheel and my foot on the gas pedal.

"'Delicate'?" She scoffed with a laugh. "You mean naïve."

"Ain't what I said."

"It's what you meant," she argued as I turned onto Durango Drive. "I live—"

"I know where you live."

Her question sounded like an accusation. "How do you know that?"

I looked at her, waiting till her eyes met mine. It was kind of my job to know where everyone lived in Wisper. Wasn't that obvious?

With a bit of attitude in her voice, she said, "Your sternly arched eyebrow doesn't exactly answer my question."

CHAPTER EIGHT

SAMANTHA

"SMALL-TOWN DEPUTY, REMEMBER?" Frank said. "I know where everybody lives."

"This is my house here," I said needlessly, pointing to my gramps's one-story house on Durango Drive. "Well, technically, it's my gramps's house, but he's in Florida." I was really feeling like an adolescent now. *Oh hi, you're really old and hot and sexy, and I live with my grandpa. You can drop me here since you had to drive me 'cause I don't even have a license!*

He didn't respond as he pulled into the driveway.

I opened my door while he climbed out the other side, sensing that it would irritate him. He probably wanted to open it for me, but something was making me want to defy him. Just a little. Seriously, we were already at odds. It was clear a relationship wouldn't be a good idea. "Okay, well, good night. Thank you for dinner."

He held the door open as I slid out of his truck, and my boots made a slopping sound in the snow on the driveway. Frank didn't mention my small act of defiance, but the tick of annoyance was clear in the way his eyebrow popped up again. "I'll walk you to the door."

"You don't have to."

"Yes, I do," he said.

This was too much. We were too different. From different places, different lifestyles. Even different eras, for crying out loud. If someone my age had driven me home after a date, they probably would barely have stopped the car. They definitely wouldn't have gotten out and walked me to the door. Or had I just been dating the wrong kind of guys?

When we were standing on the porch, I squared my shoulders, looking up at him. "Thank you for dinner, Frank. I really like talking to you, when you actually talk, that is, but I don't think this can work." It didn't mean I didn't want to jump his bones though.

I *so* did.

He gave a slow nod, lips pursed. "Already got your mind made up, huh? Without even knowin' me?"

He did have a point, but— "We're too far apart."

"Apart from what?" he asked, and he stepped forward. He was an inch away from me. I couldn't move or look away. I felt like I was trapped, but in a good way. How was that even possible? My heart was beating so hard, I worried for a second Gramps's neighbors would hear the thumping.

Without breaking eye contact, he lifted his jacket from my shoulders, the leather creaking softly as he slid his arms through the arm holes. The sweet, musky scent of his aftershave was dissipating, leaving me wanting.

He reached up to cradle my face in his hands again. Was he aware of how much it made me melt? No one had ever looked into my eyes the way Frank did. "You know, Samantha, there may be a pretty good age gap between us. I admit that it's… unusual to go out with someone almost twenty years younger. And to be honest, I don't have the first clue what I'm doin' with you…" He shook his head a little, scrunching up his nose a bit like he had at the library when I told him it was okay to break the "no pets" rule. "But the thing you're failin' to see here is that, in the nineteen years I lived before you were born, I was experiencing things you can't even imagine. And you know what that experience taught me?"

My answer was a squeak as his eyes drilled holes into mine. The scrunch fell away, and suddenly, he was as serious as a heart attack.

"Skills," he said in a low voice. A gravelly, sultry, totally sexified voice. "All manner of skills, things you probably couldn't guess." The distance between us became a thing of the past. He leaned down, and then his warm lips were pressing against mine, not asking permission, but *demanding* to be let in.

I couldn't deny him. I didn't want to.

His hands moved down my neck like the glide of warm velvet, down my arms as I shivered, and they landed on my hips, the tips of his fingers pressing insistently into my skin. It felt like I wasn't even wearing a dress. Suddenly, I remembered Juneau's "get you some" comment, and I wanted to untie the wrap dress and fling it into the snow-covered bushes.

Watching his eyes close, I opened my mouth, and he tilted his head as he began to kiss me deeper, his tongue moving in slow, firm strokes. I closed my eyes, too, and focused on how even the texture of his tongue was sexy. It was soft and warm, but his tastebuds were rough, and I couldn't help imagining what they would feel like if he were tasting some of my other, more sensitive places.

My entire body broke out in goosebumps. I breathed a

moan. Age difference? What age difference? All there was in that moment was a man kissing a woman. Ravaging her mouth, to be precise. Making her fall apart at her seams.

Abruptly, he stopped. He pulled his head back, dropped his hands to his sides, and cocked a smile. "Night," he said softly.

"Wha—"

"Sleep tight."

"Ungh?"

And he walked away, without even a backwards glance! My eyes glued themselves to his firm ass cheeks beneath his jeans as he strolled slowly down the sidewalk, like he had not a care in the world, and my mouth literally watered. Was actual drool dripping down my chin? He tossed his keys in the air and caught them, and when he was in his truck, he honked twice—two quick beeps—and backed out of the driveway, leaving me with my mouth agape, my jaw on the porch, and my underwear in a wet wad.

"Skills," I muttered, shelving books in the contemporary fiction section the next day during my lunch break, pushing my ever-sliding glasses back up the bridge of my nose. I loved my new contacts, but I hadn't gotten much sleep after that kiss, so my eyes were tired and dry. "I have skills too," I said to no one. "You think you can just woo me like that and walk away? No." I laughed at myself. Thank God there wasn't anyone around "No!"

"Sam?"

"Shit!" I spun on one foot, dropping three hardbacks when my friend Brady's voice surprised me. I hadn't even heard the door open, but there he was, chortling because he'd scared me. A hardcover copy of *The Bean Trees* landed on my big toe, and I hopped up and down in pain. "Owwwuh!"

"What's up?" Brady pursed his lips, holding back a laugh as I jumped around the library like a capuchin monkey.

My response came out a little more high-pitched than I intended. "Nothing!"

"Uh, okay? Didn't you hear me come in?"

"Obviously not." Maybe I needed to get my hearing checked. Or maybe I needed to stop thinking about Frank freaking Sims.

I shook my foot. The pain was a dull throb now. Taking a deep breath, I pulled my hair back, twisting it into a sloppy bun to keep the mess off of my face. Everything about me was a mess today. I found a pencil on my book cart and weaved it through to hold the bun in place, and Brady followed as I pushed the cart to the next aisle. "Sorry. Guess I was in my head."

"No worries," he said. "What's goin' on? You okay? You look a little flustered."

"I'm fine. I didn't sleep very well last night." More like not at all. My vibrator kept me up till the wee hours. I'd already renamed it Frank. "Everything okay with you?" I asked my lovely friend, realizing I'd missed him something awful. "I haven't seen you in two weeks. You can't ghost a girl like that."

"Sorry." A sheepish smile grew on his lips. "Theo had his winter break from classes, and it was so nice. We've been havin' a hard time gettin' back to reality. But break's over, so eventually, we had to find our way back to real life and, you know, like, go to work."

"That's what you've been doing for two whole weeks? Canoodling?" The bitterness in my voice gave me away. I was lonely.

Living with my gramps certainly wasn't doing my social life any favors, but the sadder part was that, with him gone, things were even less exciting. I didn't even have anyone to go grocery shopping with. Theo and Brady treated grocery shopping like date night, and Juni ordered her groceries online, but I loved the mundaneness of pushing my cart down every aisle, looking at cans and boxes of foods I never ate. I had been on a steady diet of microwaveable mac 'n' cheese, potato chips, and peanut butter sandwiches since Gramps left for Florida. Plus, at the grocery store, I could people watch. I liked to guess in my head what their lives were like. It was a leftover byproduct of being a lonely kid. Luckily, the Food Mart was only four blocks from Gramps's house.

It made me realize how much I depended on Theo and Brady. They'd become like family, but they were probably getting weary of me trying to inject myself into their lives like a squeaky, pink-haired third wheel.

"Sorry, Sam. I missed you, too, but it's different now, you know?"

"I know, and I'm happy you guys have each other. Really, I am, but I'm… lonely." My shoulders dropped, and I didn't like the weak way I felt when I said it out loud. Sadly, as an only child who traveled with her parents most of my life, it was kind of my status quo. Why couldn't I find my person, like Brady had Theo?

Why couldn't I have my own happy ever after? Truthfully, I was still waiting to wake up magically pregnant on some not-so-distant morning, even though no less than four doctors had told me it wasn't possible.

Brady scootched a stray strand of my hair behind my ear. "Hm. Well, that's a peculiar thing for you to say since you went on a date last night. I have it on good authority from five different sources that you looked like you were havin' a good time." His judgy eyebrow shot up. "So how was it?"

"Oh, mm," I hummed as I turned back to my cart, pretending to search for a book, but I knew where every single book in the library was, and Brady knew that I knew it too.

"C'mon. This is more than a year in the makin'. Spill. Was it fun? How'd you and the hot deputy get along?"

"It's not going to work out," I said, fitting the toe-breaking book in with the rest of the Barbara Kingsolvers on the shelf in front of me.

"Why not? You don't like him?"

I sighed and turned around, a careful look on my face. "Did you know he's almost forty-nine?" *And he still wants kids.*

"Forty-nine? Seriously? I mean, I knew he was a silver fox, but I didn't think he was *that* old."

"And did you know there's a whole sub-genre of romance books dedicated to silver foxes and younger women?" I rolled my eyes at myself. Was that what I had become? A kinky romance genre? "Anyway, I suppose it's not the end of the world. And he is *really* sexy. He's really nice too." I could feel my eyes drifting to the side, could hear the dreamy lilt beginning to take over my voice. "He holds chairs and doors for me, makes sure I'm warm and fed..." I jerked myself back to reality. "But what could he want with me? I'm nineteen years younger than him. I mean, he could be my—"

Oh, no, no. The thought flitted through my head again, but we were so not going there. I was not about to get all Britney Spears up in here. And I was not *ever* going to call Frank "Daddy."

And neither would the children I'd never be able to give him.

Was that why he was attracted to me? Was that what he wanted?

I looked at Brady. "You don't think…?"

Confusion was making him frown. "Think what?"

Whipping around, shelving books in the wrong places, I brushed off the thought. Or I tried to. "Anyway," I said, ignoring his question, "we probably don't have anything in common."

"Didn't you talk about that last night?"

"Not really. I guess I talked. Frank isn't much of a conversationalist. I mean, he talked a little. Oh, he did tell me he was adopted."

"Really?"

"Yeah, but that's all he said. He didn't expound."

Brady followed me down the aisle. "Maybe it's not an easy subject for him."

"Maybe. He said his adoptive parents are good people, but he didn't say much about his life before they adopted him." I stopped walking. I was nervous to bring up the kid subject, but I really wanted to know. "Can I ask you something?"

"Sure."

"Do you and Theo ever talk about… having kids? I mean, like, how you would go about doing that since, obviously, you don't have a uterus."

"Yeah, we've talked about it a couple times. Not seriously, but I suppose we'll probably look into adoption or surrogacy if we're ever at that place in life. Why?"

"No reason," I lied. I hadn't told Brady the extent of my infertility issues. He knew I'd had a late first trimester miscarriage in grad school, but that was it. "Frank mentioned wanting a big family, so I guess it just made me wonder." Yeah, right. It made me wonder how *I* could ever have that.

And how I could ever give that to a man like Frank. Technically, I did have a uterus. The only problem was that my uterus was a busted-up, barren wasteland.

"How was Paulo's?"

"The food was good. Have you been there?"

"Yeah," he said. "Theo and I ate there the other night. A guy he invested with a few years ago opened it. He's here now to get things goin', but he plans to put a local manager in charge so he can go back to Boston. I don't know how well it'll do. It's kinda expensive for Wisper. It'd probably do a lotter better business in Jackson."

"I know, right? My shrimp scampi was delicious, but fifty bucks for a steak? Frank paid. In fact, he *refused* to let me pay my share."

"Hm," Brady hummed suggestively. "Sounds serious."

"It was one date." I raised a brow at him this time and continued to the next aisle. "Although..."

Following closely, almost stepping on my heels, he was begging for information now. "Although what?"

"I told him I didn't think it could work between us, but then he... he kind of kissed me."

"Sam! How could you leave that part out?"

I stopped and turned, unable to hide the smile on my face. "Brady, it was so good. No one's ever kissed me like that before."

"Like what?" he asked, hanging on my next word.

"Like, sexy. Insistent. Demanding."

An "I told you so" grin slowly spread across his face.

"Yeah but..."

"But what!" He was practically jumping up and down, bouncing on the balls of his feet, waiting impatiently for me to spill the details.

"He's this older, way more mature person. He was in the

Army for years, and I'm the pink-haired little girl, dreaming of some fairy-tale love story. I got the feeling Deputy Frank Sims doesn't believe in fairy tales. Know what I mean?" I said, remembering the way Frank's eyes had sparkled when he watched the little boy at the restaurant.

Someone banged on the bell at the front desk, and then we heard, "Sam? Where are you?"

"Oh, that's Juneau," I told Brady. "She probably wants her dress back." I called to her. "Back here!"

When she found us, she popped a fist on her hip over her pink puffy coat. "Well? How was the date?"

"Oh my God, you're both awful."

"Hey," she said to Brady.

"What's up?" he said, and then they turned in unison, both fixing their eyes on my face.

"Did my dress work? You better start talking, Sam, or I'm gonna write you into one of my books and turn you into a bitter, sexless spinster."

"Okay, okay, jeez, but one of you has to buy me a green tea latte first. That's the deal, and I'm sticking to it."

———

The warmth of Coffee Shot was familiar as we entered, the three of us huddled up together to combat the cold wind before the door shut behind us. Coming here felt like seeing an old friend, if a cozy little country shop could be one. I loved being here. It made me feel like I was a part of the community because it was a hub of Wisper, everyone making their way to the Main Street café at least once a day and running into friends, coworkers, or family. It was nearly always full, and there was usually some kind of fundraiser going on.

This month it was Snowflakes for Shannon, which raised money for a little girl in the next town over who had leukemia. The owner of Coffee Shot, Walt Finkle, asked for a dollar donation with every cup of coffee he sold. Actually, it was more like a very polite demand, and when you gave it to him, he handed you a paper snowflake to hang in the front window. Customers wrote their wishes for Shannon to kick cancer's butt on their snowflakes. You could barely see through the window at this point, there were so many snowflakes. And then, at the end of February, Walt would match the donations and deliver the money and the snowflakes to Shannon and her parents to help pay for her medical care or to buy her something really special.

This was what had drawn me back to Wisper. My gramps was a big reason, too, but I'd spent so much of my life hopping from place to place, and now that I was getting older, I wanted a home base. I wanted to plant some roots. I needed stability after Florida, and the memories I had from spending summers here as a little girl were so happy. They were always at the front of my mind, pulling me to this tiny town in the heart of the West.

Juneau handed Walt a crisp twenty after she paid for our drinks, and we filled out our snowflakes at our table as we sipped them. I hummed along quietly to "Ain't No Sunshine" in the background, playing from the speakers overhead, as I typed a reminder into my phone to find some used books for Walt to take with him when he delivered the money from the snowflakes. I couldn't imagine going through something as hard and scary as cancer without some good books to get lost in, and Shannon was the perfect age to be introduced to Judy Blume. I had an old paperback copy of *Are You There, God? It's Me, Margaret* back at Gramps's house just waiting for her eleven-year-old eyes. Banned books my ass. *Are You There, God* was a classic.

Brady stuck our snowflakes to the window with the clear, sticky adhesive circles Walt had provided, then plopped back into his chair. "Thanks, Juni. Now spill, Sam."

I rolled my eyes. "Yes, thank you for the drinks," I said, and Juni winked and smiled. "And yes, he kissed me. Yes, it was amazing. But no, I don't think we're going out again."

Juni whimpered. "Really? That's all you're going to say?"

I threw my hands up, then lowered my voice, looking around and hoping only she and Brady would hear me say, "What more is there? He's almost forty-nine."

"Are you kiddin'?" Brady scoffed. "If you kissed him, then you touched him, and I definitely need to know what *that* felt like. Who cares how old he is?" He looked at Juni. "Have you seen the man's body?"

"Mmhm," Juni hummed suggestively, smirking and agreeing. "He's like one of those guys you see on TikTok chopping wood for no reason at all with their shirts off, except he's a seasoned one. He's so freaking hot. Imagine what he's capable of in the sack, Sam."

I laughed. "He actually said that when I told him it wasn't going to work out."

Her eyes grew twice their normal size. "He did? And please tell me *you* didn't."

"Yes, Juneau, I did, because it's not." I was saying it, but inside, I was knocking myself upside the head. I wanted to see him again. His smile, though rare, was magnetic, and all of his old-fashioned mannerisms were working their charms on me as I recalled them with my friends.

I kept saying it was the age thing, but now that I'd had the chance to get to know him a little, it wasn't even the biggest obstacle between Frank and me.

"Okay, fine," Brady said. "But what was his body like? At least give us that much."

"You're so bad," I said, and I smiled. I couldn't help it, and the memory had me flustered enough so that only half of my thought came out. "He was hard."

Suddenly, like in any self-respecting rom-com, a hush fell over Coffee Shot, and I watched as Brady's brown eyes rose slowly, one agonizing inch at a time, until they finally focused on someone standing behind me.

I heard a gruff grumble, a strict clearing of a throat.

Juni turned her head, looking behind and above me, and she gasped. "Oh shit."

Brady coughed at the same time and, trying to hide his smirk, said in an annoyingly amused voice, "Hey there, Deputy Sims. Can we help you with somethin'?"

I froze, embarrassment making me feel nauseated. I had to work to keep the few sips of the latte I'd drank in my digestive tract, but then I turned slowly until I was almost backward in my chair, looking up at the hard man in question.

Dressed in his brown uniform and jacket, Frank held his tan felt cowboy hat in one hand and a large to-go cup in the other, with a pastry bag dangling between two fingers. His pants were stretched tight over his strong thighs, and I'd never really noticed before, but his leather work boots were huge, at least twice the size of mine. That fact took my mind to all kinds of dirty places, and I was having a hard time looking at his face.

He was like a magnificent deputy statue, standing before me with a sexy scowl on his lips. Had he heard me? What had I said? I could barely remember.

He took in the guilty look on my face and seemed to focus on my glasses for a few seconds, but inevitably, his eyes found mine.

My mouth fell open, and Juni squeaked, "Whoops."

In a terse voice, Frank said only, "Samantha," and he flipped his hat in one deft move, fixed it on his head, and walked away! Again!

Jumping out of my chair, I yelled after him as every person in Coffee Shot turned their head in my direction. "Frank! Wait! I d-didn't mean it *that* way!"

When he was gone and conversation had fallen back to a soft din, I shrank back down into my chair, trying to hide my face with my hair. Grabbing my beanie from my coat pocket, I pulled it over my head, dragging it down until it covered my eyes.

"Well," Juni quipped, trying not to laugh at me, "that took a turn."

CHAPTER NINE

FRANK

HARD? *SHE AIN'T SEEN NOTHIN' yet.*

Leaving her stuttering behind me was more fun than I'd had in a long time. It took all my concentration not to laugh as I glided proudly out of the café with Abey's coffee order in my hand.

I knew what Samantha had been referring to. I couldn't imagine how she hadn't seen me enter the shop. I'd overheard their chatter about my body and something about chopping wood, but letting her think I was insulted that I'd caught her discussing my dick with her friends was too good, and the rosy flush that had bloomed on her cheeks was a bonus. Her eyes sparkled with something like embarrassment, but there was also a curiosity there—a question I realized I might want to answer.

But we had a long way to go before all that.

There was still our age difference. She was still hung up on it.

Maybe I was, too, but I was trying to see it more as good thing. I was past the irresponsible partying stage. Actually, I'd never really gone through one. My job was stable. I made a living wage. Owned my own home. And I had a feeling a home was what Samantha was looking for.

Not a house, but a *home*, and I could give her that.

If she wanted them, I could give her babies and support them. Just 'cause my ex-wife ripped the rearview down when she ditched town, it hadn't killed my dream of having a family. I didn't have one growing up, until I was adopted, and then it was too late. I was too jaded.

But now, maybe I was ready. I wasn't proud that it'd taken me a lot longer than most, but at least I'd gotten here. That had to count for something.

I'd thought when I married Angela that we were on the same page, even though she was five years younger than me. But she'd convinced me that when I came back from my last tour with the Army, we'd get started on a family. But everything changed when I went away.

When I met and married her at the tail end of an extended furlough thirteen years ago, two years before I retired from the service, I saw her with stars in my eyes and spent night after night while I was away envisioning our life together. But then I came back. The stars disappeared and had been replaced with a clear lens. What I saw when I looked at my ex-wife then was… disappointing.

I should've noticed it when we spoke on the phone every week, her refusal to talk about having kids. In the beginning, she was all for it, said it was her dream too, but that slowly changed to *"Let's talk about something else. I don't even wanna think about stretch marks."*

And when I was home, she stomped up a fuss when I was offered the job under Carey's leadership here in Wisper, even though it was a great opportunity for me, an honor since it was my performance in the military that had caught Carey's attention, and something she should have been proud of me for.

But all she cared about was that Wisper was a small town. It didn't have a Starbucks or name-brand shops, and her parents and friends wouldn't be here to fawn over her. It was never about us; it was about her, day in and day out. I fit in her picture while I was away 'cause I was the strong, "heroic" military man, but once that was over, I couldn't really offer her anything she wanted.

All of her eye rolls should have clued me in every time I talked about coaching peewee football, which I never ended up doing since she didn't like the idea, didn't want to spend her weekends "playing with other people's kids" until it was time for us to have our own.

Eventually, she gave in, and we moved to Wisper, but within two months, she was gone. Took the dog and an unnecessarily extensive wardrobe for a medical coding and billing secretary, and she fled town while I was out on patrol. She left her job in Jackson without a word, we settled the divorce through lawyers, sold the house, and I hadn't seen her since.

It was for the best. I hadn't really known her. Not her soul. Sex was the only way we'd known how to communicate, but there was only so much it could say without words.

It hadn't taken long for me to see that, but when she disappeared, I'd thought that was it for me. Thought I'd never see my kids running around, wearing matching pajamas on Christmas morning. Would never get to experience road trips with six arguing teenagers and two harried parents, stopping at the world's largest ball of string, 'cause why not? When you had the family you'd always wanted, you were rich in the best way, and no matter how ridiculous the activity, the point was that you were all together, loving each other and making good memories—

"Frank!"

"Jesus, Abey."

She appeared out of nowhere, holding her hands out for her skinny white-mocha latte with extra whipped cream and chocolate sprinkles on top. "What planet are you on, man? I've been sayin' your name for, like, three whole minutes."

I'd been so lost in my thoughts, I hadn't even realized I'd crossed the street and was back inside the station.

Handing over her coffee and lemon scone, I complained, "You know, orderin' that bullshit makes me look bad. I wouldn't drink that syrupy crap if you paid me."

"Oh, don't I know it, Mr. Gym Rat."

"There's no gym in Wisper."

"Sure there is. It's in your extra bedroom."

Shrugging, I admitted to it. "Sue me for takin' care of myself. You're twenty years younger than me, and I could run circles around you. All that processed crap you ingest every day's makin' you old before your time. You just can't see it yet."

Abey gasped, clutching her chest like a damsel from some fairy tale. "Don't you let José hear you say that. You'll break the poor man's heart since I'm on a steady diet of his spicy chili. He makes it from scratch every day, and you know it." She smirked. An annoying twinkle danced in her eye, and my hackles went up. "Did you see Sam?"

Glaring at her, I accused her, "Is that why you insisted on me goin' to get your coffee? You were tryin' to set me up?"

Batting her eyelashes, she turned to grab her coat from the rack in the corner. "Some detective you are." She laughed. "Besides, I was busy takin' a call. You know that."

"Yeah, about a cat stuck up a tree." It was our code for the calls we received, usually from elderly residents, requesting odd jobs. We got four or five a week. Though technically not what we were paid for, they were an unofficial part of the deputy gig in Wisper, and they were by no means emergencies.

"Oh, before I forget," she said, "you need to head next door to Ace's House. Theo Burroughs called and said he wants to talk to us about somethin'. He didn't say what though."

"Why can't you go?"

She plopped her hat on her head and flipped her coat collar up. "Gotta go save a cat."

"Deputy, thanks for coming." Theo Burroughs, the head of Wisper's new community center, greeted me as I wiped my boots on the rug in the entryway. There were a few teenagers and a couple young adults hanging out, some reading or doing homework. Ace's House was a relaxed place and, in a short time, had become a core part of our town.

I nodded, looking around at the refurbished newspaper building. I'd been here once or twice since he'd opened it but never really got a good look inside. It was a beautiful old building, and Theo had only made it better with his renovations. I appreciated the sturdy foundation and strong wooden bones. I thought about the youth football thing again and found myself wondering if I could run it from the center. A buddy and I'd talked about doing it together. Maybe it was time for that too.

"You got somethin' for me?" I asked.

"Maybe," he said, and I followed him when he waved his arm toward his office down the hallway.

When the door was shut behind us, he took a seat at a small, distressed walnut desk, but I remained standing.

"There's a kid," he started. "His name is Murphy. Or, at least, that's what he goes by. He says he's eighteen, but I think he's lying about that. He certainly doesn't look eighteen."

"I can't arrest somebody for lyin'."

"No, no, of course not." He shook his head. "And I don't want to get him in trouble, but I'm worried about him."

Finally, I sat. Sounded like this could take a while.

"He first came to Ace's House about three months ago with his mother, but now she's nowhere to be seen, and Murphy shows up here two or three times a week to eat or to get warm. He says he's just bored, stopping by after school, but I've asked around, and no one seems to know him or his mother. The other kids don't recognize him from their classes."

"What was it about him that made you think he was bein' dishonest?"

"Truthfully, I don't know. It's just a feeling. But his clothes are usually dirty, or he's not dressed properly for the weather. It's a lot colder now than it was three months ago. And any time I try to talk to him, he wiggles his way out of the conversation somehow." Theo shifted in his chair and sat back. "We gave him a coat from our donation center because the jacket he was wearing was threadbare. He wouldn't accept it, said he didn't need it, but later, when he thought no one was watching, he took the coat."

"So what is it exactly you'd like the Sheriff's Department to do, if you're sayin' he ain't causin' any trouble? Want me to do a wellness check?"

"I don't know. Maybe, but I don't have an address for you to check in on. But can you just look into it? Maybe I'm wrong about them being homeless and he's telling the truth, but what if I'm not wrong? What if this kid is alone? He's figured out our schedule, so he knows when there's going to be warm food here. José and some of the other local restaurant owners donate a couple times a week, and he always shows up on time to eat, but he doesn't interact with any of the other kids who come here or with our staff. My assistant director, Devo, has been trying to connect with the kid, but he's a brick wall."

Another cat up a tree. But maybe this one was more like a wounded kitten.

"Look, Frank, if I was sure he was an adult, I wouldn't bother. Adults can make their own choices about how they want to live. We can offer our help, but if they choose not to accept it, that's on them. I know that. I've *lived* that." He paused, taking a deep breath. "But if I'm right, he's not an adult. Just take one look at him. You'll see what I mean. And we're expecting some pretty low temperatures again. This winter has been crazy."

He wasn't wrong. "Alright then. S'pose I could try to talk to him. What else can you tell me about him?"

"Not much. Like I said, he won't let anybody in. Oh, but he loves to read. I don't think I've ever seen that kid without a book sticking out of his pocket."

Hm. Suddenly, the case of the bookstore's missing paperbacks was making a hell of a lot more sense to me.

"He's here now, actually, but go easy on him. He's not very talkative. Kind of guarded, like I said."

"Show him to me."

We stood, and Theo opened his office door. There was a kid lurking right outside with greasy dark brown hair and a look of terror on his face. I knew it was the kid in question. It was clear by his proximity to Theo's office door that he'd been trying to listen to our conversation, but before I could even attempt to talk to him, he looked up at me, taking in an eyeful of my uniform and hat and the gun on my hip, turned on a heel, and ran right out the front door into the falling snow.

CHAPTER TEN

"MAN, IT'S REALLY COMIN' down," Brady said as he drove us up Route 20 to Frank's house. "It's been snowin' off and on for weeks. I'm over it."

His old Sentra was on its last leg, so he'd borrowed a ten-passenger van from Ace's House, and I was fidgeting in the front seat. My feet wouldn't stay still, and no matter where I put my arms, I was uncomfortable. It felt like I was slouching.

It was nerves.

The cold text conversation I'd had with my dad before I'd called Brady for a ride wasn't sitting well with me, especially when he'd asked, *"And how are you doing with that whole Florida thing?"*

Like miscarrying a child and losing the ability to have more was some unspeakable mistake I'd made. But saying the words would've meant having an actual conversation about my feelings and admitting that *he* had feelings about losing the opportunity for grandchildren. And my parents just didn't do feelings. And further, admitting that they had the *same* feelings about anything would be like admitting their biggest weakness. My parents never agreed on anything on principle, except for work.

It still struck me as funny since the movies they made were always deep, emotional pieces. My parents always had the ability to pull heartrending performances from the actors in their movies, but neither of them could talk to their only daughter about her miscarriage and infertility.

Go figure.

When I hung up, I felt this pull to see Frank. I *needed* to see him, to apologize, but there was something else. I wasn't sure what it was about, but I wanted to look in his eyes and tell him that I wasn't disrespecting him when he'd overheard me, and when I experienced gut feelings like this, I tried to act on them. Who knew what life had in store for you? Why not investigate?

If I had been willing to admit it to myself, I would've known the pull to see him again was about the look in his eyes when *he* looked in *mine*. The curiosity there. The attraction.

His smile.

Activating the romance book club phone tree, I called Billie, who texted Abey, and she told me Frank owned a small piece of property past the edge of town. Brady confirmed it when he agreed to drive me out there, because of course he knew where Frank lived. Everyone knew everything about everybody in this town, even if they weren't friends.

But now, gripping the Tupperware cake holder I'd borrowed from my gramps's cupboard tighter on my lap, I was having second, third, and fourth thoughts about showing up at Frank's house uninvited.

"It's your birthday," Brady said. "You sure you wanna do this? You could stay in town. We could order dinner instead."

Peering out his windshield, he winced at the snow dropping down on us in heaves, the wind gusting it this way and that. "You might get stuck out there forever."

But I had to apologize. I was mortified that Frank had caught me gossiping about him. I hadn't actually been discussing the firmness of his—well, I guess I had been, but not *that* muscle. My face flushed and my stomach clenched just thinking about the mix-up and the irritated look on his face in the coffee shop.

He had to know I wasn't really that immature.

"Just keep driving, please," I said. "If I think too much about it, I'll tell you to turn around."

"Okay. If you're sure."

"I am." It was what my mouth was saying, but the flutter in my chest was telling me to jump out of the van. Maybe I could hide in a snowbank and hibernate until spring came. The embarrassment would've worn off by then, right?

My "follow your vibes" free-spirited personality seemed to be failing me in the moment. Honestly, I'd never had a harder time making up my mind. The desire to see Frank was strong, but his voice was loud in my head every time I remembered his words at the restaurant: "*Always imagined I'd have a family by now.*" It was like a permanent stamp in my brain.

Brady dropped me off on Frank's gravel drive, down a dark country road off the main highway, and after confirming there was sound and light coming from the house, I reached in through Brady's rolled-down window to kiss his cheek, then waved him away.

Staring up at the black sky and the crystalline snow falling in fluffy clumps, I was rethinking every decision I'd ever made up until now. Abey had also confirmed that Frank wasn't on duty tonight and that he was definitely at home, so

I was counting on Frank giving me a ride later, but maybe that hadn't been my brightest idea in this weather.

I should've asked Abey for Frank's number and called him directly to tell him I had something I wanted to give him, like an actual adult. Instead, I'd called everyone else I knew, digging for information on the hot boy I liked. If Frank had known that, he probably would've laughed at me.

Once again, our age gap reared its ugly head.

Finally, there was nothing to do but go for it. I had to walk to the door and make my presence known, or I could trudge the five miles back to town in the snow with my tail between my legs.

Here goes nothing.

Frank answered his thick wooden door three seconds after I knocked, and I could almost feel my uterus contract, trying to suck in not-yet-ejaculated silver-fox sperm, for all the good that would do. The sight of him twisted the conversation with my dad into a pretzel in my stomach. What would my parents say if they knew I'd gone on a date with a guy nineteen years older than me? One who definitely wanted kids? I could imagine their disapproval perfectly.

I could feel my own disapproval as I stood there. If he'd known I couldn't have kids, he probably wouldn't have wanted to go out with me. *"Always imagined I'd have a family by now."*

And now, there he was, trying to hide the smile on his lips as he looked me over, from the top of my beanie to the soles of my boots. Slowly. Had Abey called him to tell him I was coming? *Oh God, you should've threatened her and Billie into silence.*

I tried to ignore the guilt I felt for not being up front with him, which was *almost* easy because he was quite literally the sexiest man I'd ever seen.

Dressed in gray sweatpants and no shirt, he was breathing rapidly. Clearly, I'd caught him in the middle of a workout. The sweats fit him like cotton muscle-hugging gloves, and his brown and silver chest hair glistened, wet with sweat in the moonlight.

The seemingly enormous outline of his... manly bits, tucked snug inside the sweats, was enough to make me blush. I felt the heat creep up my neck to my face, and then it felt like a four-alarm fire erupted on my cheeks.

His feet were bare, and even they were attractive.

It was extremely difficult, but I finally raised my eyes to his steely gray ones. "Hi."

A twitch of his mouth betrayed the surprise he was trying to act out as he wiped the sweat from his face with the navy blue T-shirt in his hand. So he'd known it was me knocking on his door, and he chose to open it half naked, muscles primed and pumped?

My knees felt weak.

I held my pink sprinkle cake up in front of my chest to hide the wobbling. I'd even tried to write "Happy Birthday, Frank & Sam" on top with an icing gun, but it looked more like "Hoppy Barflay, PranK + Smm," which was even more embarrassing, but I pressed on. "Happy birthday."

His face was a stone. "Happy Birthday, Samantha."

Holding the cake up higher, grinning like a fool, I said, "I made us a cake."

"I see that. Thank you." He pressed his lips together in a flat line. "It looks..."

"It's a disaster. I'm sorry, but I think it tastes good."

Stepping back, he opened his door wider. "Would you like to come in?"

"Oh." A snowflake landed on my bottom lip. Frank's eyes fixed on it, and I licked it off. "Sure. Thanks."

I felt his gaze follow me in, but when I risked a glance at him, it flicked back out at the snowfall getting heavier by the moment. "That snow looks like it could be a problem." He shut the door, and I spun around, ignoring the masculine décor behind me. I could've sworn there was a dead deer head above his fireplace, but I was afraid to confirm that.

"A problem?" I asked as his cell phone buzzed on the kitchen table to my right.

"'Scuse me. That's the station." Taking the cake container from my hands with a nod, he set it next to his phone and answered his call, and I watched the way his abdominal muscles flexed as he turned, and then I had no choice but to explore his house. If I hadn't, I would've just been standing there, staring at his back muscles and the way they narrowed as they took my eyes down to his ass, and then I would've drooled again.

I tried to lower my bag to the floor behind his couch gingerly, but it fell to the hardwood floor with a *plop*. All the doors in the hallway at the back of the house were closed, but I heard Bruce Springsteen's "Born to Run" playing softly somewhere as I perused his living room, and it reminded me of my dad. He was the biggest Boss fan. He tried to work one of Bruce's songs into every movie my parents directed, much to my mom's dismay. She only listened to classical. And poor Bruce was probably sick of being asked for the rights.

Ugh. Get your freaking parents out of your head!

Frank's house was a cabin, basically, made out of logs, and even though there were forest-green and black plaid accents everywhere, and yes, dead animal heads fixed on the wall, it was cozy. The fire in the fireplace gave the living room a glow that had my toes warming quickly and my cheeks heating. Framed photographs hung on either side of the fireplace, the black-and-white images portraying dusty American plains with hills in the distance. Texas, maybe?

The ten-point buck in the center of the wall above the fireplace disturbed me, and I wondered if Frank had killed the poor animal himself. Probably. Why else would it be there?

Get over it, Sam. This is the mountains. You're in the Wild West. It wasn't like I'd never seen one before, just not so close-up. I hoped he'd at least used all of the animal and hadn't shot it just for decoration. But no. That wasn't Frank. I knew that already.

Forcing myself to look away, I didn't see a TV, but there was a stack of cork coasters on top of a chunky wooden end table next to a deep-seated brown leather couch, with a matching recliner closer to the fire. And hiding beneath it all was what I hoped was a black faux cowhide rug.

Frank had style. A chic Western style that was under-stated, definitely masculine, and quite lovely. I still remem-bered the first books he'd checked out of the library, and I wondered if he'd used the information he'd read in *A Moun-tain Man's Guide to Home Décor* when he'd bought his furni-ture. What a guy. It was so cute that he'd probably just converted the information into a numbered list. Number one: leather furniture. Number two: interesting rug. Number three: manly-colored matching accents throughout.

But some of it must've come from him, from his life in Texas. I liked to think it came from his soul because it was extremely inviting, even though his words and demeanor sometimes weren't.

In front of his couch, on top of an old trunk with brass locks sat a pile of the books he'd borrowed from the library, one with a bookmark sticking out halfway through. He really did read all the books he took home every week. I'd wondered.

"Sorry," he said when he was done with his call, and I turned to face him. For a split second, his eyes dipped down to my vintage carpet bag on his floor, and his left eye twitched, like he didn't like that I'd set it there. Where else should I have put it? He looked up. "This was unexpected. I'd really like to talk to you, but I gotta go."

"Where are you going?" I asked, rounding the couch, meeting him on the other side, but he passed by me and walked to his fireplace, which was absolutely stunning, made from what looked like large river stones. He stoked the coals inside with a poker, then scooped the ashes from the sides with a small clinker shovel and sprinkled the ashes over the fire. It died down, and then he placed an old-looking metal grate in front of the fireplace, on the stone hearth.

"When it snows like this, it's best if one of us is out on the roads."

"It's been snowing for a while now."

He shook his head, walking back toward me. Had he forgotten that he wasn't wearing a shirt? "Not like this."

Eyes up top, Sam! Jeez. "But if it's going to be a bad storm, won't you get stuck?"

Passing close by me—so close that I felt the heat from his workout-warmed skin—he sat at his kitchen table to put socks on. He yanked his T-shirt over his head, then walked to his front door and stepped into his boots. Lifting his brown canvas work coat from a hook on the wall, he shrugged it on and zipped it, then wrapped a matching scarf around his neck. "I got chains."

"Oh, right. Of course you do."

"C'mon. I'll give you a ride home."

"Okay," I said, feeling a disappointment I hadn't expected flooding my chest. "Thanks." I hadn't even had time to take my coat off, so I zipped it back up and pulled my lavender beanie from the pocket.

Frank stepped toward me and took it from my hand, stretching it. He placed it on my head, pulling the edges down around my face while I stared at him, trying to breathe quietly as I memorized the darker flecks in his eyes. If I looked close enough, they were just as blue as the rings around the edges, but his eyes were most definitely gray. He tucked loose strands of my hair inside the hat, then stepped back, inspecting his work. "Where're your glasses?"

"Contacts," I said, really feeling like a little girl now. A little girl getting dressed to go play in the snow with her daddy.

He gazed into my eyes for what felt like forever and no time at all, and his next words wiped the father/daughter image out of my mind. "I'd like to dance with you."

It wasn't what he said but *how* he said it, all heat and intense eye contact. My heartbeat thumped low in my belly, and I blinked in confusion. Who said things like that?

"I'd like to wrap you up in my arms and dance with you in front of my fire."

"Oh?" What in the world had just come out of my mouth? But I had no clue how to respond to that, other than to jump him, which I would *never* do. He'd probably arrest me.

"Another time," he said in a low voice, and the sound had me humming in places that should definitely not have been humming. Places lower than the heartbeat in my stomach.

Thinking about having sex with Frank made me remember why I'd come to his house in the first place. "Wait. I came to tell you that I-I—" Suddenly, the confident and extremely mature speech I'd concocted in my head as an apology became a jumble on my lips, and then it disappeared entirely. All that came out was, "I-I'm, well, sorry."

"What for?" he asked, fixing his leather deputy's badge around his neck. It hung over his chest by some kind of shiny metal chain, making me imagine the outline of his chest muscles under his coat.

I was *really* struggling to keep my eyes on his. "For… you know. The other day. A-at the coffee shop?"

Frank laughed, and it was the first time I'd ever heard it. His laugh was beguiling, a slow chuckle coming from deep inside him. "Oh, that," he said.

"Yes, that. Forgive me?"

"Didn't you just hear me, girl? If I was mad at you, would I ask you to dance?"

"No, I suppose not."

He winked at me, and all rationality left my body. "Could I ride you?" *Oh, for the love of the sweet baby Jesus, I did not just say that out loud… Did I?* "I mean, ride with you. Can I ride *with* you?"

A smirk began to form on his lips, but he cleared it from his face quickly. This man was a tough nut to crack, never letting his feelings show. "Yeah, that's what I said. I'll drive you home."

Still scrambling to cover my Freudian slip, I said, "No. I mean, can I go with you while you patrol?"

"Well," he mused, turning and lifting his hat from another hook by the door. He fixed the Stetson on his head. "Techni-cally, I ain't on duty, so I s'pose I wouldn't be breakin' any laws if I let you tag along. It'll be dull though. Lots of sittin' around, doin' nothin' but watchin' cars go by."

"Okay," I said a little too eagerly. That did sound like it had the potential to be boring, but not with him around. He may've been way too old for me, but dull was one thing Frank Sims was not. Even without saying a word, he was the most interesting person I'd met, maybe ever. I was kind of looking forward to spending the time talking to him. Maybe we could get to know each other better.

He arched a graying brow under his hat. "Thought you said you and me wouldn't work."

"I did say that." I twisted my lips, trying to think of a way I could admit to the truth but not bury myself at the same time, because, you know, women's lib and all that. "But I also said I like talking to you. We can be friends, right? There's nothing wrong with that."

"Nothin' wrong with the alternative either." He narrowed his eyes. Was he scrutinizing me? It felt like it, like I was a teenager and he the firm-handed—oh. And now I understood where the "miniskirt/spank me, daddy" thing came from I'd read so much about. I made a mental note to read more age-gap romance. Maybe I could find one for book club.

Already, and despite my feministic nature, it seemed my subconscious was warming to the idea as I pictured myself bent over his couch while he ran his hands between my naked thighs and his tongue—

"Alright then," he said, interrupting my sudden and depraved fantasies, "but if there's an accident out there, you stay in my truck unless I tell you different. Is that understood?"

Before I could stop myself, I saluted him with my pink knitted mitten. "Yes, sir."

His mouth twitched again, and I swore I felt a trickle of moisture between my legs.

"You can't wear that," he said, motioning to my skirt and boots. "I'll be right back. Stay here."

He disappeared down the dark hallway. I couldn't see him anymore, so I backed into his kitchen, turning when I got to his stainless fridge. When I opened the door and peered in— which wasn't rude; it was research—I was surprised. It was hospital clean and full of little Tupperware containers stacked on top of each other, with color-coded lids and organized by size, a half of a gallon of organic skim milk, and some kind of meat wrapped in white paper packaging, like it had come from a proper butcher, not the Food Mart. There were twelve brown eggs in an open egg carton, a blender pitcher halfway full of some kind of green liquid, and one crisper was filled to the brim with apples and oranges, the other with fresh veggies.

I spun on one foot, letting the fridge door close quietly, and inspected the rest of his kitchen. On the gray granite countertop next to a stainless steel stove sat a bunch of bananas, a line of vitamin bottles, two metal water bottles, and one made of plastic that had a colorful Cade Ranch logo on it.

And on the other side of the stove was a freaking bread maker and a loaf of some kind of dark bread wrapped in a white cloth.

Frank may've been a tough nut, but he was a healthy nut.

No wonder he looked so good. He took care of himself, and that was sexy.

He bellowed behind me, "Grum! No!" and then I was knocked forward when Grumbly jumped on my back.

My stomach hit the rough-edged counter, nearly knocking the breath out of me. "Oof! Where'd he come from?"

"This damn dog. Are you okay?"

"Yeah, it's okay." I turned, and Grumbly settled his front paws on my shoulders, jumping on his hind legs and trying to bathe my face with his tongue. "He still has puppy breath, but it feels out of place since he's the size of a small car."

"I keep him in a big crate in the back room when I'm not home. The vet says it makes him feel more secure, at least when he doesn't break out of it. I have to padlock it closed. It also stops him from eatin' my house when I'm on duty, but when I let him out, he goes nuts. I just walked in the door before you got here. Barely had a chance to work up a sweat."

Oh, I *so* begged to differ.

Wetting a paper towel at the sink, he grabbed Grumbly's collar and pulled him down, then handed me the towel, and I wiped the slobber from my face. "I dunno what to do about this ornery dog. He ain't got a lick of manners in him."

He took the towel from my fingers, wadded it into a ball, and tossed it into the garbage can behind me.

Motioning to the navy snow pants he'd draped over a dining chair, I asked, "Are those for me?" I bent, scratching behind Grumbly's ears before he trotted to his food bowl by the refrigerator. He took a bite of the dry kibble Frank dumped in there and wandered to the living room window, where he peered out, watching the snow fall and yipping quietly. Frank looked at the trail of kibble sprinkled from the kitchen to the window and shook his head. The mess clearly irritated him.

"They might be a little big, but they'll do," he said. "I have some boots here, too, and another pair of socks for you. Your feet will freeze if you wear the boots you got on. They ain't made for real winter weather."

I thought Doc Marten might have something to say about that, but I didn't argue. I wasn't looking forward to freezing toes.

Stepping closer to me, he unzipped my coat, then moved behind me, adjusting my arms out to the sides and removing it slowly. Somehow, this small, quiet kindness spoke loudly about him, and it was sexy too. Did he do anything that wasn't? My heart raced, and that pool of heat formed low in my stomach again as I listened to him breathing evenly behind me.

He pulled a chair out at his kitchen table, and I sat as he handed me the boots and a pair of white long johns tall enough to fit him.

Unlacing my own boots, I kicked them off, then pulled the long johns on under my skirt, rolling the waistband a few times so they'd fit better. When I took my skirt off, Frank lifted my boots and set them very neatly by his front door. He stayed turned away from me while I changed, which was chivalrous, but it wasn't like my legs were bare.

I folded my skirt and set it on the table because I was afraid he'd scold me if I left it on the floor. I hoped he'd never have a reason to see my bedroom at my gramps's house as I pulled the snow pants up my legs, fixing the straps criss-crossed over my shoulders like suspenders, but even then they were too big. The snow boots he'd given me looked kind of like muck boots, but they had the softest fur inside, and as soon as my feet settled into them, a wave of warm relaxation washed over me. They were that comfortable and definitely toasty warm. The extra socks helped to fill them out, but I could've fit both of my feet into one.

Without turning around, he said, "You ready?"

"Yes."

Finally, he spun on a foot, and I smiled at him. It was kind of hard not to while he was looking at me like he was proud to see me dressed in his clothes, proud to be the reason I was warm. "Should we bring water and food in case we get stuck?"

"Darlin', like I said, I got snow chains, and my cruiser has four-wheel drive." He lifted his keys from the table. "We ain't gettin' stuck."

It might've killed me to admit, but when he called me

"darlin'" or "girl" with the gravel and grump in his voice, the pool of heat in my stomach plummeted between my legs. But I would never tell him that. Instead, I asked, "Why do you call your truck a cruiser? I thought police cruisers were sedans."

"A cruiser can be any kinda vehicle, whatever an officer uses to patrol. In Teton County, a lot of us use trucks, so the truck's my cruiser. Years ago, I drove a sedan."

"Makes sense," I said, silently wondering what "years ago" meant. Ten years? Two years? How old was I while Frank had been puttering around town in a sheriff's department sedan?

The thought brought a memory to the front of my mind of my grandparents talking about the "nice deputy whose wife walked out on him." Brady had confirmed it was Frank they had been talking about. I was a teenager at the time, here in Wisper for the summer, getting ready to start my first year of college. If that didn't make me feel too young for Frank, I had no clue what would. But I remembered my Grandma saying what a shame it had been that Frank's wife had left him, but that, clearly, the deputy had to have done something to make her go. Gramps had disagreed, saying he'd met the new deputy and thought he was a good man. Grandma Josie'd had a tendency to get caught up in town gossip, so I always believed what Gramps said.

Frank stepped closer to adjust my coat when I slipped it back on, and he tugged the zipper up to my chin. "Why'd you ask?"

I shook my head to clear the memory. "Just curious." I bit the inside of my cheek and then blurted the thing I'd been thinking for more than a year. "I'm curious about a lot of things when it comes to you."

That stopped him cold, and I liked that I had that effect on him.

I smiled, not offering anything more than that, just to irk him, but he didn't respond to the huge thing I'd said, so I shrugged. "Okay, I'm ready. Let's go—wait, but what about Grumbly?"

He watched my smile fade, then said, "He's comin' with us. Can't leave him here in case we're gone a long time. I swear, if he pees in his crate one more time, damn dog's goin' to the pound." But it was clear from the way he was always petting and tending to Grum that it was the furthest thing from a promise.

CHAPTER ELEVEN

SAMANTHA

THE DRIVE into town was quiet, save for the sound of Grumbly panting and whining occasionally, wanting to jump out the window.

When we'd left Frank's house, Grumbly shot right out the door, digging holes in the ever-growing snow piles and tunneling his way through them. As soon as Frank hit the auto start button on his key fob, Grumbly ran for the truck, and I worried he'd crash headfirst into the back door, but Frank got there before he did and opened it just in time for Grumbly to torpedo himself into the back seat. Apparently, Grum liked to go for rides.

After I climbed into the front seat with Frank's hand resting gently on the small of my back, he closed my door, and I instantly remembered the allure. Since he'd recently gotten home from work, the engine was still warm, so the cab heated up quickly as he cleared the snow from the windows with a brush on the back side of a long ice scraper.

His scent was strong inside, and it enveloped me in its masculine pull. I'd caught a hint of it when he'd taken me to dinner, but tonight, with the cold outside and the clean snow surrounding us, his scent was almost hypnotic. It had me breathing deeply until he climbed into the driver's seat, and then I rubbed my mittens together vigorously, acting like I was trying to stave off the cold, hoping he hadn't noticed.

It was like every time I saw him, there was one thing building on top of all the other delicious things I'd noticed about him previously. And tonight, it was his woodsy, leathery aftershave and the quiet way he had about him inside his house. He was vulnerable there. I wondered how many people he allowed into that part of his life.

There were so many questions about him running through my mind, I couldn't keep track of them all.

We didn't come across any accidents, thankfully, as we made our way through town slowly, down Main Street past the sheriff's station and all the local shops. They were dark, the streets were mostly empty, and there was a quietness about town that was comforting. The soft crunching of his truck's tires on the clean snow could've lulled me to sleep, if my body hadn't been buzzing with its awareness of Frank right next to me.

He surveyed everything in his view, his eyes searching down every street we passed, looking for anyone who might need help, I assumed. I rolled my window down to hear the calm silence better as he drove, and he watched me as I stuck my head out the open window. My cheeks were freezing, but it felt good.

Rolling it back up with a press of my finger, I sat back, looking at Frank as Grum stuck his head under Frank's arm resting on the back of my seat. He always drove like that, and Grum seemed used to it, with his tongue hanging out and a smile on his goofy face. I reached to pat Grum's head, but really, it was an excuse to peek over at Frank. "You're not going to ask me what I've been curious about?" He hadn't said a word when I'd blurted the statement in his kitchen. Man, I really needed to pay more attention to the stuff coming out of my mouth around him.

He laughed a little at my directness. "Nope."

"Why not? You don't want to know?"

"'Course I do, but I figure you'll let me know when you're ready."

"Do you do that on purpose, the whole quiet, stoic lawman thing?"

"The what?"

"You know what I mean. You're like a big, immovable mountain. You don't really talk that much, but when you do, you grumble."

He glanced at Grumbly, as if he was only then connecting the name I'd suggested to his own demeanor. "You think I'm puttin' on some kinda act?"

"No, that's not what I—I didn't mean it like that."

"I don't see a need to fill silence with bullshit, Samantha. When I got somethin' to say, I say it."

"Of course." *Foot in mouth much, Samantha?* "By the way, you can call me Sam. Everybody does, besides my gramps."

"I like Samantha. Sam's cute." His eyes flicked to mine and then to my lips. "Samantha's sexy."

Well then. There was that.

"Oh." I did have a master's degree, didn't I? Now, I wasn't sure graduation hadn't been a dream. What a ridiculous response, but it was the only word I was able to form in my head.

It certainly made me feel sexy when he said it. The sound of his voice seemed to have a way of reaching deep inside me in places that shouldn't have been affected by any sound at all, but they were when he was around.

I really did have a lot of questions, like about his ex-wife, the same ex-wife everyone seemed to know about but Frank hadn't yet mentioned. I wanted to know about his life before he became a Wisper deputy, his time with the Army, and his experience being adopted, but I was enjoying the silence he liked so much, so I relaxed and let myself feel it for a while.

I pulled my phone from my pocket, hoping to capture how cozy the drive felt in a photo. Grum liked having his picture taken even if his dad didn't. It looked like he was posing and smiling in the back seat. Frank, on the other hand, seemed to have a hard time not rolling his eyes every time I whipped my cell out.

I'd tried to turn on music, but Post Malone was playing on the radio when I found a good station, and Frank shot me a glare, then turned it off. Okaaay then. No rap. After a minute, he turned it back on low, tapping the truck's screen until he found a compromise. A nineties station was playing "Fade Into You" by Mazzy Star. It was kind of sexy, but the only reason I knew the song was because they'd played it in an episode of *Gilmore Girls*—which I'd just binged on Netflix— where Rory dances with Dean. *Swoon*. Like I said, living without Gramps chattering my ear off at night was kind of lonely.

When we were a few blocks away from the library, Frank turned onto River Street, and to our surprise, we came upon a crime in progress at Wisper Elementary. But this crime looked like it might be fun to participate in.

Frank pulled us to a stop on the side of the road and jumped quickly out of the truck. When he opened my door, pulling me out too, he whispered, "Alright, little soldier. Our objective is to whack that man in his tall ass with a snow- ball." He pointed to the tallest of the "criminals" standing in the middle of the parking lot, who seemed to be yelling something at his friend. We were too far away to hear what they were saying, and besides, Frank was standing over me, breathing on me and shielding me from the falling snow with his big hat. The warmth emanating from his body was intoxicating. "I've wanted to smack him for years, and a snowball fight's just the excuse I've been lookin' for." Reaching behind me, he patted my ass lightly. "Go, girl. Get it."

Smiling as the desire to please him reared its head again, I assessed the situation, decided to go with the flow, and ran toward the parking lot as fast as I could, clomping through the snow in the boots he'd given me, trying to keep them on my feet. My destination was a tall pile of dirty snow made by an earlier plow. I figured we'd need something to hide behind, but it had been years since I'd been in a snowball fight. The only one I could remember was with Brady when we were, like, six, when I came to my grandparent's for Christmas break, while my parents were off, filming in the south of France or Portugal or somewhere.

After I got there and hid behind my snow heap, I bent, scooping up snow to form into balls. Frank was fast on my heels, and he slid in beside me, covering himself in the fluff as I looked out at the battle ensuing in front of me. His hat had fallen off, and I picked it up, pulled my beanie off, and donned the Stetson as I kneeled next to him. Frank took the beanie from my hand and pulled it over his own head, mumbling, "Mmhm," as he checked me out in his hat. He looked pretty good in my hat, too, like he was a boy again.

The smile I gave him wasn't one I was used to offering to anyone. My lips pursed, I could feel my one and only dimple deepening, and the look in my eyes was a heavy-lidded seduction. When he looked at me like that, like I was his temptress, I felt sexier than I ever had, and I wanted things from him, things that had never before crossed my mind.

Well, maybe they'd crossed my mind—I wasn't a virgin, obviously—but never with a nearly fifty-year-old cop.

I blinked, lowered my chin, and arched an eyebrow, and he growled at me, but not in an alarming, grizzly bear, "I'm going to eat you" way—or well, maybe exactly like that.

A snowball whizzing past my head shattered the heated moment between us, and we focused back on the two grown men whipping snowballs at each other, laughing and yelling.

Billie Cade, from book club, stepped out from behind another snowbank next to a parked row of school buses and let her own snowballs fly, one after the other, in fast succession. Her arm was like an automatic snowball gun. She must've been hiding and preparing her snow bullets while the men were clumsily forming them on the fly.

I wasn't sure who the guys were, but their voices sounded familiar. I assumed the shorter of the two men was probably her husband. "Oh, woman, you're gonna get it!"

"Really, Jay? What have I told you about calling me 'woman'?" Billie said, smiling at him in fun. And to the other man, she said, "C'mon, Finn, give me your best shot!" She stepped from behind her snow bunker, spreading her arms out wide. Her long, dark hair fell down her back, collected in a thick braid half hidden beneath her black winter hat, and her cheeks were red from the cold and exertion.

She'd told me she only joined the book club at Aislinn's insistence. I didn't know either of them well, but I knew the men were right to flee from Billie. She was fierce, and if she was threatening death by snowballs, she meant it.

Jay ran for cover, hiding behind a huge red truck with a massive snow shovel stuck to the front. Its headlights washed the snowy battlefield in their yellowy glow, while Finn, my target, tried to peg Billie with more snowballs, but she ducked and dodged, then aimed her return fire right at his face. He went down, fell back on his butt, and Billie threw back her head and cackled.

"That's our chance. Go," Frank urged, and we charged, launching snowballs as we ran, pummeling Finn with them. I felt kind of bad since I didn't really know him and he was already down, but still, it was fun.

"What?" He rolled in the snow, turning in our direction when we surprised him, shielding his red, snow-crusted face and blond beard with his gloved hands. "What the fuck, Frank? No fair. This is assault. I'm callin' the sheriff."

Frank chuckled, and he ran for Finn and slid down next to him, scooping snow into his arms and smothering Finn with it.

Coming to stand next to Billie, I smiled in greeting, and we watched the men, who looked like little boys playing in the snow. Once she'd said their names, I knew who Jay and Finn were. You couldn't live in Wisper without hearing about the Cades. They did a lot of good on and off their ranch for the community.

We cheered Frank on while Finn groaned, face-first in the snow.

Jay made his way back to Billie's side, wrapping an arm around her shoulder. "Never thought I'd see Finn playin' snow fort with a cop," he said.

"It's mother-effing hilarious," Billie said. "Finn so deserves this."

I nodded in agreement, laughing, having the absolute time of my life with a forty-nine-year-old man as he wrestled with a cowboy like he was ten.

"That was fun," I said, breathless from the cold. Frank had pulled his truck into the middle of the school parking lot, and we were alone, not another soul anywhere in sight besides Grum. The truck's bright lights illuminated us standing in the still-falling snow like a spotlight, and I removed my soaked mittens, shaking off the ice.

Billie, Finn, and Jay had gone after convincing Frank they'd stay out of trouble. They were only in town to help their brother Dean plow driveways for a few folks who needed to get to work. They weren't sure if the county plows would get to them in time, and the Cades had their own plow shovels to clear snow out at their ranch, so they did it for their friends and neighbors when they could.

But the snow had slowed. It fell lazily now, like dreamy, soft, fairy kisses landing on my eyelashes, and Frank leaned in. Trying to catch my breath, I closed my eyes, or maybe it was more like they fell shut under his spell, and I exhaled as he kissed my cheeks, melting the snow with his lips. Pressing a kiss to the tip of my nose, he pulled me close.

Uncertainty roared through my head, but my body was all too willing. How could he be too old for me after the snowball fight? He was the one joining in the fun, free and young at heart, while I stood there.

He took his hat back and tossed it into the open door of his truck, then pulled my hood above my head. And then we were dancing in the snow, swaying back and forth to the music of the crystal silence. The harder it snowed, the warmer I felt, wrapped in his arms. The only sound was Grum, snuffling and snorting the fresh powder as he ran circles around us.

Opening my eyes, I looked up at him, reaching up on my tiptoes to fit my lips to his. He pressed me closer with his hands on my low back, tilted his head, and opened my mouth with insistence from his, his beard tickling my cheek roughly.

The steam from our tangled breath rose above us, and Frank gripped my hips, holding me in place while he kissed me like he had on my front porch—had that only been last week? It felt like a lifetime had gone by.

His mouth was firm and dominant, but then his lips softened. They were intoxicating, and I was all too eager to follow him wherever it was he wanted to lead me with the kiss, until I was gasping for air, heart pounding, body tightening, my hands stealing the warmth from his neck, fingers threading through the short hair there, pulling him closer still.

And then, just like last time, he pulled away, whispering, "Slow down, girl."

"What? Why? I thought—"

In the sexiest, lowest lull of a voice, he whispered next to my ear, "'Cause this is goin' somewhere, Samantha…" The wet warmth from his lips brushing against the shell of my ear sent shivers down my spine. "But when I fuck you, it's gonna be in front of my fire, where I can lay you down and spread you open." He pulled back again, looking in my eyes, pulling a piece of hair away from my face. It was wet from the snow and sticking to my cheek. "I wanna see you and touch you. I want your nipples hard and pressin' into my chest when I make you come."

I gulped. "You did not just say that."

"Yes, ma'am, I did."

"Okay, well…" I took a steadying breath. "I want that *now*." It sounded a lot braver than I felt.

"We ain't ready for it."

Huh? I blinked, confused. "What does that mean?"

"The other day, I was too old for you. Now you want me?"

"What's wrong with that?"

"The wantin' part ain't wrong, but it's the why." He pressed against me, letting me feel his erection, hard against my belly even through however many layers of clothing we were wearing. "If we're doin' this, you better have some idea of *why* you want me, 'cause once you're mine, I ain't lettin' go."

A gasp was the only response I could muster. The nerve of this guy!

But I had to admit, I didn't think I'd want him to let go. I felt more cherished in his presence than I ever had in my parents'. How was that for a fucked up daddy/daughter dynamic?

His gaze strayed as he stepped back, focusing on something behind me. "Besides," he said, "we got work to do."

CHAPTER TWELVE

FRANK

"WORK? WAS THERE AN ACCIDENT?" Samantha asked, looking over her shoulder, trying to see what I was seeing. Dressed in the snow pants, with her pink hair under her purple hat, pink mittens, and blue winter coat, she was like a field of spring wildflowers meant just for me.

My heart was racing just being near her, and when she kissed me, man alive, it set all my instincts and insecurities on edge. What the hell was I to her? Was I too old? Was she too young?

What the fuck was this thing between us?

Whatever it was, it felt like a live wire, ready to zap and burn me if I let it.

I barely remembered the real reason I'd wanted to be out on the roads tonight. I'd kept my eyes open for the missing kid all night but still hadn't seen any sign of him.

I tried to focus. I was also trying to come up with reasons to stay with her. So maybe she wasn't the only one who needed to figure shit out. "Not yet. C'mon. You're learnin' how to drive."

"In a snowstorm?" She laughed but then glanced around

us, a worried frown taking over her face. "Frank, I thought we were out here trying to *prevent* accidents."

"We got this whole parkin' lot to ourselves, the snow's dyin' down, and if you crash, it'll be into a snowbank at five miles an hour. Can't do much damage that way." Taking her hand, I dragged her trepidatious ass to the driver's-side door and opened it for her. "Climb in."

She turned to face me. "I'm not so sure about this. There are school buses over there."

"I'm aware." This woman's hair was a wild mess beneath her hood. The wind was blowing strands of it everywhere, and it kept sticking to her face. Taking my gloves off, I couldn't seem to help myself, and I smoothed it away again carefully, then offered her my most serious expression. "Get in the truck, Samantha."

She squirmed. "Okay, jeez."

Taking a deep breath, she bit her lip and climbed up, and I watched her. She looked good in my truck. What was it about a beautiful woman driving a big rig? I had no clue, but it made my dick hard.

She slammed the door shut and rolled down the window. "What now?"

Sitting next to her, with Grum passed out in the back seat, snoring loudly, I showed her where all the controls were. The truck was souped-up a bit with four-wheel drive, my dash computer, radio base, and lights, but other than that, it wasn't much different than a regular ol' pickup. It had an automatic transmission, so it'd be easy to learn in.

"Put it in drive and hit the gas. Gently," I warned.

She looked at me with hesitation screaming out from behind her eyes. She was just as beautiful without her glasses, but I found myself missing them.

The smooth rumbling of the engine almost drowned out the quiet sound of her voice. "Okay. If you're sure?"

"I am. This ain't my first rodeo, and don't look at me. Look at the road ahead of you and go."

She got louder. "Okaaay. You don't have to be so bossy."

"Hm." If she thought that was bossy, she had another thing coming.

Mumbling expletives at me, probably 'cause she was nervous, she put the truck in gear and tapped the tip of her boot to the edge of the gas pedal. We didn't move one inch.

"More."

She winced but pressed harder, and the truck rolled forward a few feet, then stopped.

"The point is *forward* motion."

Annoyed, she mocked me like a teenager, "'The point is forward motion.' Ugh. I know that. It's just, this truck is state owned, right? And it's big. And… I'm scared, okay?"

Remembering how she'd relaxed when I told her she was beautiful on our date, I praised, "It's intimidatin', I know, but you got this, and you look *damn* good behind the wheel."

Swinging her head in my direction, a sly smile lit her eyes, but the truck rolled when she relaxed and her foot accidentally hit the gas.

"Whoa! What do I do?"

I knew there was nothing in front of us besides snow, so, looking in her eyes, I said casually, "Probably best to face forward."

She tore her eyes from mine and stomped on the brake.

"Don't stop. Keep goin'."

"I hit the wrong button. Your boots are way too big for me. Sorry."

"'The wrong button'? You mean pedal?"

"Yeah, whatever. You knew what I meant."

We lurched forward and stopped several more times, Samantha cursing under her breath the whole time, until finally, she stomped on the brake so hard, I nearly hit the windshield.

"Damn, girl! Why you stoppin'? We've barely gone twenty feet."

"I'm not a girl!" she shrieked. "And I know, okay! I'm not good at this. I don't want to do it anymore." But like a teenage girl, she lifted her hands into the air and pulled her legs up under the steering wheel without putting the truck in park, and we rolled back a foot or so. We weren't in danger of hitting anything in the flat parking lot in the snow, but I was starting to doubt she wouldn't drive my truck through the school, if she ever got it going.

Gathering my composure and trying not to lose my shit on her, I said calmly, "Samantha, put your damn foot on the gas pedal and your hands back on the wheel and *drive*."

"No," she taunted. "Why? I don't need to know how to drive. Walking's fine."

"What's this about? You really don't wanna learn, or is it somethin' else?"

Carefully, she put the truck in park, and she sighed and looked out her window. "I'm… embarrassed, okay? I should know how to drive by now. I'm thirty freaking years old. Like, as we speak, I'm turning thirty." She shook her head. "And the last person who tried to teach me yelled at me, too, and when I was terrible at it, he made fun of me, and I've just never tried again."

"Who?" I'd rip his balls off.

She waved a hand in the air. "Some jerk I used to date before I moved here."

I didn't want to think about anyone else touching her or

yelling at her, and I realized I needed to adjust tactics. "Look at me, please?"

When she did, I said, "I'm sorry for scoldin' you. I will not poke fun at you, and once you feel confident enough, you can drive me to that asshole's house, and I'll disembowel him for you. Deal?"

Looking back out the windshield, she whispered, "Promise?"

There was more to that story. The asshole in question had hurt her somehow besides laughing at her and hurting her pride. As I watched sadness cross her face, I knew it was a lot more than that.

"You're doin' great. This is a good start. So you never learned. Big deal. You're learnin' now, and I'm happy I get to be the guy to teach you."

Finally, she looked at me again. "Really?"

"Yes. Haven't you figured out by now that I don't care what we're doin'? As long as I get to look at your beautiful face and hear your laugh, I'm happy." Leaning across the seat, I slid my arm behind her head and pulled her closer, kissing her until she was moaning and melting into my hands, and *I* felt like a teenager again, making out with my girlfriend in the parking lot in secret.

Squeezing her thigh softly, my thumb smoothing closer and closer to dangerous places, I said quietly, "When you're ready, try again."

I relaxed, resting my arm along the seatback, and she nodded. Finally, taking a big, cleansing breath, she steeled herself and shifted into drive gingerly.

"The thing you wanna do is get used to how it feels when you press on the gas pedal. Your brain knows the truck will move, but you have to get your body prepared for the way it feels. That's what's makin' you nervous. We have plenty of room, so practice startin' and stoppin' till if feels natural."

We lurched forward and slammed to a stop again, but I kept my mouth shut, and she tried again. And again and again. Twenty minutes later, she eased to a stop, looking at me with the most triumphant smile on her lips.

"Good girl."

She smiled even bigger, then did a double take and glared at me. "Did you just 'good girl' me?"

Whoops. "Hm. Did I? Don't think I did."

She gasped. "You did! You know you did." After sliding the truck into park, she unclipped her seatbelt and climbed over me, straddling my legs. "I'm not a little girl, Frank."

Reaching up, I held her face between my hands, looking in her eyes. "No?"

She rubbed herself against me, and I pressed my hard-on up into the warm V between her thighs. Being this hard all the time couldn't be good for my vascular system, could it? But I was not about to complain.

"No, I'm not. Yes, I'm a lot younger than you, but I'm a *woman*. I may not know how to drive, but I know how to do a lot of other things."

My cock throbbed as she leaned down to kiss me again, her tongue snaking into my mouth, her breasts pressed against my chest. They were covered with about fifty layers of fabric, but they were there, and that knowledge alone turned me on.

I grabbed her ass with both hands. "There you go again, tryin' to start somethin'. I think I should take you home." I wasn't sure I could control myself if I didn't.

"You can't. My bag's at your house, and my keys are in my bag. Plus, we didn't eat our cake."

Wrapping my arms around her, I liked more than I maybe

should've how familiar we were with each other already. She didn't mind my hands on her. In fact, she seemed to like it, and when I eventually did take her home, I already knew I'd miss the loss of her fingers on my skin and her warmth beside me in my truck.

I teased, "Cake's just sugar."

She tsked, maybe a little offended, but she was smiling. "Whatever, Mr. Organic Veggies Only. It's a special occasion. I made it for you from scratch. Okay, fine, technically from a box, but still."

"How do you know that? Did you sneak into my fridge?"

Her cheeks turned red, and the guilty smile taking over her face made me laugh. "I may have. Just for a second, but I was impressed. It's so clean in there. Please don't ever look in my fridge." She winced, and I laughed more.

"Well then," I said, kissing her chin, thanking my lucky stars she was denying my attempt at chivalry and was even providing an excuse for us to stay together, "s'pose we better head on back to my place."

Although, I'd been dead set before when I told her she needed to know why she wanted me. I wasn't some young buck who just wanted to dip his wick and move on. Better she knew that now.

Better I knew it too.

CHAPTER THIRTEEN

SAMANTHA

WE MADE it back to Frank's cabin, but it took thirty minutes when it should've taken ten, and it wasn't without a few harrowing moments. The snow had stopped, but the roads were wet, and then the temperature began to drop. We slid for what felt like half a mile when he turned onto Route 20 and almost landed in a ditch, and it was only Frank's smooth maneuvering that steered us right. You were supposed to turn *in*to a swerve, not the opposite, which is totally what I would've done.

He threw our winter gear into his dryer when we got to his house. Our coats and snow pants were soaked, and I was cold to the bone, standing there watching him walk away from me. He was kind of a good ol' boy, possibly a little bit sexist, and definitely macho, but I'd never been more attracted to anyone.

The way he spoke to me, the patience he had with me, and the calmness about him was… sexy. I kept using the word to describe him, but that was because it was just true. I'd never met anyone more grounded or more confident and at home in their own skin.

All this time, I'd been convinced he was this shy, quiet, closed-off guy.

But he wasn't. And that was sexy too!

He still wasn't much of a talker, but I was coming to learn that his silences were just as sexy as the rest of him, because when he was quiet, it was usually because he was looking at me like he wanted to kiss me. Or bed me.

Before he returned from the laundry room somewhere in the back of his house, I grabbed my bag quickly, took out my stupid contacts, and put my glasses back on. The damn things dried my eyes out and made my eyeballs feel like they were made out of sand from the Sahara.

When he got back, he was dressed the same as me, only in long johns and a T-shirt. "Have a seat at the table. I'll get some forks."

When I sat, Grum snuggled up by my bare feet, and I was thankful for the heat coming off his body. Tucking my toes beneath his chest, I unlatched the Tupperware lid and removed it, and Frank handed me a fork and pulled a chair beside me, but he angled it so he could watch me.

"You don't have a candle, do you?"

Leaning on a fist with his elbow on the table, he shook his head and nudged my glasses up the bridge of my nose with a soft push from the pad of his index finger, smiling softly at their reappearance. "No, I ain't one of those guys who keeps a junk drawer full of weird stuff you only use once a year. Maybe when I have kids."

That one small sentence—"Maybe when I have kids"— was a bigger issue between us than the age-gap thing, but how was I supposed to bring it up now?

Taking the fork from my hand, he dug it into a corner of the cake. The pink sprinkles I'd stuck to the edges dropped onto the table as he fed me a bite and watched my lips as I began to chew. I watched him, too, letting the rush of flavor fill my mouth and the sugar liven and warm my blood, but then the look in his eyes changed.

His smile disappeared and was replaced with a look so intense that my stomach was suddenly doing flips. He dropped the fork. It fell from his fingers, making a loud clattering noise when it hit the tabletop, and then he was reaching for me with his strong arms, lifting me out of my chair and onto his lap, facing him.

He was hard—clarification: his *penis* was hard—and he held me still, his hands holding my face, forcing me to feel him, to feel our bodies touching.

"What are you doing? I thought you didn't want…"

"Didn't want what?"

I closed my eyes, trying to hide from him, trying not to let him see the immature little girl I'd originally come to his house to convince him I wasn't. "Me."

"Look at me, please." When I opened my eyes, his hand rose to the back of my head, and he held it in his palm. He didn't push or pull. It was just there, like a claiming. "You think I don't want you?"

"I mean, I climbed on top of you back in the parking lot, but you keep saying this can't happen."

"Yet. It ain't happenin' *yet*."

"Why do you get to decide?"

"Why can't I? It's my choice too."

"I'm sorry," I said, nodding. "You're right. You're absolutely right. It's just, I guess I thought, or I hoped—"

He frowned in confusion. "What?"

"Never mind."

One eyebrow tipped up in a warning. "Samantha." What would he have done if I'd disobeyed him? My pulse ran away from me when I imagined the possibilities.

But the need to please him won out.

"It's nothing. I thought that—I-I…" Resolving to get the thought out of my head, I said it quickly. "I hoped you'd be so turned on by me that you wouldn't be able to resist." *How's that for feminism?*

"You think it's *easy* for me to tell you no?" Now he pulled me closer, whispering, "Since the first day I met you, I have wanted you. Why on God's green earth do you think I come to the library every week?"

"Why did it take so long for you to ask me out?"

"Truth?"

"Yes."

He sighed. "Because I was an idiot. I thought you were seein' your friend, Brady. And once I realized you weren't, I dunno. Guess I lost my nerve. Took me a while to build it back up. And you're young. I wanted you, but I kept tellin' myself I shouldn't."

"So the age thing does bother you?"

"Not anymore."

"Then why are you denying me? I want you too."

His eyes rose from my lips until there was nothing in my view besides warm gray irises. "Because," he said, "if I make love to you, I'll fall *in* love with you, but you're not sure about me yet. You ain't ready to decide." He wasn't wrong, but was I detecting fear on his part? Fear that I might not want him for anything more than sex? "I wanna know you better. Like what happened with that guy you told me about. You got sad when you mentioned him."

"Oh." Deciding just to brush over his "I'll fall in love with you" statement because that was way too complicated in the moment, I explained. Vaguely. "It wasn't about him. I mean, it is, but it's not like I miss him or anything. It's just some old history. It makes me sad sometimes."

"Tell me."

"No." I shook my head, loosening his hold. "I'm sorry, but I don't want to talk about it. I like this thing between us, and if I go dredging up the past, it'll change."

But the truth was that I was terrified he'd reject me if he knew I couldn't have children. Everyone else had. *I* had. I was still blaming myself.

"That's life. It'll do that now and again. But I've heard talkin' makes it better."

"You don't know that," I whispered. How could he? We barely knew anything about each other at all, and if I dumped this huge thing on him, he'd run screaming for the hills.

A smile formed on his face, but it was sad, so many lines creasing around his eyes, and it was the most beautiful smile I'd ever seen. "So then, we ain't ready for sex." He licked his lips slowly, his eyes fixed firmly on mine. "It's a damn shame, too, 'cause I've been dreamin' up ways to make you come for a long time."

Had all the oxygen just been sucked out of the room? I was pretty sure it had. "That's sexual blackmail."

"No, Samantha, it's called give and take. I need more from you in order to give you more of me. Nothin' wrong with that."

Yeah, except giving him more of me was dangerous. I'd given everything to Tyler, and he'd walked away without a second thought, and that was after I'd conceived and miscarried his child.

Was there anything left for me to give?

He kissed me lightly. "How 'bout this? I'll tell you my fear if you tell me yours."

I blurted it fast. "I'm afraid you want something from me that I can't give you."

He nodded, accepting what I'd said at face value, not realizing what I'd just admitted. "And my fear is that I want somethin' you don't." He inhaled slowly. "So. Where's that leave us?"

I looked around. "In your kitchen."

He pulled my mouth down to his. Kissing me and tasting the hint of the cake still on my tongue, he whispered, "Happy birthday, Samantha."

"Happy birthday, Frank. Does my cake taste good?"

"*You* taste good," he said, and his hands slid down until he was pushing and pulling my hips, moving us together over our thermals. The fabric wasn't thick, and I could feel the wet warmth soaking through already.

His honesty was making me want to tell him everything about my life. I couldn't seem to get close enough to him. I wanted the connection to last forever, though I knew it probably wouldn't. We were all wrong for each other, and no matter what he said, I wasn't sure he was right that it didn't matter to him.

But I moaned anyway, tilting my head, kissing him like I'd never kissed anyone. It was like my tongue had a mind of its own. I was licking his lips, nipping them with my teeth, and plunging my tongue in and out of his mouth, pressing my breasts against his chest.

He stood, but I didn't stop kissing him. His chair scraped the floor, and I held onto him tightly until he set me on his kitchen table, placing his hand over my chest gently, pressing me back until I lay before him, next to our cake, in only the long johns and my damp T-shirt. The pink tips of my hair were visible in my peripheral vision, spread out around me while Frank looked me over, studying me like he was trying to commit my curves to memory, and I found myself wishing I hadn't dyed my hair. I wanted him to know the real dirty-blonde me.

His shirt came off, and the warm ache between my legs became a *pounding*. What was this thing between us? He said it couldn't happen. I'd said that too.

But *something* was happening. Whether that something was a good idea or not was an entirely other matter.

His chest was sculpted. It was the only descriptor I could come up with, like he'd been carved from stone, but he wasn't smooth.

No, Frank Sims was covered in dark chest hair that tapered down beneath his long johns, accenting the deep V between his oblique muscles, pointing to naughty, *naughty* things below.

My mouth watered when his abs flexed as he pushed the thermal fabric down his legs, revealing strong thighs and tight black boxer briefs. I wanted to look at the bulge beneath them, to trace the defined lines of his cock jutting up to his navel, but it was safer not to. Instead, my gaze flicked up to his.

Stepping forward, he tugged my pants down slowly, careful not to catch my underwear with them as he went, and he lifted my legs, pulling the soft fabric over my bare feet. It tickled, and I squirmed a little.

Kissing each foot lightly under the arch, he lowered them one after the other and then extended a hand toward me. When I reached for it, he pulled me up to sit.

He hadn't said a word, and all I'd done was lie there and watch him, but I was breathing hard, trying not to look away from his eyes, because if I did, I wasn't sure what I would do. I wasn't sure what he wanted from me.

But I *needed* him.

Would he deny me? Even though he was undressing me, I still wasn't sure what *he* wanted.

Lifting my shirt by the hem and tugging in an upward

motion, he lifted his chin at the same time as a command for me to raise my arms, and I obeyed, raising them high above my head. He removed my shirt carefully, trying not to knock my glasses off, and my hair followed slowly, falling back down over my shoulders in messy, damp strands.

It was a bit unnerving as he stood before me under his kitchen's stark light, so close, watching me. I was breathless and aching for him, but I felt an urge to cover myself with my hands. Unlike him, I wasn't so physically fit, preferring to spend my spare time lying in bed, reading, which didn't lend itself to firm muscles and a toned ass. But when I tried to cross my arms over my chest, wishing I owned lacy, black lingerie because there was no way my simple cotton undergarments were sexy to him, he stopped me, guiding my hands onto the table next to my legs. I gripped the edge of the wood, taking my nervousness out on it, digging my fingernails underneath.

"I won't have you coverin' your beautiful body, not in front of me."

Why was it that when this man decided to speak, only beauty came out? He always said the thing I needed to hear.

Dipping two fingers into the cake beside me on the table, he scooped frosting from the top and smeared it over my breasts, above my bra.

"I'm takin' you to my bed," he stated so simply, like it wasn't the single most erotic thing anyone had ever said to me, and lifted me into his arms, my legs dangling over them and my feet skimming his side. His hot skin almost sizzled against mine, or it felt that way at least. He was warming me from the outside in, and I wanted to burrow into his chest to feel more of that heat.

What was stopping me?

Wrapping my arms around his shoulders, I shifted in his

hold, turning my mouth to his neck, and I kissed my way from his ear to his collarbone, licking and nipping. He didn't moan or groan, but I felt his excitement in his quickened pace and the pulsing of his cock, pressed hard against my low back, while he carried me as if I weighed no more than a feather.

CHAPTER FOURTEEN

SAMANTHA

PLACING me in the middle of his king-sized bed, Frank straightened my legs and tangled his fingers through my hair, splaying it out on his pillow. The bed was uber-soft, it smelled like him, and I sank into the mattress like I was falling through a cloud.

The room was masculine like the rest of his house, but with mostly navy blue and dark wood accents and furniture glinting in the subdued lighting coming from a floor lamp in the corner. The bedsheets were crisp white linen, though, and I worried about staining them with the bright pink frosting.

Leaning over me, Frank removed my glasses and set them on his bedside table, but then he crawled over me, covering my body fully, holding himself above me with only the strength of his forearms.

It was quiet in his bedroom as he kissed me, his mouth moving over mine like a whisper. The only sound was our breathing. We were in sync—breathing in sync, kissing in sync—until he leaned to the side, fitting himself beside me, and he trailed a finger over my lips, urging me to open them.

My heart felt like it would beat into oblivion as I whispered, "Frank, I-I don't know if I'm the right woman for you." I didn't want to say it, but even though I couldn't find the courage to tell him the whole truth, I needed to warn him.

His finger stilled on my lips, but he didn't pull it away as he looked into my eyes. "Whatever's goin' through your head, stop thinkin' about it."

"But—"

He pushed his finger past my lips. "Lick."

I opened my mouth, and the rough pad of his fingertip settled on my tongue. I sucked, pulling the rest of his finger inside, closing my lips around it, tasting the residual frosting and moaning softly as I imagined sucking other things like that. His sharp exhale puffed against my neck as he touched his forehead to my temple.

The length of his cock throbbed beneath his boxers against my thigh as he pulled his finger out and dragged it between my breasts, catching on the little strip of elastic there, and down lower to my stomach, avoiding the frosting.

He followed the discolored line of my surgery scar with his finger, but he didn't stop to ask about it. It was so faded that, for all he knew, it could've come from a bad scratch. I clamped my legs closed. The whole night was swirling around in my head like its own snowstorm, making me miss what Frank's hands on me felt like.

But then he slid his finger beneath my underwear, and my legs fell open and stayed that way. His tongue in my mouth as he kissed me again was hot, thrusting against mine, and then his finger slipped deeper between my thighs, playing in the slick there.

It was almost shocking to me how good that felt. It had been a long time since I'd been touched by a man the way Frank was touching me, and I'd been through hell and back since.

But then he began to rub.

I gasped and flexed my hips, digging my heels into the sheets, seeking more of his finger, so he added another and dipped them inside my body as he pulled his head back so he could watch me.

"Frank." The whisper was a plea for more, and he knew it.

He licked my ear, nuzzling his nose behind it. "I promised you when I fuck you, it'll be in front of my fireplace. We're not doin' that yet, but I wanna watch you come. It's your birthday. I need to make you feel good, and then I want you to turn thirty in my arms."

I panted, "But w-what about you? It's your birthday too."

Pushing in deeper, he crooked his fingers carefully. I cried out, whimpering at their thickness, riding them, listening to the suction as he moved them in and out.

His voice was pure seduction in my ear as I closed my eyes. "Don't worry about me, Samantha. You're givin' me everything right now, writhin' in my arms while I touch you."

"Orgasms can't fix every—"

His thumb found my clit while he worked his fingers faster, whispering, "What's that you were sayin'?"

I breathed, "Faster."

"Say please."

"Please, Frank. Please!" I was chasing release now. It was so close, and he knew that too.

He withdrew his fingers and sucked them into his mouth, clearly enjoying the shock the swift move elicited from me. He arched an eyebrow and smiled a smile so alluring that I was chasing it, wanting those lips on mine again.

He didn't allow it.

Instead, he slid between my thighs, slipping my underwear down my legs. When they were off, he moved back up and leaned over me, licking the frosting from my skin.

He was slow about it, and he never moved his eyes from mine. I tried so hard to control my breath, but it rushed out of my mouth fast and loud, my stomach moving up and down against his chest as he bathed the tops of my breasts with his tongue.

He collected a dollop of frosting on his finger and sat back, hooking my knee over his shoulder.

Wordlessly, he locked both of my wrists in one hand and lowered his head while he guided my hands to where he wanted them, placing them on his head. His hair was soft, softer than I'd imagined it would be, as it tickled my palms.

I closed my eyes, releasing a pent-up breath, and then he smeared the frosting over my clit. I froze at the sensation, my whole body locking in place as he lapped it up while his fingers slid back inside.

I didn't mean to, but my hands formed fists around his hair, and I pulled. "Oh God."

Grumbling between my legs, he said, "Ain't no God here, girl. Just me."

He flicked his tongue faster but in a specific rhythm. Flick, flick, flick, pause. And with each drugging flick, the pause became longer until I was nearly in tears, begging him for more. Again he denied me, stopping just to breathe on me, to watch me, making me wait with his fingers still inside but not moving. It felt like forever.

I wiggled under his gaze as he wound me up, showing me he could control my pleasure. Pulling his fingers out slowly, he licked the length of my leg, from the apex of my thighs to the back of my knee. Tickling me there, he moved lower, kissing and laving my calf with his tongue until I was stretching and flexing the muscle because I wanted more.

Whatever he had to give, I wanted more.

I was already begging, my body arching toward his, my eyes fixed on him, watching what he was doing to me. It was sinful and erotic and delightfully wrong in some way. No one had ever kissed my body like that, but it was delicious. I moaned, relaxing the lower he moved. The wet trail his mouth left on my leg made goosebumps rise. They began a slow ascent, moving over all the places he'd already kissed, until the rush went rogue and reached my nipples, making them ache.

He said nothing and moved lower still until he reached my foot. My feet had certainly never been touched like that, but with Frank caressing them, licking and massaging, digging his thumbs into the tender muscles in wide circles, I had to admit, it felt amazing, like some kind of erotic massage, because, with each swipe of his thumb, need *throbbed* in my core.

When he finally made his way back between my thighs, I was a writhing, sweating mess. Beads of perspiration collected at the back of my neck, but the second I felt his hand cupping me, his fingers pushing inside me again, and his tongue hot on my clit, I came.

Hard.

I cried out and squeezed his head between my legs. I couldn't stop it.

The anticipation had made me come. I felt his pleasure deep inside, the euphoria traveling slowly until I felt it in my breasts, too, and he'd barely touched them. I felt it in the back of my throat.

My body gripped his fingers, and he tugged them gently in and out while he climbed over me again, kissing me and making me taste myself.

I liked the sweet, musky flavor, and that he was feeding it

to me through his kiss was sexier than his tongue inside my body. More intimate.

"Best cake I've ever tasted," he murmured against my lips, and he rolled beside me, tucking me against his chest, his hard cock pressed against the curve of my ass, but it was still sheathed beneath his boxers. He didn't seek friction, didn't rock against me, and we fell asleep like that, me basically passing out from pleasure and him hard as a rock behind me, kissing my neck and pulling me closer.

In my dream, I'd been wrapped in silk like a cocoon. There were children outside the cocoon, running around it, giggling and talking in whispers. Warm arms hugged me, tucking me closer to an even bigger warmth.

A lovely, low voice said, "Mornin', Samantha. Can you open your eyes for me?"

"Mmm." I knew the voice in my ear, but the face that went with it was just beyond my sight. A name was trying to form in my head, but it was barely a breath on my lips. "Still sleeping," I mumbled.

A husky chuckle behind me made me lift my lids, and I found myself looking into two shiny brown orbs. I caught a whiff of puppy breath, and then a long, wet tongue slurped in my direction.

I yelped, backing into the warm boulder behind me on the bed. "What is that?"

Frank's voice made it clear where I was. "Grum, mind your business. Go lie down."

Duh. Grum. I laughed at my reaction.

Grum trotted off, and I sat up, covering my breasts with Frank's down comforter, but I was still wearing my bra.

When I felt the soft cotton, the blanket fell from my hands as a rush of everything that had happened late last night washed over me: Frank's mouth on me, his fingers inside me, oh God, the frosting, and the most intense orgasm I'd ever experienced. The memory had my heart pounding and my breath quickening.

"It's just me. You're in my bed. Did you forget?"

Turning toward the sound of his voice, I was greeted with the most handsome smile as he lay behind me on his side, his head propped up on his hand. There was a twinkle in his eyes. It was a seductive twinkle, and it only intensified while he looked my body over, noticing how my nipples had hardened and peaked. It was his fault. I would never look at him again without getting turned on. And that was it for me and cake. I'd never be able to eat it again without creaming my underwear.

"Sorry," I said. "Guess I was sleeping pretty deeply."

"It killed me to wake you, but I gotta go into the station. I didn't wanna leave you here without a way back to town."

"Oh." I rubbed the sleep away from my eyes with my knuckle. "Is everything okay?" He was already dressed to leave, and it made me feel exposed.

"Everything's fine, but Abey ain't feelin' good. I need to spell her."

"Spell her?"

"I need to take over for a while. Carey's wife and kids caught a chill or somethin', too, probably from the weather, so he's on nursin' duty. He'll be in and out today, so there's likely to be some accidents on the highway I'll need to see to."

"Oh. I hope they aren't bad accidents."

He pushed a strand of hair out of my eyes, tucking it behind my ear. His breath was minty fresh.

"No coffee?"

"Hm?"

"You don't smell like coffee," I said.

"Never drink the stuff."

"Me either. Not very often anyway."

He laughed as he moved away from me and stood from the bed, walking to his dresser. "Then why'd you ask?"

I shrugged one shoulder, rolling over quickly, reaching for my glasses on the bedside table so I could see him properly.

Wrapping a brown leather-banded watch on his wrist, he checked the time and then grabbed some kind of deputy holster thing from an armchair in the corner. There was a black metal gun in the holster, and he slung it over his waistband, threading the strap through his belt loops and fastening and adjusting it so the gun was right where he wanted it on his hip.

I shivered. It was a serious-looking gun, but it wasn't the reason my body was reacting. Watching Frank dress and get ready for work was damn sexy. I could only imagine what I looked like. It definitely wouldn't be categorized as sexy. I knew that much as I puffed my cheeks and blew more hair out of my eyeline.

"So," he said, watching me watching him.

"I don't want to go home." It was cold at Gramps's house. And lonely. And if I stayed, I could pretend a little longer. "Can I stay here? Is that weird? I could keep Grum company. The library will stay closed all day. If the roads are bad tomorrow, I might not even open it then."

The look on Frank's face changed. The twinkle was back in his eyes, and he stalked toward me, trapping me between his arms on the bed, pressing me to lie back. "Girl, you could stay in my bed for the rest of time, and I wouldn't kick up a fuss." He kissed me. Or maybe it was more like he scorched me with his lips and tongue. I didn't even care about my morning breath. Finally, he pulled back, licking my kiss off his lips. "But the roads have been cleared already. Schools are open."

"Well, that totally sucks. I had this dream of lazing about all day in pajamas, reading and sipping hot tea."

He growled low in the back of his throat, grinding his hard cock through his uniform pants between my bare thighs. I moaned and wrapped my arms around his shoulders, pulling him closer and kissing the ever-loving crap out of him too.

Looping his arms behind my back, he rolled me on top of him.

"Careful! What if your gun goes off?"

"Safety's on," he said, but he unbuckled the holster and slid it out from under his hips. As soon as he'd set it on the bedside table, he thrust upward, pressing me down with his hands on my hips, and I rolled against him. "I, on the other hand, have no such capability. We better cut this out, or you're gonna make me come in my uniform. I'm still hard from last night."

Scraping my teeth over my bottom lip, I looked down at the body part he was really talking about, then flicked my eyes back up to his. "I could… take care of that for you."

His eyebrows rose, and he shook his head once. "No."

CHAPTER FIFTEEN

FRANK

"NO?" The nervous smile on her lips dropped like a rock in the river. "Why not?"

I pushed harder, burrowing my dick between her thighs, trying to make contact with her clit through my work pants. I was hoping her scent would stay with me all day, like she'd marked me.

Her eyes rolled shut when I hit my mark, and I pressed harder. "Trust me, Samantha, there's nothin' I want more, but not before I make love to you."

"What?" She froze, then pushed with her hands flat on my chest and sat up. "Why not? That's ridiculous."

Relaxing my head into the pillow, I was confused. "Ain't ridiculous." Why was that ridiculous? Was it ridiculous for me to want some certainty from her before I gave away the last chance I'd probably have at… the last chance I'd maybe ever get at falling in love?

Was that what was happening?

Shit. Well then, I really needed to be careful. What was stopping her from ripping me apart and running away?

"Yes, it is. It's antiquated and old-fashioned. Are you trying to preserve my virtue or something?"

"What virtue?" I said with a smirk. The irritated look on her face made me think she hadn't gotten the joke. "If that's what I'm doin', why'd I bring you back to my house in the first place?"

She scoffed.

"You like to argue just to argue?" Or maybe she was arguing 'cause whatever it was that had ruined her mood last night was still bothering her and she was trying to distract me. Or maybe sex was all she wanted from me.

"I'm not arguing with you. I'm disagreeing with you."

"Whatever you wanna call it. No, I'm not tryin' to protect your virtue, but I s'pose maybe I am old-fashioned." I pulled her back down, kissing her chin and cheek. "You have no idea how much I want inside you. But, like I said, we ain't ready for that."

"*I'm* not ready, you mean." She jumped off me and yanked my comforter out from underneath my ass. Seeing her femininity in my house was highlighting just how "single bachelor" my furniture was. Her softness stood out from all the dark bulkiness and sharp edges. "Maybe *you're* not ready." Wrapping the blanket around her body like a towel, tucking it closed over her breasts, she whipped around, the thing trailing behind her, and stomped out of my bedroom.

It was the single sexiest thing she'd ever done, and my dick hardened even further when I caught a glimpse of the angry red flush flashing across the side of her face and neck beneath her pink glasses.

She grumbled all the way down the hall, muttering, "Not ready? What does that even mean? Where are my clothes?"

Jumping up, I followed, adjusting my dick, wishing we had all the time in the world to explore each other, that I could spend hours making her flush for other, kinkier reasons. The thought had me imagining her handcuffed to my bedpost while I fucked into—

Whoa. Slow down, old man. That might send her running even sooner.

I caught up to her standing in the middle of my kitchen, the blanket slipping down her back, curling around her hips. It allowed the curve of her spine to show below her delicate shoulder blades and the hint of her ass just beyond my sight.

When I spoke, she yanked it up, clutching it tight.

"I folded your clothes and put 'em on the bathroom sink. You can use my toothbrush. It's brand new. I threw away my old one and opened it for you this morning after I brushed my teeth. Your boots are by the door, and your bag's hangin' from my hat hook. That's where it goes, by the way."

I smiled, and she turned. "You're condescending."

I advanced slowly, letting her know I'd stop if she wanted me to, and she backed up two steps but no further. "If it pleases you, you can throw your bag any old place," I said, taking her in my arms carefully, like we were dancing, fitting one hand on her low back over the blanket. I backed her up against the wall next to my kitchen window, looking in her eyes. "But I'm right about this."

"No, you're—"

"Yes, I am," I whispered, kissing her cheeks and neck, making my way lower. I tugged the blanket down and bent, sliding her soft bra to the side and sucking a flushed nipple into my mouth.

I couldn't stop the groan that came out of my mouth. *Fuck*, her breasts were soft.

She tried again, but the argument fell from her lips like a slur. "No, y-you're n-not." She moaned, and the blanket dropped and pooled around our feet on the floor.

I was so hard, I could barely move, but I kneeled before her and made my way even lower, showing her my intention with my tongue, licking down her belly to her pussy, spreading her open with my fingers. Pumping two inside her, I looked up at her beautiful face. She was nothing short of magnificent when she was angry and turned on at the same time. There was some kind of fire behind her hazel eyes. She was still mad at me, but she wanted me, and the way she pressed her teeth into her bottom lip was sexy as sin.

"Want me to stop?"

I didn't want to. I wanted my body inside hers.

But I couldn't let things go that far yet. I needed to protect us both.

She shook her head, making strands of her hair fall over her breasts, and I licked hard between her pussy lips, from her cunt to her clit. She gasped a long, slow intaking of air through her mouth, and then let it out even slower in a moan. Her head hit the wall when it fell back, and she widened her legs.

"Good girl."

She whimpered.

"We can talk about all the things you wanna do to me and why I ain't gonna let you later. We got some issues to iron out between us first."

She breathed, "Th-that's not fair."

"Fair's for fools," I said, and I buried my face in her slick, running my nose up her wet channel, breathing her in, letting her taste fill me up.

She made me fucking wild.

Wild enough that I could ignore the fact that I was being a hypocrite. I wasn't without my own past, and I hadn't said word one about it.

Another gasping inhale was the only indication I had that

she was still breathing. She wasn't moving, but then her legs began to shake. They quivered, and the harder I pressed my tongue to her clit, the harder she shook.

Pulling my fingers out slowly, feeling how soft and warm she was inside, I reached around, grabbing her ass, one cheek in each hand, and I squeezed while I fucked her with my tongue and chin. They were wet with her juices, and my beard was sure to add some texture to her orgasm.

She cried out and clutched my hair in her hands. "Frank!"

It wasn't only her legs shaking now. Her whole body was trembling. And when I released one ass cheek and penetrated her with three fingers again, she came so hard, she fell down into my lap, breathing a moan.

It was difficult and definitely painful not to whip my cock out and jack my cum all over her beautiful body and the one rosy nipple I could see, but I didn't. If my pecker made an appearance, the fucker was going in. Nothing could stop it. I knew I couldn't.

Already, my shirt was wet with sweat from the effort of holding back. I was shaking now, trying with everything in me not to pop my fly and impale her on my cock. I wanted her on her knees or leaned over the back of my couch, ass high and tight. I wanted her breasts to bounce in front of my eyes while she rode me. Fuck. I'd take her right here on the hard floor.

But we weren't ready.

We'd both been burned before, and I didn't want Samantha to become another ex. Something about her made me almost desperate for her to be more.

Instead, I wrapped her in the blanket and carried her to my bathroom. I set her on the counter, and the satisfied smile on her lips began to fade as she looked up at me.

"Take a quick shower if you want," I said. "Get dressed,

brush your teeth, and I'll drop you at the library. Text me later?"

"I don't have your number."

"Yes, you do. Abey gave me your cell, and I texted you this mornin'."

"I'm hungry. Can I make a quick egg before we go?" Jesus, just the thought of her standing half naked in my kitchen, cooking breakfast, was enough to make me come without her even touching me.

I kissed her forehead. "Another time. I'll shoot José a text and ask him to whip somethin' up to go. You like to cook?"

"No. I only do it because apparently I'll die if I don't eat."

Chuckling, I said, "Well, I love to cook, and next time, I'll make you some whole-wheat pancakes that'll knock your socks off. They're my specialty."

Wide-eyed, she asked, "Next time?"

"Yeah, next time, when you're gonna tell me what the hell changed your mood last night, and we're gonna discuss whatever this is between us and why you think it can't work."

And why I wanted her to be dead wrong.

Grabbing the toothbrush next to the faucet, she pointed it at me. "Why do you like me? Is it because I'm so much younger than you and you want a submissive little girl to play with?"

My eyebrows must've hit the ceiling. *This* was the feisty librarian I'd been coveting like she was water and I was drought-ravaged dirt.

"First of all, are you always this disagreeable? And second, since when are you submissive?" I smiled—couldn't help myself—and wrapped my hands around her hips over the blanket. Squeezing, I said, "And third, do I look like the kinda man who wants to play around?"

She swallowed loudly, the sound like a bullhorn echoing off the bathroom walls.

"I know what I want, Samantha, and I don't have time to fuck around playin' games. Been there. Done that. I want more."

She tapped my chest three times with the end of the toothbrush. "Okay, but I feel like this might bear repeating: I'm *not* a little girl."

Moving in between her spread legs, letting her feel the hard-on I still had for her, I tugged at the blanket, and she released it, baring her body to me. Her pretty breast was still exposed, but I looked only in her eyes as I adjusted her bra, covering her. "Noted." I winked. "Now, get cleaned up. Daddy's got work."

CHAPTER SIXTEEN

SAMANTHA

FAIR'S FOR FOOLS?

What did that even mean? I tried to contemplate the ridiculous thing Frank had said as I pulled my emergency eyeliner from my purse after Frank dropped me at the library. There was a blow-dryer around here somewhere. Maybe under the sink in the downstairs restroom.

God, that man. He was infuriating.

We weren't allowed to have sex yet, but he could penetrate me with every other appendage of his body? Just not his dick?

What was the damn difference?

And it was frustrating that he could read me so well already. He'd noticed my change of mood in the parking lot last night without me even saying a word.

But I hadn't wanted to disappoint Frank, and I didn't want to tell him the truth because I was ashamed of my past. It made me feel like I'd failed at life before I'd even really lived it. Would someone like him want me, someone with so much experience as he'd said? Could Frank really want me if he knew the truth? Me, the poor, immature, *barren* librarian?

What the hell could I even offer him?

Five minutes ago, I was in denial that a relationship could even work between a forty-nine-year-old man and a thirty-year-old woman, and now I was searching for a reason that it could, even though he made me insane sometimes. He thought he was so cute—"Daddy's got work." Ugh!

Plenty of people had successful, non-"daddy" age-gap romances. All I had to do was look to the books I loved so much. Jo March and Professor Bhaer in Louisa May Alcott's *Little Women* had a huge difference between their ages. Huge!

But maybe it was smarter for me to find a reason to end this… whatever this thing was between us.

Before he could find out that I was inadequate.

And how dare he try to protect my… *Wait. What exactly are you complaining about here, Sam?*

My phone buzzed on the check-in desk behind me, and I grabbed it, then sank into a reading chair by the window with one of the veggie breakfast burritos José had so kindly delivered to the cab of Frank's truck when we pulled up in front of the diner, with orange juice and a cream cheese Danish, which Frank had said he'd ordered in case I wanted "sugary crap instead of nutritious food for breakfast."

I watched an elderly couple as they walked down Franklin Street holding hands, crunching carefully through the snow on the sidewalk, as I answered my phone, wishing I had a sweater or a blanket. Man, the library was cold. "Hey, Juni."

"What's up with you? Where've you been? Are you opening the library today? It's book club, right?"

"What time is it?" I looked around for one of the five thousand clocks on the library walls, forgetting there was one on my phone.

"It's only nine."

"Yeah, I just got to work. The roads are already clear."

"Oh. Cool. You sound disappointed though. Were you hoping for a snow day?"

I paused. I knew if I told her about last night, she'd flip a stitch, but I really needed to talk this out. "I stayed at Frank's last night."

"Oh my God, you did? Wait. I thought you said it wouldn't work between you two."

"I did say that."

I fidgeted with the hem of my shirt until I realized I was still wearing the same clothes I'd worn to Frank's house last night. I'd changed back into them after I'd taken a shower using his shampoo and soap. I basically stood under the spray of the water, letting the warmth coat my skin, sniffing his toiletries until I was satisfied, like I was filling a reservoir to keep me drowning in Frank's scent until I could see him again. I'd barely had a chance to wear my skirt before I changed into the long johns he'd provided, so it was still clean, but I needed to change my underwear at least. Good thing I kept a change of clothes in a closet upstairs. Not that I'd ever anticipated a walk-of-shame emergency clothing-change situation, but I was kind of proud of myself for being prepared for it anyway.

"But then I got to know him a little."

"Did you go on another date?"

"Kind of."

"So then," she said, "what's wrong with you? You sound sad."

"I don't know. I feel sad, but it's kind of hard to explain."

"Try."

"You're sure you're not busy?"

"Not too busy for you," she said. "I'm self-employed, remember? I can take a break whenever I want."

"Thanks."

She and Brady were slowly convincing me that I was worth loving and that I wasn't a burden. Except for when I was with my grandparents, I'd felt that way my whole life, but I'd never had friends like Brady and Juni before.

"So Frank's this great guy. I mean, *really* great, Juni. Like, I thought he was too old for me, you know? There's a huge age difference. But when I'm with him, it doesn't feel like that."

"You like him."

It wasn't a question. She already knew the truth. She could probably hear it in my voice.

"Yes."

"Okay, but isn't that a good thing?"

"I don't know." I sighed. "Yes, it's a good thing, until you get to the logistics of it all. He's almost fifty. He hasn't had a family yet, but he wants one, and like, the clock's ticking."

"You don't want children?"

"I do, but I…" Taking a deep breath, I released it and just said it. "I can't have children."

"Oh, Sam. I'm so sorry. I didn't know."

"Of course you didn't. I've never told you. I don't really like talking about it."

"I understand. But you know, there are lots of ways to have a family."

Like I'd never heard that before. Duh. I *knew* that. I didn't need anyone to tell me. There was surrogacy and in vitro. Unfortunately, those options would never be available to me. If I was ever going to be lucky enough to have kids, I would have to adopt. And with my salary, my lack of good health insurance, and the fact that I lived with my grandpa, I was sure to be on the top of every adoption agency's list. *Right.*

"I know, Juni, but it's different than having your own

kids. And Frank told me he wants a big family. He was adopted, so I'm sure he meant his *own* family."

"I know it must feel like that to you." Her next question was tentative. "But can I tell you a story?"

"Okay."

"My friend Teonna adopted a little boy, and she told me, before he came along, she felt an emptiness inside her because she could never carry a child, but as soon as she held that kid in her arms, all the emptiness melted away. She's so in love with her baby, and it doesn't matter one bit that he isn't hers biologically." Juneau cleared her throat quietly. "Can I ask what happened? I mean, *why* you can't have children?"

"I had really bad endometriosis. They did surgery three times in my teens and early twenties to remove scar tissue because it was so painful, but it kept coming back. And then, in college, I dated this guy, and the condom broke and…"

"Oh, Sam."

"Yeah, but my body couldn't handle it. It was a tubal pregnancy, and I lost it. Things were damaged beyond repair."

"I'm so damn sorry."

"Thank you, but now I feel like I've failed as a mother already. You should've seen how Frank's eyes lit up at the restaurant when he talked about having a family someday. And besides, we barely know each other. How can I dump this on him? What would I say? 'Oh, by the way, we haven't even had sex yet, but let's talk about the whole "Do you want kids" sitch.'" I sighed. "He'll kick me out of his house."

"If he's as nice of a guy as you say he is, he will not. Just talk to him, Sam." She waited a minute before asking, "So you haven't had sex with him yet?"

"No. Not… quite."

"'Not quite'? What exactly does that mean?"

"Well, there were moistened body parts involved, heavy petting, and throbbing members. And tongues. *Lots* of tongues. But no Ps in Vs."

Juni snorted. "That was a very clever way of saying you made out with the good deputy."

"Made out? Nuh uh. He *blew* my mind, Juni. Twice. Once last night and once this morning."

She meowed like a leopard.

"It was… fucking delicious."

"Tell me."

"I can't. I have to open up and get ready for book club."

"Okay, then you can tell all of us when we get there. After all, it's a *romance* book club."

If I could've seen her face, I was certain she would be winking like a villain in a black-and-white movie, twisting an imaginary mustache between her fingers.

"I cannot believe y'all forgot to invite the owner of the *only* bookstore in Wisper to your little book club. So rude," Aubrey George said jokingly when the ladies were all there.

She was right. I hadn't even thought about inviting her, but Carly laughed. "Oops. That was my job. Daisy asked me to call you, but I totally forgot. You know I'm scatterbrained, Aubrey, and it ain't like pregnancy makes that better." She shivered kind of violently. "Is it cold in here? Maybe it's just the hormones." She lifted a knitted wrap from her bag and pulled it around her shoulders.

"I'm so sorry, Aubrey," Daisy said. "I missed the first meeting, so I assumed Carly told you. I should've double-checked."

"S'pose I forgive you," she said. "Anyway, I'm here now. What'd I miss?"

"Not much," I said. "Does everybody know Aubrey?"

Everyone nodded, and Billie said, "Yep. I've gotten to know her 'cause Aislinn *devours* audiobooks, and Aubrey gets lots of free download codes." Aubrey smiled, tipping her shoulder up in a "Yeah, I'm the best" kind of way. "Actually," Billie went on, "I'm surprised it's taken us this long to form a book club. I'm also surprised I'm a member of it. I usually don't like people."

"It's true," Daisy said, laughing, fondness clear in her eyes for her daughters-in-law. She was a great addition to the club. The woman had already read every single historical and vintage romance in the library. I'd placed an order for more from another library in Cheyenne. She had two different e-readers, but she said she preferred used books from the library. The soft, papery feel of their pages reminded her of being a teenager and holing up in the library to read during summer breaks.

I laughed too. "Well, I'm glad you're here."

I had arranged the weathered armchairs in a circle in the reading room and asked Vern to pick up and deliver a big round reclaimed barn-wood coffee table I'd found at a local resale shop. Aubrey had brought a portable box of fresh-brewed coffee and cranberry scones from Coffee Shot, and we arranged them on a side table against the wall. I added a bowl of plain M&Ms in the middle of the coffee table so we'd have something to snack on. "Oh, um, Abey isn't feeling well today, so I don't think she's coming. And Juneau—"

"I'm here! I'm here!" Juni came skidding into the room with a fresh bouquet of flowers in one hand and a clear plastic bag filled with white chocolate-covered pretzels from a sweet shop in Jackson in the other. She set them on the table, handed me the yellow daisies already situated in a simple clear vase with water, then plopped her butt in the chair next to me. "Sorry. I swear, I'm not usually late to things. Hi." She waved to the group. "I'm Juni."

"Thanks, Juni. They're gorgeous."

"Welcome," she said as I set them in the middle of the table next to the M&Ms. "I thought they'd brighten up this dark room."

Carly gushed at Juni, "I freakin' love your Billionaire Brats series. Stone's my ultimate book boyfriend."

"Thanks," Juni said shyly. "That's really cool of you to say."

"Who's Stone?" Billie asked.

"He's the billionaire from Juneau's first book," Aislinn said. "It doesn't come in audiobook format, though, so I had to have my computer read the e-book to me. It's very inconvenient, and the computer doesn't do the voices."

Juni winced, getting her first dose of Aislinn's directness. "Sorry. I'm working on the audiobook now."

"Good," Aislinn said, crossing her legs. "I liked the first book. I'd like to listen to the rest."

"Okay. I'm sure we could talk about Juni's books all day, but should we talk about *Forever Your Man*?"

"Oh, is that our first book?" Aubrey asked. "Good. Already read it."

"Yeah," Billie said. "I'm not done reading it yet, but I don't like it."

"Hold on," Juni interrupted. "Has Sam told you about Frank yet?"

Aubrey perked up. "Frank Sims?"

"How'd you know?" I asked, feeling my cheeks flushing.

"C'mon," she said. "There's no other Frank in town, is there? At least not one who you went on a date with."

"Yeah, but how do you know that?"

Everyone laughed, and Billie rolled her eyes. "*Everyone* knows that. And she's been on at least two dates with Frank. We saw them out last night."

"Right," I said, blushing harder. "Small town."

"Yeah." Aubrey laughed, settling back into her chair, flicking her strawberry blond hair over her shoulder. "And Juni's right. You need to tell us about him. He's *so* sexy."

My face was the color of a baboon's ass as I remembered just how sexy he was last night and this morning when he'd made me come.

"So, a second date? How'd it go?" Aubrey pressed again.

"It was good, but he's a lot older than me."

"How old are you, and how old is he?" Aislinn asked.

"I'm thirty, and he's forty-nine, as of last night."

"Wait," Juni said, turning toward me and leaning forward. "Wasn't yesterday your birthday too? Happy belated birthday, by the way." She smirked.

Everyone repeated "happy birthday," and I tried not to wilt under their attention. I wasn't used to it. "Thank you. And yes. Frank and I have the same birthday."

Carly cooed, "Isn't that the cutest thing ever?"

"Yeah," I said, looking around the circle, wondering how much to tell them. I barely knew most of the women. But it did feel good to have girlfriends who wanted to hear about my life. "But nineteen years is a pretty big difference."

"What does that matter?" Phil said. "Once you get to be my age, you'll realize it don't make a bit of difference. Do you like him, honey?"

"Yeah. Maybe a little."

"Don't listen to Philomena," Cal disagreed in her uppity

way. "I think you'd be better suited to someone else. You can't possibly be in the same stage of life as he is with that age difference. It'll only end in heartbreak."

"Way to be supportive, Cal." Billie tsked. "Can't you see how nervous she is talking about him?" She waved a hand in my direction. "That tells me she likes Frank more than a 'little.' Who cares about age or social class or whatever. Like in this stupid book." She held *Forever Your Man* in the air, shaking it. "That ridiculous prince dude is so freaking hung up on the fact that Myra grew up poor in a Kentucky mining town. Like, for real. Who gives a shit? People are always using those things as excuses, but if you love someone, you should go for it. I learned that the hard way."

"Exactly." Phil glared at Cal. "You used to be more of an optimist."

"Well, losing a *friend* will do that to a woman."

Phil softened toward Cal then. It was easy to see from the sad look in her eyes, but she didn't respond.

"Actually," I said, "I'm kind of worried Cal may be right."

"Why?" Carly asked. "Where are you from?"

"No." I laughed. "It's not about where I'm from. It's about—" I looked at Juni for encouragement. I still wasn't sure how much to say. She raised her eyebrows, nodding her head toward the other women, so I continued. "It's about possibly wanting different things in life."

Carly asked, "Like what? Like he wants to buy a new pickup but you want a sensible minivan for all the babies you're gonna have? In that case, I say go for the truck. More fun when you're datin'. Then, later, you can trade it in for the kid wagon."

"Actually, I c-can't have kids." *Oh.* I hadn't realized how much it would hurt to say that out loud to a group of women.

Logically, I knew they wouldn't judge me, but that didn't stop me from darting my eyes around the room to check their facial expressions.

"Oh, babe," Carly said. "Stuck my foot in my mouth yet again. Please forgive me."

"It's okay," I said, trying to smile.

"Sweetie," Phil said, "I'm so sorry. But did you two discuss that on your date?"

"No. The subject didn't come up." Because I didn't bring it up, even after Frank said he definitely wanted a family.

"That's not *exactly* true," Juni hedged. She turned toward me in her chair, asking with the look in her eye and a tilt of her head if it was okay for her to explain more.

I whispered, "Okay."

"So Sam thinks, because of Frank's age and some personal things in his life, that he'll want biological children. Plus, he's not getting any younger, if you know what I mean. But I told her biology doesn't matter. I'm not speaking from experience or anything, but I think, if you adopt or go through surrogacy or whatever, the result is the same. You'd still love that child more than your own life."

"Yeah," Billie said. "I bet there's lots of kids out there who need a mom."

In my head, I rolled my eyes. Like it was that easy. Like I could just order a kid and have DoorDash deliver him or her.

"Juneau's right," Cal said. "I couldn't have children either, but Herbert and I adopted our two girls, Lilah and Shawnee"—she lit up, smiling and looking happier than I'd ever seen her—"and they made our lives so full. Sure, there were issues now and then that were probably different than biological parents have to deal with, but it was worth it, Sam. And now I've got grandchildren."

I shot out of my chair before I could stop myself. "I *can't* adopt. Please stop saying it like it's so easy! It's not."

Looking around at all their faces, my heart was pounding, and I was embarrassed and ashamed of my reaction, but they seemed to take it in stride. In fact, they felt sorry for me. It was dripping from the sad expressions on their faces.

Except for Cal. She looked personally offended. "Well, I don't see why not," she said. "Are you opposed to adoption?"

"No. I'm sorry," I said, taking my seat again, trying to calm the scream I could feel inside my chest. "Of course not, but I've been hearing that for years. 'Just adopt.' Does no one understand that it's expensive and it's a really complicated process? And does no one care that I lost the ability to have my *own* children? The thing I've been dreaming about since I *was* a kid. What about that?"

And that was the real issue between Frank and me. It didn't really matter what he wanted or expected from someone he was dating. The big thing between us was that I was still grieving my loss, and I didn't know if I could get over it on his timeline. Besides, he was a private man, and I didn't want to gossip about his personal history, so I apologized again for my outburst and left it there with the ladies, steering them back to our book.

Thankfully, they were tactful and forgiving enough to let it go.

CHAPTER SEVENTEEN

FRANK

"WHAT'S GOIN' on, ol' man?" Carey greeted me when I got to the station after lunch. "Ain't like you to take a long lunch."

I'd been sitting in my cruiser, daydreaming about Samantha and the way she'd let me command her body last night and this morning, even when she was mad at me. I could still see her indignant expression. I found myself having a hard time paying attention to much else all morning.

Grabbing the updated daily call printout from Shelley's desk, I looked it over. "You scoldin' me, boss?" There wasn't anything pressing on the list besides lots of winter cats stuck up trees.

He snorted. "Like I could. How were the roads last night?"

"Not too bad. Abey comin' in at all?"

"You haven't talked to her yet? I'm surprised she hasn't called you to complain in your ear like she did me. She won't be in today or tomorrow. Said she's feelin' awful. That woman's whinier than a little kid when she's sick. She said her mama's already at her apartment, prayin' over her and stuffing vitamins down her throat."

His phone dinged, and he pulled it from his jacket pocket, clicking the screen a few times. "Ah shit. I'm getting reports that the winter storm we got comin' next week will be pretty bad. Worse than the last one. Record lows and snow that'll stop our world from spinnin' for a couple days. Let's check that the roads have been properly cleared and prepped before this one. And it's probably best to check in with the elderly community when we can, make sure they have what they need before it hits. We'll have to set up our usual roadblocks so nobody gets stuck up on the pass south of Cade Ranch." He paused. "Hear what I'm sayin'?"

"Heard. Hey, you haven't gotten any reports about that kid—the one from Ace's House I told you about?" The one popping into my head more and more as the days went by with no sign of him. I'd gone through Mrs. George's receipts and called everyone I could track down, but nobody had noticed anything suspicious.

"No. Haven't heard a word. Why?"

"Just hopin' we woulda found him by now."

"Well, we don't really know if the kid is actually homeless. Could just be what he told Theo Burroughs, that he's bored, lookin' for a place to be instead of home."

"Yeah. S'pose."

Carey dug through a stack of papers on Shelley's desk, tsking at the disorganization, as usual.

"But what if he ain't?"

"Well," he said. "Ha! Here it is. Damn woman puts shit in the weirdest places." Whatever paper he'd been looking for had been stuck under a potted plant. "Anyway, if he is homeless and he's a minor, which again, we don't know, then we'll have to get state services involved. You know that. If we can even find him. Could be he was just passin' through." Carey shrugged. It sounded cold, but without more to go on, we couldn't allocate too many resources on a hunch.

"Hm." But what if it wasn't a hunch? What if Burroughs was right and the kid was alone and scared? What if he was hungry? That was the worst feeling, not knowing where your next meal was coming from. "Just keep an eye out, would ya?"

"Will do. That reminds me. You remember I was out at Milson's ranch a while back?"

"Yeah."

"Buckey Mann reported that they'd had some food stolen from the bunkhouse. I told him it was probably just the construction guys workin' on the new buildin' who ate the food or maybe one of the other cowboys, but Buckey swears no. He keeps track of that shit like a military cook. It just occurred to me now, but I wonder if your boy had anything to do with that."

Huh. "Could be. And now with another storm comin'… I'll look into it."

"How was your date?" Carey asked, probably trying to distract me. He knew how focused I could get when something was bothering me.

"It was, you know, good."

"You and the librarian goin' out again?"

Leaning over my desk and pulling up the call log on my computer, I double-checked if he was right that there hadn't been any new reports about the kid, but there wasn't anything new. "Since when do you talk gossip?"

"Ain't gossip if it comes from the horse's mouth. I'm just checkin' in with you, man. You alright?"

I straightened. "Yeah, Carey. I'm good. The date went

well. Saw Samantha last night, and I plan to see her again tonight."

"Good," he said. "I'm glad you found somebody. I was startin' to worry about you, ol' man."

"Fuck off. How many times in one conversation are you gonna call me an old man?"

He laughed. "As many as I can, ol' man. So's you don't forget. Alright, well, enough of that. I gotta make some stops and then check back in on my girls. This cold or virus or whatever's wreakin' havoc on my house. Even the baby has it." He yawned. "I was up with her, tryin' to clear the snot from her nose by foggin' up the bathroom. I think I managed maybe two hours of sleep last night. Poor Frannie just lay there in bed this mornin', moaning. She said she's achin' somethin' awful. Gracie's not too bad. She's just happy she gets to play hooky from school. She's binge-watchin' those *Harry Potter* movies."

Lucky him. Not the aching or the snot part, but the family part.

"Hope they feel better. I'll see you later. Gonna get goin' on these calls."

***

As I made my way across town to Milson's ranch, I thought about what it would be like to have a family like Carey's. Time wasn't exactly on my side.

And then I thought about Samantha. Was she right? Not that I wanted her just 'cause she was younger, but was it part of the reason I was attracted to her? Because she was still young enough for the possibility of a family? It wasn't my intention to find a woman I only halfway liked and then knock her up 'cause I was that desperate for a family, but I did *want* a family. I didn't really care what it looked like, just a family.

I wanted a reason to stop home in the middle of the day. Technically, I had that now with Grum, unless I brought him to work with me, but he didn't count. I wanted loud plate-clattering dinners and melting snowmen in the front yard. But more than that, I wanted someone I could share my life with. Someone to talk to late into the nights and make love to in the mornings before the world woke up.

But not just anyone. I wanted someone who was passionate about life. Someone I could laugh and argue with. Somebody who could put up with my grouchy bullshit. Maybe someone who made me *not* grouchy.

Samantha could be my someone. Was it too soon to think that we could make each other happy?

It was. I knew it was fast, but I liked how I felt around her. I liked taking care of her. I liked that she made me think. Being around her had all kinds of things running through my head. The football thing, kids, a future. Love.

The family part would come, or it wouldn't. The important thing was the love. That was what I really wanted. Someone who loved me enough to stick around.

Old man Milson's ranch was right at the edge of town. Head of a big cattle operation, Milson owned more land than the whole of Wisper that reached out northwest of Route 20. He had seven full-time cowboys through the winter. Always seven—never six, never eight—'cause he believed the number was lucky. In the spring, summer, and fall, though, he hired day workers to help with calving season, branding, and all the rest of whatever it was that made cattle such a hard business to be in.

Cowboys from all around Wyoming sought jobs at Milson's every year. He paid well, offered up a nice place to live, and treated his employees like family. Max Gordon ran the place like a well-oiled machine, and I knew he and Buckey, one of the other full-timers, would help me if I asked.

I parked on the south side of the bunkhouse and knocked on the door, and a short man with a round belly answered.

"Just the cowboy I wanted to see," I said.

His belly jiggled under his Coors T-shirt when he jabbed his arms in the air. "I'm innocent, Deputy. I swear!"

"Shut up, Buckey, you ol' fool."

He laughed. "Come on in, Frank. You want a beer?"

"It's one in the afternoon."

"There's only two times of the day for a man: coffee time or beer time. You want coffee?" He turned, motioning for me to follow with a wave of his hand.

"No, thanks," I said, removing my hat and stomping the snow from my boots by the door. "Max here?"

"Yeah, he's around. He'll stop in when he sees your truck out there. So what can we do for you? Oh, hey, you thought any more about what we talked about? The youth football thing? My kids are still too young, but it won't be long."

"Yeah," I said. I'd been mulling it over long enough. Why not? What was stopping me? "I was just thinkin' about it actually. We should do it. What do you think about talkin' to Theo Burroughs over at Ace's House, seein' if we could run it from there?"

"Well, Frank, I think you're smarter than ya look," he joked. "That's a damn good idea."

"We can talk about it more later, but right now, what can you tell me about the food that went missin'?"

"Shoot. I already told Carey about it."

"I know you did, Buckey, but I'm lookin' for somebody. I'm hopin' you can help."

"Oh. Okay. Um, so it's been a while, but whoever broke in here took a bunch of perishables."

"Perishables?"

"Yeah, you know, like fruit, couple green peppers. Well, and nonperishables too, come to think on it. Bags of chips, boxes of crackers. We had a couple of them air-sealed packages of tuna. What else? Uh…"

"I know what perishables are, but that's it?"

"No, now, lemme think." He pursed his lips as he sat at the supper table in the kitchen.

I'd never seen a nicer bunkhouse. This one had seven small bedrooms built around the perimeter of the building so each full-time guy had his own space. Max and Buckey didn't live on the property, though, so the extra rooms were unoccupied till spring, and then the two fastest cowboys to rope a calf on the first day of the season claimed use of the rooms. They were a hot commodity since a lot of the guys spent their time off at the rodeo and often came home with a buckle bunny or two. The rest of the workers slept in bunkbeds in the open main room of the bunkhouse or in long-term tents they pitched out on the property every spring. Old man Milson was in the process of building a second, bigger bunkhouse, but with winter being so bad this year, the project was on hold.

"Frank? Everything alright?" Max asked when he walked through the door, knocking his boots against the frame. Clumps of snow fell to the pile I'd just made as I turned toward the sound of his voice.

"Hey," I said, shaking his hand after he took off his gloves, and we both sat at the table. "Everything's fine. I was just checkin' in about the missin' food, though I'm thinkin' Buckey might've overreacted."

"I didn't overreact," Buckey argued. "There were cans

stolen, too, but only the kind with the pop tops, not the ones you need a can opener for. And there was a big bottle of antibiotics stolen from the med cupboard in the barn."

"Meds? Carey never said anything about that."

"Yep." Buckey nodded. "Told him about it."

"Liquid or pills?"

"Pills."

"What's this about, Frank?" Max asked. "By the way, you ever find out who broke into my cousin's bookstore? I meant to text you about that. I put the cameras up for her and showed her how to use the software." He poured himself a mug of coffee from one of them fancy French presses sitting in the middle of the table, holding it up in my direction, asking if I wanted a cup. They weren't just well-paid cowboys; spoiled cowboys was what they were.

I shook my head. "No, thanks. It's funny you ask. I think it's the same person. We got a report of a missin' kid—possibly missin'," I amended, "and I don't even know if he's technically a kid. I'm pretty sure he is. Mr. Burroughs over at Ace's House thinks he's homeless. I'm not sure, but with the weather lately, I'm worried he's out somewhere alone."

"None of the guys have said anything, and I haven't seen any kids. Have you, Buckey?"

Buckey sipped his coffee, pinky up. "Only kids I've seen are my own when they're screamin' at me and holdin' out their grubby little hands for my money when I get home every night. How Carly talked me into havin' another, I'll never know." He winked at me.

"No kids," Max confirmed with a shake of his head. He took off his winter cap, dropping it on the table in front of him and running his hand through his hair.

"Alright, well, keep your eyes peeled, eh?"

He nodded. "You got it."

"Mind if I drive around the property a bit this mornin', just to take a look?"

"Sure," he said, "but there's places on this ranch a truck can't get to. If the kid's here somewhere, ain't no guarantee you'll find him."

"I know, but just in case. Maybe he'd stay close to more food."

"Yeah," Buckey said, "but then we'd notice him."

Max saw the worry on my face. "G'on then. Call if you need help. Buckey and I got a bunch of upkeep shit to do today, but we'll be around."

"Thanks."

Damn. I really hoped Murphy wasn't out here.

These mountains were a harsh place for a kid to try to survive, but the Grand Tetons were some of the most beautiful parts of America I'd ever seen, especially topped with snow. The prickly green edges of the fir and pine trees poked through two feet of the white fluff, and steam rose from the curving river in the distance.

I'd driven up an old access road and parked, and I stood there, looking out at nothing and everything all at the same time.

This right here was what I wanted. A real cabin somewhere in the mountains. I'd take my family up for summers, and we'd fish and hunt and enjoy life the way it was meant to be lived. Free.

The silence was the thing. I could hear myself think up here, could block out all the ugliness I saw every day.

A tree creaked to my right, a clump of snow fell, making

a plopping sound, and I turned my head just as a doe stepped through into the clearing. She saw me, but she didn't run.

I was hoping to find smoke from a burning campfire somewhere on the horizon, but I didn't. There was nothing to see but gleaming white snow, mountains, and a cold blue sky.

I watched the doe, silently conveying my wish that she'd look for the boy too. I wasn't sure how she could've helped him, but just another soul witnessing him would've made me feel better.

As if she'd understood me, she lowered her head slowly but then turned and leapt back into the trees, and I was alone again, looking out at the beautiful nothingness, worried, but my heart was warm and aching to see Samantha.

If anybody could cure the heartbreak I was feeling for this kid, it was her.

CHAPTER EIGHTEEN

SAMANTHA

JUNI STAYED after book club to make sure I was okay after I'd melted down in front of everyone, and we made plans to go for a drink after I closed the library. She drove us out to the Duck & Bowl, Wisper's "finest" nightlife establishment. They had beer from a keg, which they served in red plastic cups. You could order a whiskey and Coke if you didn't like beer, but it tasted more like gasoline and Coke, if you asked me. But the draw was the live ducks.

There were flocks of them out back. They raised them and sometimes brought the babies indoors. If the owner's daughter Jacinda was working, you could hold and pet them. Unfortunately, she wasn't here tonight, so Juni and I sat at the counter, sipping our five-dollar swill, watching the bowling teams as they played their slow games and listening to the crack and tumble of the pins echoing down at the ends of the lanes, while I tried not to imagine exactly what they were raising the ducks for.

It had only just occurred to me. Why would anyone raise ducks? At a bowling alley? They were well cared for, but seriously, not knowing why was starting to disturb me.

"So how was the rest of your day?" Juni asked as I made a face while a mouthful of beer slipped down my throat. Budweiser was definitely not my favorite, but it seemed to be the unofficial beer of Wyoming. We should've gone to Manny's Bar. He had IPAs, but he *didn't* have ducks.

"Oh, you know," I said with a wave of my hand, "it was fine. How was yours?"

"Good. I had an idea for a new series, so I spent the afternoon jotting down notes." Juni seemed to be hedging her next words. "Are you… feeling better after the thing at book club today?"

"Yeah. I'm fine. I just…" I hung my head, still ashamed of my reaction earlier in the day. "I'm sorry." The ladies were becoming my friends, just like I'd been hoping, and then I turned around and yelled at them?

"It's okay, Sam. There's nothing you need to feel sorry about." She took a sip, too, and then groaned. "Ugh. This stuff is disgusting." Pushing her cup to the edge of the counter, she turned on her stool to face me. "When you're ready, will you talk to me about this? I'm no expert, but I think maybe you have something in your head about adoption that might not be right. If you'd allow me to, I'd be happy to help you investigate. We can find out together." When I looked up at her, she amended, "Only if you want. If I'm off base, just smack me." She winced. "Are you gonna smack me?"

I shook my head, rolling my eyes, exasperated with myself inside, and Juni laughed.

"Thank you, Juni. That's a really nice offer, and I would love the support, but I don't know if I'm ready. I think I still… blame myself for what happened. I should probably get over that first before I look into adoption or anything else."

"Yeah, I get that. But Sam?" Tilting her head, she caught my eye. "It wasn't your fault. You didn't do anything wrong."

"Yeah." I knew she was right. Logically, I knew that, but somebody needed to tell it to my heart. I mean, why me? Why *my* body? Why was my reproductive system a traitor when all I'd ever wanted was kids? I used to dream about it as a little girl, probably because I was always alone while my parents were off on their movie sets, ignoring their daughter and making masterpieces. I'd be this weird ever-pregnant earthy mama, with a clutch of kids, running around on some English moor, like in *The Secret Garden*. They'd have wild hair and would wear haphazard clothing, reading poetry and solving scientific equations. What? So the kids in my dreams were geniuses. Sue me.

"How are you gonna tell Frank? You are going to tell him, right?"

"I don't know." I turned back to my beer. God, why was this so hard? When I pictured telling him, actually pictured the words coming out of my mouth, I could never see the look on Frank's face. Would he be angry? Sad? Disappointed? Would he hate me for leading him on? Was that what I was doing?

And why? Why did I care so much what he thought of me?

"Girls?"

Juni and I both turned at the sound of Cal's voice, and when I spotted her walking across the bowling alley toward us, I smiled. I should've known Cal was in a bowling league. She was dressed in the official bowler's uniform, black slacks and a rose-colored league shirt, with flowery lettering like the Pink Ladies jackets from *Grease*. Her team's name was The Wisper Willows. She'd wrapped her wrist in a brace, and I wondered how she was able to fit her fingers into the holes on her bowling ball with those long red nails of hers.

"Hi, Cal," I said, motioning to her wrist. "Are you okay?"

She looked at it and then held it up in the air. "Oh, this? Yeah, this thing gives me an edge. Makes my wrist even stronger so I can get more strikes. But shhh, don't tell the Barton Belles. They don't need to know our secrets. We're gonna beat them so bad this year."

Juni laughed. "Your secret's safe with us."

"Are you bowling tonight?" Cal asked.

"No," I said. "We just came for a drink after work." I grabbed my Solo cup and went to take another drink but, when I caught a whiff, decided against it. I set it back down, thinking that I should probably brush my teeth when Juni dropped me off at home before Frank picked me up for dinner at his house.

"Excuse me, ladies," Juni said. "I need to run to the little girls' room."

Cal took Juneau's bar stool when she was gone, looking me square in the face. "Why don't you want to adopt?"

Sputtering at her extremely forward question, I didn't quite know how to answer. "I-I, um, I mean, there's just a lot to it, and I don't have a lot of money. I'm young. I'm not married. I don't know. I just don't see it happening for me. I-it's *hard* to imagine."

"Well, there are different ways to adopt. Some are more expensive than others. It depends on a lot of things."

"I know," I said. "I'm sorry. I didn't mean to offend you earlier. I'm sure your experience with adoption was really positive."

"You didn't offend me, but I don't think it has to be all you're making it out to be. And it wasn't always easy. Herbert and I did have money to spare, it's true, but we waited years before we got our girls. I thought it wouldn't happen for us either. I cried myself to sleep many nights."

"You did?"

"Yes," she said, plucking imaginary lint off of her black wrist brace. "I had a uterine tumor when I was about your age and had to have a full hysterectomy at thirty-one. So I understand. I just wanted you to know that."

"Thank you." Taking a deep breath, I asked, "But how did your husband handle it? I mean, how did it affect your relationship?"

She looked at me, and I wondered if, in the confines of Cal's mind, she was deciding how much of her wisdom to impart to me. Sometimes I got the feeling that Cal was on the top of the world, looking down at the rest of us.

After a minute-long silence, she answered, "He mourned the loss, just like I did. Of course, he got over it faster than I did, but he was a good man. He waited for me patiently. The right man will for you too."

I nodded, hoping she was right.

"You have my cell phone number, don't you?" she asked.

"Yes."

Stepping down from the stool, she said, "Well then, maybe use it. You may be young, but you aren't the only one who can text up a storm. I'm on TikTok."

I laughed. "Thank you, Cal. I will."

"Alright, then," she said. "Say good night to Juneau for me. It's my turn, and I'm about to knock Elsie Cartwright down a peg or two. That awful woman's been preening around here, acting like she's queen of the alley because she got some fancy new bowling shoes." She turned back toward me. "Unfortunately for her, new shoes don't make a bit of difference when you're going up against bowling royalty. The Willows won best in state two years in a row. We almost made it through the first round at nationals." She walked away, waving her hand in the air. "Bye."

Juni dropped me at home, and I checked the mail before heading in. God, Gramps's place was quiet. It hit me square in the face every time I walked in the front door and was the reason I spent so much time at the library. It was quiet there, too, but all the stories living between its walls made it seem loud to me sometimes.

Tossing the new pile of mail onto the old pile on the kitchen table, I watered the mint and chives I'd been trying to grow in the kitchen window, then dropped my bag, too, and headed to get cleaned up before dinner. A green thumb was not something I'd been born with, but my little plants were eking their way out of the dirt slowly, crawling up toward the limited winter sunshine.

Frank had promised pancakes, so I zipped my toothbrush into a plastic baggie after I brushed my teeth and tucked it into the inside pocket of my purse in case I needed it later. Like maybe if I stayed the night at his house again. Or if he fed me some of the vegetables he seemed to love and they got stuck in my teeth, although I couldn't imagine any vegetable pairing well with pancakes. And when I really thought about it, I was surprised Frank would even eat pancakes because, inevitably, you needed sugary syrup and butter to go with them. Or maybe you didn't. Maybe he ate them dry.

Yuck. I was contemplating smuggling a bottle of syrup in my bag when the doorbell rang but decided against it. I would trust Frank to feed me something delicious. Actually, I could think of a few things he could feed me that would be oh so yummy.

The thought got stuck in my throat when I opened the door to see him standing on the other side, just dripping sex.

The man should arrest his damn self. This was too much. How was I supposed to concentrate on talking about all the things he'd said we needed to discuss with him looking like that? Ripped and tall and strong. It should've been illegal how freaking sexy he was. His jacket wasn't a stiff traditional motorcycle jacket. It was made from soft leather that molded to his body in the nicest way. Instantly, when I saw him, I wanted to slide my hands beneath it to feel the heat coming off those muscles.

And I wanted to confess everything to him, but then he spoke, and I lost my nerve.

"Hi," he said, and his skin creased up at the corners of his eyes when he smiled, like just seeing me made him happy. Like I lit up his world.

I breathed, "Hi."

He cocked his head a little, eyebrows up. "You ready?"

"Yes." I stepped forward, out the door, but he stopped me with his warm hands on my shoulders.

He turned me gently. "Get your coat, girl. It's twenty degrees out here."

"Right." I grabbed my coat from the back of the couch and shrugged it on, then slipped my purse's handles over my shoulder. "Okay. Now I'm ready."

"You know," he said, peeking past me at the colorful sixties and seventies mixed décor in Gramps's living room. "I bought a copy of that decoratin' guide I borrowed from the library the first day we met. You might wanna loan it to Jessup when he gets back."

I snorted, and it sent me into hysterics. "Oh my God. I can't wait to tell him you said that."

"Girl, don't you dare!"

"Too late. You said it out loud."

Frank laughed, too, placing his hand on his stomach. He was beautiful when he laughed, and I knew instinctively that seeing it was a privilege many people didn't get.

I locked up, and as we walked to his truck and he opened the passenger-side door for me, he said, "I actually know Jessup."

"Yeah. I remember him saying he knew you too."

"He'll probably mention it if you, you know, tell him we're…"

"I haven't told him yet." Honestly, I was a little nervous to tell my gramps that Frank and I were dating. Frank was a lot closer to Gramps's age than I was. Would he have something to say about it?

But then, I kind of doubted he would. Gramps was a happy guy. He believed in love, even if his only daughter, my mother, didn't.

"Anyway, always thought he was a nice guy."

"He is," I said. "He's a great guy. My best friend."

That made Frank smile again as I climbed up into the seat, and he shut my door with a nod and a cute purse of his lips.

When he was sitting beside me, he started the truck. "A while back, I was thinkin' of puttin' an ad in the *Wisper Gazette* about startin' up a Pop Warner club. I stopped in to talk to him about it once. That was before he closed the paper though."

"What's Pop Warner?"

"Youth football."

"You want to teach little kids how to play football?"

"Yeah," he said. "I was gonna do it when I first moved here, but it just never worked out. Me and Buckey are thinkin' about doin' it now though." He looked at me as he backed out of the driveway. "Whatcha think about that?"

"I think that's a great idea! I even know some kids and parents who might be interested. Do you need help setting it up?"

"Yeah," he said, smiling from ear to ear. "Think I'd love that."

CHAPTER NINETEEN

FRANK

"TOLD you I wanted to dance with you in front of my fire."

"You did," Samantha said against my chest after dinner as we swayed together in my living room to "Born & Raised" by Shane Smith and the Saints, our arms wrapped around each other, hands resting low. Grum was fast asleep in the corner on the new oversized dog bed I'd bought him, possibly swimming in his dream, his big, clumsy paws scooping at nonexistent water slowly. "You promised other things in front of your fire too."

"I did."

"When can I have *that*?"

"You're a greedy little girl, ain't you?" I teased, running my hand over her shoulder, lifting her hair and letting it fall behind her, hugging her closer.

I was right. I loved dancing so long as I got to hold her in my arms while I did it.

She swatted my ass. "I am not. But the last time I was here, we did things that... make me want that."

Oh, me too, girl. Me too.

"Yeah, but I also said we had some things to iron out between us first."

Pulling out of my arms, she spun away, and her hair whipped against my shirt in an arc. She padded on her bare feet over to one of the built-in bookshelves on the far side of the fireplace, next to my desk. Grum twitched but didn't wake up. Damn dog was worn out 'cause I'd bought one of those plastic tennis ball thrower toys. He probably ran ten miles back and forth in my yard before dinner. My shoulder would be a little worse for the wear tomorrow, too, aching and creaking for sure.

"This desk is beautiful," she said. "Is it old? It looks old."

"No. Max made it for me."

"Really? Wow. He's talented. It looks like it's from the early nineteen hundreds." She stepped to the right, inspecting the books she saw lined up on the shelves. "You don't own any fiction, do you?"

"Never really developed an affinity for it."

"How come?"

"Dunno. Fairy tales and daydreams just ain't my thing, I guess."

Laughing softly, she pressed up on her toes, touching her finger to the first book on the top shelf, tilting her head to read the title, and her hair slid over her shoulder. I never would've thought I'd have a favorite shade of pink, but I did now. Samantha's hair was a pale rose color, and somehow, even though I knew it wasn't, it looked natural.

She moved on from there, touching her slender finger to every book I owned. "You read a lot about war."

"Mm." I sat in my chair, taking a drink from my water glass, balancing it on top of my thigh while I watched her. When she bent to read the titles on the lower shelves, I averted my eyes from her ass. It wouldn't help me resist her if I stared at the thing I wanted more than my next breath.

"What are all these unopened letters on your desk? They look like Christmas cards."

Shit. I thought I'd put those away. I meant to.

"They are. Christmas cards, birthday cards, and the like."

She turned, smiling at me. "'And the like'?" God, her smile came from Heaven above. It must have. There was nothing in this world more beautiful. "I like the way you talk sometimes. Is that a Texas thing?"

With a quick lift of my shoulders, I said, "It's a country thing, I guess." I took another drink, trying to distract myself from the fire building up inside me while I watched her. Whiskey probably would've been a better choice, but I never drank it.

When the song was over, the playlist on my phone came to its end, and silence rang around the room as she continued examining the cards on my desk. "These are all from Texas. Are they from your family?"

"Mmhm."

"You don't want to read them?"

"They all say the same thing."

She turned her head but not her body, frowning at my answer. "They can't *all* say the same thing."

Sure they could. Happy Birthday, Merry Christmas, Happy "Gotcha" Day—the anniversary of the day a kid got adopted. The list went on, but the words written inside the cards were usually the same: *We love you, Frank. Maybe you can get a little time off work soon so you can come down to see us. We hope you're happy and that you're still enjoying your job. It sure is hot/cold/rainy this year. How's the weather up in Wisper? We miss you. Love, Mama K and Dad.*

Samantha stalked over to me, a curious look gleaming in her eyes. "You're not going to explain?"

"Nothin' much to say about it. Family sends a lotta cards."

She climbed into my lap, straddling me and taking the glass from my hand. It felt like we could've caught fire from the heat between us. Setting the water on my side table, she tsked when I reached over to move it onto a coaster and centered it in the middle. "Is that where you were back in October, when you were gone for two weeks?"

Lifting her phone from the table, she held it up in front of my face and snapped a picture. Good grief. Another picture? What in the world could she possibly need them all for?

The flash blinded me for a second while I thought, *She'd noticed I was gone? Hm. Interesting.* All that time I'd been going to the library, debating whether to ask her out or not— if she'd noticed me the way I'd noticed her, I could've asked her months ago.

"Nope."

She set her phone down, then fixed her eyes back on mine, peeking every few seconds at the open top buttons on my flannel and licking her lips like a hungry lioness. "Where'd you go?"

Resting my hand on the side of her neck, feeling her pulse on my palm, I pressed my thumb to the hollow dip below her throat, watching with fascination as the skin lost its color and flushed pink again when I lifted my thumb away. "The sheriff made me use some of my vacation days, so I drove around for a couple weeks, campin' and fishin'."

"Where?" Leaning her head to the side, baring her soft neck to my eyes, she waited for my answer.

"Nowhere. Just here and there." Damn. I was hard as a

rock, and I wanted to slam her body down against mine and bite that neck like a fucking vampire.

"You know you're doing it again?"

In the low voice she seemed to like, the one that made her eyes darken, I asked, "What's that, Samantha?"

But she gave up the hunt and sat back, her thighs balancing over mine. "One-word answers. I want to know about your family. Your time with the Army. Your… ex-wife." She winced, maybe nervous that I'd get mad at her for asking, but that was an easy topic.

"You heard about that?"

"Yes," she said with a guilty smile. "Actually, I remember hearing about it when it happened. From my grandparents. I didn't know who you were then, and I was just a kid." She blushed, and our age gap tugged at the connection between us, like an angry bee sting.

"Ain't much to it. Got married and then left soon after on my last tour with the Army. I was gone for about two years, and when I came home, I realized she wasn't who I thought she was. It wasn't a messy divorce. There was no fightin'. It was just over. Haven't spoken to her in over eleven years." I cleared my throat a little, realizing the subject made me uncomfortable. The same way I didn't like thinking about Samantha with some other man, I didn't want to bring my ex into the equation either. But I wanted to be honest with her. "It's the reason I stayed away from you this last year. Why it took me so long to really talk to you. I guess it… I dunno. Guess it kind of took a toll. Relationships, marriage, all that stuff seemed like a priority when I was younger, but now… Maybe I don't trust so easy."

She listened, taking everything I said in stride. "What's her name?"

"Angela."

"You didn't want kids with her?"

"I did. I've always wanted kids. She said she did in the beginnin', but"—I shook my head—"guess she changed her mind. She never really explained her change of heart. Just kinda walked away. It was a good thing though. We weren't right for each other."

Her eyes flicked down, and she tried to back off of me, but I wrapped my hands around her hips, pressing the tips of my fingers into her backside through her skirt. They twitched to explore lower, but she'd said it herself; I was stubborn. I wasn't giving in, no matter how much she tempted me.

I needed her to be sure. It'd be torture if we went all in and then a few months down the line she decided I really was too old for her. And I needed her to trust me enough to open up to me. What good was sex and love if we didn't have trust? She had to trust that I'd protect her heart, and I needed to trust that she'd guard mine.

I *wanted* to trust her, and for the most part, I did, but until she told me what she'd been holding back, I couldn't give in. Didn't matter how much I wanted to. I'd been alone a long time for a reason. As much as I felt like some crybaby to think about her "guarding my heart," it was the bare truth. It took me eleven years to get over my ex-wife stealing away with my dreams of a family in her hands. I had a feeling getting over Samantha Russo might be a lot harder, and it would take the rest of my life. What was left of it anyway.

"Your turn," I said.

"What do you want to know?"

"I wanna know why you got sad in the school parkin' lot. What'd that asshole do to you?"

Suddenly, my furniture became really interesting to her as she picked at the upholstery stitching on the arm of the chair.

"Samantha."

She sighed loudly. "He was just a bad boyfriend, and then we broke up, and I was left feeling… I don't know. Less than."

I was trying to see the truth in her eyes, but she was having a hard time looking at me. "He hit you?"

"No, nothing like that. He was just a jerk. When I—when I needed him, he made me feel like I wasn't worthy of his time." Under her breath, she mumbled, "Or basic human kindness."

"That son of a bitch." Disembowelment was too good for him.

She smiled at the curse, giving me eye contact again. "You're very protective of the people in your life, aren't you?"

"I could be." If I'd let anyone in. If she wanted to stay in my life, I'd protect her forever.

"I think I should go."

What? "Why?"

"This"—she motioned between us—"it's too much. You want something from me that I don't know how to give you."

"It's true," I said. "I want you, but I want more than just sex."

"I want you, too, but every time you breathe in my direction, my underwear gets wetter. They're soaked clean through right now. I can't think around you. But you're not going to do anything about it tonight, are you?" She blinked, then looked down, twisting the bottom of her sweater between her fingers. "I think, for you, sex is something you do after you let someone in. Maybe the difference is in our ages, but for me, physical intimacy is the thing I need *in order* to let you in. Does that make sense?"

My hold on her hips got tighter, my fingertips pressing harder into the soft give of her skin. If I gave into her now, before we really hashed things out, what did that say about me? No, I wasn't willing to relent, but it seemed she wasn't quite ready to bare her soul to me. But I also wasn't willing to leave her wanting. I'd found myself desperate for her to let me in, but there had to be a way to achieve that without risking the pain I'd surely feel if she bolted. I had to be honest with myself.

It would hurt.

"You want more?" I asked. "Right now?"

"Yes. I do. Is that wrong?"

"It ain't wrong. Kiss me." Relaxing back in the chair, I spread my legs wide, and she leaned over me tentatively. She remembered her glasses, though, and slipped them off quickly, setting them on the table by my glass. Refocusing on me, she smiled, and when she slid closer and her lips touched mine, that was when she felt my hard cock beneath my jeans. She gasped into my mouth, and I pressed up.

"Oh."

"Think I can make you come with your clothes on? No hands?" Resting my elbows on the arms of the chair, I held my hands up.

She looked from one to the other, then her eyebrows arched for the ceiling.

"Bet I can," I said, pumping up between her legs, reaching up to kiss her like I was a baby bird looking for a meal.

She fed me. She held my face in her hands, her thumbs rubbing circles over my chin as she kissed me. Her eyes were closed, and her quiet moans flowed into my mouth.

She'd worn a long skirt, but the fabric wasn't heavy, so I lifted my thigh, pushing the skirt higher. I did the same with my other leg till the skirt was pooled in my lap.

"You didn't say I couldn't use *my* hands," she whispered,

and she readjusted the fabric, rolling it up and pushing it back and to the side, exposing her panties. The silky pink cotton matched her hair.

I rolled my hips into her, pushing the bulge of my dick against her mound, working at it over and over till she was wet and her pussy lips spread apart for me beneath the panties. Her head fell back. Her mouth was open, and her heavy breaths were all I could hear.

Some dumb schmuck could've paid me millions of dollars not to smile in that moment, but I would've failed. I was a poor man for her. She responded to my body like a dream, just like I'd been picturing.

Leaning all the way back in the chair, I placed my hands flat on the arms so I wouldn't break my own rule. Her legs opened wider, and I knew I was hitting her right where she needed me to, especially 'cause my cock was as hard and huge as it had ever been. It was like a heat-seeking missile aimed right at her, bumping up into her clit in an explosive rhythm.

She was panting, the sound mixing together with my own quick breaths, still with her head back, her hair falling behind her like pink champagne and her knees rubbing against the cool brown leather of my chair.

I wanted my mouth on her breasts. I'd promised not to use my hands, but I couldn't get her top off with my teeth unless I stopped dry humping her, and I wasn't planning on doing that until she came. But it was no matter, 'cause she seemed to know what I wanted. Raising her hands, she lifted her oversized yellow sweater by the neck and pulled it over her head.

She wasn't wearing a bra, and the sight in front of my eyes was almost too much. I'd gotten a glimpse before, but now, those perky handfuls were right at my eye level, just begging to get sucked.

She bumped one against my lips as she rolled her hips, and I slid my tongue between my teeth, aching to pinch her swollen nipple between them, but she must've known that, too, 'cause she looked in my eyes and leaned forward, placing them within my mouth's reach again.

When I latched on with my lips and tongue, she groaned, grinding down on my dick harder, rolling her hips faster. She threaded her fingers through mine on the arms of the chair while I sucked a nipple into my mouth, flicking it fast with my tongue and then catching it between my teeth. I bit down gently, and her whole body jerked in response. She squeezed my fingers, but she moaned loudly, so I felt pretty confident she liked it.

All the while, we were rubbing our bodies together below, grinding our sexes together as hard as we could through our clothes, and I was starting to feel the damp heat from her pussy through my jeans. The inside of my boxers wasn't that dry either.

Letting go with one hand, she breathed, "You feel good," and she pushed my flannel up, her eyes locking onto my bare chest beneath it.

I wouldn't be too proud to say that I felt like a little bit of a peacock. She liked my body. She moaned again, and her hips moved faster over mine when she saw it. I was glad I took care of it. Maybe she was the reason why—so I could take care of her, please her, and turn her on—and I'd just never known.

She ground down harder, and I was trying not to lose my mind. The need to throw her on the couch and fuck her mouth was becoming harder to ignore the faster she panted, breathing out in quiet, sexy "ah" sounds.

"Talk to me," she whispered. "I want to hear your voice."

"Samantha," was all I said, and she planted her hands on my pecs, making a loud slapping sound and digging her fingernails in.

"More," she begged, looking in my eyes, using both hands on my chest now as leverage to ride me harder.

"Don't you boss me."

Groaning, her head dropped forward, and her hair fell down around her face like a curtain, trapping us together inside as she leaned her forehead against mine.

I wanted to smack her ass. Would she like it? "I think you like when *I* boss *you*."

Her eyes darkened, her lips lifted, and her eyebrow popped, betraying her and exposing her wild side to me. My cock *throbbed*, and my heart leapt into overdrive. My whole fucking body was on fire, begging me to let it release. I couldn't even imagine how good it would feel to fuck her.

Well, I *could* imagine, and now, holding back everything I wanted to give her, I was dying inside, and my voice was as tight as a drum. "That's my good girl."

My praise elicited a whimper, and I could tell she was close. She was working hard for it now. Her teeth began to chatter the tiniest bit as she writhed against me, using my body to find her release, so I leaned up to warm her lips with my tongue as I rolled my hips again and again.

"I need to taste you." It was a command, and she gasped, but then, slow as molasses, she dipped her fingers beneath those pale pink panties, rubbing herself in her juice, her eyes locking onto mine.

I waited. Thrusted. I was just trying to breathe and not pass out from the anticipation of the flavor of her desire bursting on my tongue.

She rubbed harder, distracting herself for a few seconds,

eyes closing in rapture, and my breath hitched at the sight of her playing in her own cum. My dick hurt, it was so hard, and my heartbeat was trying to strangle me as it crawled up my throat.

She opened her eyes, dragging those thin fingers out and up, and I watched as they rose to my mouth, centimeter by centimeter.

I opened it, and she pushed past my lips, fucking my zipper as hard as she could now, her drenched, swollen pussy moving over me in fast little waves. Drawing those fingers deep into my mouth with my tongue, I sucked them clean.

"Kiss me," I said again, except this time it was a growl, and as soon as I licked into her mouth, her body locked in place, and she filled my lungs with her raspy cry, then collapsed down onto my chest. The ends of her hair tickled my stomach, and her soft tits warmed my pecs, her nipples hard and pointing into my skin. I gripped the arms of the chair so hard, I was afraid I'd rip through the leather.

She looked up, seeing the strain on my face and the stress in my jaw as I grit my teeth, still trying to hold back. Why? I'd never been so turned on in my life.

"Come, baby," she whispered, centering her soaked underwear over my dick. She rolled hard against me one more time, rubbing me in exactly the right spot as she begged and shivered, dragging her wet pussy up and down my dick. "Please," she begged again, and I let go, imagining pounding into her naked body.

Her voice was all I needed, and it surprised me that I hadn't fucked a hole right through my jeans.

CHAPTER TWENTY

"THANKS FOR COMING, Vern. I've tried everything, but I can't get this window to shut."

Leading him up the stairs to the library's second floor, I gestured to the room straight ahead of us at the top.

The windows in the old brick two-story house were original, and they took a lot of muscle and a good push to get them open in the summer or closed in the winter, but this window just wouldn't budge no matter how hard I tried.

I'd slept in Frank's arms again last night, fully clothed but well sated. We'd made out for hours like a couple of randy teenagers. He came like a teenager when I slipped my hand inside his jeans and gripped his cock before he even knew what I was up to. The look of lust on his face when I'd licked my hand and then pumped harder and the way his every muscle had hardened told me he liked it, but he still wouldn't budge from his "no sex till you tell me everything" rule. But I was starting to understand that maybe he was just as scared as I was. For different reasons, but maybe that meant he'd understand if I told him why I'd been holding back.

That wasn't the hard part though. The hard part was *what*

I wasn't telling him. When he found out I couldn't ever get pregnant, it would change how he saw me. It had changed how Tyler saw me. *"This is really messing up my plans for the future, Sam."*

It changed how I saw myself.

But we talked about other things. I told him about Ireland, one of my favorite places I'd traveled with my parents, and he told me about basic training and his first tour with the Army. He was just a kid back then. I couldn't imagine going off to some war zone at eighteen, but it was who Frank was. He had a need inside him to protect people, to make them feel safe. He made me feel that way.

"No problem," Vern said, and the memories from last night evaporated, dissolving before my eyes like a scene in a movie.

"All the heat's leaking out," I said, "and it's making the furnace run for its life. When I got here a few minutes ago, it was almost as cold inside as it is outside. I really appreciate you getting here so quickly."

"I'll take a look. Probably just stuck." Vern wasn't wearing his black cowboy hat this time, but he removed his winter beanie and tucked it in his coat pocket. "It was nice to see you and Deputy Sims at the restaurant. The food was good, huh?"

"Really good. Did you and Millie have a nice time?"

"Uh, well, I did. Not sure 'bout Millie. She didn't eat much."

"Oh, um—"

"It's alright, ma'am. I know I ain't the most eligible bachelor in Wisper, but she said yes when I asked. Guess I'm still hopin' I can wear her down and maybe she'll go out with me again."

My heart was breaking for him. "I bet she will, Vern. I

think you're a great guy. It's this window here." Vern blushed, and I pointed to the stuck glass pane, thinking I was kind of glad I hadn't known him before his transformation. People had told me he used to be a menace, but since I'd met him, he was the nicest guy, always making himself available to help someone in need. I didn't know what they had going on between them, but I thought Millie could do worse.

He approached the window, inspecting the frame and the lock. With more strength in one arm than I had in both of mine, he lifted it all the way open, then leaned forward and stuck his head through. "Uh, I think I see your problem."

"Really? That fast?"

"Yep. Somebody stuck a pocketknife right here." He yanked, and his hand appeared through the window, holding a small flip knife with a tortoiseshell laminate decoration on the side. "Looks like it was jammed in the frame so the window couldn't close. There's also a piece of tape coverin' the lock."

"Tape?"

"Yeah," he said, ducking back through. "Like duct tape?" He scraped his fingernail under the lock and then pulled off a gray piece of tape. "Here."

I frowned, confused, taking the knife and tape from his fingers. "Why would anybody do that?"

"Maybe it's been here a while."

"But the window was closed and locked last week when I washed it."

He shrugged. "Maybe just some kids messin' 'round?"

"Hm. Maybe." But I was pretty good at keeping track of the teenagers who came into the library, on the extremely rare occasions they did. I didn't want anyone taking a quick drag of a cigarette or a joint in the library and then burning the place down. All those poor books!

"If that's all you need, ma'am, I'll be headin' back to the

center. We got a big delivery comin' in. Everybody's gearin' up for the big storm headed our way."

"Another storm?"

"Yeah," he said. "Thursday, I think. Heard it's gonna be a record breaker."

"Jeez. Well, there goes my dream of having a Georgian tea party here. I was planning to pull out all my Jane Austens for book club."

"Huh?"

"Never mind. Thanks, Vern. I could've done this myself, but it never occurred to me to check the lock or look for a"—I held the small knife in the air with my thumb and index finger, wondering who the hell stuck it in my window—"knife."

"Sure thing."

"I'll walk you out."

I escorted Vern out to his blue Ace's House's pickup truck parked on the side of the street in front of the library, thanking him again. When he drove away, I hurried back inside. Hugging myself, I shivered off the cold outside air and wiped my boots on the rug by the front door, and then my eyes immediately flicked to the stern, silent sheriff's deputy waiting by the check-in desk. He was so quiet, Vern and I hadn't even noticed him on our way out.

"Hi," I said. God, if Frank wasn't the most handsome man I'd ever seen, I was a liar. He'd ruined all other men for me. No one could compare to him, to his tall, strong body, or to the smile he offered only to me. Once we'd gotten over the nervous get-to-know-yous, Frank wasn't shy or stingy with his catching smile.

He was waiting for me, hat in hand. He had this adorable habit of dragging his fingers through his hair when he wasn't wearing his hat, like he was self-conscious of his hat hair, and it pushed the thick locks up off his forehead. Gray hair was taking over the rest of the younger dark brown color, and I found myself chasing the waves with my eyes, trying to follow the silver streaks.

"That your new boyfriend?" he asked, totally deadpan.

"Yes," I teased. "We're going to the honky-tonk for Sunday supper."

"Hm."

"Oh my God, Frank. Speak!"

His lips curved up, but only at the edges of his mouth. "I was hopin' you'd come back to my place again tonight. I wanted to feed you, but if you wanna go with Vern, that's fine. Have fun then." He flipped his hat onto his head and nodded, then walked past me like he was really going to leave.

I grabbed his arm and yanked. His hat fell to the floor, and he spun back around, reaching for me.

"Oh no you don't," I said breathlessly. I jumped up, wrapping my legs around his waist as he lifted me with his hands firmly planted under my ass. It was like climbing a tree, he was so tall. His fingers dipped between my thighs from the back, jamming my skirt up there, his thumbs rubbing circles over my ass cheeks.

He smiled fully, and I melted right there in the middle of the library as I began to tingle in places a librarian should never be tingling, at least not while they were *in* a library.

If I'd had to, I would've guessed Frank was a breast man, if the way his eyes were always drawn to my chest was any indication, but when he touched my ass, my body lit up in ways I would normally have been embarrassed about. If we ever had actual sex, I was certain there were things he could do to me there that would positively scandalize me.

I shivered again, and he kissed me, murmuring against my lips, "Miss me?"

"I did, actually."

Truly, I'd been aching for him. I couldn't stop thinking about what he'd said the other night before he'd taken me to ecstasy and back without laying a finger on my body.

There was a tug-of-war going on inside my head every minute of every day, with the scared, sensible part of me on one end and the dreaming little girl on the other, both yanking the rope, one trying to convince me to set free all my insecurities and fears, and the other trying to convince me to hold them tighter.

But both of them were afraid to tell Frank the truth. Both were becoming terrified my shortcomings would send him running.

As I had done a million times already, I pushed the thought out of my head as he squeezed lightly, his fingers one measly inch away from where I already knew they could offend my better sensibilities, and the hum inside my body began to burn.

"What was Vern doin' here?" he asked. "You gettin' a little somethin' somethin' upstairs?"

"Ugh." I swatted his burly bicep. "You're terrible. No, one of the upstairs windows was stuck open. Vern helped me get it unstuck."

He frowned, a frustrated look taking over his face. "Now, why didn't you call me? I woulda fixed that for you."

"Oh, well, I—"

"I rebuilt my house pretty much from the ground up. I think I could manage a window."

"I didn't know that, and besides, you have kind of an important job. I didn't want to bother you."

"I told you Max and I renovated my house."

"No, what you said was that he helped you with 'some renovations.' I thought you meant new kitchen cupboards or something. I didn't know you rebuilt the entire house. And now I'm extremely impressed."

Setting me on the desk, he worked his body between my legs. He was always doing that, like he couldn't stand to be too far away from me, and it was... sexy. There was that word again. He pushed my skirt over my knees and ran his warm hands up and down my calves. "Well, did he fix it?"

The heat radiating off his body warmed mine, and I sighed. I was doing that a lot when he was around too. "Yes. It wasn't broken. Someone stuck a knife in the window frame on the outside. Look." I pulled the offending tool from my handy skirt pocket and held it up for him to see. "And there was duct tape on the lock. Probably just kids being dumb, but it's been so cold in here. One of my book club ladies asked if we could get a space heater for the reading room."

Frank's face changed. He looked very much the serious sheriff's deputy all of a sudden. "Show me."

When I led him upstairs, he inspected the room and then the whole freaking library with his sharp eagle eyes, and when we didn't find anything suspicious, he followed me back to the front desk and plonked his big hands on his hips. "I'm an asshole for not even considerin' this, but how've you been gettin' to work?"

"I usually catch a ride with Brady. He picks me up if he's working at the center, but if he's working in Jackson or out at the reservation, I walk. Gramps's place is only half a mile from here. Why?"

"Two things," Frank said. "One, you're learnin' to drive. Period. This ain't a big city. You can't hop a bus or a train, and with the weather this winter, you need a vehicle. I drive my cruiser usually, but I got an old pickup out behind my house. You can learn in that. And two, let Brady know I'll be drivin' you till you can drive yourself. I'll work my schedule around it, but if there's a day I can't, I'll call him myself."

"Excuse me?"

"You heard me right."

"No," I said and scoffed. "I don't think I did, because what I heard were a bunch of demands from someone that sounded eerily like my father, which you *definitely* are not. You don't get to make decisions for me like that. I didn't ask you to do that."

He nodded once, then fixed this look on his face like he was about to put me in my place—which he did when he opened his mouth. "Someone's been breakin' in here at night."

"I… Wha—?" I sputtered into speechlessness. "How do you know that? I mean, just from one open window?"

"From one open window with a knife jammed into it," he replied. "And from this big ol' wad of tape I found stuck to the lock on the back door."

"What?"

He shoved a bigger crumpled piece of duct tape than Vern had shown me into my hand and dared me with the look in his eyes to argue.

"Okay," I argued anyway. "But that doesn't mean anything. It could still be from kids screwing around." I held the tape up in the air. "This doesn't mean there's any danger."

"Oh no?" he said coolly. "Let's play a little game, Samantha. A treasure hunt. I want you to go through the library and point out three things to me that don't belong."

"Frank, you don't have to be a jerk about it."

"I'm not tryin' to be a jerk. I'm dead serious."

I huffed a breath, rolling my eyes. "I looked when you did."

"And you didn't see anything outta place?"

"No," I said, shaking my head.

He lifted his hands in front of his chest. "Just do me this favor and look again. Please?"

"Fine."

He followed me through the first floor. I looked down every aisle, in the bathroom, in the resource center, and in the—

"That wasn't there a few minutes ago."

"It was, but you missed it. Now that you're lookin' with the knowledge that someone was here who shouldn't have been, you're seein' it."

Walking to the window facing the back alley in the reading room, I bent to pick the pine-green winter cap off the floor. It was still damp, and the color matched the library's ancient carpeting, which was probably why I'd missed it. "Okay, but this doesn't prove anything. Somebody dropped their hat yesterday. Big deal." Except if someone had lost their hat yesterday, wouldn't it be dry by now?

Frank nodded, one small lift and drop of his head. "Keep goin'," he said.

"Frank, this is—"

There was something in his eyes that made me uneasy. "Humor me, please?"

I sighed. "Okay."

When we got to the rear hallway, I looked all over, but I still wasn't seeing anything nefarious. But then he pulled a small, hand-sized flashlight from his coat pocket and shined it on the floor in front of the back door. There were dried shoe tracks there, and they certainly didn't look like they'd come from my boots. They were way too big.

No one used the back door but me, or sometimes delivery

drivers, but I hadn't had any deliveries in more than three weeks, and I'd mopped the floors the last time I was here.

Frank was right. As he led me from room to room this time, I noticed a bunch of things that didn't fit. Trash filled the bins in the book club room and in the small bedroom-turned-conference room upstairs—food wrappers and bandages with small drops of blood and dirt on them, and even an empty can of French-cut green beans, but I knew for a fact that I'd emptied them the night before, and no one had been upstairs since, other than Vern and me. Besides, who the heck would bring a can of green beans to the library? Why?

"I think I may have an idea who your burglar is," Frank said.

"You do?" I asked, turning to him behind me. But he didn't look angry or macho protective. He looked… worried. "Who is it?"

He pulled a chair out at the conference table and sat, placing his hat in front of him. I sat, too, and scooted my chair closer. Something was making me want to hold him, so I reached for his hand and held it.

"There's a kid…"

CHAPTER TWENTY-ONE

FRANK

"HE'S HOMELESS?" she squeaked when I explained my suspicion that the teenager I suspected of breaking into the library was also the book thief.

I hadn't even met the damn kid yet, but my gut was screaming at me that it was the same person.

"I dunno for sure, but I'm guessin' he is. I tried to look him up, but all I have is a nickname. I didn't find anything. There's no missin' or unaccounted-for kids in Wyoming or any other state fittin' his description or with that name."

"What's the name?"

"Murphy."

"And what were the titles of the stolen books?"

"Don't remember, but he turned his nose up at *The Great Gatsby*. I wrote the books down. Here." Pulling my notebook from my jacket pocket, I slid it across the table toward her. "Flip through to my last page of notes."

She did what I asked, then surprised me with, "Frank, your penmanship is beautiful. I wasn't expecting that."

I laughed. "Thank you?" What was I supposed to do with that compliment?

"Okay," she said, reading the list, and her eyebrows dipped a little, "so the stolen books are *The Catcher in the Rye*, *Journey to the Center of the Earth*, *Of Mice and Men*, and *Oliver Twist*."

"What?"

"It's nothing really. I was just wondering if the books all had something in common. And I mean, they kind of do. For example, they're all classics, and I suppose they all have a sense of... I don't know. Adventure? Maybe that's not the right word. The main characters in these books are all searching for something."

"Hm."

She laughed at my response and leaned her head to the side, gazing over at me, a relaxed smile on her lips. "I love the sound of your voice, even when you grumble and growl. Which is kind of a lot."

Now, that was a compliment I could get behind. I already suspected she liked my voice, and it was something I could use against her. If she liked it, I'd remember that, and when the time was right, I'd aim it right at her.

I tried it out, low and slow. "Thank you, darlin'."

Her cheeks turned the blushed peach color I loved, and despite the potentially serious situation, something stirred beneath my zipper again.

"But how do you know the person who stole the books is the same person you think is breaking in here?"

"C'mon. Missin' books, missin' food, and now someone's hidin' out in here? How many delinquent teenagers you think we got in Wisper?"

"Okay, well, do you think something happened to his mom?"

"I hope not, but I'm thinkin' it probably did. If Burroughs is right and it was his mom who came with him to

Ace's House the first time he showed up there, where is she now?"

"What could've happened to her?"

"Maybe she abandoned him." Maybe she was dead.

Samantha gasped. "Frank. Why would you say that?"

Why? 'Cause I knew all too well it was a possibility. "It happens," was all I said.

"I really hope you're wrong, but I'll stay here tonight in case he comes back."

"You will not."

The obstinance in her eyes and the way she cocked her head was adorable. "Uh, yeah, I will."

"Not alone, you won't. Besides, if he knows someone's here, he won't show."

She deflated a little when she realized I was right, her shoulders slumping and her lips twisting to one side. "Okay, so what do we do?"

I smiled, imagining another night in my truck with her. "You up for a stakeout?"

"Success!" she declared when she came rushing out of the Food Mart and hopped in my truck.

We'd closed up the library but left the upstairs windows unlocked. It wouldn't be hard for someone to get to the second floor from the outside if they climbed the wooden trellis, where honeysuckle vines grew in the summer on the east side of the building. It led right to the conference room window.

She dug through a grocery tote filled with cholesterol-inducing goodies. "I got all the good stuff—Twizzlers, Reese's Pieces, and I grabbed these all-natural fruit roll-up things to balance out our stakeout diet. Oh, and I picked up a six-pack of soda."

"What'd you do, stick up the Food Mart?"

"Huh?"

"You came runnin' out here pretty quick." I laughed. "Like an outlaw."

She rolled her eyes. "No, Frank, I paid for our snacks."

"Did you get Nerds?"

"Nerds?"

"You've never had Nerds? It's candy."

"Of course I've had them, but *you* like Nerds?" She shook her head, laughing and reaching for the door handle. "I can run back in and get some for you."

I stopped her with my hand on her arm. "Thank you, but I was kiddin'. I don't eat that junk anymore. And by soda, do you mean pop?"

"Yeah," she said. "Soda, pop. Same thing. Then what do you eat when you go on a long drive or have to do one of these stakeouts?"

"Usually just bring water and fruit. Carrots. Couple sand-wiches. Homemade venison jerky." She made a disgusted face at the mention of venison jerky as she opened her package of licorice. "Besides, if we drink all that pop, we'll have to leave our post for latrine breaks."

"Oh, well, I wasn't thinking about that." She looked up. "Why are you so careful about what you eat?"

I shrugged and motioned to her candy and cans of carbon-ated liquid sugar. "Makes sense to me to give my body what it needs. Can't you tell the difference when you eat something healthy compared to when you eat all that?"

"I don't know. I guess not."

Before I could stop myself, I said, "You're still young."

She caught her bottom lip with her teeth and stared at me for fifteen seconds, but she didn't respond to my comment.

I changed the subject. "There's a ranch on the edge of town called Milson's—"

"I know it. One of my book club ladies said her husband works there."

"Who's that?"

"Carly Eaton."

"Yeah," I said, "that's Buckey Mann's girl. He's the friend who's gonna help me with the youth football thing."

"Doesn't Max work there too?"

"Yep. They called Carey out there recently, and I followed up. They had some supplies go missin'. I think our burglar might've made a stop out there, lookin' for somethin' to eat, but there's also a bottle of antibiotics they can't seem to find. We found those bandages in the trash at the library, so I'm thinkin' this kid is hurt somehow. I don't think it's bad though. Or at least, I hope it ain't."

She sighed, frowning, and looked out the window as I slipped the truck into gear and headed for the street behind the library, the one that intersected with the back alley. There was a nice nook for us to park in by an old, unused one-horse stable at the back of the Zimmerman's property. I'd already called them to get their permission to park out there overnight. I'd had to do some quick thinking to come up with an explanation about why I needed to do it. If they knew someone had been breaking into the library, that shit would've spread through Wisper like diesel fire. I told them there was a menacing racoon on the rampage, and I didn't want to wait for Game and Fish to deal with it. It wasn't the best excuse I could've come up with, but it worked in a pinch.

"I can't imagine being on my own like that at his age. He must be so scared."

"He is."

She looked at me. "Do you know something about this?"

I didn't want to lie outright, but I also didn't want to bring my traumatic past into the equation. That was a conversation for another time, although it did occur to me that I kept finding reasons to delay the inevitable. "Just my experience on the job."

"Oh, well, what do you see happening? I mean, if we catch him breaking in, what will we do?"

"I'll have to bring him in."

"What? Frank! You can't arrest him. He's just a kid."

"We think, but he's also a thief. He didn't just steal books, Samantha. He stole money and medication. I have to at least pick him up to find out why, and the safest way to do that is to take him down to the station."

She was glaring at me now. "We could just ask him."

"That ain't the law."

"Frank, sometimes laws need to be broken."

"Not by me."

She was pissed now, and she sat back into the passenger seat as I parked between two big fir trees and killed my headlights. We had a perfect view of the library's back door and east-facing windows. "You live your life by the book, don't you?"

I laughed in my head when it occurred to me what she was accusing me of, this beautiful lover of books. "I do."

"Why? I mean, don't you ever break a rule?"

"No." Breaking rules was what landed me in a situation much like the one Murphy was in, though it wasn't me who'd broken them.

She sighed again, but this time, frustration clogged her voice. "You're doing it again."

"What?"

"Nothing. Never mind." Crossing her arms over her chest, she snuggled into her coat. "Well, before you came back to pick me up, I put food on the table in the conference room, and I left a hat, scarf, and gloves on the check-in desk."

"What? Why would you do that? I told you we don't wanna do anything to spook him, and I distinctly remember tellin' you to act normal."

"I know that, Frank, but I also know that it's wet and cold outside. Besides, I left them in a pile, made it look like I'd just forgotten the hat and scarf. And the food is all snacky stuff. It looks like I was eating my lunch but left the rest on the table."

"And is that normal for you? Are you usually that forgetful?"

"Well, no."

"So what makes you think the kid won't know that? He's probably been watchin' you. He's been watchin' the library at the very least. Since you haven't seen anything suspicious, he obviously knows what time you leave at night and what time you get there in the mornin'. And if he's been comin' in at night, he would've noticed if you'd left food out. As hungry as he probably is, he would've eaten it."

"I didn't think about that." She peeked at me. "I'm sorry. Are you angry with me? Did I ruin the stakeout?"

Reaching for her hand, I held it. "No, we just have to be more careful."

"I still think we should've stayed the night in the library. I mean, then even if he got spooked, we could've caught him."

"But if he's payin' attention like I think he is, he'd notice if we didn't leave when the library closed."

She laughed under her breath. "I think it's good that you're the detective in this scenario and I'm not."

We sat there for a while, not talking, and I held her hand the whole time. It was nice, and I kept trying to picture a life with her, but there was a bit of a divide between us now. It was small in the truck, but somehow, inside my chest, it felt as big as a mountain.

It sounded so simple. She didn't mind breaking rules. I did. It wasn't like we were talking about murder or tax fraud, but it still had me gripping the steering wheel tighter.

I had my own rules, and to be with her, I'd need to break them. I'd have to give myself to her, open up, put my pain out there for her to see and know. I'd have to be vulnerable and risk her running away with my heart in her hand. Even if we both opened up about our pasts, I would still be risking everything.

But opening up seemed like the way to bridge our gap. Or maybe part of the way. If I explained why I lived my life so rigidly, she'd have more of a reason to understand.

She'd told me a little about her past, but did she really think I was buying that what she'd said was the whole truth? She was still keeping something from me too. It was easy to see in the way her eyes would wander when I asked her about that time in her life. All I knew was that she'd dated some jerk in graduate school in Florida, but she hadn't made a peep about *why* he was a jerk or what it was she'd gone through because of him.

Maybe if I broke my precious rules and told her about what happened when my mama died, she'd finally tell me about whatever it was still hurting her.

Technically, we'd known each other for more than a year, but we didn't really *know* each other until recently. I hadn't forgotten that. I wasn't expecting her to give me everything she had in the span of a few weeks.

Or was I?

Maybe I was. Maybe I was 'cause she was everything I'd ever wanted, and I was afraid to lose her already.

And who was I to talk? I'd never told anyone about what I'd gone through, not even my ex-wife, which should've been my first clue we weren't right for each other, especially 'cause she'd never asked, even though she'd known I'd been adopted.

The whole thing was pissing me off. What was the big fucking deal? So Samantha would know about my sad past. What difference would it make?

But as I watched her, eating her red licorice ropes in my truck, it became this big, festering thing in my mind. I'd worked it up into something I couldn't see around. And I knew, if I told her, she'd feel sorry for me, and that was something I just could not abide.

And maybe her pity would be the thing that would make the whole bridge fall. We'd be two lonely mountains with no path through the valley between them.

Several hours had gone by with both of us staring at the library's back door through my truck window in silence. Nothing happened. The kid never showed. Samantha nodded off, snuggled against my side, snoring lightly. Eventually, she moved down, resting her head on my leg while I pulled my fingers through her hair, feeling the silky strands fall out of my grasp.

Maybe Murphy had gone in the front, but no lights ever came on. There was no movement from inside, and finally, at three-thirty in the morning, I flipped my headlights on to drive her home. The stakeout was a bust.

"What?" She woke slowly and sat up, looking around like

that doe in the forest as I drove down the alley, back out to Franklin Street. The apple of her cheek blushed red where it had been pushed against my thigh. "Where are you going?"

"Takin' you home," I said as the wind outside the truck kicked up. Trees were swaying, and the snow on the ground was starting to swirl in circles on the road.

She wiped the sleep from her eyes with her fingers. "But we didn't find Murphy." When I didn't respond, she asked, "Frank?"

"You expect to find him with your eyes closed?"

"I'm sorry. I didn't mean to fall asleep, but let's go back. I'm awake now."

"If he was comin', he woulda already. It's late. I'll try again tomorrow."

When I dropped her off at her grandfather's house, she smiled tentatively at me. "Can I see you tomorrow?"

Listening to trees creaking and the howl of the wind building up high in the mountains, I said, "Yeah. I told you I'll drive you to work."

"Oh, right, but I meant after work. Dinner?"

"We'll see," I said. I was planning another stakeout, but maybe it would be better if I did it on my own.

"Frank? What's going on? I feel like something changed between us tonight."

"Just tired," I said, and I lifted her hand to my lips, brushing them over her knuckles. "Get some rest. I'll be here at 8:45."

When she leaned across the seat to kiss me, I kissed her back, watching the way her eyes fell closed, trying again to see through this thing between us. Trying to navigate our divide. Whatever she was holding to her chest about her past was blocking my view, and the things I was keeping in were creeping up everywhere, making mountains out of molehills.

"Night, Samantha."

"Okay. Good night. See you in the morning."

"How's it goin' with your girl?" the other Little Miss Nosy in my life asked when I got to the station to write down some thoughts I'd had about where to look for Murphy. I didn't want to forget. "I'm gettin' all kindsa reports about you."

"What're you doin' here, Shelley? You don't usually work the night shift."

"No, but I could use the extra cash, and my mom don't mind. Since Liam and I moved in with her, it's kinda like a vacation when I can get outta the house for a while." She nodded toward the TV in the corner with a paused image of a young man and woman lip-locked in some kind of embrace. What was it with the women around here? Sappy love bullshit everywhere. "I get to watch my shows uninterrupted all night, and I could even read a book if I wanted to."

I flashed her a doubtful look, and she laughed.

"Okay, fine, so I don't read, but the point is that I *could*." She cocked her head a little. "So? You gonna tell me, or do I gotta coax the info outta Carey and Abey?"

I didn't answer as I looked over the nightshift call list. There wasn't anything on it that could be related to the kid.

"Really? You're not gonna tell me about the librarian?"

"Shelley," I warned.

She laughed. "*Frank.* Hey, you're not supposed to be on duty. Why you out and about this late anyway?"

"Just lookin' into somethin'. I'm headin' home now."

"Alright. Have a good sleep."

"Yeah, I will, but call me if you get any odd reports tonight."

"Carey's on duty—"

"I know, but call me anyway."

"Okay," she said, lifting the TV remote to restart her show. "Will do."

The next few days were a goddamn bust.

I searched and searched for the kid and found nothing. He was nowhere. There were no more break-ins, nothing suspicious at all.

Murphy and Samantha had all kinds of memories bashing around in my head. I didn't usually think about my time on the streets, but I was now. Couldn't get it out of my mind. Every alley I searched looking for Murphy was an alley in Dallas, or any of the handful of smaller towns I passed through as I made my way east on my own, a thirteen-year-old kid with no money, no parent, no food, and nowhere to stay at night.

When my father passed away, my mama never recovered, and I was still paying for it, even though she'd been gone from my life for years.

I had been so pissed at her for dragging me around the night before she died, 'cause I had a math test the next day and was afraid I'd fail since it had been hard to do my practice problems with the loud music thumping and vagrants wandering in and out while she gave into her demons in the back room with her dealer.

The ruckus started up again at seven the next morning, and that stupid song, "Everybody Have Fun Tonight" became the soundtrack to my misery. I'd never forget the greasy sound of the devil's voice when I woke in his living room as he stumbled on his way out the door to buy cigarettes at the Circle K. He said, "Your ma's dead. Run along now."

There had been no one for me to call, no one to come for me, to take me home with them and tell me everything would be okay. No one to care if I passed my test or not—no one to care that I never showed up to take it. Our hovel of an apartment was a respite for a few days, but then people came knocking, wanting rent or money for electricity, and the little food I had ran out, so I left.

Being arrested for stealing a year later was the best thing that could've happened to me. It was what led me to the home for boys where my adoptive parents later found me. It wasn't their fault that I was already closed off, that I could never let them in.

The military became my family, and later, when I moved to Wisper and my ex-wife left, I became a part of the community here. I wanted to be more to the community, and I had planned on it with the football thing, but maybe I'd been holding back there too. It was time. I needed this community just as much as it needed me. Wisper used to be a fresh start where no one knew me. No one knew the sad, neglected kid I had been, but now, it was my home. It had come time for me to treat it that way.

A twinge of regret tugged at my stomach, though, when I thought of my adoptive parents still down in Texas, still begging me to be in their lives.

Those cards Samantha had found on my desk were only reminders. I'd always felt like my adoptive family wasn't missing anything without me around. I made the required trips home every once in a while for a quick Christmas visit or every now and then for Mama K and Eugene's anniversary, but mostly I stayed away. I'd always figured they preferred me to stay away, the kid who'd rejected their love.

But now I'd started to think maybe there was more to all that than I let myself believe. Maybe they really did want me in their lives. And maybe I wanted them in mine. Maybe I had something to offer my family. Wasn't I the guy always thinking about wanting one? Well, I already had a family. I just had to show up more.

Sitting in my truck outside the station, I called Mama K.

"Hi, Frankie. How's your day?"

I didn't think before I said it. "I wish you'd stop callin' me that. I ain't a kid."

"I'm sorry," she said. "I know you're not a kid. It's just… when I think about you, I see a fourteen-year-old version of you. Quiet, skinny little thing. Stubborn and rigid."

I hung my head. "I'm sorry. I didn't mean to snap at you… I wanted to ask you something. I'm hopin' you'll be honest with me."

"'Course I will. Don't you ever doubt it."

"Did you… Do y'all regret adoptin' me?"

"What? No! How could you think that?"

"It's just, I've pushed you away. I've been so closed off since my—since you found me, and I… Didn't that piss you off?"

"Oh, my boy. No. It made me sad. It frustrated me 'cause I didn't know how to reach you. Then you joined the Army, and it was the first thing in your life to put a light back in your eyes, so we went along with it. But I missed you somethin' awful. I still do. I hoped you'd come around after you had a little distance from all the sadness in your young life. I still hope for that." She paused. "But Frank, if we ain't what you need, that's okay. As long as you're happy, that's all we want for you."

If that wasn't a kick to the ass, I didn't know what was. They loved and wanted me, even though I'd been nothing but a point of pain in their lives. I rejected them and acted like I didn't want them, but still, they loved me, and I didn't even share their DNA.

Finally, on Thursday morning before my shift, Shelley called me early to tell me about a possible break-in at the gas station, so I headed there before I picked Samantha up. When I pulled up in front of the Stop and Go, the manager, Ted, met me outside, bundled up like a snowman, holding a shovel.

"'Bout time," he said, leaning on the handle as I parked and got out of my truck.

Okay, yeah, I wanted to be more accessible to my community, but I wasn't starting with Ted. He had an uncanny ability to cause a headache any time I talked to him. "Show me the broken window."

He turned, waving me inside with his hand, setting the shovel against the building. "You wanna tell Shelley to stick to her job? I don't need her guesses about what *might've* happened. I called to report a damn crime, but she kept on and on about how it was probably just a tree branch bangin' around in the wind we had last night."

"The window, Ted?"

"Deputy of the year right here. *So* friendly." He rolled his eyes. "C'mon."

Did he want to build a snow fort together, or did he want me to investigate the crime he was yammering on about?

When we were standing in the storage room in the back, I looked around, seeing a whole lot of nothing. "G'on then. Tell me what happened."

"Nothin' happened. It was like this when I opened up this mornin'." He pointed to the door leading out to the back alley. The small square window set into it was cracked but not breached.

"Uh, Ted, that's a cracked window, not a broken window. And this back room doesn't look disturbed."

"No, but there's blood outside in the snow by the back door."

Well, why the fuck hadn't he shown me that first?

He led me out the front of the store and around the side of the building to the back. And sure enough, there were a few drops of blood in the snow to the right of the back door. He should've shoveled the shit days ago.

I called Carey on my radio. "We need dogs."

"What?"

"I've got blood behind the Stop and Go. I need a K9."

"Hold on, Frank. We don't know who it came from. Is there damage to the store?"

"Cracked window."

"That's it? Nothin' was stolen?"

"No, but maybe I missed somethin'."

"I doubt that. I can't put a call in for dogs for that, and you know it."

"Carey, it could be the kid's blood."

"It could," he said, "but we need more to go on. Why are you so fixated on this? We have zero evidence. We don't even know if this kid is missin'. He coulda just been out fuckin' around."

"Dammit."

"Frank, I know you're frustrated, but we need more."

Fuck. I hung up. I'd apologize later.

When I got back to my truck, my cell rang, and I barked into it, "Yeah?"

"Deputy Sims?"

"What?"

"This is Gina Horowitz. I own the Stop and Go. Listen, I just spoke to Ted. He called earlier, but I've been in the ER getting stitches. I stopped by there early this morning to check on things after that wind last night. We've been having the craziest weather. My husband usually checks all the properties we own after bad weather, but he's out of town. Anyway, the back lock was frozen over, and I cut my hand trying to get in. That's my blood Ted showed you. No one tried to break in. There was a big tree branch on the ground out there. I'm guessing that's what caused the damage."

Fucking Ted had probably moved it so he could deny Shelley was right.

It had nothing to do with the kid. And now Shelley would *know* she was right. Great. That was bound to make my life hell for a long time.

"Thanks for lettin' me know."

"Sure thing. Ted said you were headed out on some manhunt, so I wanted to call before it went too far. Sorry for causing a commotion."

"Alright then."

And that was how the rest of the day went and the five days before that. Every call sounded like it could be about the boy, but when I got there, it didn't take but a minute to figure out that it wasn't about him. I still had no leads, and I still had a rock in my gut about it all.

I was projecting my own shit on the kid. I knew next to nothing about him. Carey was right. He could just be some delinquent, fucking off around town, trying to get into trouble. I had not one goddamn iota of evidence that he needed my help.

CHAPTER TWENTY-TWO

WHEN HE PICKED me up Thursday morning to drive me to the library, Frank was exhausted.

"Did you get any sleep last night?"

"Some," he said, looking out his back window as he reversed out of my driveway. His truck had a back-up camera, but he rarely used it. Sometimes, it felt like he was allergic to technology. He rolled his eyes every time I went to order something online. "I'll drive you to the store," he'd say with a smirk. "Besides, that keeps things local. Don't you young'ns like doin' that?"

Except lately, he wasn't doing much smirking or smiling at all. He was back to not-very-talkative, grumpy Frank.

It had been several days since our stakeout, and he picked me up every morning and every night after I finished up at the library, but he was closed off, speaking in one-word sentences again. I'd tried talking to him to find out why there was a sudden cold front being aimed at me, but he shut me down pretty quickly, saying he was just busy with work.

We went to dinner once at José's Diner, and he grumbled through the whole thing and took me home the second I'd finished eating my fried chicken platter. Man, was it good. I resisted the urge to lick the grease off my fingers. Frank wasn't a fan of grease. He was so rigid with his diet, I thought he suspected it could harden his arteries just by being near it. Even José knew this. He didn't even bother to ask Frank what he wanted to order, and when he delivered my fried chicken, Frank got grilled chicken with brown rice and steamed broccoli as sides. Blech. Where was the flavor?

I had the feeling that whatever his recent bad moods were about, they had to do with this kid Murphy.

Frank still hadn't found him, and he'd told me he'd done nothing else but search. Murphy hadn't been back to the library, at least as far as I could tell, and Frank checked my windows and doors and every single garbage can in the building when he dropped me off in the mornings and picked me up in the evenings. Sometimes on his lunch break too. I didn't get bad periods since the miscarriage and all the surgeries, but I still *had* a period. Ruined though my uterus and ovaries were, they still existed, and occasionally I did have to pee, so I would've noticed a homeless kid hiding out in the bathroom.

I'd even tried to talk Frank into another driving lesson, with promises of another make out session after, but he'd said only, "Yeah, maybe tomorrow." But tomorrow came and went, and he never brought it up again.

We were barely speaking.

"Listen," he said, turning out of my gramps's neighborhood, headed toward downtown. "That storm's comin' tonight. I don't want you to be alone if things get bad. Would you stay at the station?"

I was surprised. I hadn't expected that. Honestly, from the lack of communication from him over the last week, I was half expecting him to find an excuse to end things. Something had changed between us, but he wouldn't say what it was. Maybe he'd realized things really couldn't work. Maybe I was too young for him after all. Or maybe I was putting off some kind of "don't pick me, I'm infertile" vibes.

"Please? You could keep Grum company. I have to be on the roads tonight, but I'll be in and out. Abey and Shelley will be there though. I'll worry if you're alone."

"O-okay. Or maybe I could hang at Ace's House. Brady and Theo will be there."

He smiled, but it didn't reach his eyes. "Okay. Good compromise. Thank you. I'll check in when I can."

God. The angst pouring out of him was practically choking me. I wanted to shake him. In fact—

"Frank, talk to me, please? What the hell's going on with you? You've been distant for days. I don't know what I did wrong, but would you please just tell me so I can fix it?"

He sighed, and his voice was a quiet rumble when he said, "You didn't do anything wrong, Samantha. Why do you immediately assume it's something you did? It's not. Work's been busy, and I… I'm just tired."

I scoffed. He expected me to keep believing that? "That's a lie. I mean, maybe you are tired, but that's not all that's going on here. Whatever it is, I'm sorry it's upsetting you, but you're the one who said I wasn't ready for this relationship, and now *you're* the one acting like a sulky teenager. So it's up to you to fix whatever's wrong."

He pulled up in front of the library and stared at me as I got out. He didn't follow me in like he usually did, and I didn't ask him to. He didn't even say goodbye.

Freaking men. He may've been nineteen years older than me, but he was acting like a little boy.

And how did it work out that the one time he didn't come in with me to check the doors and windows, the second I crossed the threshold and stepped inside, it was glaringly obvious someone had been there?

The garbage can had been kicked over next to the armchairs in the main room, and trash was everywhere. I thought I'd emptied the bins, but I must not have. Books lay scattered across the floor next to my overturned shelving cart. The downstairs bathroom light was on, shining off the wall in the back hallway.

As Frank drove away, I closed the door behind me and called out, "Hello?" I walked through the first floor slowly, ready to run at any second, but from everything Frank had told me about Murphy, I wasn't too afraid. What was the kid going to do to me? Clobber me with a paperback copy of *The Adventures of Tom Sawyer*? "Hello? Is anyone here?"

I should've called Frank the second I'd realized someone had been there, but something stopped me, and I knew exactly what it was.

If I'd called him, Frank would've arrested Murphy, and I didn't think Murphy deserved that. He'd been through so much already. How did Frank expect this kid to handle the sheriff's station or a child advocate from the state who looked like Miss Trunchbull from *Matilda* and was just as mean? He was only looking for a safe place to sleep.

I was not about to help Frank punish him for that.

"Hello? If you're here, please talk to me. I won't hurt you."

My head whipped up toward the ceiling when I heard a chair or something scrape across the floor upstairs. There was a loud *thump*, and I ran up there, skidding to a stop in the open conference room door because there was a child lying in front of it, clutching his side and rolling on the floor.

"Oh my God. Are you okay? What happened?"

He looked up at me, his dark brown eyes scared and squinting, probably trying to discern if I could be trusted.

I held my hands up in front of me to try to convince him I wouldn't hurt him. "I'm Sam. I'm the librarian. I promise you, I don't care that you're here. You're not in trouble. I want to help you."

Kneeling next to him slowly, I looked him over, trying to find where he was hurt. His royal blue winter coat was filthy and wet, and it looked slightly too small for his frame. He couldn't have been more than fifteen years old.

"You're Murphy, right? Where's your mom?"

He didn't answer, but his eyes wouldn't stray from mine.

I kept talking, hoping to put him more at ease. "I'm going to move your coat so I can see what's going on, okay?"

When I reached for it, he jerked away, but he winced, and I warned him with my eyes to stay still. "Please don't be scared. I only want to see." I moved his coat aside carefully, noticing his ratty tan sweater underneath. It was filthy and covered in holes from constant wear. "How did you hurt yourself? I saw the bandages in the garbage. I was hoping you'd come back, but you never did. Where have you been sleeping?"

He didn't make a peep, but when I finally lifted his sweater, it stuck to his skin, to the dried blood on his side underneath, and he hissed in pain.

"I'm sorry. Let me go get the first aid kit. We should clean this up."

"No."

My eyes flicked up to his. "So you *can* talk."

He was holding back tears. "I didn't mean to fall asleep, but I-I couldn't keep my eyes open. I gotta go."

"Murphy, I promise, you're safe here."

Whispering, he said, "The cop comes here."

"That's Frank, my boyfriend. He's been trying to find you. He's worried about you."

"No." He pushed my hands away and, with effort, sat up. "No cops."

"O-okay. Um, well, can you tell me what happened at least?"

His voice cracked when he said, "Climbed over barbed wire." This kid was still going through puberty. There was no way he could've made me believe he was eighteen.

I leaned forward, trying to show kindness through my eyes, and he relaxed a fraction as I lifted the sweater off his skin slowly. I was hissing now, too, trying to unstick the fabric from his wound carefully. The six-inch cut across his lower ribs was an angry dark-red color, and it extended to his back. "I think it's infected."

He reached for his backpack beside him and pulled out a humungous brown bottle of some kind of medication, then handed it to me.

Reading the bottle quickly, I said, "Penicillin? Murphy, these are for animals. It's not the right dosage for you."

"Th-they make me throw up."

I nodded. "Yeah, well, that's not surprising."

He was watching my face while I spoke, and I was getting a look at him too. He looked gaunt and malnourished, and his skin had a pale, waxy quality to it, with dark bruise-like smudges beneath his eyes.

"It probably doesn't help that you're not eating well. Have you eaten today?"

He shook his head.

"I'll go get my lunch for you. I'm afraid it's not very exciting. PB&J and potato chips."

A glazed look took over his eyes.

"Oh yeah, I bet you're hungry. I'll be right back."

He gripped my wrist with a bony hand. "I'll go with you."

"Are you sure you can get down the stairs?"

He nodded again, watching my eyes when I spoke.

"You don't trust me, do you? I promise, I'm not going to get you in trouble. Come on. I'll help you."

He crawled onto his knees, then stood. He was as tall as me, so I wrapped his arm around my shoulder to help carry some of his weight. I felt the weakness in his muscles as we hobbled down the stairs, one at a time, and when we got to the bottom, he swayed and leaned against the wall.

"Sit down. My lunch is right there. See my tote bag in the entryway?"

"'Kay," he mumbled, sliding down the wall and parking his butt on the bottom step.

"Let me just—"

A car door slammed outside, and when I turned back to him, panic had filled Murphy's eyes. He stood, looking at my face, then in the direction of the front door, and then back at my face.

I jabbed my thumb behind me to the rolling cart under the book drop next to the front door. "Maybe it's just a library patron returning books."

He shook his head, eyes wide, and I jumped to the side, trying to see out the front windows.

Shit. Frank.

I held my hands up in front of me again. I didn't know what to say to make Murphy stay, but it didn't matter. He bolted. I had no idea how he could move that fast, as weak as he was, but he disappeared in a flash, and as soon as Frank pushed in through the front door, I heard the back door slamming shut.

Frank heard it too. He missed nothing. He took one look

at the garbage still on the floor, my overturned book cart, and the guilty wince on my face. "Where'd he go?"

"Out the back. Just now." I hung my head. It made my stomach hurt to think of Frank finding Murphy and arresting him, but he really didn't look good. I was afraid Murphy needed more help than I could give him.

It felt like there was barbed wire in *my* stomach when Frank whipped around and jumped down the steps outside, letting the door slam behind him. And when he peeled out, kicking up dirty snow behind his truck's tires, I was so scared for Murphy, I felt like I might throw up.

"Dammit, Samantha! Why didn't you call me as soon as you knew he was here?" Frank boomed at me, slamming the front door closed behind him when he returned. "I've been trying to find him for weeks!"

"You didn't catch him?"

He'd been gone for over an hour, and I just sat there on the bottom stair, my mind racing with all the really bad possibilities.

Yanking the gloves off his hands, he threw them to the floor, and his hat followed. "No!"

I stood, following him into the main room. "I'm sorry, but you didn't see how scared he was, Frank. He can't be more than fifteen years old. Why do you have to arrest him? I know you don't like it, but not everyone has to live by the rules all the time. Why can't you go with the flow a little? Nothing bad is going to happen if you do, you know."

"Yes, it will!"

"What, Frank? What bad thing will happen?"

"Life! Goddammit. Life will happen, and it ain't always

hippie roses and good times." He pushed his hand through his hair. "You come in here, and you—you're messin' everything up. Why can't you just leave it be?"

"Leave what be?"

"Nothin'," he said, turning away from me, shaking his head.

"I know life isn't always easy." God, did I ever. "But that kid was terrified of you finding him. He knows, as soon as you do, you're going to arrest him."

"Yeah?" He wouldn't look at me. He stepped to the front windows and stared out, breathing in loudly and releasing the breath silently. "Well, he's gonna be scared shitless tonight. The storm headed our way is s'posed to be really fuckin' bad, Samantha. Polar temperatures, high winds, and we're gonna get dumped on. A whiteout. Abey's already out there, blockin' off roads."

Oh God. The storm. "I wasn't thinking about that."

"No, you weren't," he said. "I'm so angry with you right now."

"Frank—"

"I gotta go. I *have* to find him. You have no idea what it's like to be out there all alone."

I didn't want to make him any madder, but I couldn't stop myself from asking, "And you do?"

He didn't reply. He turned and bent, swiping his hat and gloves off the floor, then walked to the door and stopped, but he still wouldn't look at me. As he fixed the hat on his head and yanked his gloves back on, he said, "I'll be here to pick you up at six. Earlier if the storm hits sooner. If he comes back, you had *better* call me."

"I will," I said, because now I knew that there was a hell of a lot more to this than Frank was letting on.

"Hey." Brady called on his way back to Wisper from Wind Reservation, talking really loudly into his cell phone. "This storm's s'posed to be a monster. The snow's already startin'. I'm on my way home from the res now. My mom's gonna stay with her cousin out there."

"Okay, but drive slowly. I can't handle it if you get hurt."

"Okay, boss," he joked. "I'm glad you're staying at Ace's House tonight. Theo ordered a bunch of sleeping bags and supplies. We've got a huge generator, we got that big ol' fireplace, and we got food. There's a bunch of people plannin' to come. When the power lines go down, it can be days before they get 'em back up and runnin' for some of the more rural residents."

"Yeah, I don't want to be alone. But, um, do you mind if I bring a dog?"

"A dog? I guess so?" He laughed. "I doubt Theo will care, but whose dog?"

"It's Frank's dog, Grum."

"How's it goin' with you two?"

"Well…"

"Well what?"

"I don't know. There's something bothering him. I have no idea what it is. He won't talk to me, and it's affecting… us."

"Ooo, so it's 'us' now?"

"I thought it was, but maybe I was wrong."

"And the age thing?"

"It doesn't matter. Age doesn't matter at all. He's such a good man, Brady. I think I… Well, I like him. Like, a lot." I kicked my boot against the bottom of the check-in desk as I leaned over it. "And now that I've figured that out, he's pulling away."

"I'm sorry, Sam."

I sighed. "It has something to do with that kid. The one Theo told Frank about—Murphy."

"Oh, really? Did Frank find him?"

"No, but he was here. He's been breaking into the library at night. He cut his stomach trying to climb a fence, and I think it's infected, but Frank scared him off again. And now Frank's angry with me for not calling him right away. He's really worried about Murphy. You don't know Frank though; he's really strict. I just didn't want the kid to get arrested. It's not his fault he's homeless."

"I'll be there to get you in about fifteen minutes, and we'll go pick up the dog. Then you can tell me all about it. Maybe the kid will reach out tonight. Everybody's talkin' about the storm. I'm sure he knows it's comin'."

"I'm leaving the library unlocked just in case. The county might fire me for it, but I don't care. If he comes back here, I want him to be able to get in without hurting himself again." I looked out at the dark, ominous afternoon sky already spitting snowflakes. "Okay. I'll close up. See you soon."

CHAPTER TWENTY-THREE

"GRUM! NO!" The silly dog launched himself at Theo, and they both landed on the hardwood floor in the hallway at Ace's House. I rushed forward, arms out, trying to help. "I'm so sorry."

I thought it might be a good idea to give Frank some space, so I called him and told him Brady was picking me up. He followed through on his promise and called Brady himself to make sure Brady was aware of the situation, even though I'd already told Brady. I wasn't three years old. I could speak for myself. But he was still so angry, so I hadn't argued.

As soon as Brady and I walked in the front door at the center, Grum pulled on his leash, detaching it from his collar by sheer will, and I was holding my breath, expecting to get yelled at for bringing such an unruly puppy into the community center. Instead, Theo laughed, and then he just lay there, rubbing his hands back and forth vigorously over Grum's fur, while Grum gave Theo's face a tongue bath.

"I don't think an animal has ever reacted to me this way," he said, laughing. "Usually, it's my sister they love. She's always had a special connection with them."

"I'm glad you're laughing," I said. "I was half expecting you to kick me and Grum out."

"What kinda name is Grum anyway?" Brady asked.

Looking around, I saw at least six different families in the center, playing card games or huddling up by the fire in the main room, trying to convince their kids that a night stuck in the community center would be fun, probably with no cell service or internet for their phones and tablets.

I shrugged. "Short for Grumbly." I couldn't stop the smirk from forming on my face as I thought about Frank's grumbling tendencies.

Brady chuckled. "Makes sense."

"Well"—Theo moved Grum to his side and sat up—"you and Grum are both welcome here. I'll ask Vern to shovel a little patch out in the back parking lot for him to do his business."

"Thanks, guys."

"Frank is welcome to wait the storm out here, too, you know," he said as he stood, dusting himself off. Grum sat next to his legs, looking up at Theo.

"Thanks, but he's patrolling tonight in case anyone needs help."

"He's still looking for Murphy," Brady told Theo. To me he said, "He was pretty intense on the phone."

"I know. I'm sorry. He's worried about Murphy, but I think I made things worse. Murphy was right there, and I let him get away, and now Frank can't find him. It's really upsetting him."

"Does he have any idea where Murphy could be?" Theo asked. "He hasn't been back here."

"I don't think so. If he does, he's not telling me anything. This kid seems to be good at hiding, but I think maybe there's more to it than just a cop looking for a missing kid. I think that's why he's so focused on finding Murphy." Looking down at my boots, I shook my head. "I don't know. I wish he'd talk to me."

Theo came to stand beside me, hooking his arm around my shoulder. I turned into his chest and tried to hide the tears welling in my eyes. I'd really messed things up with Frank, but how could I have known? He still hadn't told me anything about his childhood, and I was betting there was a lot there to unpack. And this whole thing was doing nothing but convincing me further that I wasn't the right person for Frank.

He'd never treated me like I was immature because of my age until today.

Theo steered me into his office. Brady followed and sat next to me in the office chairs, flicking his long, silky black hair over his shoulder. It had grown so long that it fell to the middle of his back. Usually he wore it in braids or pulled it back into a low ponytail, but this evening, it was loose and wild.

As Theo shut the door behind us, Brady's warm voice was a comfort. He rarely used the nickname he'd given me when we were five-year-olds, running around Wisper, getting sunburnt and voyaging out on the adventures I'd told him about from the books I'd read. "It's gonna be okay, Sunny Samshine."

"Will it? I've really fallen for Frank. God. Like, he's all I think about. And now, I'm pretty sure he's too angry with me for us to get past this. I should've trusted him, but I thought I knew better, and now, what if Murphy's really hurt? What if he dies in this storm?"

"We should help Frank look," Theo said while Brady patted my back.

"You can't go out into this storm, Theo," Brady said.

"Look outside, love. The snow's already startin' to dump on us. It's gettin' darker by the second, and even my bones are cold. The temperature's definitely droppin'. It's not safe."

"You're right," Theo said as my cell rang in my bag. "I know you're right, but—"

Pulling the phone out, I checked the caller ID. "It's Frank."

Brady nodded silently, standing and wrapping his arm around Theo's waist. I felt a small twinge of annoyance at how easy it was for them to be so in love. But almost instantly, I remembered when I'd first moved to Wisper and how miserable they'd both been before they found each other. Could Frank and I ever have what they had? Was this our "miserable" phase?

I wanted my happy-ever-after, too, damn it. Didn't I deserve it? Didn't Frank?

As I sat there, staring at Frank's name and the purple smiling devil emoji I'd assigned to his profile in my phone after he ate my cake, I realized that no matter how angry I was with Frank for not talking to me about how he felt, I was the one dumping obstacles in our path. I was lying to him. Well, not outright, but a lie of omission was still a lie.

I wanted to be with him, no matter our ages, no matter my inability to give him children, but if I didn't tell him, he couldn't decide if he wanted me too.

"Hi," I answered. "Grum and I are at Ace's House. Is it getting bad already?"

"Yeah," Frank said quietly. "I'm sittin' here in my truck, just watchin' it dump down. It's intense. Thanks for keepin' an eye on him. I just wanted to hear your voice. It's gonna be a long night. We got a few deputies from Jackson stayin' in town to help. Two of 'em are already out at accidents, and you know more people are gonna try to drive in this crap."

"A-and Murphy? No sign of him yet?"

"No," he said, and my heart sank at the dejected tone of his voice.

"You were right. I should've called you. There's something I need to talk to you about but I-I—but you said you would arrest Murphy, and all I could picture was that poor kid in handcuffs, scared and freaking out."

"I know," he said. "I know that's what you saw, but Samantha, there's somethin' I need to tell you too." He took a deep breath. "I was homeless and alone when I was thirteen after my mama overdosed. I had no other family. I got arrested for stealin' from a store, and it was the best thing that ever happened to me. I'm sorry I didn't tell you before, but" —he paused, and it was almost shocking to me to hear so much uncertainty in his voice—"it's n-not my favorite subject."

Tears were streaming down my face now. "Oh, Frank. Baby, I'm so sorry."

He sighed. "I didn't want you to feel sorry for me. To see me different."

Picking up on the seriousness of my conversation, Brady and Theo quietly excused themselves, leaving me in the office alone.

"I don't feel sorry for you. My heart is breaking for the little boy you used to be, but you're the strongest person I've ever met. There's nothing about you now that makes me pity you."

He was quiet for a minute. "You know, I really love the sound of you callin' me baby."

Scooting deeper into the chair, I pulled my knees up to my chest and tried to relax the stress out of my shoulders. "Yeah?"

"Yeah. A lot."

I smiled, wiping the tears from my cheeks. "Will you tell me about your mama?"

"I will when we can sit down together, and then you can tell me your thing, too, okay?"

"Okay. Thank you, Frank."

He smiled. I heard it in his voice. "When you say my name like you just did, I can picture it, you know? Wakin' up with you in my arms on a Sunday mornin', havin' a lazy day with our kids. Watchin' a game while you read in my lap or goin' for a drive in the mountains together. You'd be by my side, callin' me baby." He paused. "I could love you. I think… I think I already do."

Oh no. I couldn't wait. I had to tell him now. It was so not the right time, but I couldn't let him go on believing—

"Shit!"

There was a loud groaning sound over the phone, like the complaining of metal being scraped and bent, and then a loud whooshing and a popping sound.

"Frank? What happened? Are you okay?"

His voice was stressed and far away, like he wasn't holding his phone anymore. He grunted and hissed in pain. "Ah, fuck."

"Frank? Talk to me!"

I heard shuffling as he moved the phone, and then his voice returned. "Somebody just slammed into my truck." His breath hitched. "Dammit. I'm bleedin'. I gotta go."

"No, wait!"

"I need to check on the other driver. I'll call you back as soon as I can." Right before he hung up, he said, "I'm fine. Promise. I love you."

What? No! I'd read enough romantic suspense to know if someone said, "I'm bleeding" ominously and in the same breath as "I love you" right after being hit by a car, it probably wasn't going to end up being a good thing.

Jumping out of the chair, I yanked my bag off my shoulder, dropped it to the floor, and threw open the door. I had no idea what to do. I didn't know where Frank was, but he was hurt.

"Sam?" Brady's voice registered behind me, and Grum barked as I ran down the hallway toward the front door. "What's wrong?"

"There was an accident."

"Where?"

I turned, my heart plummeting as I thought about Frank out there alone, injured. *Oh God*. Grum whined, circling me nervously. "I don't know!"

"Okay," Theo said, "let's take a breath. Um, maybe we can call over to the sheriff's station. They'll know where Frank was."

"Yes! Frank said Abey will be there—"

Just then, the front door opened, and a cold blast of snow rushed in at us, and then there she was. Deputy Abey Lee. "Hey, y'all. Just checkin' in. Frank wanted me to make sure you—" She looked at me, clearly seeing the panic on my face. "What's wrong?"

"Have you talked to Frank?"

"Yeah," she said, "'bout half an hour ago. Why?"

"He's been in an accident. I was just talking to him on the phone when it happened. I think he's hurt."

Abey nodded. The few times I'd met her, she was usually smiling or joking, but now, a seriousness was taking over her face. She held her thumb over the microphone button on her shoulder radio, raising it closer to her mouth. "This is Deputy Lee. I need a location for Deputy Sims. Shelley? You there?"

"Yeah, here," a woman replied. "Frank's over by the library. He's still lookin' for that boy."

That was all I needed. The library wasn't far. Pulling my mittens on, I ran out the open door and down the icy steps. I nearly slipped and fell on my ass, but sheer determination kept me on my feet as I slid across a patch of ice until my feet found purchase on the snow again. I could barely hear Brady and Theo behind me, holding Grum back and calling after me, begging me to stop.

Frank had been right. It was an utter whiteout. I couldn't see two feet in front of my face, but I kept going. I could kind of tell where the sidewalk was, though the snow was already deep enough that it was hard to see, but as long as I stayed in my current direction in the middle of Main Street, I'd eventually end up on Franklin, and the library was only one block to the west once I made it there.

The freezing air was making it hard to keep a fast pace, though, and I wasn't the most physically fit person in the world. I slowed. I had to. I couldn't run and breathe at the same time, not in this cold, but a truck rolled up beside me. Its tires crunched on the snow beneath them, and then I heard Abey's voice and saw blue and red lights reflecting off the vortex of white surrounding me.

She called out her window, "Hop in, lil' lady. I'll take you over there."

I stopped, looking over at her with frozen tears stuck below my eyes. Grum's nose was pressed against her back window as he whined and yipped for me.

"You comin'?"

When I climbed in the passenger side, she waited for me to click my seatbelt into place and then took off at one freaking mile an hour, and Grum leaned over the seat to lick my face.

"Hi, buddy." Panting hard, breathing in the warm air blasting through the heater, I was trying to thaw my burning lungs, but it was still cold enough in her cruiser for my breath to come out in a white huff. "Can you go faster? Please?"

"Actually, no, I can't. It won't do for us to get in an accident too. How's that gonna help Frank?"

"I know, but—"

She glanced at me for a second but then fixed her eyes back on the blizzard swirling angrily in front of us. "You really like him, don'tcha?"

"Yes. I love him."

I did. When that had happened, I had no clue. It was just a couple of weeks ago that I was trying to convince myself we were too different. But somewhere between our first date, our epic cake-eating and dry-humping sessions, and now, Frank had lured me in. His dedication and insistence on finding Murphy, the way he never spoke, and all the lovely things that came out of his mouth on the rare occasions when he did —all of it was beautiful.

I'd never felt so cherished, so loved and protected. Even earlier today, when he was so angry with me, he made sure I had a ride to a building only a few blocks away so I wouldn't have to walk in the storm, and he called me just to hear my voice. He was out in a seriously scary weather situation, risking his life for this little town and all her residents. He was risking his life for a boy he knew nothing about.

How could I not love him?

"Well, ain't that somethin'," Abey said. "I'm glad to hear it. The grouch deserves some happiness." She reached over to pat my hands folded in my lap. I was squeezing the crap out of my own fingers. "He's a tough ol' bastard. He'll be okay."

But she couldn't know that.

It felt like it took three days, but we finally pulled up beside Frank's truck another block west of the library. His lights were turning and flashing on top, and the car that had hit him was still there, still rammed into Frank's driver's-side door, but there wasn't anyone in it. I couldn't even determine the color of the car, there was so much snow piled on top of it already.

Frank was nowhere to be found. His passenger door was open, the interior light was on, and the airbags surrounding his seat were out and deflated. Grum jumped up, sniffing the seat and the steering wheel.

"Where is he!"

Usually in Wisper, when there was a car accident or someone was hurt, neighbors would flood the streets, trying to help or at least find out what had happened so they could call everyone they knew, but now, there was no one. The storm was so loud, the wind so powerful, that I didn't think anyone had heard the accident.

Abey called the station on her radio again, and I turned, searching, looking everywhere for Frank. I thought I could see a light on at the library in the distance, but I knew for sure that I'd turned them all off. I ran in that direction, and this time, Abey and Grum followed me on foot, but once Grum caught Frank's scent, he took off like a flash of furry yellow light.

CHAPTER TWENTY-FOUR

FRANK

GODDAMN AIRBAGS.

Looking at myself in the mirror in the library's downstairs bathroom, dabbing the little bit of blood on my forehead with a piece of toilet paper, I pressed against the bruise I could already feel forming underneath.

I heard a bang out in the front room and then a dog barking.

"Frank? Frank!"

Samantha?

Grum beat her there, but when she appeared in the doorway, a vision and a soaked mess, I was confused. "What're you doin' here?"

"Are you okay?"

"I'm fine."

She took one careful step toward me. "You're not hurt?"

"No."

Launching herself at me, she jumped up and threw her arms around my shoulders, knocking the first aid kit in my hand to the floor and locking her legs around my waist, hiding her face in my neck.

Grum settled around my feet as I wrapped my arms around her back, holding her against me. I wanted to hold her like that forever. Her heart was pounding. "Did you walk all the way here in this weather?" I leaned back so I could see her face, but she hugged me tighter.

"I tried," she mumbled against my coat, "but Abey found me and drove me the rest of the way. Are you sure you're okay?"

"Promise. Just a little cut on my forehead from the airbag. I think a little piece of the plastic dash covering broke off and flew against my head when the bag deployed."

Finally, she leaned back to inspect my face, her eyes landing on the cut. She reached up with her pink mitten, soaking up the blood with it. It wasn't too bad of an injury, all things considered.

Abey appeared in the doorway, her eyebrows doing a caterpillar crawl up her face when she saw Grum hugging my feet and Samantha latched onto me the way she was. "Mrs. Bettison crashed into you?"

"Yeah," I said. "She was on her way to her sister's house, but she hit some ice and couldn't stop the car before it collided with the side of my truck. She's okay. We needed shelter from the storm, so I brought her here."

"Is that the woman sitting out in the front room, looking guilty?" Samantha asked.

Abey chuckled. "Yep. That's Cal's sister."

"Myrna?"

"Yeah," I said.

I'd turned my shoulder radio down so I could hear Myrna over the roar of the wind, but Shelley's voice came through over Abey's. "Report back. Everybody okay? Frank? Abey?"

Abey replied, and I looked down at Samantha, smirking. "I broke in. Broke the law."

She hugged me closer, still clinging to me like static. "I think you'll be forgiven this time, especially since I left the door unlocked."

When she was done filling Shelley in, Abey shifted on her feet, resting her hand on the butt of her gun tucked snug in her holster. "I'll take Myrna on over to Cal's. You sure you're okay?"

In any other circumstance, I probably would've been uncomfortable with Samantha's affection in front of my co-worker, but now, there wasn't anything more important in the world than having her in my arms. I squeezed her tighter, nodding over her shoulder. Besides, Abey was family, whether I liked admitting it or not. "Yeah, thanks, partner."

Abey slammed the front door shut when she and Myrna left, and as soon as I knew we were alone, I lowered Samantha to the sink, and she widened her legs to let me between them. The snow packed into the tread of our boots was melting and dripping down to the floor around Grum, but he didn't seem to care.

"You were worried about me? Here," I said, "gimme your glasses." They were fogged over and covered in dots of moisture. Reaching under my coat, I pulled the bottom of my undershirt out and cleaned her lenses when she handed the glasses over, then set them back on her face.

She was the most beautiful woman on the fucking planet, even wet and looking like a drowned rat, her makeup streaking black down the sides of her face. Concern clouded her eyes when she looked in mine, and she had me believing in destiny and soul mates. In that moment, with her in my arms, I knew dreams could come true. She was everything I'd been wishing for.

"I was terrified, Frank. You said you were bleeding. You were hurt."

Touching my finger to her bottom lip, I said, "Thank you. It feels good to have your worry aimed at me." I kissed her softly, trying to quiet the sudden need I felt for her, but it was no use. I was already hard, and my heart was pounding just looking at her. "I'm about to break another one of my rules."

Her voice was raspy from yelling for me. I loved the sound. "Which one?"

Without preamble, I confessed, "I need to be inside you. We don't have a warm fire, but I wanna make love to you. Right now."

"In the library?"

"Yes."

"Without me telling you everything?"

"Yes."

"I'm ready, Frank. I'll tell you anything. I need to tell you. I'm scared, but I want you to know."

"Later."

Releasing a breath, her eyes fell shut like she was relieved, and I kissed each closed lid, feeling her lashes flutter against my lips.

I unbuckled my holster and set my gun on the counter, checking to make sure the safety was locked, then popped my fly. Samantha opened her eyes.

"I need you now," I whispered, letting the moment and the quiet of the library take me where it wanted. The storm was raging outside, trees banging against the building, the wind howling its anger, but we weren't letting it in. "I'm in love with you."

She didn't say anything, but a fire had begun to build behind those eyes, and she responded by leaning back a little and opening her legs wider.

It didn't take long then. She pushed my pants below my ass, and when she tried unsuccessfully to kick her boots off without untying them, I tugged on the laces, slipping the knots and pulling them off her feet. She wrapped her legs around my waist again, and my hard-on was like a white flag between us.

She hadn't worn her hat when she came running to my rescue, so her hair was wet from the snow. It was a damp mess. I moved it away from her eyes, cradling her face in my hands, dragging them down her neck. Finally, I slid them around her back and lifted her.

She moaned as I carried her, searching for somewhere I could lay her down. The front desk caught my eye, so I headed there. Grum must've understood the situation, 'cause he stayed where he was.

All the lights were on in the library's main room, the blinds covering the windows pulled up and open, but it didn't matter.

The only thing that mattered was us. Samantha and me.

Setting her atop the long wooden counter, I pulled her leggings off quickly, and then her white cotton panties. They dangled from her ankle as I lowered my head, finding warm perfection between her legs. I swooped in, latching onto her clit with my lips, sucking it into my mouth.

She was already sopping wet for me, her slick coating my lips and chin.

She cried out and bent her knees, planting her socks on the counter, letting her legs fall out beside her. I snatched the panties from her foot, stuffing them down my pants and wrapping them around my cock beneath my boxers, letting the fabric that had just kissed her pussy fuck my shaft as I palmed myself. I groaned at the imagery, and she lifted her head to watch me. Once she realized what I was doing, her head fell back, and then she was moaning, making those sexy panting noises I'd loved so much in my living room.

They spurred me on, and I licked at her faster, collecting her essence on the tip of my tongue and plunging it inside her, and she rode my face, rolling her hips, her ass slapping the hardwood surface. Her taste coated my throat as I swallowed. I wanted inside her, but I needed her to be inside me too.

Anyone could've walked in or seen us through the windows, if they could see through the snow, but I couldn't stop. It did occur to me that Abey could come back at any moment, so I lifted Samantha again, and she kissed me, reaching underneath my shirt as I carried her.

There had to be somewhere more private, but her wet heat was positioned above my cock as I walked, and getting inside her was all I could think about. I knew I wouldn't make it all the way up the stairs. The urgency between us was overwhelming. My hands shook, so I dug my fingertips into her skin.

She reached between us, trying to grip my dick in her hand, but if I let her get that far, this would be over before we'd even started. Lowering her as I stumbled down an aisle between two bookcases, I anchored my hand on the back of her neck and held her down as I pushed up inside her, and then I couldn't think at all anymore.

Her eyes fluttered closed, and suddenly, I couldn't breathe. I was so fucking in love with her. She hadn't said anything about how she felt, but it didn't matter.

Seeing the wall and heading toward it, I admitted everything I'd been thinking since I'd met her 'cause her warm pussy walls around my cock were like some kind of truth serum. "I want you in my life. In my bed. I wanna build somethin' with you. I'm sorry I yelled at you earlier. I'm sorry I wasn't open with you about my past—this kid has me all fucked up—but I know what I want, and what I want is you."

She gasped as I pushed her hard against the wall, finally fucking her.

But fucking her had become about loving her, and I couldn't get enough.

She begged me for release. "Frank, *please*." Her hands were everywhere, her heels digging into the backs of my thighs as she kissed me. She stole the breath from my lungs, the thoughts in my head, and my heart.

I couldn't respond. I made some kind of noise in the back of my throat, and she groaned and tilted her hips.

With the wall bracing her, I could fuck into her harder. The commotion we were making was loud, but I couldn't stop. Grum whined back in the bathroom, probably confused about the noise as I banged us against the wall. Samantha stared into my eyes, lifting her hands to my face, rubbing her palms over my jaw.

I was lost to her. Lost in her eyes, lost inside her body. And without her, I would be lost in the world.

There was no going back for me, no matter how she felt.

I loved her, and it was my mission now to make her mine.

"Take your sweater off," I commanded, pushing her down on my dick and punching up into her. I needed to feel her skin against mine.

She whipped it over her head, and her hair fell down around her shoulders. I used my thighs, pressing us against the wall, and pulled the cups of her bra aside. Her breasts popped free as she pulled at my shirt, then ripped at it, and buttons pinged on the floor when they fell. She lifted my undershirt and arched her back, smashing her breasts to my chest.

I felt more animal than man as I growled and bent,

sucking and licking her tits, rubbing my face all over them, marking her with my saliva, scratching her skin with my beard as they bounced.

Her fingernails dug into my shoulders, and the sharp pinch had me hissing and fucking her harder.

I felt so out of control. "Oh God, Samantha."

She whispered, "You feel so good. I knew it would feel like this."

I moaned and raised up to kiss her, capturing her mouth in mine. She was panting around my lips, thrusting her hips against mine, calling out.

"I can't get enough," I breathed. "I can't... Samantha. *Fuck*."

More bookshelves were banging the walls beside us, and one began to teeter.

"Frank! Oh God, but don't stop."

I couldn't have stopped if my life had depended on it.

As she chanted in rhythm with my thrusts—"Yes, Frank! Yes, baby!"—books began to drop from the shelves. The whole world was falling down around us, and it felt so good.

"I fuckin' love you," I rasped, kissing her harder, *pounding* my cock inside her. Did she know what that meant? I'd never loved anyone. Not like this. I would kill to protect her. I'd break every fucking rule in the book for her. I'd give her anything she ever wanted.

She owned me.

When I looked in her beautiful hazel eyes, the fire in them was blazing now, but she closed them, and her head fell back, hitting the wall. She was moaning as her thighs pulled me closer, raking her nails across my back, tears streaming down her face.

I understood. It felt like finally coming home, but it was a place I'd never been to before. It was a place I'd never dared to dream.

"I love you too," she whispered, "so much," and her body gripped my dick like a fist. She came on a cry as I clenched my ass cheeks, straining to get as far up inside her as I could. Lifting up on the toes of my boots, I held her there, pinned to the wall as I spilled my soul inside her with a shout.

And without a condom.

We slid down to the floor, still connected.

"Oh my God," she breathed.

"That went a little faster than I meant for it to."

She laughed, the sound like a summer breeze warming my skin in the chaos of the frozen storm. She kissed my nose. "It was perfect."

Catching my breath, I tried to figure out how to tell her I might've just knocked her up. "I wasn't thinkin' straight. I'm sorry. When I said I wanted to build somethin' with you, I didn't mean right this minute."

Her eyes grew big, and she blinked. "What?"

"I didn't use a condom."

"Oh." It was like an invisible wall slammed down in front of her face. Everything changed, like somehow I'd just hit her "off" button. She shook her head. "Don't worry about it."

"It's irresponsible—"

"Frank. It's fine." She took a deep breath. "I can't have children." Closing her eyes and breaking our connection completely, all the color drained from her cheeks. "Like, ever."

The world stopped spinning for a minute. She held her breath.

"I-I should've told you before. I'm sorry. I understand if this… if it changes things for you."

"Changes things?" The way she'd said it was cold. Detached. Almost robotic. It was a side of her I'd never seen.

Pushing me back gently, she disconnected us and stood. "Do you see my underwear anywhere?"

"Samantha?"

She reached for her sweater on the floor and pulled it over her head, straightening her glasses and tugging her long hair loose so it lay wet down her back, and then bent to pick books up off the floor. I stood, too, zipping up and righting my shirts. I had another uniform in my truck that still had its buttons, if we could get to it.

What did she mean? The words resounded in my head. *"Can't have children. Like, ever."*

"Samantha, talk to me. Would you come back, please?"

She dropped the books from her hands into a chair and then found her underwear and pants by the front desk. Turning away from me, she dressed and said, "It's not a big deal. I had really bad endometriosis in my teens and early twenties, and that caused an ectopic pregnancy in college. Remember that jerk I told you about?" She waved a hand in the air, like what she was telling me didn't mean anything.

But I was starting to understand just how much it did. She'd never mentioned kids, even when I had. Any time I talked about wanting a family, she'd gone quiet. How had I not noticed it before now?

"It was a whole thing. I was in the hospital—I almost died, actually—but I'm fine now. They had to remove one of my fallopian tubes, and the other one is scarred closed. So don't worry. You didn't get me pregnant, and I haven't had sex in almost three years, so you don't have to worry about STIs." She stood completely still. "I know it's not what you were expecting to hear, so I understand if that changes how you feel about me."

"It doesn't." How could it?

"This thing you want," she said, still facing away from me, "the family you *deserve*—I can't give you that, Frank. Are you hearing me? You want a whole boatload of kids, right? *Your* kids? Well, I can't have them. Ever. My reproductive system is dust. The damage extended to my ovaries and uterus too. No in vitro for me. No surrogacy. So that's it for that dream. It was dead a long time ago. If you want a family, you'd be better off finding someone else, maybe even someone younger who can pop out a brood for you. I can't."

When she turned, I could see on her face she was imagining it—me with another woman and kids—and my heart broke for her. The sadness on her face made me ache inside.

No. I couldn't imagine it either. Samantha was it for me. Kids or not.

I opened my mouth to tell her it didn't matter. If she loved me, too, and we were meant to have a family, I would find a way, but the door blew open, whirling a blast of snow into the foyer, and then Abey was there, hands on her hips. How did she always appear out of thin air?

She looked back and forth between Samantha and me, then took in an eyeful of the mess we'd left behind us. Grum shot out from the bathroom and ran to her, jumping up, trying to convince Abey to pet him. She patted his head. "While y'all were here gettin' jiggy with it or whatever, we might've gotten a beat on your boy. Tilda Granger just called the station. She thinks somebody broke into the Oswalds' house down the street from her. There's a light on inside, but they're in Arizona till April. I already called 'em, and Mr. Oswald said there shouldn't be anybody in there."

Samantha turned and looked at me. "Go," she said.

I nodded. "But you're comin' with me."

CHAPTER TWENTY-FIVE

SAMANTHA

RIDING in Abey's back seat on the way to hopefully find the kid I'd let come between Frank and me, I was kicking myself. Why had I told him like that? I could've let the moment pass between us without ruining it. And now, every time he thought about the first time we'd made love—the first and probably the only time he'd ever tell me he loved me —he'd remember this huge thing I'd dumped on him and the way I'd tried to brush it off, like it wasn't this big, important thing.

Like it didn't change *everything*.

I'd made the decision that he wouldn't want me if I couldn't have children, even though, when I thought about it, he hadn't actually ever said that, and I'd decided I wasn't good enough for him because of it too.

I felt like a fool. An immature child. And I felt like I was proving that our age difference did matter, even though I'd been doing everything to convince us both it didn't.

I hadn't even had a chance to think about the fact that we'd had sex without a condom, forcing me to admit the truth I'd said I was ready to tell him but was still terrified of.

I wanted to go back, to start the conversation over so I could do it better. He deserved better. So did I.

"Lights off," Frank said, checking something on his phone as Abey crept down the street the Oswalds lived on, and she flipped off her headlights. "Ain't like they're helpin' us see any better. Damn. There goes cell service." He shook his head, stuffing his cell into his front coat pocket and snapping the button closed.

The storm was out of control. I'd never seen anything like it. We still couldn't see our elbows from our asses. It was a good thing both Abey and Frank knew this town like the backs of their hands. Now I saw the benefit of him knowing where everyone lived in Wisper. We couldn't see road signs, let alone read them.

I couldn't even tell if the houses on this street were one story or two.

"Samantha," Frank said when Abey parked, "the Oswalds live two houses down on our right. Stay behind me. I doubt Murphy's a threat to us, but just in case this is somethin' else. And please..." He turned in his seat, looking at me with some ambiguous look in his eyes as I smoothed my hand over Grum's neck, trying to calm the both of us. "I know you're worried about him, but please, trust me?"

I did trust him. I knew he wouldn't do anything to hurt Murphy. I knew he wouldn't do anything to hurt me, so I decided, as soon as we found Murphy, I would lay it all out for Frank like the grown-ass woman I should've been in the first place.

"I do."

"Thank you."

We left Grum in the running truck, much to his consternation. Frank walked ahead of Abey and me, and she held my hand, maybe as a reminder to stay behind Frank or maybe so she wouldn't lose me in the blizzard, but whatever the reason, I fell in love with her in that moment. She became my sister. She could probably feel the tension between Frank and me, and holding her hand was the only thing stopping me from crying.

She looked at me, squinting against the squall of snowflakes, bending her neck so her hat took the brunt of them, but it seemed like they were coming from every direction, even up from the ground. "Stay quiet. We don't want the boy to know we're comin', or he might run right back out into this mess."

I felt numb, but I bobbed my head and fixed my eyes on Frank's back.

Abey left us on the front porch to stand guard at the back of the house. How she was going to navigate the snow, I had no idea, but Frank trusted her and was confident she had his back, so I did too.

He turned to me and brought his glove up, raising his index finger in front of his lips. Our boots on the porch were noisy, but the wind was so loud, I didn't think it mattered. He had been right that first night at his house; my boots were doing a shit job of keeping my feet warm. The snow was getting in between the laces, melting and leaking into my socks, and the leather was stiff and uncomfortable in the cold. My feet felt like painful blocks of ice.

Frank rarely wore anything other than his cowboy hat, so looking at him now with a brown Teton County Sheriff Department winter beanie pulled down over his ears, I was realizing just how handsome he was. Yes, he was hot. Yes, he was sexy, and his smile could melt me from the inside out, but more than all of that, the love he had inside him, the care for his friends and his community, for Grum—the care and love he had for me was the sexiest thing about him.

I saw it in his eyes. Even though we were in this crazy and potentially deadly situation, there was still a hint of a smile in those eyes for me.

Because he loved me.

I remembered thinking of him as a bear, and I knew in that moment that *nothing* would ever stop him from loving me, if I'd let him. Not even my worthless reproductive system. He would be as fierce as a grizzly with his love, and I was the luckiest woman on the planet to be offered such a gift.

And those age lines around his eyes and the worried wrinkles in his forehead, the ones that had made me so nervous before? They were only markers of all the people in this life, and strangers, too, that he loved and protected, though he'd never say it. He wouldn't want it to be recognized. It was who he was.

He turned toward the door and took a deep breath. I watched his shoulders rise and fall with a breath, and then he leaned to the side and put his hand on the doorknob. When he tried to turn it and it didn't open, he threw his powerful body against the wood, busting through it on his first push.

I guess I'd expected there to be a big commotion once we were inside—maybe Murphy would freak at being surprised—but silence and stillness greeted us. There was a light on toward the back of the house, but there was no noise or movement that we could hear or see back there either. The only sound in the world was the storm behind us. The wind was so loud, it grew silent, too, like white noise.

I followed Frank inside, watching where he stepped so I could step there, too, in case that mattered somehow.

He stopped in the middle of the Oswalds' conservatively decorated living room. Light beige carpet and white accents were everywhere. Seriously, after all the snow, I was so freaking sick of the color white.

But Frank must've seen something from his taller height that I couldn't because he rushed forward toward the brightly lit kitchen behind a half wall. He slid to the floor, and when I caught up and peeked over his shoulder, he was checking Murphy's pulse with two fingers on his neck as that poor boy lay deathly pale and unconscious on the white-tile floor.

Frank yelled into his radio. "Abey! Call a bus. *Fuck.* They can't get here. Okay, pull up out front. Let's try to get him to Doc Whitley."

There was static for a few seconds, but then Abey's voice rang out. "10-4."

Frank checked everywhere, digging in Murphy's pockets, pulling off his soaked shoes and socks. He grabbed Murphy's backpack sitting a few feet away and dumped the stolen paperbacks and the rest of its contents on the floor.

"What are you looking for?"

"Needles. Pills. Anything. I have naloxone."

"No, Frank. He's just a baby. He's not on drugs. It's his cut. It's so infected, and he's not eating, probably not drinking."

He lifted the hem of Murphy's sweater, and the wound looked fifty times worse than it had when I'd seen it at the library this morning. It was oozing now, and I'd never seen that color on skin before.

"Oh my God."

"Jesus Christ," he said in the smallest breath. "Samantha, see if you can find some blankets. He's freezin'."

I turned, searching desperately for a sofa throw or something, but there was nothing. It looked like the Oswalds had packed those kinds of things away before they'd left for Arizona. There weren't even any decorative pillows on the couch, so I ran, finding a staircase at the end of the front hallway.

When I got to the top, I rushed into the first bedroom I saw and ripped the comforter and blanket off the bed and practically jumped back down the stairs, trailing the blankets behind me.

"Here."

Frank took them from me and spread them out on the kitchen floor, one on top of the other, and then he lifted Murphy and laid him in the middle. He wrapped that kid up as if he had been made of glass, tucking the blankets around Murphy's body, making sure every part of him was covered, and then took the hat off of his head and put it over Murphy's. He lifted the bundle into his arms, like Murphy was three years old instead of fourteen or fifteen, like he wasn't already the size of a man.

"Get the door," Frank said, and I ran for it, opening it and trying to clear the snow on the porch with my boots.

He walked swiftly but carefully, each step urgent but confident, and when Abey pulled up in front of the curb, Frank climbed in the back seat, holding Murphy carefully in his lap. I hopped in the front, and Abey drove.

"How's his pulse?" she asked.

"Weak."

"Goddamn this snow," she said. "When this shit's over, I'm movin' to Bermuda."

I turned in the front seat, scrambling up on my knees so I could see Murphy and Frank behind me. Grum was on the floor in the back seat, trying to lick and sniff Murphy back to consciousness.

"Samantha, please, for the love of God, put your seatbelt on. Abey can't see oncomin' traffic, and if you get hurt..."

I didn't say anything but turned and refastened my seatbelt. Everything I did, everything I said, was childish, and Frank was scolding me like a parent.

It was okay. I deserved it.

And if Murphy died, I would never, *ever* forgive myself.

"His prognosis is guarded," Doctor Whitley said.

Abey took Grum with her when she went back out to help another driver who'd slid into a ditch while Frank and I waited for news about Murphy in a small waiting area in a medical clinic in the middle of downtown Wisper. It registered on some level as weird to me that a clinic would be located inside a house, but the thought flitted from my mind as I watched Frank's hands clench and unclench into hard fists as he paced the length of the small waiting room, which was really just a living room.

"His body temperature is almost back to normal, but his heartbeat and respirations are too fast, and he's severely dehydrated. I'm giving him fluids, but the bigger problem is the infection from his injury. I believe he's septic."

"What does that mean?" I asked, anxious to get back to the library so I could look it up. Cell service was out. I couldn't just pop it into my search engine. Besides, I'd stupidly left my bag and phone back at the community center.

"It means the infection's in his blood stream," Frank said grimly.

"Yes," the doctor agreed. "I won't know for sure until I can get some of his blood to a lab, but since I have no way to do that now, I'm going to treat him for sepsis. He'll most likely need to be hospitalized for some time. Blood pressure can become an issue."

Tears were streaming down my face. "But will he…recover?"

The doctor patted my shoulder. "I don't know. It will depend on the severity of the infection and if we've caught it in time. If it gets to his heart…"

I sank into the chair behind me, and it felt like the edges of my world were freezing from the outside in. Things were icing over in my vision. Everything in my view looked like it was quickly crystalizing.

My stupid decision not to tell Frank when Murphy had broken into the library for the last time might've cost this child his life.

"What can you tell me about him, Frank?"

"Not much, Doc. Mr. Burroughs over at Ace's House thought he might be in some trouble, and I've been lookin' for him. He's been breakin' into places all over town, I assume tryin' to find shelter and food. He stole antibiotics from Milson's ranch meant for their horses."

"Do you know what kind of antibiotics?"

"Penicillin tablets."

"And do you know how old he is?"

Their conversation faded away as I thought about Murphy out in the storm, fighting to stay alive, trying to find a safe harbor. He was alone when he passed out. The fear he must've felt was settling inside me like an anchor, and suddenly, I couldn't catch my breath. I just kept seeing Murphy's brown eyes, looking up at me, begging me to help him.

I was trying to blink through tears, trying to find oxygen, gulping air into my mouth.

Frank knelt in front of me on the floor. "Samantha, take a slow breath." He held my hands, squeezing them hard. "Look at me." When I looked up, the doctor had disappeared, and Frank said, "Focus on me. Nod if you can hear me."

I nodded quickly. "I-I'm sorry."

"Carey's outside waitin' for you. He'll take you back to the community center. G'on, get some sleep. I'll come see you soon."

Carey drove me back to the center, trying the whole time to convince me everything would be okay. I wasn't so sure. When he dropped me off, Juni was at Ace's House, riding out the storm there, too, since Max was stuck out at Milson Ranch.

As soon as I walked in the door, she was there, hugging me. "Sam, are you okay? How's Frank? Brady said he was in an accident."

As I looked around numbly, I realized half of Wisper was there. They had a film projector in the gym to my left that was casting *Legally Blonde* onto a huge white screen hanging on the wall. There were at least twenty-five people snuggled up on cushions and sleeping bags, watching and eating popcorn while the storm wrought havoc outside.

"Frank's okay," I said, and my knees gave out. I collapsed to the floor in the foyer, landing in a puddle of melted snow. Oh, what did it matter? My clothes and coat were already soaked.

"Sam? Oh my God, Sam!" Juni dropped to the floor next to me, and then Brady was there, wrapping a blanket around me.

"It's all my fault. I think I killed that boy."

"Who died?" a man asked, and I looked up to see Carly from book club standing next to a chubby man with a beard.

She was cradling a toddler in her arms, her two older children attached to her hips.

"Sam? What's goin' on?" she asked.

"There's a missin' kid," Brady explained. "Carey and Frank have been lookin' for him."

"Well," the chubby man said, "did they find him? Frank was out at Milson's askin' about the food that was stolen. Is it the same kid?"

I nodded.

"Here," Carly said. "Take the baby. I'm gonna help Sam." She shoved her baby into the man's arms. "Don't worry," she told me with a sly smile. "This is my Buckey."

"Oh, hi. How come you're not at the ranch with Juneau's boyfriend?"

I didn't know why I'd asked. I wasn't thinking straight, but he laughed. "Howdy, ma'am. Nice to meet you. I've heard quite a lot about you girls over at the library. I ain't at Milson's 'cause the roads out that way are closed. We live out in the country on the opposite side of town. We knew we'd lose power, so we came here to camp out till tomorrow. Max and the other guys will be fine without me."

"Oh."

"Kids, help your daddy with baby Drew," Carly said, and her family wandered off while baby Drew tried to climb over his dad's head like it was a jungle gym.

Juni and Carly pulled me up, and we went upstairs to find dry clothing in the center's donation room. Brady called it the "free clothes store."

Thinking about Murphy was making my stomach hurt, but something else was building up inside me as I thought about why he was out there alone. Where were his parents?

Come to think of it, where were mine? I wasn't injured like Murphy, but I was still hurting, and they should've been there for me. No movie could be more important than your own family. Nothing should be more important than your child, no matter how freaking old they are.

"What happened out there?" Juni asked while I dressed in a pair of gray men's sweatpants and a mustard yellow Buckin' Broncos T-shirt three sizes too big for me.

I sat next to them on the floor, crossing my legs like a little girl. "They found Murphy, but he was hurt. Dr. Whitley's treating him, but he told us Murphy is septic, and he doesn't know if he'll be okay."

"Oh my gosh," Carly said.

"Yeah." I hung my head.

"But how's that your fault?" Juni asked.

"Oh God." I sighed. "There's so much I haven't told you."

"Tell us now."

After I'd explained about Frank looking for Murphy and about how it had been bringing things up from Frank's past, and then how I didn't call him when I should have, I told them about tonight, when Frank told me he loved me and we'd had sex.

"Wait, so you had sex in the stacks?" Juni squealed. "That is so freaking hot. I'm putting that in a book."

My laugh was weak. "That's all you got out of everything I just told you?"

"Of course not, Sam." She squeezed my hand and held it. "I was trying to cheer you up."

I squeezed back, soaking up the warmth from her skin. My parents really did suck, but I had found another family here. Juni, Carly, Theo, and Brady had all become my family. Frank was my family. "Thanks."

"Babe," Carly said, "it ain't your fault. That poor kid's been dealt a crap hand. You were tryin' to help him."

"What if he dies?"

She held my other hand, looking in my eyes. "He won't."

"I hope you're right."

Juni cocked her head. "What's going on, Sam? Besides the boy. *Something's* going on. I can see it in your eyes."

"I don't know. I'm scared, I guess. Confused. I told Frank tonight I can't have children. He barely had enough time to react before we went looking for Murphy, but he didn't freak out. Didn't tell me I was ruining his plans for a family. He said it didn't change anything, which was when I realized it's not Frank's reaction I'm so afraid of." I took a deep breath, ready to admit the truth to myself. "It's mine. All this time, I've been thinking I'd be ruining someone's life if they shackled themselves to me. I'd be taking away Frank's opportunities."

Scooting away from them, I stood. I needed to move. "It's the same feeling I've had all my life. It's the way my parents always made me feel. Like I was in the way. Like them having to drag me around from job to job was a pain in the ass. I always felt like a burden. The only time I didn't feel like that was when I was here in Wisper with my grandparents."

And finally, after years of beating myself up for something I'd had no control over, everything became clear.

I ticked the reasons why I *wasn't* burden off on my fingers. "But first of all, my parents *chose* to have me. I didn't ask to be born, so that's on them. I didn't deserve to be dragged halfway around the world *and* ignored at the same time. And second, I didn't ask to have endometriosis. I didn't ask to miscarry the only child I'll ever get to be pregnant with. I didn't do anything wrong. It wasn't my fault. So why the fuck do I feel guilty about it? Why am I always telling myself I'm worthless? That my body's worthless? It's not. I'm *not* a burden.

"And I'm thinking… Maybe I'm thinking all of this was meant to happen. Maybe I was meant to do something else. Maybe Frank was, too, and that's why we met and fell in love now. I mean, it's not like the two of us make sense together, the grumpy, stoic deputy and the weird librarian nineteen years younger?" I snorted. "It makes no sense. We're all wrong for each other, but it works. I *love* him."

"Aw," Carly said. "Yeah. Y'all were meant to be."

I looked at my friends. "I'm sorry I yelled at you guys at book club. You were just being good friends, and I was rude to you."

"I told you, Sam," Juni said. "It's okay."

Carly nodded in agreement. "What're friends for if you can't freak out on 'em every once in a while?"

"Thanks," I said. "It's just that I thought if I heard the phrase 'just adopt' one more time, I'd scream. I don't know why. I've been so angry at my own body, I didn't even bother to really look into it. Maybe I could adopt someday."

"We should research it," Juni added as I began to pace in front of them.

"You should see their faces," I said. "Maybe it's because I was so young when it happened, but whenever someone finds out I can't have kids, they say that—'don't worry, you can always adopt.' The pity on their faces makes me so angry.

"And I guess I built it up in my head that if I couldn't have my own kids, I'd never have *any* kids. And that made me feel like a burden, too, you know? Like it would be a burden to anyone I was in a relationship with, but you know what? It *should* be their burden if they love me. If he loves me the way he says he does, Frank will love me through infertility."

Stopping on a dime, I turned back to them still sitting on the floor, watching me work this out in real time. "Right?"

They were nodding. "I bet he already does," Carly said.

"Yeah, I think he does," I agreed. "And you know what else?"

Juni seemed a little concerned about the crazed look I could feel growing in my eyes. "What?"

"I'm calling my parents. Right now."

She winced. "You sure? Right now?"

"Yep. Oh wait. No signal. Damn it. Okay, that's fine. I'll text my mom. She'll probably get it in the middle of the night, but it serves her right."

Taking my phone from my bag on the floor, I unlocked it and clicked till I got to my mom's number and then hit the little message bubble. My parents were still in Norway, as far as I knew, and I had no idea what time it was there, but who knew when we'd get service back?

Who the hell goes to Norway in winter? I imagined the wind howling around my mom, messing up her perfectly styled hair on a movie set in some fjord or something.

I texted, *"Mom. Listen, I need to say something to you. My whole life you've treated me like I was in your way, like your jobs were more important than your daughter. I had a miscarriage, Mom, and you and Dad couldn't be bothered to come see me because you said your project wouldn't allow for you to take time off."*

I started to write, *"I'm sorry if I'm waking you up…"* but then deleted it. I didn't care. In fact, I was kind of hoping my message woke her up.

Carly and Juni watched me, their faces morphing from nervous smiles into wide eyes and open mouths as I schooled my mother with my thumbs.

I snorted, talking to myself. "Right, like she isn't still working. Ha. Wait till she reads *this*."

"You guys have been jerks to me. Instead of making me feel bad about you having to worry about me when you're so far away or you have a big project or whatever, why weren't you by my side? I NEEDED you. And by the way, if you don't love each other, get a freaking divorce! Even Gramps thinks you should. You're miserable together. You've made me miserable having to watch you my whole life, trying to make me think everything was perfect, but the truth is that life isn't perfect. It's messy, and there isn't a fucking thing wrong with that."

Hm. Someone else needed to learn that lesson, too, but I suspected my confession earlier had clued him into that fact. I still felt a little worried about how Frank would react when we got the time to hash it all out, but I knew he wouldn't make me feel inadequate. I knew he'd help and support me, like family was supposed to.

I finished my string of texts with, *"I've been in Wisper for almost a year and a half, and you haven't been out to see me once. You didn't come home after the miscarriage. Oh, and you forgot my thirtieth birthday, by the way, so when you read this, don't bother calling. Instead, go book a fucking plane ticket, Mother. I deserve that much at least.*

"Oh, and tell Dad everything I just texted, and then get over yourselves and get out here. There's someone I want you to meet. Pick Gramps up on your way."

Tossing my phone on top of my bag, I turned to my friends again. "You were right, Carly. Frank and I were meant to be, and if he'll forgive me for not being honest with him, I think I know the reason why."

CHAPTER TWENTY-SIX

FRANK

WISPER LOOKED like some fairy-land bullshit, the snow blanketing roofs and trees. Power was still out in most of Teton County. The power lines had iced over, and some snapped right in half. Thick icicles dangled from the eaves of every house in town. The dark morning sky didn't seem settled to me, and I wondered if we were due for even more of this mess, though the National Weather Service had reported it over.

Traffic was nonexistent, thankfully. People were home, most of them trying to dig or snowblow themselves out from the snowmageddon. County plows hadn't made it to Wisper yet, but a few residents were out, doing what they could with their own trucks and shovels, but there was so much snow, it barely looked like they were helping matters. When Abey drove by it on our way to find Samantha, the piles someone had plowed in front of the library were taller than her truck by twice.

Abey waved to residents as we drove by, and we pulled over a few times to check in with people to make sure they were okay. The ones we didn't pull over for wouldn't have waved back or would've flagged us down if they needed help, so I was relieved to know they didn't. Most people out this way had generators and fireplaces, so at least they'd be warm as we all waited for power to be restored.

I'd have to use a loner till my truck was fixed. It would need some time to dry out 'cause I'd left the door open and the cab was filled to the roof with snow this morning. A little body work, new radio and computer, and I was hoping it'd be fine. I was pissed at myself for being so irresponsible, but my head had been such a mess last night.

Today, things were a little clearer. A lot clearer, actually.

We checked in at the station, and then I walked to Ace's House with Grum following on my heels. Vern was out front, shoveling like the rest of Wisper. "How's the kid?" he asked, bending to pet Grum's head.

I sighed, my breath blowing out in front of me in a cold cloud. "EMTs picked him up to transfer him to the hospital in Jackson. The highway's still closed, but emergency vehicles can get through with a plow and salt escort. He's pretty sick, Vern, but Doc said he did okay through the night, so hopefully he'll fight through it."

"That's good. Doc Whitley knows what he's talkin' about." He nodded. "Miss Sam's been a wreck all night. She's real worried about him."

"I know she is," I said. "Thanks for lookin' out for her."

"Oh, well…" He looked at his feet, shuffling them and kicking a pile of snow. "Welcome." He didn't seem at ease accepting my thanks, but he'd have to get used to it. It was weird to me that all of a sudden he was this pillar of the community, and maybe that was overstating things a bit, but I was glad he was there.

We shook hands, and I headed inside.

People were sucking down coffee and milling around in

pajamas inside Ace's House, including Brady Douglas and Theo Burroughs. There was a buffet set up on a long table in the gym next to a few gas camping stoves, and I spied a huge pan of scrambled eggs and a baking tray filled with bacon. Grum sniffed in that direction, drool dripping from the side of his mouth, but I held his lead tight. It was a rope from the back of Abey's truck since she told me Grum had snapped his leash last night.

My stomach grumbled, and I couldn't remember the last time I'd eaten, but I ignored it. I had more pressing issues to attend to.

"Mornin'," I said to the guys. "Everything okay here?"

"Yeah," Brady said, and he nodded back toward the staircase down the hall. "She's upstairs."

"How's Murphy doing?" Theo asked. It looked like he might be holding his breath while he waited for me to answer.

"So far, he's hangin' in there," I said. "He's at the hospital."

"What will happen to him?"

"Social services will come, probably try to find any family he may still have, but if they can't…" I shrugged.

"Thanks, Frank," Theo said. "Thanks for what you do. It can't be easy."

I should've been more used to thanks myself. "You're welcome."

Leaving them to tend to their guests, Grum and I climbed the stairs, looking for my heart.

When we found her, she was fast asleep on an old couch in a room filled with computers and printers.

I sat next to her on the edge of the couch cushion, rocking her shoulder gently, and Grum lay next to my feet, resting his head on his paws and sighing. Like me, he was relieved to be in the same room with her again.

"Samantha."

"Sleeping here," she mumbled. "Buzz off."

"Wake up," I said, trying not to laugh at her. I was a dead-tired wreck after last night, but seeing her beautiful face, her messy pink hair, and hearing the spit and fire in her voice could make me smile any day of the week.

She gasped and sat straight up, spearing me with her puffy, sleep-filled eyes. "Is he… Did he…?"

"He's at the hospital. He's alive."

Tears seemed to burst right out of her, and she threw her arms around my neck. "Oh thank God. I should've called you when I found him at the library. I'm sorry. And I'm sorry I didn't tell you about my infertility."

"It's okay."

"It's not. I should've been up front with you, but this whole thing's made me realize some stuff."

"What?" I pulled back so I could see her eyes. There was some kind of glint in them this morning.

Leaning back, swiping the tears from her cheeks with her knuckle, she said, "Can I ask you something first?"

"Ask me anything, my love."

She smiled, and her breath hitched when I called her love. "Why do you always follow the rules?"

So we were getting down to the nitty gritty first thing.

Okay then. Here goes nothin'. "'Cause I thought if I didn't, somethin' bad would happen, like it did when I was a kid. I dunno. I guess it's just how I processed what happened back then."

"You followed every rule. You joined the Army so there would be more rules for you to follow."

"Yeah, I did. I followed the rules for years, and look where it got me."

"What do you mean?"

I sighed, shaking my head and sliding down to my ass on the floor, and Grum grumbled at me for disturbing his nap. "This damn dog," I said, and Samantha laughed.

"Yeah, I followed all the rules, and the only thing it ever did for me was make me lonely. I've been so fuckin' alone for so long. Then I saw you, and my gut told me to leave you be 'cause you were too young for me. Too alive. You were perfect. Why would you ever want me? And if I fell in love with you, you'd want me to break down my walls. The walls I'd spent years buildin' so no one could hurt me. My ex left. My mama left. I hid myself away so I wouldn't feel the kinda pain I felt when she died."

It was all coming out. But now I *wanted* Samantha to know. I needed her to so she could understand me.

I needed her to know everything in my head so she'd know how much I loved her and how much I needed her to let me.

"All these years, I've been so angry at her. Still am, I s'pose, but I think I understand her better now. She was wrecked when my dad passed away overseas. It was like there was no light on inside anymore. And I always thought she was so damn selfish for that. But now? Now I have you? I understand. If I lost you like she lost him, I'd die inside too.

"It's no excuse for doin' drugs and abandonin' her kid, but I guess it makes more sense now."

"Baby, I'm so sorry. You didn't deserve that. Man, she missed out on the best son in the world."

I smiled. "Yeah, she did. You know, Mama K and my dad, Eugene, beg me to be in their lives. They call and write. They love me, but I never let 'em in. But do you know, since our first date, I've been rethinkin' things, tryin' to understand why I pushed 'em away for so long? You did that for me. You made me wanna be loved again."

"*I* did that? How?"

"You made me laugh. You made me want somethin' different than my stupid rules, day in and day out. There's a light inside you. You're like the sun, and you warm me up. All this time, I've been tryin' to prove to you that I'm not too old, but I think I proved it to myself." I laughed under my breath. "I'm old, Samantha, but I ain't too old for you. I'm just right. And you're just right for me."

She bolstered herself, straightening her shoulders and taking a deep breath, but she didn't take her eyes away from mine. "I can't have children, Frank. I will *never* have them. The miscarriage took the use of my only properly working ovary and fallopian tube, and it damaged my uterus beyond repair. The only reason I opted to not have them removed was so I wouldn't go into early menopause, but I may still need to have a hysterectomy at some point. My body still makes hormones, so I have a period, but I am infertile."

I squeezed her hands in mine, and tears began to well in the corners of her eyes. "Stop that now. None of that matters to me. I'm so fuckin' sorry you had to go through what you did. I'm sorry for what you lost, but it doesn't change a thing for me. It doesn't make me love you less. And I do, Samantha. I love you."

"But you said you wanted—"

"Yeah, I know what I said. I wish it'd never come outta my mouth, but you never bothered to ask me what my definition of a family is. Yes, it's true, I said I wanted a family, and I do, but the only person I *need* is you. Two make a family, don't they? And there's other ways to have kids in our lives, if that's what we choose. It don't matter to me how we do it. As long as we do it together, that's all I care about. Think about it. Next year, I'll be *fifty*. If we could get pregnant and had a kid right now, I'd be almost seventy years old by the time they graduated high school. No, I think there's a better way."

She released a huge breath. "Good. I'm glad to hear you say that."

I smiled, but I was confused. How had we gone from despairing Samantha to this? Had I missed something in the night?

"You're glad?"

"Yeah," she said, sliding off the couch and crawling into my lap. "I noticed something about you recently; you became really fixated on finding Murphy."

I shrugged. "Yeah, it's a personality flaw. When I get somethin' in my head, I just can't let go. Like you." I kissed her nose.

"I do that, too, sometimes. Obviously." She rolled her eyes but then smiled. "But I have another question."

"Okay," I said carefully. "What?"

"Could you ever believe in true love?"

I laughed and shook my head. "Girl, I believe in it now. I'm *lookin'* at it."

The smile on her face blinded me. It put this hopefulness in my heart that had me wanting to move mountains to be with her.

"I love you, too, Frank. I think I've loved you since our first kiss on my Gramps's front porch. I was so worried about letting you down. I was terrified of disappointing you if you knew about me not being able to have kids, but after Murphy, I think maybe everything I went through happened for a reason. I was meant to come to Wisper, and I was meant to meet you. To love you."

Pulling her even closer, I kissed her. "You really think that? You really think we were meant for each other? This is like somethin' outta your books, ain't it?"

"Yeah. It is. And I do believe you were meant for me. Wanna know why?"

"I'm on pins and needles, darlin'."

She wrapped her arms around my neck. "My parents hate each other, but they still managed to raise a good kid. Imagine what two people who love each other like we do could give to kids who need a family?"

"You read my mind," I said, and you couldn't have wiped the smile off my face for anything.

She loved me, and she made me feel like everything bad that had ever happened in my life was worth it. Every lonely night. Shit—every lonely day. Every dream I'd had that I thought had died.

In that moment, I felt like I was sixteen again with my first girlfriend. And what did a young man do when he found the girl he wanted to be with forever?

"By the way, you ever been to Texas?"

The kid was out for almost two days, but his infection was finally improving, and his heart was out of danger of being infected. He would need to be monitored for a while, and he still had a long way to go to gain some strength back, but at least he was headed in the right direction. At least he was eating three square meals a day. Plus, Abey'd packed him a whole backpack full of junk to eat from a crap stash she kept in a drawer in her desk at the station—Ho-Hos and Twinkies and such—and she made me promise I'd deliver it.

Law enforcement across Wyoming was looking for her, but so far, Murphy's mama was nowhere to be found. He hadn't said much about her to the hospital staff or to the protective services caseworker assigned to him, except that he thought she was dead or gone and he didn't know where.

When he woke, Samantha and I were there in the hospital. Normally, she wouldn't have been able to visit with him, but my job afforded us a little leeway.

She followed me to his room, but she was so nervous, biting the inside of her cheek and gripping my fingers so hard when I held her hand that I thought she might break them in two.

When we knocked on his door and entered, Murphy was stiff and scared. It ate at me to see him alone in a strange place like that. Man, did I know how that felt.

"How d'you do?" I asked him, almost laughing at the look on his face when he didn't answer. I'd seen that face before, in the mirror when I was almost exactly his age. "I think you've already met Samantha." Reaching behind me for her hand again, she grabbed mine, and I pulled her forward. For somebody with such big ideas, she was acting awful shy. "And I'm Deputy Sims, but you can call me Frank. You mind if we sit?"

I wasn't expecting an answer, and I didn't get one, but the kid's heart rate was steady, beeping away slowly on the monitor next to his bed, so I figured he wasn't about to bolt. Plus, he was connected to an IV and a bunch of other machines, so where could he go? I held the chair next to his bed while Samantha sat, then pulled another from the corner closer to Murphy's bed, thinking that I had no fucking clue what to say to this kid. What would I have said to myself?

Before I said anything, though, I looked at him, and I realized he wasn't anything like me. Yeah, sure, we had similar pasts, but Murphy was still innocent. There was still light in those big brown eyes. Maybe he hadn't been too jaded yet. Maybe he could let someone love and take care of him.

"So, um, I want you to know that I wasn't chasin' you to get you in trouble. I was… I, uh, I had a similar thing happen to me when I was your age, so I know how it feels to be hungry and scared, and I wanted to help you."

Samantha squeezed my hand.

Murphy hadn't moved an inch since we'd stepped through his door. His eyes were locked onto mine, like if he looked away for even one second, I'd pull a fast one, and he'd end up behind bars.

"Anyway," I said, "the weather's been so bad, and the temperature was droppin' quick, so I wanted to find you so you'd be safe. That's all."

"Are you feeling better?" Samantha asked. "We were so worried about you."

His eyes were as round and as big as golf balls, but still, he didn't say a word. I remembered not wanting people to force me to talk either, so I stood and nodded. I was planning to come back later to try again. Maybe if I showed up a few times, he'd warm up to me.

"We'll let you rest, but if you need anything, you just tell the nurse to call me. I left my number at the desk. And here." I held my work card out for him, with my cell number high-lighted.

He wouldn't take it from my hand. He still wasn't talking, and that was okay. I set the card on the table next to his bed and turned to go.

Samantha looked a little defeated, but she stood, and I pulled her with me to the door. I grabbed the handle, but then I heard a quiet voice.

"Frank?"

Had he forgotten to tell me to fuck off? That was what I would've done.

When I turned back, he fixed his eyes on his blanket.

"Yeah, Murphy?"

"What did you mean, a 'similar situation'?"

"Oh, um…" I settled my shoulders, trying to convey relaxation. "My mama died when I was thirteen. My dad was already gone, and we didn't have any other family. So…"

"What'd you do?"

"I did what you did. I found food where I could, slept outside, but I was in Texas that whole year, so it was a lot warmer."

He looked up, searching my face, desperate for answers. "Y-you were alone for a whole year?"

"Yeah," I said, slowly sitting again, and Samantha stood behind me. I scooted the chair a little closer to his bed. "Yeah, almost a year. From April to April."

He was quiet for a minute, and I didn't try to fill the silence. All the people I'd had yammering in my ears after I was arrested had made me want to punch someone.

Finally, he whispered, "What's gonna happen to me now?"

Right. The burning question. "The state will investigate and try to find any family you have out there."

"There's no one."

As if the sound of Murphy's voice had relaxed her, too, Samantha sat again. Nervous though she was, she'd told me she thought we were meant to meet Murphy. Actually, she was pretty adamant about it. "Your mom didn't have a sister or brother? Cousins? Do you have grandparents?"

"No. They died before I was born. At least, that's what she said, and she said her sister died a long time ago, too, like when she was my age."

My next question made me nervous, but I had to ask, "What about your dad?"

"Don't know who he is. Never met him."

"Well, still," I said, feeling relieved, but it made my heart race to think about why. "They'll look for him. But if they can't find anyone, you might have to live in a group home till they can find a foster family or an adoption situation."

Fear clouded Murphy's eyes, and he looked between Samantha and me. "Strangers?"

"Maybe, but it was a good thing for me. I went to a boys' home, and that's where my adoptive parents found me."

"You got adopted? And they treated you good?"

"They did," I said, realizing again what a big fucking idiot I'd been where my parents were concerned. "They were real good to me. They still are."

He was picking at his blanket, pulling at a loose string. "You know my name ain't really Murphy, right?"

"Dakota. The nurse told us."

"It's a cool name," Samantha said.

He shrugged.

Cool or not, I wanted him to feel some kind of control over his own life. "What would you like to be called?"

He looked up, surprised he had a choice. I doubted anyone else would use the nickname, but he'd always be Murphy to Samantha and me.

"I like Murphy."

I smiled. "Me too, kiddo."

We were quiet for a minute while he thought things through. Then he asked, "Could I live with you guys?"

"Uh—"

"Oh, Murphy." I could hear in Samantha's voice that tears had already started.

I'd tried, but I couldn't stop myself from imagining that

very thing. We'd discussed it with CPS, but there were still too many moving parts: Samantha and I weren't married, we didn't have a license to foster, they were still looking for his family, and he hadn't even been released from the hospital yet.

"Never mind. You guys probably got your own family. It was a stupid thing to say."

"No, w-we don't have a family," she said. "But it's a lot more complicated than just saying yes."

We'd been instructed not to tell him we were looking into it. We weren't allowed to give the kid hope of anything.

But maybe he saw it in my eyes.

Murphy sat up straighter in his bed. "But you could ask, right? I mean, you're a cop. They'll trust you."

It was the hardest thing I'd ever had to do not to smile then, 'cause I was trying like hell not to get my hopes up too.

"Samantha, come *on*," I said to the bathroom door.

"Frank, chill." She was locked behind it, getting ready to meet my parents.

In the blink of an eye, three weeks had gone by, and my parents were currently on their way from Jackson Hole Airport, by way of Dallas International.

It had been too long. I was ashamed of that, but I was really looking forward to having them in my life again. Mama K nearly had a heart attack when I called to invite them up, and my dad cried in my ear over the phone.

Everything felt hopeful.

"At least open the door so I can see you."

"Hold on!"

I looked at my watch, counting down from sixty seconds,

and then I ran out to my loaner truck and grabbed my lock pick kit. When I came back inside and broke into the bathroom so I didn't end up busting through my own damn door, Samantha was standing in front of the mirror on her tiptoes, leaned forward over the sink, pulling at the side of her eye as she swiped a black line over her eyelid with something that looked like a pointy black marker.

Squinting into the mirror, she looked at the tool in my hand out of the corner of her eye. "Did you pick the lock?"

"Yes, I did. What's takin' so damn long? You don't need all that. They're gonna love you no matter what you look like. Where're your glasses? You know how much they turn me on."

She laughed. "Oh my God, you're such a guy." Swiping the marker over her eye one more time, she set it on the counter. "There. Done. I'm wearing my contacts today. I don't think you want to be 'turned on' in front of your parents."

"Good point."

I sighed in relief, following her out of the bathroom as she whizzed past me, darting through the house, checking to make sure each room was clean and tidy. They were. Hello—*I* lived there.

She hadn't changed her address at the post office, but it was only a matter of time. She was right that it was fast, but when you found your person, you kept them close. Her family had made arrangements to visit in a few days, after some strongly worded texts she'd told me she sent during the big storm, but Jessup wasn't due back permanently from Florida for another month or two, and I didn't want her staying alone in his house anymore.

Besides, she wanted to sleep in my bed now that I was giving her what she wanted—and what I craved like air—

every night. And every morning, and on our lunch breaks. Before supper. After supper. She was insatiable, and I would die trying to please her if that was what it took.

Who knew? I was forty-nine fucking years old. Not even one more year and I'd be f—*shit*. I didn't even like to think the number in my head. I certainly didn't feel half a century old with Samantha in my life. I'd never laughed so much or had so much sex. I felt sixteen again every morning.

And there were some even bigger changes in the works. I just had to wait for the green light.

When she emerged from the bedroom, carrying the blanket I'd bought for her 'cause her little feet were always cold, she griped, "There's nowhere to put this blanket." She held the pink throw in the air. It was as soft as fox fur, and it matched her hair.

"Just toss it on the couch."

"'Toss it on the couch'? Who are you, and what have you done with Frank?"

I laughed. "I'm sure Mama K likes fluffy blankets as much as the next lady."

"It doesn't match the rest of the house."

"But it keeps you warm, so it's perfect."

She smiled up at me, and I snatched the blanket from her hands, flinging it over my shoulder. Grum yipped behind me, and then I heard him snuffling around. Reaching for her, I pulled her close and wrapped her up in a hug, feeling her breasts against my chest and her legs between mine.

She leaned around my bicep, looking at Grum. "Great. Now I have to wash it again. Look at him. He was just outside, stomping around in the snow and mud, and now he's rooting underneath the blanket with his wet nose and paws. Ugh. He's chewing it!"

Tightening my arms, I sighed into her neck. "I'm nervous."

She hugged me tighter. "Why, baby? They love you. That's more than obvious by the amount of time it took them to book their flight up here. I think it was only three minutes after you called."

"There's so much I need to say to 'em. So much I wanna tell 'em."

"The words will come when you need them." She pushed up on her toes, running her hand through my hair and kissing me. "I can't believe you never mentioned your mom used to be a librarian too."

"I didn't know. Honest. She only told me when I told her about you. It was before they adopted me, and it ain't like I spent a lotta time gettin' to know 'em before I left for the Army."

She patted my chest. "You will now."

"Yeah," I said, listening to the sounds of a vehicle pulling into my gravel drive. "Showtime."

We walked outside, my arm slung over Samantha's shoulders and hers around my waist, and she tucked her hand into my back pocket as Mama K rushed from their rented SUV, attacking us both in a hug. Samantha stepped away to give us a minute and to greet my dad as he got out of the car. I smiled at him as I hugged the only mother who'd ever truly cared about me, who did still, whispering in her ear while she cried quietly, telling her again how sorry I was for keeping them at arm's length for the last thirty years.

"Oh, Frankie. I dreamed you'd come back to us someday."

"Thank you," I said, "for lovin' me and for not givin' up on me."

CHAPTER TWENTY-SEVEN

FRANK

"MY MOM and dad will be here in two days," Samantha told my parents as she, my dad, and I sat around the table and Mama K busied herself in my kitchen. "I'm excited for you to meet, but I should probably apologize now. They're kind of weird."

"How so?" my dad asked.

"Mm, well, they're kind of arty. They get so consumed by their projects. It's literally the only thing they agree on."

"Well," Mama K said, "I'm sure they're fine people since they raised you." She looked over her shoulder and winked at Samantha. "So how's Murphy doin'?" she asked, turning back to the stove to stir the chili she'd been working on all day. I'd told my parents about him and how he and Samantha were the catalysts for me finding my way back to them finally.

And Grum, that damn dog. Dr. Masterson had suggested I make Grum a therapy dog, and I grumbled at the idea, but that was exactly what he'd turned out to be. He was like our kid. I reached below the dinner table to scruff up his ears and scratch behind them while we chatted as Mama K finished cooking. I hadn't eaten her food in a long time, which, according to her, was a sin. Food was Mama K's love language.

"He's better," Samantha said. She seemed pretty at ease with my parents, which made me love her even more. "A lot better. Frank and I went to see him this morning. He's staying in a boys' home in Jackson temporarily. And his name isn't Murphy. It's Dakota Chaska. He just turned fourteen. I thought he might've chosen the nickname Murphy because he loves to read, and maybe he'd taken the name from a Samuel Beckett book, but no. He told me he chose it because, of all things, he likes that show *Murphy Brown* with Candace Bergen. She played a TV journalist. He said he watched the reruns a lot with his mom."

"Oh, I remember that show," my dad said. "We used to watch that. Remember, Kathy?"

"Mmm, yes, it was a good show," she said, clicking the stove off and pulling a baking tray from the oven. "I love that Candace Bergen. She's a feisty one."

Mama K was a traditional Texas woman with long, white hair, but she never wore it down. She'd fixed it up into some kind of braided bun thing on the back of her head. It looked the same as it had when I was a teenager. I remembered 'cause the woman was always cooking, so I'd gotten a good view of her back. My dad's hair was white now too. He was always happy, always glad to go fishing or watch a game if he knew it was what I liked to do. I was taller by a foot than both of them, and it was easy to see we didn't look alike, but it didn't matter to me now like it had when I was younger.

They loved me, and that was all that had ever mattered.

"Do you know how he ended up in Wisper?" my dad asked. "He and his mother weren't from here, right?"

"No," I said. "She's from Oklahoma originally, but they'd

been livin' in a little town in eastern Wyoming with a man she'd been datin', but that guy kicked 'em out, and they lived in their car for a while. Murphy admitted he'd broken into the bookstore and stole the money and antibiotics. Said his mama used to make him steal for her. She up and disappeared after they stopped here in town months ago, lookin' for somewhere she could find a job, and Murphy hasn't seen her since. He did okay findin' places to sleep and food in the fall, but winter made it a lot harder."

"It's just heartbreakin'," Mama K said.

"Yeah." It was a fucking tragedy, and it broke my heart more than I could say.

My dad took a swig of his root beer. "What do you think happened to her?" He and Samantha already had something in common. They both drank too much pop.

"Murphy thinks drugs. He told me it wasn't unusual for her to come home high on somethin'." I hated to think it, but my gut and my own experience had convinced me she was dead. The ex-boyfriend had been questioned, but he didn't seem to have any idea where Murphy's mama was. The local police believed he was telling the truth. He didn't give a shit about the kid, and he wasn't a relative, so he had no reason to take Murphy in. Thank God. Another deputy from the area had called to fill me in. The ex-boyfriend sounded like a real peach of a douchebag, and local law enforcement was convinced he was dealing drugs.

"Well," Mama K said, setting Texas amounts of food on the table, "at least he's safe now. Alright, g'on, y'all. Wash up for supper." She winked at me this time, and I smiled, squeezing Samantha's hand and pulling her with me to the bathroom while my dad washed his hands in the kitchen sink.

"I think they like me," she said, perched on the counter

while I washed my hands, too, like a good little boy. "Did you tell them about the infertility?"

"I think they *love* you. I knew they would. And yes, I did. Mama K said if you ever wanna talk to her about it, she went through some similar things."

"They're really great, Frank."

After drying my hands on a towel, I turned, spreading her legs with mine, stepping closer. "Yeah, they are. I'd forgotten, you know? I blocked out their kindness all these years 'cause it was easier to pretend I wasn't missin' out on anything."

"I can understand that. But you're done with that now, right?"

"Right." Sweeping her hair over her shoulders with the backs of my clean hands, I ran my thumbs up and down her neck.

A little twinkle formed in her eye. "You know, Mama K even said she'd come to book club with me."

I laughed and rolled my eyes. "Oh boy."

"What?"

"You wanna talk about sex with my mama in the room?"

She tsked. "No, but I'd love to talk to her about *books*."

"Yeah," I said. "Sex books."

She swatted my arm. "They're romance books, Frank."

Using the voice she liked, I said real low, "Whatever you say, darlin'."

"Kids!" Mama yelled from the kitchen. "Hurry up. What's takin' so long?"

Samantha chuckled. "She sounds just like you."

"She knows I ain't a kid, right?"

"You're her kid, no matter how old you are."

"S'pose you're right." Wrapping her legs around my waist, I slid my hands under her ass and lifted her, and she locked her feet together behind me. "Time for supper."

"You can't carry me to the dinner table. How would it look?"

"It'll look like I love you, which I do." I kissed her nose. "And it'll look like I don't wanna stop touchin' you, which I don't."

"I'm going to kiss you now, and then you're going to put me down. You can hold my hand, but we're not cave people."

"Oh no?" I teased. "So when I took you from behind this mornin', ruttin' into you like a Neanderthal, that didn't do anything for you?"

She blushed, lowering her head and looking up at me through her black lashes. "I didn't say that."

"Mm," I grumbled low. "Thought as much. Wanna try that again tonight?"

"Yes, please." Her blush was crawling down her neck now, kissing the tops of her breasts under her V-neck sweater.

"Good girl," I whispered, lifting my hand into her hair, twisting it in my fist, and pulling a little, and her head fell back so I could kiss her. And, oh, I did. Who needed food? Her mouth was the only sustenance I required. Her tongue was soft and pliant. She let me kiss her and take her any way I wanted.

"Kids! You comin'?"

She winced. "We better go."

"I ain't through with you yet."

"Your mom's been talking about feeding you all day. If you don't get out there, she'll be mad at me."

"Well, we can't have that," I said, stepping back and lowering her to her feet.

"I thought you were sick of chili," she said, fitting herself under my arm and draping it over her shoulder. She twined her fingers through mine.

"No." I opened the door, pulling her through it. "I said I

was sick of Abey *eatin'* chili. Besides, it ain't really chili if it's got beans in it. You'll see what I mean when you take your first bite. Mama K makes the best damn chili in the whole state of Texas, and she serves it over baked potatoes. It's one of the only things I remember lovin' about livin' there."

"Is it weird that I'm kind of excited to see you eat unhealthy food?" she whispered.

I whispered back, like we were in cahoots, "Don't you tell *her* it's unhealthy. That wouldn't be the right foot to start off on."

She laughed. "I would never. Besides, I'm not the one who thinks it's unhealthy. I love chili, beans or no."

"Well, since I'm so much older than you, you want me takin' care of this body for you, don'tcha?" I patted my stomach. "So I can live forever?"

She stopped walking, tugging on my fingers, and I turned back to her. "So you can *love* me forever."

Like an oath, I swore, "I will. Till the end of time and back again."

But Mama K was getting impatient. "Frank Sims! Dinner. Now."

I kissed my heart, the one living outside my chest, and pulled her to the kitchen, and when we sat back down at the table, my mama flurried around us, filling our glasses with sweet tea. I drank it without complaint, the whole time thinking about how many workouts it'd take to counteract all the sugar.

But by now, my mouth was watering, just waiting for the unhealthy chili.

"You know," Mama K said, "we could try to apply for an emergency placin' for Murphy if they can't find anyone. I know we're old, but we still have love to give."

Blinking back emotion, I cleared the clog from my throat. When I was kid, I thought they were crazy for taking me in, for offering to deal with an orphan and all his issues, but seeing them now, hearing Mama K—who was seventy-three years old—talking about disrupting their lives for a kid they'd never even met, I was falling more in love with them than I'd ever allowed myself to before.

My phone vibrated in my pocket with a notification. I pulled it out, hoping it was the message I'd been waiting for.

It was.

I took a deep breath. "Someone's already stepped up."

"What? Who?" Samantha asked, the octave jump in her voice betraying her. She'd been trying to act like her hopes weren't sky high, but they were.

I hadn't told her what CPS had told me this morning while Murphy was giving her a tour of the boys' home. Fostering him was the only thing on our minds, besides each other, but nothing was official… *yet*, and I was sure she felt like it was something that would never come true.

But it was about to. And I was about to lay all my cards on the table.

I shook my phone in the air. "Just found out. Walt and Terre Finkle have offered to take Murphy temporarily till the state can find a more permanent situation for him."

"Really?" She looked relieved and disappointed at the same time.

"Yep," I said. "But…" Turning my chair toward hers, I leaned forward, holding both of her hands. "If we want him, we can have him. He can live *here*."

Mama K covered her mouth with her hand and stared at us.

"Are you serious?" Samantha asked, looking deep in my eyes. "What would that mean?"

"His case worker helped me, and if we're willin', they'll release Murphy to me because of my job and standin' in the community on a kinda contingency basis, until we can fill out all the paperwork and go through the official process."

Samantha gulped.

"We'd have to go to family therapy once a week, and there'd be people checkin' in on us. I suspect they'll go through our whole lives." It was a lot. I knew it.

Samantha didn't respond. The words seemed to be stuck in her throat.

Oh boy. Here we go. "I know this is fast. It's all so damn fast, but whatcha think? Do you want... Are you really ready? Will you help me look after him?"

"You want me...?"

Did I want her? Hell yes. That was the easy part.

Lowering down in front of her legs on my knees, I looked up at her, holding her hands so tight. "Yeah, I want you. Forever. Murphy doesn't know about this, so if this is too fast, Walt and Terre can take him, but the you-and-me part is what I'm askin'."

My mama squeaked, "Oh, Frankie."

I could hear my dad already starting in with the water works behind me.

I focused only on Samantha. "If we want this, it can be the start of our family. S'pose we'd probably have to get hitched if it works out that we wanna adopt him—"

"I-I—What's happening right now?" Samantha's heart was pounding. The veins in her neck were ticking away to the rhythm of her heartbeat, her eyes moving back and forth between mine. "What are you asking me?"

"Will you be my family? I love you. I don't ever wanna let you go... Marry me?"

CHAPTER TWENTY-EIGHT

SAMANTHA

"YOU SURE?" Frank asked me. He stepped in front of me, lifting the bottom of my sweater as I looked up at him. "Kinda put you on the spot earlier."

"Yes," I said breathlessly, raising my arms and tilting my chin up for a kiss. "I'll marry you." I'd never wanted anything more.

I was still really nervous about raising a teenager, but Frank believed in me, and I wanted Murphy in our life just as much as he did. He *belonged* in our lives. I was sure of it. I'd seen it in his eyes that first day at the library. And taking Murphy in was healing a little bit of the abandoned boy in Frank's soul. It was easy to see the change in him when he smiled, like it came easier to him now. Maybe it had a little something to do with me too.

We'd spent several days in the hospital with Murphy before he'd been released, getting to know him and hanging out so he wasn't alone, and already, we felt like some kind of family. He loved word puzzles, and we talked endlessly about books. His favorite was *The BFG*, one of my faves too.

Frank moaned softly, only stopping his kisses to tug my sweater over my head. "I love you."

"I love you too," I promised as he offered that smile to me, leaning down to kiss my lips again. "Do you think your parents will be comfortable in Jackson?"

"Yeah," he said, kneeling in front of me. He pulled me down with him, and we were face to face in front of the couch. The flames crackled slowly in the fireplace, warming us. "I'm pretty sure they could tell I needed to be alone with you. Besides, the hotel room I got 'em is pretty fancy. They'll love it, and we'll see 'em tomorrow."

Reaching for me, the glint in his eyes now promised naughty things as he lifted me into his arms and turned, laying me down on the rug in front of the stone hearth. He'd replaced the dead deer above the fireplace with the collage I'd made for him with all the pictures I'd been taking since our first date: selfies he'd grudgingly allowed me to take of us together in his truck on our birthday, a picture of us on our date at Paulo's, of our barely eaten birthday cake, and pictures of Grum, always with his tongue hanging out. There were candids of Abey and Murphy when we visited him, of the library and Coffee Shot, and of Main Street after the storm. Frank still made a face every time I pulled my phone out for another picture, but when I gave him the framed collage, he was so choked up, he couldn't speak. It was picture proof of our love.

"This might be our last chance to do this for a while. We're gonna have a teenager livin' with us soon. But I promised to make love to you in front of my fire, and when I make a promise, I keep to it."

"Oh," I breathed, and he laughed at me.

Lifting my skirt around my waist and bunching it up, he ran his hands up and down my legs, his fingers pressing into the outsides of my thighs and his thumbs inching closer and closer to the ache that had formed between them.

"Goddamn, you are so fuckin' beautiful. I can't believe you're mine."

"I'm yours?" I asked as he changed his mind and pulled the skirt down and off. My underwear went next, and then his eyes zeroed in between my legs.

"You are," he whispered, his eyes moving up my body slowly. "Take off your bra."

I did what he commanded, watching the lust descend over his face when it had been discarded. I was completely naked, my hair spread out beneath me on the floor.

Frank licked his lips, like he was starving. "Spread your legs for me."

Bending my knees, I opened them slowly, exposing myself to him, and he clutched a hand to his bare chest. I'd never felt so beautiful.

But he was still wearing his jeans. "Get rid of those," I said, reaching up to finger his fly. "Let me see you too."

A sly smile lifted his lips. "Yes, ma'am." He stood, unzipping his jeans, and he pushed them down.

I watched as the bulge beneath appeared. My heart was hammering against my ribs inside my chest. His boxer briefs came off next, and I was reeling just looking at his body. I'd never seen anything bigger or stronger or more beautiful, and I'd never met anyone more capable of love.

He was beautiful everywhere I looked, and suddenly, I wasn't on my back anymore. I scrambled up on my knees in front of him, and then his cock was in my mouth, my fingernails digging crescent moons into his ass cheeks as I sucked him down my throat.

"Fuck," he breathed, and he tangled his hand in my hair, guiding me gently as he pumped slowly into my mouth.

"Samantha," he whispered, and I looked up, loving how his eyes closed in pleasure and his head fell back on his shoulders. All that graying chest hair turned me on like nothing else could. Well, other than the muscles beneath. But then he spoke, and I was flat-out done for. "Oh," he breathed. "Good girl."

Those two words were my undoing, no matter when he said them, and they made me wild.

But they made him wild too.

I moaned around his cock, and then somehow, I wasn't on my knees anymore. I was on my back in front of the fire, and Frank was between my thighs, tasting me and growling against my pussy, making me even wetter.

He rose up, fitting his body between my legs, pushing inside me.

There was no warning. He was just there, and then he was fucking me with abandon, thrusting hard, over and over, his gruff breath in my ear.

Nothing had ever felt so good. I whispered, "Yes, baby."

"Oh God," he said. "Love when you call me baby."

"Ain't no God here, baby," I teased, reaching down to clutch his ass cheeks in my hands so I could feel the power in them. "Just me."

He fucked me harder then, his hips rolling into mine again and again, his lips chasing mine, his tongue in my mouth.

He rolled us, lying on his back while he adjusted me on top of him, watching my breasts bounce as I fought for balance. "Ride me hard."

He didn't have to tell me twice. With him beneath me, I could control how fast and hard he fucked me. I wanted him deep, and I descended till his eyes rolled shut and his hands grabbed for me, landing on my hips, gripping them and pushing me down further.

I gasped when he hit home, his cock so far up inside me that I couldn't move anymore. With my hands on his chest, feeling the hair there, rough beneath my palms, I began to grind my hips slowly.

"You're mine too."

He opened his eyes then, and he watched me as I rode us both to ecstasy. He lifted a hand to my breast and held it, thumbing over my nipple as his other hand reached down and found my clit.

"Yes," he said, working wet fingers over it as I vibrated from the overwhelming sensation.

Planting my hands on his chest, I fell forward, working harder to make him come, my knees digging into the rug under us, using the leverage to push and pull his cock with my body. The wet slide of his length in and out was too much. It felt too good, and I couldn't hold back anymore.

"Oh yeah," he panted. "You're such a good girl. Just like that."

I was taking him in and out, faster and faster, slamming down on his cock, over and over, my thighs getting a workout like none they'd ever had before.

"You're mine," I said again. It was a declaration and a promise.

He vowed, "Forever."

My orgasm seized his cock inside, and I lost control. He punched his hips, bucking into me and jerking my whole body. My back arched and my head fell back, my hair tickling us both behind me as the euphoria spread, and he lifted us off the floor with the power of his thighs as he came.

There was nothing in the world sexier than Frank when he came. It was like I could feel every emotion he held inside, and I heard it, the rough sound of his telltale shout, like he was releasing all of those emotions to me. So I could help him carry them.

So I could hold his heart.

He pulled me down onto his chest, whispering against my temple as he kissed me there, "Forever your man."

Book club was loud.

We hadn't been able to meet because of the big storm, and then Frank's parents came into town, so we'd had to reschedule twice. My parents finally made the trek to the Wild West too. They met Frank and his parents, which went much better than I had anticipated, and then we talked.

They were a little skeptical about how fast things were moving with us, but I gently pointed out that they hadn't participated in my life much up to this point, so they didn't get to have an opinion now. They apologized for not making me a priority, and I had hope that they would in the future, but they were already back to work, this time somewhere in South America.

Honestly, it was fine with me. I had other people in my life now that *I* wanted to make a priority.

And like I'd thought, Gramps didn't care about Frank's and my age difference. He was just happy I was happy.

And I was.

Frank and I made an appointment with the doctor in Jackson so he could understand what had happened in Florida a little better and so we could be absolutely certain we couldn't get pregnant. But I knew I couldn't. Still, a little part of me wished so hard for it. Hearing another doctor tell me no would be good for me. I needed some kind of closure.

But then I thought about Murphy, who would be coming

to live with us in two more days, and that was the last I thought about infertility for a long time.

The ladies were talking a mile a minute, not about the book they were supposed to have finished reading, but about the storm and what happened with Murphy. And a couple of them were talking about Frank and me, knowing full well I was standing right there.

But they hadn't heard the latest gossip yet.

Mama K took a seat in the middle of the group, looking at ease around a bunch of women she'd never met as she pulled her knitting project from her bag and grabbed her needles and a green ball of yarn. Small towns were the same everywhere, I supposed.

"Oy!" I shouted. "If all you wanted was to talk smack, you could've done that on the phone. I thought we were here to finish talking about the damn book club book."

"Keep your pants on, Sam," Billie said. "Nothing juicy ever happens in this town, so when it does, we have to talk about it."

Aislinn snorted. "This is coming from Billie Acker Cade. The queen of Wisper gossip herself. As if."

"When in Rome," Billie replied with a smirk.

Phil and Cal were in a corner, whispering to each other.

"Um, Phil, Cal, sorry to interrupt, but can we get started?"

"Hold on," Carly said, pointing a finger at them. "At the last meetin', y'all two were glarin' daggers at each other, and now you're best friends? What gives?"

Abey rolled her eyes, shaking her head, clearly in on their secret. She was in on mine too.

"Nothing 'gives,'" Cal said. "Phil and I had a chance to talk things over. That's all."

"Well," Carly snarked, "are you gonna fill the rest of us in, or what?"

The two women looked at each other, and Cal shrugged.

Phil sat next to Aubrey. "I'll tell 'em, Cal. You just rest."

"Are you sick, Cal?" I asked as she took a seat next to Phil.

"No, I'm perfectly fine. This is not a big deal at all."

"*What's* not a big deal?" Aubrey asked while Juni and Daisy nodded next to her.

"Some years ago," Phil said, "Cal and I had an argument. She claimed her lemon chess pie was better than mine. Now, my pie had been winnin' contests for years, so I mighta challenged her on that, and I ain't too proud to say I mighta been a little rude about it."

"Yes, and I was a"—Cal lowered her voice—"I was a B-word about it."

Juni looked back and forth between Cal and Phil, with her mouth open and a dumb expression on her face. "Seriously? That's what your feud was about? Pie?"

"Oh yes," Cal said. "It's a very serious subject."

"Exactly," Phil agreed.

Billie added, "You ever heard that expression, 'show, don't tell'? I think you're gonna have to bake us some pies so we can weigh in on this. Next TikTok lesson, I want pie."

"Ach, Billie." Cal adjusted the charm bracelet on her wrist, her long nails clinking against the metal, but then she sat back and smiled at her friend.

"But *how* did you resolve the argument?" Juni asked.

"Well now," Phil said, "we just talked it over."

Abey snorted under her breath.

"Something you wanna share with the class?" Billie asked.

"They didn't talk nothin' over!" Abey jumped out of her chair, pointing at Cal, knocking her hat from her lap to the floor. "Her sister drove in the storm and ran into Frank's truck. Then, after we found Murphy and took him to Doc's clinic, Myrna drove off the road again! After her first accident, she decided she wanted to run to the store for lima beans. Lima beans in a whiteout! So she took Cal's car, and I had to go pull her outta the ditch by the Food Mart. By the time I got her back to Cal's—for the second time—she was wet and shiverin' up a ruckus. Well, both of 'em got sick, picked up that cold or flu that's been goin' around. Next day, Father Jed told Phil about it at church, so then Phil showed up at Cal's house with soup. She nursed Cal and Myrna back to health, and all of a sudden, they're besties again."

She stopped and looked up at the ceiling. "You know, it's a wonder I like women, 'cause I really don't *like* women. Y'all make no sense." Bending to pick up her hat, she looked at Phil and straightened. "You two have hated each other for years, and all it took was a damn bowl of soup?"

Phil and Cal both shrugged and said, "Yep."

Carly raised her hand. "What kinda soup? I'm hungry now."

Frank's mom was laughing beside me, and finally, everybody noticed her.

"Who're you?" Billie asked.

"I'm Kathy, Frank's mama, and I was just laughin' 'cause y'all sound like my friends back in Texas."

Cal hmphed, and then the Frank questions started.

Aubrey asked, "Did you know how handsome your son would turn out to be?" and she wiggled her eyebrows.

I stomped my foot. "Hey!"

She winked at me, and Abey said, "Did you know your son would grow up to be such a pain in my ass?"

I stood next to my chair, listening to it all, wondering if we'd ever talk about the damn book, but then I realized it didn't matter. We could talk about the color of the walls, and

I'd be entertained. I hoped we'd get around to books, too, but I was just glad for the friendships I'd made. Glad for the community I was a part of now, and glad for the love I'd found in Wisper.

It was better than any book in the world.

Frank's voice behind me was a welcome interruption though. "Hey there, good-lookin'. You keepin' these ladies in line?" With his rough hands on my arms, he turned me and planted his lips on mine, taking off his hat and hiding us from my nosy friends with it while he kissed me stupid, and a hush fell over the reading room.

"I'm trying," I whispered when I could breathe again after being ravaged by his tongue so thoroughly that my knees wobbled.

"You tell 'em yet?"

I shook my head. "I'm kind of surprised your mom hasn't said anything. Or Abey."

Looking around his hat, I peeked at Kathy. And yep. She was about to burst as she smiled up at us.

I counted down in my head. *Three, two, one...*

"They're gonna foster Murphy, and they're gettin' married!" she announced, and the whole room erupted.

Visions of *Pride and Prejudice* danced in my head as I laughed, and I realized that Frank was my Mr. Darcy. We weren't rich by any means, but we were rich in love. We *were* a walking romance novel. Our grumpy sunshine age gap was one for the books.

How fitting that we'd fallen in love at the library.

Like a torpedo aimed for the sheriff's station, Grum pulled Murphy through the door.

Abey had agreed to take custody of Grum for the weekend so Frank and I could take Murphy to see Frank's parents in Texas. They'd been up to see us two more times since their first visit, but this was Frank's first trip back to Risk, and Murphy's and my first time there ever.

Frank was excited to show us around but nervous because his brother and sister would be there with their families, and I was happy to be going with him so I could help to keep him stress free. He was in his truck, checking in on the airline website, while Murphy and I ran in to do the last thing on our checklist before we left town.

Spring had come to Texas, and Frank promised Murphy and me fields full of bluebonnets.

When I caught the door and Murphy pulled Grum to a stop inside the station, we found ourselves standing in front of Devo from Ace's House. She was handcuffed, her wrists held together in front of her, swinging her legs back and forth in Abey's chair behind her desk with her black-and-white-striped tennis shoe pushing off the floor.

"Devo? Are you okay?"

"Oh yeah," she said in too chipper of a voice for someone who had just been arrested.

"Why are you in handcuffs?"

She nodded over her shoulder in Abey's direction. "Ask her." She smiled at Murphy. "'S'up, Murph?"

"What'd you do?" he asked her.

Devo was a saint. What could she have done to land herself in handcuffs?

I looked at Abey in question, and she planted her hands on her hips. "Oh no you don't," she said. "Don't you give me that sour puppy-dog look. I was just doin' my job is all."

Devo snorted, and she snubbed her nose at Abey, turning the chair away with a toe press.

"Hey," Abey said. "It wasn't me who decided to go all liberal warrior on the biggest redneck in town. And you parked your truck in front of a fire hydrant. I warned you, missy, and then you got all sassy."

"Don't call me missy," Devo said.

"Sorry, Devona. I warned you, *Devona*." Abey frowned. It looked like maybe it was upsetting her to be the reason Devo was stuck in the sheriff's station. "It is kinda funny, though, that you got arrested at an LGBTQ rights protest by a lesbian."

Devo whipped around so fast that she teetered on the edge of the chair as it tipped to the side. I worried she'd fall on her butt on the floor, but she kept herself in the chair by sheer will, then righted it and planted her feet, glaring at Abey. "You're gay?"

Abey looked down at herself, like the brown, polyester

uniform she always wore held the answer, and then back up at Devo. "Obviously. Last time I checked anyway."

"Do you want me to call Theo?" I asked, my head swinging back and forth between their faces while Murphy led Grum to his dog bed in the corner.

He'd brought a whole backpack full of chew toys, and he pulled them out, one by one, letting Grum sniff them. He'd also brought one of his T-shirts from his laundry basket because he thought if Grum had something with his scent on it, he wouldn't be sad while we were out of town.

"He's on his way," Devo answered me, and to Abey she said, "How do you 'check' your sexuality?"

"Seriously? It's an expression. I—"

Devo narrowed her eyes further. "What?"

"Nothin'," Abey said. "I was about to say somethin' kinda rude. Sorry. Bad habit."

I snorted. "I've never known you to stop yourself before."

She ignored me, her eyes fixed squarely on Devo's. Walking closer with her hand on the butt of her gun sticking out of its holster around her waist, she leaned over so they were face-to-face, but Devo pushed off the floor again, backing away.

Abey removed the holster, setting it on Frank's desk, and then she stepped closer again, but she clasped her hands behind her back. I stood there like a spectator at a baseball game, watching some kind of tension explode between them. Neither one of them acted like they even remembered Murphy and me were in the room.

But Abey smirked and leaned in closer, whispering so Murphy wouldn't hear, "I was gonna say, 'I check my sexuality every time I'm down between a woman's legs'... but I didn't wanna be *rude*."

Devo's eyes widened infinitesimally, and Abey licked her lips.

The front door swung open behind me, and Frank barreled into the station in a huff. "What's takin' y'all so long? We coulda made it to the airport already."

He took in the look on my face as Abey backed up two steps, straightening and fastening her holster back around her hips, but stayed locked in a battle of wills with Devo.

Devo watched her, but the *way* she was eyeing Abey had Frank backing up too. "Uh, yeah, so how 'bout we head out? Murph, hop to it. Say your goodbyes. Grum'll be fine."

"I don't wanna leave him." The heartbreak in Murphy's voice was killing me. I'd even tried to convince Frank to let us take Grum with us to Texas, even though I knew it was ridiculous. We were only going to be gone for a few days. "Why can't we take him with us?"

Abey and Devo were still locked in a face-off, but Abey was listening to Murphy. She was a really good aunt. "Don't you worry, Murph. Grum and I got plans. My brother's havin' a cookout this weekend, so Grum'll get to swim in a creek and roll in the mud. And if he's a good boy, I'll let him chase me when I go four-wheelin'. He's gonna have a ball."

Devo rolled her eyes at Abey. I hadn't known Devo to be argumentative or rude in the past, but cordial was the last thing on my mind as they glared at each other.

What was on my mind, though, was, *Whoa! Get a room already.*

"Okay," Murphy said, "but if you give him a bath, you gotta make sure the water's warm. He don't like it if it's too cold. But don't make it too hot. And you have to brush him after. It's good for his skin. And you gotta brush his teeth every night. His toothbrush is in this backpack. There's chicken-flavored toothpaste too. Don't use your toothpaste.

He don't like mint, and it makes him look like he's foamin' at the mouth."

"*Doesn't* like mint," I corrected.

"Right," he said. "He doesn't like mint, and he likes to sleep in bed with me, so make sure you let him up on your bed at night, Aunt Abey. I ain't gonna be happy if I find out you made him sleep on the floor."

Frank laughed and grabbed my hand as I rolled my eyes. "No, he *ain't*. Alright, Murph. Think you've covered all the bases. And remember what I told you. Abey has Dr. Masterson's number in her phone, so if there's a problem, she'll call her. Right, Abey?"

Still staring at Devo, Abey said, "Right."

Murphy hugged Grum, snuggling into his neck, and Grum licked Murphy's hair. "Love you, buddy. Be good. I'll be back in three days." He stood and nodded once, trying to pep himself up before he had to leave his best friend, then turned and walked to Frank and me still standing by the door. Grum settled down onto his bed, laying his head over his paws.

Looking between Abey and Devo, Murphy said, "And whatever this is"—pointing a finger, he shook it back and forth between them—"y'all better get it figured out. They need Devo at the center. She's doin' movie nights, and she asked me to help her when I get back from Texas."

Smug was the word I would've used to describe the smile on Devo's face now. Abey turned away and barked a laugh. "Oh, well then, I'll just let her go, shall I? If she's doin' movie nights. That's way more important than followin' the *law*."

Murphy rolled his eyes, sighing, and he turned. "Well, you guys ready? Let's go. We don't wanna miss our flight. Besides, I ain't never had a grandma before. I'm thinkin' maybe I can get me a new Nintendo outta this whole deal and maybe some homemade biscuits."

Abey and Devo both turned their heads at the same time, and together they said, "Murphy, that's rude."

He laughed knowingly, grabbing Frank's and my hands, tugging us toward the door. "See you in a few days! C'mon, guys. Let's go do this family thing."

THE END.

If you liked *Mountains Divide Us* (or loved it, I hope), please leave a review—even just a few words would help—on your favorite bookseller website, Goodreads, or Bookbub. Self-published indie authors rely heavily upon reviews to get our stories out to the masses. And thank you. I know it takes time to do this. I appreciate the time out of your day and the effort.

DEAR READER,

Thank you for coming along on Frank and Sam's journey with me! If you want more, you can sign up to receive my newsletter on my website, gretarosewest.com, or join the Wisperites Unite Facebook group. That's where all the gossip is, and if you read this book to the end, you know how good the gossip can get! Plus, you get a free short story, a steamy little introduction into the Wisper world.

This book! Man, did I have fun writing it, diving into Frank and Sam's heads. The chemistry between these two had me fanning myself more than once! But more than that, to me, they're a lot like Billie and Jay from the Cade Ranch series—once they figure out *how* to love each other, they do it fiercely.

I, myself, am quickly creeping up on fifty, so it was fun

for me to incorporate that aspect of life into Frank's point of view, though, he's A LOT healthier than I am, by a mile. And I don't hate technology. I'm not saying I'm always a whiz at it, but I don't detest it. :D

Up next is Abey Lee's story, *Light Betrays Us*. I hope you'll come along for that story too!

Love always,

Greta

The fourth book in the Wisper Dreams series, Light Betrays Us, is a small-town Western, FF romance about accepting who you were born to be and following light, wherever it may lead you.

GET THE NEXT BOOK IN THE WISPER DREAMS SERIES, *LIGHT BETRAYS US,* ABEY LEE'S STORY.

The fourth book in the Wisper Dreams series, Light Betrays Us, is a small-town Western, FF romance about accepting who you were born to be and following light, wherever it may lead you.

GET THE NEXT BOOK IN THE WISPER DREAMS SERIES, *LIGHT BETRAYS US,* ABEY LEE'S STORY.

ALSO BY GRETA ROSE WEST

WILD HEART: WELCOME TO WISPER

A Short Story

Join the newsletter for this short introduction into the Wisper world and for extra goodies and scenes. Sign up on my website:

gretarosewest.com

THE CADE RANCH SERIES IN ORDER (Series #1)

BURNED

BROKEN

BUSTED

BRAVED

BLINDED

THE WISPER DREAMS SERIES (Series #2)

RIVERS BETWEEN US

STORMS INSIDE US

MOUNTAINS DIVIDE US

LIGHT BETRAYS US

WANT MORE?

Become a Wisperite!
Join my newsletter for exclusive stories, Wisper news, and
The Cade Ranch Sexcapades—naughty little interludes for
my subscribers ONLY!
Jack and Evvie's wedding scenes are there!
Sign up for your first FREE short story,
Wild Heart: Welcome to Wisper
on my website:
gretarosewest.com

I would love to hear from you, email me at
greta@gretarosewest.com.
I'll reply.
You can find me on the usual social sites, but I mostly hang
out on Instagram, Facebook, and Goodreads.

Scan the QR code below to take you straight to my website.

ABOUT THE AUTHOR

 Greta Rose West was a floundering artsy flake until cowboy Jack Cade showed up, knocking on the door of her brain, pounding on it, and then he just plain kicked it down. She's a boy mom to a grown freakin' man, and she lives in NW Indiana with her husband and her two precocious kitties, Geoff Trouble and Sally Mae Midnight. When she's not writing, she's reading and devouring music. She enjoys indie films no one else likes, and her favorite food is Aver's Veggie Revival pizza.

You can find her on Instagram @gretarosewest, in her Facebook group, Wisperites Unite!, or on her website.

gretarosewest.com

facebook.com/gretarosewest

instagram.com/gretarosewest

bookbub.com/authors/greta-rose-west

goodreads.com/gretarosewest